JULIE CORBIN

A family held
together by lies –

about to be torn
apart by a secret...

Do Me No
Harm

HODDER

First published in Great Britain in 2012 by Hodder & Stoughton
An Hachette UK company

First published in paperback in 2012

2

A CIP catalogue record for this title is available from the British Library.

ISBN 978 0 340 91896 8

Typeset in Plantin Light by Palimpsest Book Production Limited,
Falkirk, Stirlingshire

Printed and bound by Clays Ltd, St Ives plc

Hodder & Stoughton policy is to use papers that are natural, renewable
and recyclable products and made from wood grown in sustainable
forests. The logging and manufacturing processes are expected to
conform to the environmental regulations of the country of origin.

Hodder & Stoughton Ltd
338 Euston Road
London NW1 3BH

www.hodder.co.uk

For Bruce

Special thank you to: Inspector Paul Matthews of Lothian and Borders Police and Mr David J Steedman, A & E Consultant at the Royal Infirmary of Edinburgh for patiently answering all of my questions and for helping me to bring the plot into focus; Justine Saunders for putting me right about prescriptions; Paula Healy for her detailed input on the Irish strand of the story, and Susannah Waters at the University of Sussex for her inspiring lessons and forensic examination of writing techniques.

Special thanks also goes to the team at Hodder, most especially my editor Isobel Akenhead whose advice and enthusiasm is invaluable to me. And to my agent Euan Thorneycroft who continues to be a great sounding board and whose support I very much appreciate.

Finally, as ever, big thank you to my writing friends and my family for coming on the journey with me.

'The physician must know the present, and foretell the future and have two special objects in view with regard to disease, namely, to do good or to do no harm.'

Hippocrates, *Epidemics*

I

'Are you his next of kin?'

'Yes,' I say, elbows and shoulders jostling me as a group of four men push into the queue behind me. 'I had a phone call from one of his friends to say he'd collapsed and was being brought here in an ambulance.'

'And your name is?'

'Olivia Somers.' More jostling. I hold my ground and grip the edges of the counter, leaning in towards her. 'I'm his mother. I'm also a doctor. And I want to see my son.' I let each statement roll into the next, then realise I'm sounding threatening. That won't help. The receptionist's face is tightening into an expression of practised tolerance, so I take a deep breath and make an effort to slow myself down. More space would make this easier and I step back, straight on to the foot of the man behind me. I say a quick sorry, feel him yield just a little, and stare back at the receptionist. 'Can I see my son, please?'

'Yes, of course.' Her attention focuses on the computer screen. 'I just need to take a few details first.'

'But is he okay? Is he conscious?'

'I'm sorry, I don't have that information.'

'I know that you're only doing your job, but can we please just—'

She eyeballs me over the top of her glasses. It's a look that says, *we're doing this my way*, so I grit my teeth and patiently tell her everything she wants to know – vaccinations, current medication, name of GP, etc. She keys my answers straight on to the computer and that's just as well because my hands are shaking too much for me to fill out any forms.

Three minutes and a dozen questions later, my cooperation pays off and she lifts the phone. 'Robbie Somers's mum is here. Yes. Mm. Fine.' She stands up and without looking at me says, 'This way.'

I grab my bag and follow her. It's Saturday evening, the pubs are shut and the Accident and Emergency waiting area is crammed full of the after-hours crowd. There's a potent aroma of blood, sweat and alcohol mingling with the fresher smell of disinfectant. Those who haven't been able to find an empty chair are pacing up and down holding their injury close, or, in the case of one man, a bloodied sweatshirt up to the cut on the side of his face. The whole room simmers with discordant energy and I know it's only a matter of time before the air heats up and people start to get stroppy. Being in pain, waiting too long, tired, drunk, worried – it's not a great mix.

The receptionist is wearing chunky plastic shoes, bulbous at the toes. They give an extra spring to her step and she moves with pace across the room. I'm wearing three-inch heels and a knee-length dress that's tight at the hem, so I'm forced to trot along behind her in staccato steps as we wend our way between the wounded and their relatives towards a set of double doors.

She pushes through the doors and into the treatment area. I trained in this hospital, but that was over twenty years ago and since then it has relocated from the rambling Victorian buildings in central Edinburgh to a purpose-built facility southeast of the City. I glance around me, registering the signs on the doors as we pass: Toilets, Relatives' Room and several doors marked Staff Only. Trolleys line the wall space in between the doors, half of them taken up with people who look in need of a more comfortable place to lie.

Ahead of us, over a dozen treatment bays branch out from

a central island. All the bays have curtains pulled across, apart from one, where an elderly man is propped up on the trolley, his bony hands gripping the cot sides and an oxygen mask over his face. Nurses are bustling in and out of the bays giving reassurance and carrying out procedures – 'try not to scratch', 'tip your head the other way', 'it'll only hurt for a second' and then, 'oh dear, never mind', as vomit splashes on to the floor and a sour, acidic smell permeates the room.

I look along the floor beneath the curtains searching for signs of Robbie, his jacket or his shoes, anything that identifies him. I see other people's bags and heaps of discarded clothing and legs from the knee down, but nothing to let me know Robbie is here.

'Wait a second,' the receptionist tells me, bringing us both to a halt next to the nurses' station. 'I'll get one of the doctors to come and speak to you.'

I expect her to pop her head behind a curtain but she doesn't; she goes into a room at the end. There's a sign on one of the double doors that says Resuscitation.

Sweet Jesus. Panic flashes through me like lightning. My heart starts to race and my legs collapse inwards so that my knees knock together. I press one hand over my mouth and hold on to the counter with the other. It takes almost a minute for the feeling to pass, and as soon as it does, I start to talk myself round. Robbie is seventeen years old. He's young; he's healthy; he's strong. And he's in the right place. God forbid that his heart has stopped, but if it has, there's all the necessary expertise and equipment here to deal with it. I need to keep calm and I need to ring Phil.

Keeping an eye on the Resusc room, I move into a nearby cupboard and stand next to a stack of crutches and wheelchairs, rummaging around in my bag for my mobile, stopping short at emptying the whole lot out on to the floor when I remember I zipped it up in the side compartment. I've managed to avoid speaking to Phil for over a month now and, as immature as it sounds, I'd be more than happy never to speak to him again. But we were married for almost seventeen years and he's the father of both my children, so I have to find a way to communicate with him without it degenerating into our usual slanging match. This is an emergency. *Be an adult, Olivia,* I tell myself. *Just do it.*

I press the numbers and his phone starts to ring, five times, and then the answering service clicks in. 'Phil, it's me. Please call me as soon as you get this message.'

I end the call, but before my mobile's even back in my bag, I'm mentally kicking myself. Bugger. I'm going to have to ring him again. He'll ignore my last message because he'll think I'm calling for myself. When he first left me, I went through a phase of phoning him late at night – two or three large gin and tonics, the children in bed and I couldn't help myself. At first he picked up the phone, but after a couple of times of telling me I needed to 'move on' and accept that our relationship had 'come to a natural end', he just let me ramble into the answering machine. Each and every time I ended up feeling humiliated and sore as if I'd taken a penknife to an open wound. I'm past that stage now, but because the divorce papers only came through yesterday, he'll think I've slid back down there again.

I pace around in a small circle, then have another go. 'It's me again, Phil. I should have said that it's not about me. Robbie's in the infirmary. He collapsed up town. I'm not sure but I think they might have been drinking. I don't know any more yet. I'm waiting for the doctor to come and talk to me.'

I drop the phone back into my bag and breathe deeply. Right. That's that done. At least he can't accuse me of withholding information about the children. I come out of the supplies cupboard, side-stepping an elderly woman who's pushing a Zimmer frame and being walked towards the exit by a nurse. Someone is crying loudly behind the nearest set of curtains and a young voice shouts, 'You shouldn't have done that!' followed by a woman's soothing tones.

I stare at the windowless doors to the Resusc room, willing them to open. *What's happening in there?* Surely the receptionist should have come out ages ago? I contemplate just walking in on them, but the truth is I'm afraid to. Familiar as I am with illness and injury and the workings of a hospital, I don't want to see Robbie on the patient end of a defibrillator and witness the horror of him being treated for . . . for what? Truth is I don't really know what's happened to him. His friend Mark Campbell called me less than an hour ago. I was having dinner in a restaurant and the background noise from both his end and mine drowned out most of what he said. All I'd been able to work out was that Robbie had collapsed outside one of the pubs on the Royal Mile. Emily Jones, a friend of theirs, helped with first aid until the ambulance arrived. I told Mark I'd meet him at the hospital, said a rushed goodbye to my date and left the restaurant immediately. All the way here in the taxi I imagined that Robbie had drunk too much and was being brought to the infirmary to have his stomach pumped. But now I'm not so sure. The amount of time it's taking and the fact that he is in the Resusc room rather than one of the treatment bays is flooding me with increasing anxiety. And where is Mark? He can't be in the room with Robbie. He must be waiting around here somewhere.

'Please!' The old man has pulled his mask to one side and is waving at me, his voice croaky and weak. 'I need a bottle.'

'You have a catheter in, Mr Darcy,' a nurse calls across from the central station. She is balancing several files over one arm and pushing a trolley laden with sterile dressing packs ahead of her. 'Try to relax.' She looks towards me and smiles. 'Bless him. He's waiting for a bed upstairs but nothing's available yet.'

She's the first nurse who's been willing to catch my eye and I seize the chance to talk to her. 'My son is in Resusc and the receptionist has gone in there to get a doctor but that was at least five minutes ago and she hasn't come out yet.'

'There's another door out of that room. Takes you round the outside of this area.'

'I see. Sorry.' I follow her a few steps along the corridor. 'You wouldn't happen to know how my son is?'

'Robbie Somers?'

'Yes.'

'Dr Walker will be with you in a mo. They're just sorting him out.'

'So he's all right?'

'Getting there.'

'Thank God.' For the first time since the phone call, the knot inside me loosens. 'His friend accompanied him in the ambulance. Do you know where he is?'

'He was feeling sick and went outside for some air. I think both boys might have had a bit too much to drink.' She widens her eyes. 'And the rest.'

My gut tightens again. 'And the rest?'

'Dr Walker will give you the details.' She steers me ahead of her. 'Robbie's a lucky boy. It's been touch and go.' She opens the door signed Relatives' Room and ushers me inside. 'Doctor shouldn't be a minute. Make yourself a coffee if you'd like one.'

I sit down on one of the seats, red imitation leather squeaking a protest underneath me. The room is painted an off-white colour with bland prints at regular intervals breaking up the expanse of wall. There's a fridge in the corner, a kettle and half a dozen mugs on a tray next to it. A low coffee table has two piles of *National Geographic* magazines stacked neatly in the centre. The carpet is a busy pattern of blue-, green- and cream-linked chains and I stare at it while I think about what the nurse was implying when she said 'and the rest'. It doesn't take me long to surmise that there's only one thing she can mean – drugs. Robbie's collapsed because he's been taking drugs.

The realisation sends my thoughts sparking off in all directions. I see words, neon-bright – ecstasy, cocaine, GHB and heroin; words loaded with risk and significance. All teenagers experiment, but surely Robbie hasn't been foolish enough to take drugs that would cause him to fall unconscious? Especially when, as recently as last month, we talked about drugs. There was a programme on television about substance abuse and it led us to have what I thought was an honest conversation about the dangers. He assured me he wasn't interested in taking drugs. Yes, he'd smoked marijuana a couple of times, and once he'd taken ecstasy at a party but he hadn't liked it much; as for hard drugs – they were 'for losers'. I remember being absolutely sure he was telling me the truth. And perhaps he was. It could be that recently something has happened to change his mind. I can't think of anything specific, but then if he's fallen out with one of his friends or been knocked back by a girl he likes, he's not necessarily going to share that with me.

'Right you are then.' The same nurse is back and she has Robbie's friend Mark Campbell with her. 'You two wait in here together. I'll find out how much longer the doctor's going to be.'

Mark looks terrified. He's breathing heavily, his dark eyes are bleak and his hands are pulling at the hem of his T-shirt. His mum is my best friend and I've known him since he was born. I stand up to give him a hug, then notice that the reason his T-shirt is bothering him so much is because there's a large bloodstain across the front of it.

'Is that . . . ?' The crème brûlée I had for dessert curdles in my stomach. 'Is that Robbie's blood?'

Mark's body sways from side to side. 'I'm sorry, Liv. Robbie banged his head when he hit the kerb.' His voice breaks and he coughs into his hand. 'He fell down so quickly I didn't have time to catch him.'

'Sweetheart.' I hold his upper arms, trying to reassure him while at the same time keeping myself away from the stain. 'You did everything you could. I know you did.'

'I don't get it. I don't get why he collapsed.'

'Sit down here.' I nudge him backwards into a seat, then sit down opposite him and take both his hands. Ordinarily the sight of blood doesn't faze me, but this is Robbie's blood and there's so much of it and what if the head injury is serious? Once again, panic closes in on me and I talk myself round, remind myself that liquid spreads. It always looks like more than it actually is. And as for the head injury – Robbie banged his head a couple of years ago when we were skiing. He was out cold for four minutes and still made a full recovery. 'Tell me what happened, Mark,' I say, keeping my voice steady. 'From the beginning. Take your time.'

'After hockey practice, we decided to go up town.'

'Just you and Robbie?'

'No.' He shakes his head. 'We went with the usual crowd. There were about ten of us. We were just going to have a couple of drinks then get the bus back home.'

'But you ended up drinking a lot more than that?'

'No.' He shakes his head again, this time emphatically. 'We only had two. It's too expensive to drink in pubs.'

'Did you drink before you left the hockey club then?'

'Just . . . well . . .' He hesitates. 'Just one vodka. It wasn't much.'

'You know you can tell me the truth.'

His face falls into his shoes.

'Mark.' I lean in closer towards him. His shock of

blue-black hair, the colour of old-fashioned ink, is covering both his eyes, and I have to bend my head to see up into his face. 'I won't deny that I'm disappointed you lied to me about where you were going this evening. And I've already worked out that the two of you must have fake IDs, otherwise you couldn't have been served. But I'm not interested in blaming you for either of these two things. The truth is important because it might affect the treatment Robbie's given.'

He looks at me then, his eyes a soft brown and in stark contrast to his bone structure which is all sharp angles. 'We shared a half-litre bottle of vodka before we left the club but we've drunk loads more than that before.'

'And in the pub?'

'Two pints of lager.'

'Anything else?'

'No. And the doctor already asked me whether we took drugs.' His stare is fierce. 'We didn't.'

'So if you didn't drink too much and you didn't take drugs, why did Robbie collapse?'

'I don't know.' He pulls his hands from mine and wipes them over his thighs. 'I really don't know. We were finishing our second drink and then he started acting weird.'

'Weird in what way?'

'Like he was seeing stuff.'

'What sort of stuff?'

'He said at first he thought the walls were moving and then he started seeing people who weren't even there.'

'Hallucinating?'

'Yeah.'

'And then what happened?'

'We went out to get some air and the next thing he fell down. I shouted for help and some guy called an ambulance and then everyone came out of the pub to see what was going on. Emily knew what to do. She put him in the recovery position but then his heart stopped and so she gave him mouth to mouth.'

'Jesus.' I bring my hands up to my face and try to press away the tension around my eyes.

'I'm really sorry, Liv.' Mark's on the edge of tears. 'I know you were out on a date and everything.'

'That doesn't matter.' I give a short laugh, briefly remembering how I spent the evening. His name was Fraser and it was the first time we'd met. Organised by mutual friends, neither of us were ready to date again. He spent most of the evening bitching about his ex and I spent most of it wondering how quickly I could get home again.

I stand up and walk towards the door. Still no sign of the doctor, but there's a rush of urgency in the corridor. A trolley is being pushed at speed towards another one of the Resuscitation rooms. A small boy is lying on it, naked apart from his nappy. He is completely still, his lips are blue and a rash blooms on his lower limbs. The toddler's mother is crying and hanging on to her husband's arm. My heart goes out to them but I pull away from their anguish and look back at Mark. 'The thing is, Mark, I'm not really understanding how this could have happened. Is there anything else you can think of that might be relevant?'

He shakes his head, at a loss for an answer, and then a doctor walks in wearing blue scrubs and an air of importance. 'Doug Walker.' He holds out his hand. He's about six feet tall, early fifties and has experience written all over him. I immediately feel that Robbie will be getting the best possible care.

'Olivia Somers.' We shake hands and he gives me a prolonged stare, as if working out whether or not he knows me. 'How's Robbie?' I say.

'Stable. He's had a rough time but he's just regained consciousness.'

Relief relaxes my facial muscles and I'm able to smile. 'Thank you.'

'Mark and I have already had a chat about the sequence of events that led to Robbie's collapse.' He gives Mark a significant look. 'Have you been able to think of anything else that might help us?'

'No.'

Dr Walker folds his arms across his scrubs and doesn't let up on the look. 'It's vital you tell us the truth.'

'I am telling the truth!' Mark pushes his chin out towards the doctor. 'Why would I lie?'

'To protect yourself or Robbie or whoever supplied you with drugs.'

'We didn't take any drugs!' He's shouting now. 'I'm not saying we've *never* touched drugs. We've smoked weed a few times, but that's about it.'

'It's okay, Mark.' I take hold of his arm. 'You're not being accused of anything.'

'Honestly, Liv.' He looks me full in the face. 'Robbie didn't take anything.'

'And he couldn't have gone off into the toilet and taken something without you knowing?' Dr Walker persists.

'We went to pee at the same time,' Mark replies. 'And then we both came back and sat down.'

'Okay.' The doctor claps him on the back. 'Why don't you go off to the waiting room? I need to have a chat with Robbie's mum and then we can think about getting you home.'

Mark gives me a concerned backward glance then slopes off, the ragged hems of his jeans trailing the floor. Dr Walker closes the door behind him. 'Have they been friends for a while?' he asks me.

'Since they were small.'

'You trust him?'

'Yes. His mum and I are old friends. We were at university together.'

'The receptionist mentioned that you're a doctor.'

'I'm a GP.'

'Your name's familiar. I thought you might work here.' He frowns at me – not unfriendly, just thinking. 'I know!' He clicks his fingers. 'I read an article about you in the *Edinburgh Courier*. You're up for one of the City Women awards.'

'That's right. I volunteer in an outreach centre in the Grassmarket.'

'My wife tells me you have a good chance of scooping an award.'

'That's kind of her.'

'Not so much kindness as admiration. Sounds as if you do some very good work down there.'

'I'm a small part of a very committed team but yes, we've helped quite a few youngsters get back on track.'

He smiles. 'Well, best of luck with your nomination.'

'Thank you.'

He gestures towards the seats and we sit down opposite each other. 'So, Dr Somers . . .'

'Please call me Olivia,' I say.

'Olivia.' His expression grows serious. 'Your son collapsed outside one of the pubs in town. He was helped by a friend who knew first aid and when the paramedics reached him she was administering CPR.'

'Yes. Mark told me.'

'When he arrived with us, his conscious level was still depressed. We ventilated him for twenty minutes, then he started breathing for himself.'

'And the cut to his head?'

'Superficial. We glued it together. It should heal without any problems but, of course, it's worth looking out for a concussion.'

'Will I be able to take him home tonight?'

'While we don't expect any further problems, we'd like to keep him under observation in our Toxicology Unit until lunchtime tomorrow.'

'But Mark's adamant that neither of them took anything. Or could his collapse simply be drink related?'

'Olivia.' He makes a point of holding my eyes. 'There's no doubt in my mind that your son has taken drugs. Most likely GHB.'

'GHB?' I know from my work in the centre that there's a surplus of GHB on the streets of Edinburgh. 'Are you sure?'

'We don't do routine assays for drug abuse, but his recovery is consistent with a GHB overdose. As I'm sure you're aware, a typically flat patient arrives in A & E, is given IV fluids and prepared for CT scanning when he's suddenly pulling out the ET tube and trying to climb off the trolley.'

'I can't believe . . . Well, I mean . . .'

'He's not the first young man who's taken too much.'

'Robbie doesn't take drugs.'

Dr Walker raises his eyebrows at this.

'I know, like Mark said, they've smoked the odd joint, and I know they drink too much – but this?' I tense my jaw and try to swallow but can't get saliva past the lump in my throat. 'I can't believe he'd be so stupid.'

'It's not such a big step from alcohol and marijuana to other, so-called recreational drugs.' Dr Walker shrugs tired shoulders. 'And I'm afraid there's always a first time.'

'He's just not the type.'

My body slumps back in the seat but my mind stays active as it mulls over the likelihood of Robbie taking GHB. I'm not an unusually protective mother, and I'm not blind to the temptations that teenagers are under, but still I'm convinced that Robbie would not endanger himself in this way. Although he felt unhappy and insecure when Phil and I separated, he's never been reckless. He understands that every action has a consequence. I know he doesn't tell me about everything that's going on in his life, but neither is he secretive. I find it hard to believe that I wouldn't have noticed warning signs that he was heading in this direction. 'Perhaps he took it by mistake,' I say, searching for an explanation. 'Perhaps his drink was spiked?'

'Sometimes friends spike each other's drinks,' Dr Walker says, moving his head from side to side as he considers it. 'But I'm afraid it's far more likely that the drug was self-administered.'

My eyes fill with tears and I try to blink them away. In the nicest possible way, Dr Walker is forcing me to face the fact that I don't know what my own son is capable of, that he has his own life and makes his own choices. As a GP, I've said similar things to parents myself. And when working at the centre, I treat young people who find themselves, in a matter of a few short weeks, on a downward spiral of drug abuse.

But still I can't believe this of Robbie. He has a solid core of common sense – doesn't he?

Dr Walker hands me a tissue. I scrub at my cheeks, then scrunch the soggy paper up in my hand. 'He's alive and he's going to be fine,' I say out loud, the sound of my own voice definite enough to reassure me.

'Is there anyone we can phone to come and help you through this?'

I shake my head. 'I called Robbie's father, my ex-husband, about an hour ago and left a message and it's too late to get friends out of bed.' I straighten my back and stand up. 'I'll be okay. It's all a bit of a shock. That's all.' I find my businesslike face and clasp my hands across my middle. 'So what happens now?'

'You can see Robbie.' He opens the door and ushers me ahead of him. 'He's groggy but he's able to talk.'

We walk along the corridor and Dr Walker pulls aside the curtain into one of the bays. Robbie is lying on his side on a trolley. He's wearing a hospital gown and a sheet covers up to his waist. He has a gangly frame, all arms and legs, and no matter how much he eats he doesn't put on any weight. His feet are sticking out the bottom, hanging over the end of the trolley, and I notice he's wearing odd socks.

Dr Walker brings a chair up behind me. I thank him and sit down. 'I'll leave you to it,' he says, pulling the curtain closed behind him.

Robbie's eyes are shut and he's breathing slowly and deeply, as if this was any other night and he was in his bed at home. 'Robbie.' I stroke his hair. 'It's me.'

'Mm.'

'How are you feeling?'

'My throat hurts.'

'The doctor had to put a tube down it.'

'I know. I tried to pull it out but it was stuck.'

'The balloon has to be deflated before the tube will come out.'

'Yeah. They told me.' He opens his eyes then quickly closes them again. 'The walls are still moving a bit.'

'You'll be back to normal in no time.' I take hold of his hand. 'By midday tomorrow, when the effects of the drugs have completely worn off, you'll be as good as new.' I wait for him to comment and when he doesn't I say, 'Have you any idea how you came to have drugs in your system?'

'No.'

'Robbie.' I stroke his hand, feel the calloused patches on the ends of his thumb and forefingers where he strums the guitar. 'We can talk in more detail when you feel better, but I need to know – and please be truthful: did you take GHB this evening?'

'No.'

'You're sure?'

'I didn't take any drugs and all I drank in the pub was a couple of pints.' His tone is weary, his defences down, and he sounds as though he has barely enough energy to talk, never mind think through a lie. 'And some vodka before we left the club.'

Exactly as Mark said.

'You're not going to tell Dad, are you?'

'I already left a message on his machine.'

He says something under his breath. It sounds like 'such a wanker'.

'He's your dad, Robbie. He loves you.'

'He'll build it into a mega-deal. You know what he's like.'

'Robbie, it is a big deal.' I hesitate before saying quietly, 'You could have died.'

'Yeah, but I didn't.' He turns his body over so that he's facing the other way, his shoulders hunched against me.

I stand up and lean across him. 'Would you like me to sit by your bed for a bit?'

'There's no point, Mum. I'm really tired.' He opens one eye. 'Thanks for coming, though.'

'I'll go home then. Let you sleep it off.' I bend down and kiss his cheek. 'I'll be back tomorrow with some clean clothes.' I kiss his cheek again. 'I love you, remember?'

'I know.'

That's as much as I'm going to get, but it's enough to reassure me that he's doing all right. He's on the mend. Thank God. I leave the curtain open behind me and walk back towards the waiting area, letting go of the breath I seem to have been holding, and stretching out my back and neck. Tension dissipates and I start to feel like this is manageable; this is doable. There's no point jumping ahead, even although my gut feeling tells me that both Mark and Robbie are telling the truth.

So how, then, did the drug get into his system?

Don't worry about that now, I tell myself. Take it slow. The main thing is that Robbie's recovering. He's going to be fine. No doubt, within the next couple of days, we'll find out what happened and then we'll be able to put the whole sorry incident behind us.

My self-reassurance comes to an abrupt halt when, up ahead of me, I hear a voice saying, 'I'm not looking for special treatment but I am looking for speedy answers.'

I round the corner and find Phil talking to Dr Walker. He's dressed in casual trousers and an expensive-looking polo shirt with different widths and shades of grey stripes running across it. I don't recognise the clothes because he's changed his whole wardrobe since he left me. All part of shedding his former self. He sees me approach and looks me up and down. 'Were you out?'

'Yes.' The dress I'm wearing is silk and feels like warm water against my skin. I think I look good in it but I turn away before I'm tempted to examine Phil's expression to see whether he thinks so too. Even after a year of living without him, I'm still programmed to seek praise and comfort from him. It makes me angry and impatient with myself.

'Who's looking after Lauren?'

'She's at Amber's for a sleepover.'

'Have you told her about Robbie?'

'I'll tell her tomorrow.'

'I'll collect her from Amber's and tell her.'

'I'd rather you didn't,' I say forcefully. 'And anyway, it's not your weekend.' I try to sound matter-of-fact but suspect that all I sound is petty. Dr Walker is watching us both, his face giving nothing away, but still I feel embarrassed behaving like this in front of him. 'I'm going to take Mark home.' I look at the doctor. 'Thank you for everything.' We shake hands. 'I'll be back tomorrow for Robbie.'

2

I walk away from both men knowing I'm leaving Dr Walker with the brunt of Phil's questions, but I'm sure he's coped with worse and I'm too tired to share the load. Phil is a consultant psychiatrist, and at the moment, he'll be Rolodexing through his memory until he comes up with the best of his medical or surgical contacts. My gut instinct tells me that Dr Walker is an experienced professional but that won't be enough for Phil. He'll be seeking a second opinion. He'll want one of his cronies to verify Dr Walker's credentials. And he'll do that in front of Dr Walker. Conventional wisdom tells us that people don't change but Phil is rapidly becoming someone else: a more uptight version of his former self. He's increasingly pedantic and pernickety and, at times, downright insensitive. It makes me want to divorce him all over again.

A & E reception has reached boiling point. The men who were waiting in the queue behind me are talking to the security guard, jabbing accusing fingers close in his face then pointing back at a nurse who's standing with her arms crossed, her expression rivalling stone for immobility.

I hover close to the reception desk and look for Mark. All the chairs are taken and at least twenty people, in various states of insobriety and ill health, are milling around. There's heartbreak in the corner where a nurse and a doctor are trying to calm a middle-aged couple who've clearly just been given bad news. The husband is sobbing so much that his small frame is convulsing in on itself. 'There but for the grace of God,' the woman standing next to me says, and we acknowledge this with grim faces and tight lips.

I can't see Mark anywhere so I dodge and excuse my way through the throng of people and out on to the forecourt which is flooded with light. Edinburgh isn't known for its generous weather but today was sunny and upbeat enough to make Milan or Barcelona proud, and the night air is unusually balmy and warm. Three ambulances are parked in front of the building and have their rear doors open. The paramedics are standing on the tarmac, drinking from Styrofoam cups and chatting to each other in humorous tones.

Mark is about twenty yards away on a grass verge, smoking a cigarette and talking to a group of their friends – two boys and a girl – Simon, Ashe and Emily, all of whom I know from the hockey club. Mark sees me coming, stubs out his cigarette with his foot and steps forward to greet me. 'Liv! How's Robbie? Is he okay?'

'I've just spoken to him. He's groggy, but after a good sleep he'll make a full recovery.'

'Thank God!' Mark says, and all four of them smile with relief.

'And thank you, Emily,' I say, turning towards her. She is petite, no more than five feet tall, and she leans in to me as I give her a grateful hug. 'Without your help he would have been in a far worse state when the ambulance arrived. And then who knows how it would have panned out?'

'I'm glad I could help. It was horrible to see him like that.' She gives an involuntary shudder, her eyes bleak. Her mascara has run and she's wiped it to the sides so that grey streaks track into her hairline. 'I was really scared.'

'You did brilliantly,' 'You didn't look scared,' 'You were great,' the boys say all at the same time, and I can't help but smile. Emily is often round at our house and I know how popular she is with them all.

'I learnt first aid in fourth year but never imagined it would come in handy. I'm planning to become a doctor actually.'

'Right,' I say. 'And have you applied to any medical schools?'

She nods. 'I'm hoping for a place at Glasgow, dependent on next year's exam results.'

'Good for you! It's not easy to get into medical school these days.'

'No, it's not.' She stares off towards the main road, her teeth worrying at her lower lip. 'I'm really glad Robbie's okay again but I should be getting home. My parents will be wondering where I am.'

'Of course. Let me call a couple of taxis.' I glance at Simon and Ashe. 'Tell me where you all live and we can work out the best routes.'

'We can get the night bus,' Simon says.

'No, really.' I already have my mobile out of my bag and am dialling City Cabs. 'I appreciate the effort you've made to come and support Robbie.'

'We're the West End,' Simon says, pointing to Ashe and then himself.

'And I'm Murrayfield,' says Emily. 'So it makes sense for us to share one.'

I make the call and the controller promises two taxis within ten minutes. The boys talk about football and Emily asks me whether I plan to go to anything at this summer's festival. I say I haven't seen the programme yet and she tells me about a couple of the fringe events she's interested in. We're just discussing the merits of various venues when the first taxi pulls up. I offer it to Emily and the boys, hand the driver the fare and say to Emily, 'Listen, if ever you want some work experience in a GP's practice, let me know.'

'I will.' She smiles at Mark and me. 'See you soon.' As the taxi pulls away, all three of them wave to us through the back window.

Mark's kicking a small stone with his right foot, balancing it on the end of his toes then sending it up into the air. His T-shirt is still stained with Robbie's blood but it doesn't seem to be bothering him any more. 'You're not going to tell Mum about this, are you, Liv?'

'I think I'll have to, don't you?'

'She's not going to be happy.' He lets his foot drop and the stone rolls off into the gutter. 'I'll be grounded for about a month.'

'Unfortunately, it might get worse before it gets better.' I fold my arms across my chest. 'The thing is, Mark, Dr Walker's sure that Robbie ingested a fairly large quantity of GHB.'

He stares at me blankly.

'We need to find out how this could have happened.'

'The doctor must be wrong.'

'He's too experienced to be wrong. And if you and Robbie are telling the truth—'

'We are telling the truth!' He tugs at his hair. 'Jeez! Why does nobody believe us?'

'Because it's more likely he took it himself, and is lying about it, than someone else gave it to him.'

'He's *not* lying.'

'So how did it get into his body?'

He thinks for a moment, doesn't come up with anything.

'I'm wondering whether his drink was spiked,' I say.

The stone is back on his toes, teetering and then falling. 'Except that none of our group would do that,' he says.

'So you can see why people will think Robbie was trying the drug, took too much and ended up collapsing.'

'I suppose so.' He glances at me through the floppy pelt of his hair. 'But you believe us, don't you?'

'I do, as it happens. Even although you lied to me about where you were spending the evening.'

'That was kind of more of a white lie.'

'A white lie is when you're trying not to hurt someone's feelings.'

He screws up his face.

'But, anyway, if Robbie's drink *was* spiked then it's a crime and it needs to be reported to the police.'

'Shit.' Mark's mouth hangs open and he rolls back on to his heels. 'Mum will go fruit loops if I get expelled.'

'Why would you get expelled?'

'We shouldn't have been in the pub and if the police start asking questions . . .' He gives a resigned sigh. 'The head's been freaking out about drink and drugs and fake IDs. It gives the school a bad reputation. There'll be zero tolerance if we get caught.'

'Well . . .' It's on the tip of my tongue to say, *You should have thought of that before you went into the pub.* In fact, if they had, Robbie wouldn't be lying in a hospital bed recovering from the after-effects of an overdose. But I don't say this. It's neither the time nor the place to start berating him. 'We'll cross that bridge when we come to it. If necessary your mum and I will go to see Mr Wellesley.'

A taxi screeches around the bend and comes to a halt in front of us, its diesel engine idling noisily at the kerbside. We climb in, I shout my address to the driver and we begin the fifteen-minute drive home. For the first few minutes Mark's quiet, staring out of the window as the cab speeds through streets, empty of all but the odd cat slipping through the shadows. We pass by rows of darkened tenement buildings, their rooftops silhouetted against a sky that's bright with an almost full moon and a cascade of tiny stars. The traffic lights are with us and the taxi keeps up a steady thirty miles an hour; then the driver takes a corner at speed and Mark and I are thrown together on the seat.

'He thinks he's in a rally car,' Mark says as we both use the handles above the doors to pull ourselves upright again.

'I expect he wants to get home too,' I say. 'The lucrative time of night is long past.'

'So, do you think . . .' Mark sighs and looks around him. 'I can't believe Robbie almost *died*.' He slumps forward and rests his forearms on his thighs. 'It's such crazy shit.'

'You're telling me.' An echo of the fear that gripped me in A & E returns and the air in the taxi cools. I take my cardigan out of my bag and cover the goose bumps on my arms. 'Was there anyone in your group who doesn't like Robbie? Or thought it would be funny to spike his drink?'

'No, we all get on okay. Well . . . like there's Dave Renwick but Robbie and him are cool now.'

I lean forward, mimicking his posture, my arms and face level with his. 'And was Dave in the pub?'

'We're all mates now. He wouldn't do anything like that.' He frowns, as if he's having trouble processing the whole thing, and I realise it's better to wait until he's had a sleep. I don't want to force him to speculate, so that he ends up coming up with what he thinks might have happened rather than with what did happen.

The taxi comes to a stop outside our house. I pay the driver and we walk up the path, the scent of overgrown honeysuckle worth breathing in deeply for, cleansing me of the smell of blood and vomit and other people's sweat. I unlock the front door into the porch where shoes and bags take up most of the floor space. I move as much as I can to one side with my foot and then we go inside the hallway where our dog Benson immediately launches himself on top of Mark. Benson is a four-year-old Jack Russell terrier who has a kamikaze streak that has him leaping off stairs. He is full of canine charm, a one-off, and unlike most small dogs he's not prone to incessant barking. We all love him.

'I won't wake you in the morning, Mark,' I say. 'I'll fetch

Lauren and Robbie and we'll be back after lunch. Then I thought we could all have a relaxing afternoon together.'

'Sounds good.' He brings Benson's wriggling body off his shoulders and on to the floor where he tickles him into submission.

'The emphasis is on *together*,' I say. 'Because I'm not letting either of you out of my sight.'

'Cheers, Liv.' He stands in front of me, his shoulders sloping, head lurching forwards on his neck. 'I'm really sorry about everything. I know you thought we were just hanging out round at my place and then coming back here.'

'I don't appreciate being lied to,' I say.

'We shouldn't have done that.' He takes a step closer and hugs me awkwardly. 'It won't happen again.'

'No, it won't.' I give him a friendly cuff around the ears and push him towards the stairs. 'Off to bed and don't forget to clean your teeth.'

I go into the living room and sit down next to a toppling pile of ironing that's waiting to be done. I rarely wear high shoes and my feet are killing me, so I bring them up beside me on the sofa and massage the soles until they feel as though I'll be able to walk without them hurting. Benson jumps up too, his button brown eyes fixed on my face as he waits for me to give him a clue as to what's happening next. 'What are we going to do about Robbie, Benson? This has been a bad scare. A very, very bad scare.' Benson's eyes soften. He can do kamikaze but he can also do comfort. He rests his head on my lap and stares up at me. 'How could this have happened? Do you think somebody wanted to scare him?' He gives a sympathetic, throaty growl. 'Or maybe the drug was meant for someone else and it got into his drink by mistake?' I tickle the spot between his ears. 'I don't know what to think. I don't know—' The phone starts to ring and I jump, then stumble the few paces across the room and grab the receiver. 'Hello?'

'I'm calling to give you an update.'

It's only Phil. My shoulders immediately relax. I thought it might be Dr Walker telling me that Robbie's condition had deteriorated.

'I'm leaving the hospital now. Robbie's obs are stable.'

'That's a big relief.'

'He's fast asleep.'

I bet he is. Eyes tight shut so that he doesn't have to answer any of Phil's questions.

'I asked Bob Nichols in neuro about Walker.'

'And?'

'He's only been in the post six months, so that explains why neither of us knows him. He's very experienced. Worked in St Thomas's in London for a long time. Even spent three stints in Afghanistan as part of the volunteer doctor service.'

My gut feeling was right then.

'Have you spoken to Leila and Archie?'

'Mark's sleeping here tonight. I'll speak to them tomorrow when they get back from Peebles.'

'What're they doing in Peebles?'

'They're staying at the Hydro. A weekend of luxury.' I pause. 'It's Archie's birthday. They've been looking forward to it for ages.'

This cuts no ice with Phil. 'They need to know what Mark and Robbie have been up to.'

'I know and, as I said, I'll call Leila tomorrow.'

'Did you know the boys were going to a pub?'

'Of course not!'

'Where did they say they were going?'

'Round to a friend's and then back home.'

'And you went out?'

'Robbie's *seventeen*, Phil. In six months he'll be eighteen.'

'We need to have a serious talk, Olivia. Not only is our son lying about how he intends to spend his evenings, but he's drinking in pubs – presumably with fake ID – and, worst of all, he's taking illegal drugs.'

'I don't believe Robbie took any drugs.'

'You think Walker has the wrong diagnosis?'

'No,' I say slowly. 'What happened to Robbie is consistent with a GHB overdose. I accept that. What I don't accept is that he took the GHB himself.'

'And your opinion is based on what?'

'Both boys are adamant that they didn't take any drugs.'

'Olivia.' He sighs. 'Teenagers lie.'

'I'm aware of that. But based on what I know about our son, I think he's telling the truth.'

'And yet he lied about how he was spending the evening?'

'In his mind, I think there are different types of lying.'

'Meaning?'

'Meaning that he doesn't want me to forbid him from going to the pub so he lies about that. As far as he's concerned, he's not putting himself in any danger and I'm never going to find out, so what does it matter?' I sit back down and pull my knees into my chest. 'But taking drugs to the point of collapse is something else. Think about the sort of child he's always been . . .'

'Robbie's no longer a child. And, as you well know, drug taking is something that needs to be swiftly addressed.'

'He's not impulsive or reckless,' I continue. 'He mixes with a good group of kids who work hard, play sport. I mean . . . Just take a moment to think about it, Phil.'

'I am taking a moment to think about it and the conclusion I'm coming to is that you want to believe he's not lying because it saves you from having to take control.'

'*What?*' I drop my feet on to the floor and stand up again.

'Both Robbie and Lauren need more active parenting.'

'I *am* an active parent,' I say, incredulous. 'I talk to them; I care for them. I cook and clean, make sure they've done their homework and are behaving respectfully towards others. I take them out, give them opportunities and have fun with them. But most of all, *most of all*,' I repeat, my voice cracking with pent-up emotion, 'I love them, Phil. Absolutely and completely.'

'Erika says—'

'It's two in the morning,' I snap. 'I'm hard pushed to care about what Erika thinks at midday on a sunny Sunday, never mind at this time of night.'

'Olivia, this—'

'Good night, Phil.' I put the phone down and climb the stairs to bed, quietly seething. I know I'm on a hiding to nothing trying to get Phil to see my point of view, but I'm not going to allow him to bully me into disbelieving Robbie. I also know that, objectively, it looks as though I'm being naïve, but I do believe Robbie. Yes, teenagers lie to their parents, but not all the time.

Neither am I going to let Phil twist this around so that he feels justified in pushing for shared custody. When we separated we drew up a custody agreement and he requested that Robbie and Lauren stay with him every other weekend. That's what he wanted and that's what he got. But recently he's been asking to spend more time with the children and it's been the children themselves who prefer to stick to every other weekend. They're more comfortable here, in this house, with me, than they are with Phil and his girlfriend Erika. And, like it or not, Phil will just have to accept that.

Next morning I collect Lauren from her friend Amber's house. There's a gaggle of giggling girls in the living room and they all shout hello to me apart from Lauren. She says an effusive goodbye to each of her friends, grabs her stuff and follows me out of the room.

'Why do you always have to be the first mum to arrive?' She throws her overnight bag on the back seat and then launches herself in beside me. 'It's so *annoying*.'

'I'm sorry, Lauren, but we have to go to the hospital and I was worried that if I picked you up afterwards I would be too late.'

'*The hospital?*' It's a wail of refusal. 'This is *not* my Sunday to be with Dad.'

'I know. We're not going to Dad's hospital.' I swivel towards her in the seat, determined to do this carefully. Lauren and Robbie are close. She's six years younger than him, which could mean he would find her a pain, but in fact there's always been a noticeable lack of friction between them and, good times or bad, they have fun together. I know that when I tell her about what's happened she'll be worried about Robbie and cross with me for not letting her know immediately. 'I have something to tell you, but before I do, I want you to know that there's no need to worry.'

'What do you mean?' She's frowning but there's a tremble close to her lip because, underneath all this attitude, she's afraid.

'Robbie got into a bit of trouble last night.'

'What sort of trouble?'

'He had to spend the night in hospital.'

'Why?'

'He collapsed in town. Mark called an ambulance.'

'Why?' she shouts back. 'Why did he collapse?'

I tell her what happened. I don't bring emotion into it. I don't say he could have died. I don't say that it looks as if his drink was spiked. But what I do say is still enough to make her face blanch and her lips shake.

'He's my *brother*. You should have called me.'

'I thought about it, but it was already after midnight—'

'I wasn't asleep!'

'And I felt that A & E wasn't a good place for you to be.'

'Like I don't know about hospitals!' she shouts. 'I've spent hours waiting for Dad and saying hello to his patients. People who dribble and cry and look completely weird.'

'Yes, I know but—'

'And, *and* Robbie would have wanted me there.' Her eyes are ice blue and she uses them to good effect, pinning me to the seat with an arctic glare.

I break eye contact with her, start the engine and leave Amber's street behind while Lauren stares straight ahead, completely still apart from her hands that busy themselves on her lap. She has developed a habit of tearing at the edges of her nails, creating hangnails for her to bite and chew on. Often she does this with such intensity that she makes them bleed. Occasionally she lets me take her hands and rub calendula cream into them but mostly she keeps them out of my reach.

'I thought that on the way to the hospital we could stop at the supermarket and buy all Robbie's favourite food,' I say, glancing over at her. She's still showing me her profile. 'What do you think?'

'Where's Mark?'

'In bed. In our house.'

'Shouldn't we go straight to fetch Robbie?'

'I called the hospital. He's had a good night – what was left of it. They won't let him leave until midday anyway.'

'Did you tell Dad?'

'Yes. He was at the hospital when I left last night.'

'Did Robbie speak to him?'

'I'm not sure.' I turn into the supermarket car park, slowing down for the speed bumps. 'He didn't seem very keen.'

'You shouldn't have called Dad.' Now she's looking at me. 'You shouldn't tell him about private stuff that happens to me and Robbie.'

'I had to, Lauren. He's Robbie's father. He has a right to know.'

'He left us. He shouldn't have any rights.'

'He didn't leave you two. He left *me*.'

'That's just crap that parents say to try and make children feel better. It's pathetic.'

She climbs out of the car and I do too. We've had this conversation many times before and she settles into the familiar groove of 'he rejected all of us, he left the whole family.' Last year, when he told her he was moving out, she was so stunned that she was slow to believe him. 'We're the perfect family. You can't leave,' she said, following him from room to room as he packed his belongings. 'You're making a mistake, Daddy. This is all wrong.' He was kind to her, he explained himself to her, but still he left, and all her little girl's trust and faith was trampled on. 'How could Dad leave? I don't understand!' she shouted at me. 'We have to stop him. What can we do to stop him?' On and on, until, finally, she accepted it. No more crying, no more asking me to try and get him back, just a nut-hard acceptance that he'd let her down. We'd both let her down.

'He pretends to care about me and Robbie,' she says, following me into the store. 'But really he only cares about himself and that silly bitch Erika.'

'Don't say words like "bitch", Lauren.'

'For God's sake, Mum!' She stamps her foot. 'You care about all the wrong things. You're just so stupid!'

'Okay, that's it!' I stop walking and hold up my hand, forcing my temper low in my chest. 'I have been through enough for one weekend and I am *not* going to have you being rude to me like this.'

She stands mute and angry for a couple of seconds before her face becomes first pinched and then stricken. 'I'm sorry.' She throws herself at me and hugs me as though she never wants to stop. And then she starts to cry, silently, as if her tears are worth nothing.

'Listen, sweetheart.' I hold her away from me so that I can look into her eyes. 'I know times have been hard, but Daddy loves you very, very much. He absolutely does.'

'I don't care about Dad.' She gulps in a mouthful of air. 'I only care about you and Robbie.'

'Well, Robbie and I, we care about *you*.' I kiss her forehead. 'And we're doing fine!' I manage a laugh. 'We could be better – especially your brother – but nothing that can't be sorted by some treats.'

She looks up at me then, her eyelashes wet with tears. 'How much is he allowed?'

'As much as you think he can eat. Fill up those hollow arms and legs of his.'

'No limits?'

'None.'

'Cool.' She wipes her tears on to her sleeve, grabs a trolley and runs a few steps before jumping on to the back of it. 'We can buy him that ice cream with the caramel pieces in and tortilla chips and dips. Oh, and the spring rolls with the prawns in them and raspberry trifle.'

I nod and nod and nod again and in ten minutes we have a trolley full of enough treats to last a month. She watches my face as I pay for it all. I know she's wondering whether we can afford it and so I give her a confident smile, waving my credit card around as if it's a magic wand.

One of the conversations I regret Lauren hearing happened six months ago when Phil and I sold the family home and split the proceeds. He combined his share to buy a place with Erika and I combined my half with a mortgage on a house for the children and me, much smaller but still convenient for school and work. Although my salary is decent, after the mortgage and household expenses, there's barely anything left over. Phil was complaining to me one day about the fact that I'd stopped buying organic food for the children and I told him in no uncertain terms why this was the case. Unfortunately, Lauren heard me, and she's been worrying about money ever since.

Before we climb into the car she grabs my arm. 'I'm sorry I'm a bit-ch-*eeky* to you sometimes.'

'Well recovered.'

'You know that's not even a bad word.' She stares up at me through a fringe of straight blond hair. 'Not like the f-word or the c-word.'

'Neither of which I want to hear coming out of your mouth.'

'Well actually, Mum.' She's holding a stick of liquorice and she bites the end off. 'I heard *you* say the f-word once.'

'Must have been in a moment of extremis.'

She rolls her eyes.

'Must have been!'

'And I can't have moments of . . . whatever?'

'I just don't think it's very becoming for young ladies to swear.'

'La-di-da!' she affects a posh accent. 'How very Jane Austen.'

We both laugh and our light mood continues until we pull into the hospital car park. 'Take some change and get a ticket, will you, Lauren?'

She stares at the change but doesn't take it. 'Will he look the same?'

'Robbie? Of course!'

'Will he smell funny?' She climbs out of the car. 'Will he have memory loss?'

'Hah!' I pretend to think. 'You might have missed a trick there.' I walk across the car park and slide one coin after another into the machine. 'This was your opportunity to claim his bedroom.'

'You mean I could have stayed at home and moved everything over and he would be none the wiser?'

'Would have been a plan.' I hand her the keys and the ticket and she skips back to the car.

'He could have had the shoebox at the back of the house—'

'Your bedroom is hardly a shoebox, Lauren!'

'And I could have had his attic room.'

'It's cold up there in the winter.'

'Benson would keep me warm. Do you think it's too late? Do you think he might swap with me?'

'You can ask him.' I offer my hand. 'Come on. Let's go inside.'

She takes my hand and falls into step beside me. When we're a few feet away from the building, I feel her hand grip more tightly on to mine. Both my children have been subjected to too much time waiting around in hospitals. Even before our separation, Phil would take the kids to work with him at weekends if he was on call. Emergency admissions for acute symptoms of self-harm, episodes of hypermania or psychotic hallucinations – it all kicks off over the weekend. While Robbie sat in Phil's office and lost himself in comics or hand-held game consoles, Lauren absorbed all the activity like a sponge takes in water. She saw far too much distress and confusion, but whenever I asked Phil to please not take her, he insisted that it was a good learning experience for her. The public only shunned the mentally ill because they didn't understand what was happening. Stigma came about because of lack of information, and while I didn't exactly disagree with him, exposing Lauren to the sharp end did her no favours and she is rapidly developing a hospital phobia.

'I never, *ever* want to be a doctor or a nurse. All those smells and naked bodies and crying and . . .' She shudders.

'Don't worry, hun. This isn't like your dad's unit. It'll be fine. I promise.'

I'm relieved to see that the A & E reception is a different place from last night. The queue has been cleared and there's a feeling of calm about the place. A couple of small children, looking tired but cute, are playing with the toys in the corner while their mother sits in a chair, holding her baby close to her chest, mewling sounds coming from within the blankets. I tell the nurse I'm here to collect Robbie and she points me through the double doors. As we're walking along the corridor, I look through an open doorway and see Doug Walker sitting behind a desk. 'You're still here?' I say.

He stands up. 'Catching up with patient records.' His scrubs are rumpled and drops of blood are dotted across the material. 'This latest government hasn't done anything to simplify the process.' He takes his glasses off and rubs the bridge of his nose. 'And you must be Lauren?'

She nods.

'Your brother's been telling me about you.' He moves from his side of the desk to ours. 'Would you like to see him?'

She stares up at me. 'Is that okay, Mum?'

'Of course. Here!' I hold out a carrier bag. 'Take him his clothes. I'll join you in a minute. I need to have a quick chat with Dr Walker first.'

Dr Walker calls over to one of the nurses and she comes towards us. I give Lauren a gentle nudge and she follows the nurse into the adjacent ward where Robbie has spent the night.

'She's very sweet,' Dr Walker says.

'She can be.' I follow him back into his office. 'Do you have any children?'

'I have two sons.'

'It's hard on family life when you have to work on a Sunday.'

'The youngest is twenty. Neither of them lives at home any more. They're both at Edinburgh University.'

'That's why you moved up from London?'

He raises his eyebrows at this.

'I'm sorry.' I hold up my hands. 'It's none of my business. Phil was speaking to a colleague and—'

'Checking me out?'

'Checking you out,' I acknowledge. 'It was rude and unnecessary.'

'It's not a problem. Parents show their anxieties in different ways.' He pushes the door almost closed and returns to his side of the desk. 'Have a seat.'

'I just wanted to ask your advice.' I sit down opposite him. 'Robbie's adamant that he didn't take any GHB last night and so I really feel this incident should be reported to the police. Don't you?'

Dr Walker rests his elbows on the desk and steeples his fingers in front of his chin. 'Your husband—'

'Ex.'

'I beg your pardon.' He gives a half smile. 'Your ex-husband seemed to think that Robbie might be lying.'

'Yes . . . well, I don't. And spiking someone's drink is a crime, isn't it?'

'Absolutely.'

'I noticed there's a sign for Lothian and Borders Police at the entrance to A & E.'

'They have a small office there. It's not routinely manned but you might be lucky because I know there's a policewoman in this morning taking down details of another case.'

'I'll have a word with her.' I stand up. 'And if she wants details about Robbie's treatment, shall I point her in your direction?'

'We'll need Robbie's permission before giving out any information.'

'Okay. I'll speak to him first.' I hold out my hand. 'Thank you, Dr Walker.'

'Good luck with getting to the bottom of it.' His eyes are kind as he shakes my hand. 'And congratulations again on your nomination for the award.'

I leave him to his paperwork and follow the signs round to the Toxicology Unit. It's not quite visiting time and a Sunday hush pervades the corridor, empty of people, the only sound the soft squeak of my trainers on the linoleum floor. As soon as I walk on to the ward, Lauren sees me and comes across, slipping her arm through mine before she whispers, 'Robbie's behind the curtain getting dressed.'

'Great.'

I discuss Robbie's care with the charge nurse, then the curtain is pushed aside and Robbie appears fully clothed, walking gingerly as if the floor is hurting his feet. After thanking the nursing staff, we head towards the exit, and I ask Robbie whether I have his permission to report what happened to the police. 'Because if you didn't take these drugs yourself, then someone gave them to you.'

'Okay.' He shrugs. 'Whatever.'

'And you didn't take them yourself, did you?'

'No, I didn't, Mum.' He stops and looks fully into my face. 'Honestly, I didn't.'

His eyes are an icy blue, exactly the colour of Lauren's, and of my own, and I'm convinced I can read them. I've caught him in lies before and every time his gaze automatically avoided the scrutiny of mine and his lips tightened at the corners. None of this is happening now, and I give him a hug, relieved that I'm able to trust him.

Dr Walker's right and we're lucky enough to find the policewoman at the A & E reception. Robbie and I tell her about what happened overnight and she promises that we will have a follow-up visit before the day's end. Then the children and I go out into the sunshine and stroll back to our car. All the while, Robbie's laughing at Lauren's attempts to persuade him out of his attic bedroom and into her smaller one '. . . if you think about it, Robbie, you'll be nearer the kitchen and the bathroom and . . .'

We begin the drive home and I quieten the voice in my head by reminding myself that we need to be thankful we've got through this without any serious harm done. This works for a little while but, before we've even reached our house, a worry worm settles itself in the comfortable hollow beneath my sternum, reminding me that, glad as I am that Robbie didn't take the drugs himself, it raises the questions of who gave them to him and why. Much as I want our journey home to mark the end of this incident, I know that it's far from over yet.

3

'Obviously drug abuse of any sort is something that we in the police service want to clamp down on.' Detective Inspector O'Reilly looks around at each one of us. 'But drink spiking is particularly corrosive and if found guilty the person can be sentenced to up to ten years in prison.'

It's late Sunday afternoon and we're all jammed together in the living room – Phil, Leila, Archie, Mark, Robbie and myself, spread out on the three couches and two easy chairs, facing each other. I prefer not to invite Phil into the house, but it was either this or we all went down to the police station, and Robbie, despite his assertion that he feels fine, has dark smudges under his eyes and looks as if he hasn't slept for a month.

Lauren has gone for a walk with Benson and Erika. On her way out she gave me an injured look as if she'd drawn the short straw being stuck with Erika. Phil denies that he left me for Erika but he did, and much of my own and the children's animosity has been directed her way when, in actual fact, she isn't so bad. A bit serious, but essentially well-meaning, and I don't envy her the task of trying to persuade a moody and anxious Lauren into conversation.

Leila is sitting forward on her seat, her expression unusually solemn. Even at forty-one she has an exotic beauty that always draws a second glance. Her hair is jet black and lush with natural curls that sit on her shoulders. Her eyes are tiger-orange, a blend of old gold and autumn leaves, and normally her teeth flash white against the caramel warmth of her skin, but at the moment she isn't smiling.

I telephoned her as soon as we got back from the hospital and told her what had happened. She listened in silence – very un-Leila like – until I got to the part where I was waiting in the hospital, aware that Robbie was in the Resusc room but with no idea as to how critical he might be.

'Why didn't you call me?' Leila said.

'I would have if you hadn't been an hour's drive away and celebrating Archie's birthday.'

'You should still have called me! I can't believe you've had to go through this on your own.'

'Fortunately I wasn't kept in the dark for too long but it was scary while it lasted.' I told her that the police were taking the possibility that Robbie's drink was spiked seriously, and were due at my house later in the afternoon.

'We'll drive back straight away.'

'You don't have to.'

'I think we do.' She inhaled a sharp breath. 'Are you sure the boys are telling the truth?'

'About taking drugs? Yes, I am. Phil isn't, though. He thinks Robbie's lying and that I'm being naïve for believing him.'

'Well Phil's going to disagree with you, isn't he? But still.' She paused. 'I know we read a lot about drink spiking these days, but isn't it usually for date rape?'

'Not exclusively. I've heard about cases through the centre. I think it might be more widespread than either of us realise. I'm hoping this incident with Robbie will be part of a pattern that the police already know about.'

She gave an impatient sigh. 'Wait till I get hold of Mark.'

'It wasn't his fault, Leila. The boys shouldn't have been in the bar drinking but I think their mistake ends there.'

'But haven't we always told them that they should be honest and that they should look after each other?'

'He did look after Robbie. He was very brave actually. And he came to the hospital in the ambulance.'

She mumbled something I couldn't hear. Leila has four children but Mark is her eldest and her only son and she has high expectations of him. When, almost two hours later, she arrived at my house, there was no stopping her taking Mark aside and giving him an earful. I watched him make repeated attempts to argue back, but Leila wouldn't listen and finally he simply stood with his head bowed, stoically taking the verbal punishment.

Since the two policemen arrived, we have all sat listening as they talk us through the investigation. DI Sean O'Reilly is doing most of the talking. He is broad shouldered and dark haired and, although he has an Irish name, he talks in a very definite Scottish accent. More Glasgow than Edinburgh, the rhythm of his speech has a relaxed, singsong quality unlike most east coast accents. His colleague is PC Harry Bullworks, and on the few occasions he speaks, he sounds as though he's come down from the Highlands. His hair is red-blond, his freckled skin covers delicate, almost feminine features, and he writes everything down with a hurried hand and a watchful eye towards the boss.

'Two officers are at the bar in the High Street having words with the manager,' O'Reilly says. 'Checking CCTV footage and finding possible witnesses. All the staff who were on duty that night will be questioned and officers will go back every evening next week to speak to clientele.'

'Do you think this could have been perpetrated by someone who's already known to the police?' I ask. 'What I mean is – are there people who routinely commit this sort of crime?'

'Possibly. In cases of date rape, for example, the perpetrator may have acted before. But an incident like this is most likely to have been perpetrated by somebody Robbie knows.'

We all look at Robbie. It's hard to tell what he's thinking.

He's staring down at his bare feet, curling his toes into the carpet. He looks vulnerable and I want to hug him to me, but I know he won't appreciate my show of affection and protection when there are so many of us in the room.

'Friends sometimes spike each other's drinks. Usually it's just for jokes. Other times it's malicious,' DI O'Reilly says. 'In light of Robbie's condition when he arrived in A & E, it appears he ingested a hefty dose.'

'Hardly a joke then?' I say quietly.

'It's possible whoever did this made a mistake with the amount but . . .' His expression is reluctant. '. . . I'm inclined to think it's malicious.'

'But why? Who would do that?' Anxiety churns in my stomach. Phil is next to me on the couch and I catch myself in the act of reaching out to hold on to his arm, diverting my hand at the last minute to grab at a cushion. I hug it tight to my middle. 'It doesn't make sense.'

'It can't have been any of my friends,' Robbie says.

'But you don't know the hockey crowd that well,' Phil says.

'*You* don't know the hockey crowd that well,' Robbie says, glowering at Phil. 'But *I* do.'

'The fact remains, that if you didn't take the GHB yourself—'

'For the hundredth time,' Robbie says, leaning across the space between himself and Phil, '*I didn't take anything.*'

'So one of the crowd must have a grudge against you,' Phil pushes on. 'Could you have offended someone?' Robbie's face shuts down. He says something under his breath and slumps back against the sofa, his feet jerking a frustrated rhythm on the carpet. Phil glances along the couch at Mark. 'Can you think of anyone Robbie might have upset, Mark?'

'For God's sake!' Robbie says before Mark has a chance to answer. 'They're just not like that! None of them take GHB themselves, never mind giving it to me!'

'We have to consider every possibility,' Phil says. 'Otherwise you'll never find out how the drug got into your system.'

'So what if we don't?' Robbie challenges. 'It's happened and it's over and I just want to get on with my life.'

'What we'd like to do now,' O'Reilly says, interrupting the palpable current of animosity flowing from Robbie to Phil, 'is to take statements from both boys.' He looks at Mark and Robbie then turns to me. 'Is there another room where PC Bullworks can take Mark's statement?'

'Yes.' I shoot to my feet. 'We have a small study next door.'

'Are we allowed to be present?' Leila says, indicating herself and Archie.

'That's up to your son. At seventeen, we're legally entitled to question him without parental consent.'

We all look towards Mark who steals some quick eye contact with Robbie before saying, 'I can handle it.'

'Are you sure?' Leila says. 'Because I'm not.' She squeezes Archie's sleeve. 'Do you think he should have one of us in there with him? Or a lawyer even?'

Before Archie can answer, O'Reilly says, 'Neither of the boys is being charged with anything, but they are perfectly entitled to have legal representation if they wish.'

'It's fine, Mum,' Mark says, impatience showing in the tight expression on his face. 'Stop making such a big deal of everything.' He marches off through the door and Bullworks follows him. Archie takes Leila's arm and says something quietly into her ear. I expect her to argue her point but she doesn't; she follows him out of the room and into the kitchen.

'Help yourself to tea and there's plenty of food in the fridge,' I shout after them. 'Would you like some tea, Detective Inspector?'

'No, thank you.' He smiles at me before swivelling round to where Robbie is standing by the window staring out into the overgrown back garden, a climbing rose encroaching on the light and reminding me that I need to get out there and put some time into the garden before it gets away from me and becomes more than I can manage. 'Robbie, would you mind if I talk to your parents first and then we can have a word?'

'Sure.' Robbie's mood brightens at once and he makes a beeline for the door. 'I'll be in my room.'

'Glad to be off the hook,' O'Reilly comments as the door slams behind Robbie.

I've yet to retake my seat and now that there's more space I don't need to sit back down next to Phil. He knows more intimate details about me than any other man on the planet – not just the sort that involve sex, but all the other stuff that counts for just as much, if not more: dreams and ambitions, fears and regrets, all my day-to-day realisations and concerns. I trusted him with all of me, felt our confidence-sharing engendered closeness. For over twenty years he was the repository for everything I thought and felt, and yet now that counts for nothing and we keep a distance between us, a polite space, safe from each other's heat and touch. It still makes me sad that what started out as a deep and meaningful connection has ended up like this.

'Can I just ask,' I say. 'Could this be a case of mistaken identity?' I sit down in an armchair several feet from both men. 'Or simply a random crime? I mean, I know Robbie's friends and he's right – they're all very supportive of each other.'

'What about the fight he had at school?' Phil says, and I sense O'Reilly's ears pricking up.

'There was a problem at school last term with a boy in his year,' I tell O'Reilly. 'They ended up having a fight in the common room and were both suspended for a couple of days.'

'We never quite got to the bottom of it,' Phil says. 'And neither did the headmaster, but it seemed like Robbie was as much to blame as the other boy.'

'They're good mates again,' I say.

'How do you know that?'

'Mark told me.'

'Mark's going to side with Robbie. For all we know, their dislike of each other may have continued out of school and this could be the boy retaliating.'

Phil's only following the same line of thought as I did when I questioned Mark in the taxi but, hearing him talk like this, in front of O'Reilly, feels like a betrayal of Robbie's trust, and I try to prevent a cold expression closing down across my face. It's a bit like trying to stop a sneeze and I know I'm not succeeding.

'What was this boy's name?' O'Reilly says.

'David Renwick.'

He writes it down in his notebook.

'But I really don't think he could have had anything to do with it,' I add. 'Otherwise the boys would have flagged him up as the obvious suspect.'

'That's for the police to decide,' Phil says.

Irritation spikes in my chest and I try to breathe through it. I once participated as a facilitator in an anger management course and I practise one of the techniques now, visualising a scene that makes me feel calm: a sandy beach, Mediterranean sunshine, a lounger placed just in the shade, a good book, a cold drink by my side, the children playing happily in a turquoise sea. Not a care in the world.

'I'm wondering,' Phil says to O'Reilly, 'whether you think Robbie's reaction is normal for a teenage boy?'

'In what way?'

'He doesn't seem to care about who did this to him.'

'Well . . .' O'Reilly shrugs. 'Teenagers generally think adults are making a fuss about nothing. As far as he's concerned, it's happened, it's over and he wants to get back to what interests him. Or – ' he tilts his head – 'he might have something to hide. Do you think that's a possibility?'

'Yes,' Phil says. 'I do.'

I give a deliberate sigh before staring down at the floor.

'I think there's a possibility that he willingly took the GHB,' Phil says.

'I *completely* disagree.' My voice is loud. 'I think—'

Phil holds a hand up towards me and I stop talking, not because he's commanding me to, but because O'Reilly is watching me and I want to keep my cool, put forward my opinion as calmly as possible.

'I find his lack of interest in who's done this to him suspicious,' Phil reiterates. 'It's as if he knows there's no point pursuing it.'

I stay quiet as Phil and O'Reilly discuss the likelihood that Robbie and Mark are both lying. This goes on for a couple of minutes, Phil talking in his psychiatrist's voice about the unreliability of adolescents and O'Reilly listening with, I'm pleased to observe, a noncommittal look on his face.

'Several times in the room just now, they glanced . . .' Phil pauses, '. . . slyly at each other.'

'They weren't sly glances,' I say into my hand. 'They just don't like being under the spotlight.'

O'Reilly turns to me. 'You don't think the boys might be lying in order to protect each other?'

'No,' I say.

'Do you think they could have bought the GHB and what happened was an accidental overdose?'

'No, I don't believe they bought the GHB.'

'And as far as you know your son does not use drugs?'

'Well . . . nothing stronger than alcohol and the odd smoke of marijuana. And if you look at his record, you'll see that – apart from that one incident at school – he's not a child who's ever been in trouble before.'

'With all due respect, Dr Somers, most parents don't know the half of what their teenagers get up to.'

Phil is pleased at this comment and stares at me as I reply. 'That's as maybe. But I think it extremely unlikely that my son is using drugs.'

'No changes in his behaviour over the past year?'

'No . . . well, yes,' I admit. 'But that's been because Phil and I separated.'

'Robbie has shown signs of situational depression and anxiety,' Phil chips in, and I turn to him, aghast.

'*What?*' I say.

'I think anxiety over the break-up has caused him to kick back against us both and to question his own place in the family. You know that children from broken homes are more likely to have problems—'

'Not exclusively,' I cut in.

'Significantly. Marital breakdown is not good for children.'

'And who caused the break-up, I wonder?' Out of the corner of my eye I see DI O'Reilly lean forward in his seat.

'This is neither the time nor the place to discuss our relationship,' Phil says in his calm but firm voice.

'No, you're right, it isn't,' I say with a forced steadiness. 'And I would appreciate it if you would comment as a father rather than a psychiatrist.'

'All I'm trying to establish here,' DI O'Reilly says, his palms upwards as he appeals to us both, 'is whether or not you think Robbie might know who did this but is either too afraid to tell us or is protecting that person.'

'I don't believe for one second that Robbie knows who did this or is protecting the person who did,' I say firmly.

'What DI O'Reilly wants to establish, Olivia—'

'Don't *patronise* me, Phil. I'm not stupid.' I hold his eyes. It's difficult, because resentment has filled my mouth with bitterness and I want to spit words at him, words that have nothing to do with Robbie and everything to do with us. 'I'm not taking Robbie's side because I'm naïve. I'm doing it because I believe he's telling the truth.' I look back at DI O'Reilly. 'I am a trained doctor and I have not noticed signs of depression in my son. He has been moody and awkward at times but nothing beyond the realms of the ordinary. I am one hundred per cent sure he's as much in the dark about this as we are.'

'Good.' O'Reilly gives me a reassuring smile and there's a sympathetic expression in his eye that makes me feel he's no stranger to marital discord. 'So . . .' He looks down at his notebook. 'One final point. You're linked to the shelter in the Grassmarket, aren't you?'

'Yes. I volunteer there two evenings a week.'

'That's the reason you're up for the City Women award? I recognise you from the papers.'

I nod. When, way back in September, I saw I'd been nominated for the award, I was pleased at the publicity it would give to the centre, never imagining it would turn me into a reluctant mini-celebrity.

'Does Robbie ever go with you?'

'To the centre?'

'Yes.'

I think I see where this is going. The centre has a zero tolerance policy on illegal drug use, but most of the people the centre aims to help are, or have been, drug users, and I've no doubt that drugs are sometimes brought on to the premises and hidden in places where the staff can't find them. 'He's only visited the centre once. Both children came with me on Christmas Day last year when we joined in with the party. Otherwise neither of them ever accompany me because I don't think it's appropriate. The clients deserve their privacy and the children would gain nothing by being there.'

'And Robbie has no connections to the centre otherwise?'

'None.'

'Okay.' DI O'Reilly smiles at us both. 'I think I have everything I need from you. I'll have a word with Robbie now.'

'And will you be questioning all the young people he was with that evening?' Phil asks.

'Absolutely. We'll get the names from Robbie and follow them up.'

'I'll call him.' I open the door, walk the few steps to the bottom of the stairs and shout up to Robbie, breathing a sigh of relief that I got out of the living room before I had a proper go at Phil. I don't remember when he started speaking to me in his oh-so-tolerant tone, as if I'm one of his patients, but it's become one of the triggers that snap my antennae into attack mode. While I wait for Robbie to appear, I can just about hear Phil conversing with DI O'Reilly. I catch phrases like 'everything I can', 'putting the children first' and 'my experience with adolescent behaviour' and it makes me groan. 'Sod off, Phil,' I say under my breath. 'You're full of hot air.'

Robbie thumps his way down the stairs and I give him a quick hug before he can sidle past me. 'Would you like either myself or Dad in there with you?'

He shakes his head. 'Like he says, I'm not being charged with anything. I can do this on my own.'

'Be absolutely truthful, hun, won't you?' I hold him still so I can look up into his face. 'It's important they catch this guy before he does it to someone else.'

'I don't have anything to hide, Mum. Honestly, I don't.'

I give him another hug then send him towards the living room. There's a short exchange between Robbie and Phil when Phil suggests to Robbie that he stays in the room during the questioning and Robbie point-blank refuses, folds his arms and braces himself against the doorframe, his posture challenging. I don't wait to see what happens next. I walk through the kitchen and outside where there's a wooden table and four chairs at the bottom of the back garden on an old stone patio that has split in places and has weeds growing up through the cracks. Archie and Leila are sitting in what's left of the sunshine, two glasses and a bottle of wine between them.

'We spurned tea in favour of the wine bottle.' She holds it out to me. 'Want to share what's left?'

'I won't yet. I need all my faculties about me when I'm dealing with Phil. I wanted to brain him in there. He's so bloody full of his own importance.'

'I never liked him that much,' Leila says.

'Leila,' Archie warns her.

'Well I didn't!' She takes my hand. 'I'm not saying I actively disliked him, but I never thought he was good enough for my best friend.'

We really are best friends and I pull a chair up next to her and lean my tired head against her shoulder. We first met at the evening social before the start of medical school, back in the eighties when we were both eighteen. I was standing by myself in a roomful of strangers, overcome by crippling shyness and wanting nothing more than to blend into the dusty, russet velvet curtains that hung from ceiling to floor across the rectangular windows. Our eyes caught and held for a couple of seconds and then she worked a path towards me across the polished oak floorboards, dodging through groups of students who were striking up tentative conversations with each other. She was holding two drinks, and she handed me one, then linked our free hands together and said, 'Come on, I want to show you something.' We went up a flight of red-carpeted stairs with an ornately carved banister and then through a door and up some cold concrete stairs that were narrower and dirtier. At the top of this there was another door and more stairs, metal this time, and a sign that said 'emergency access only'. Leila took no notice of this and led us both through the door, up the final set of steps and on to the roof. I gasped. We were on top of the world and the view was breathtaking: Edinburgh Castle, the city lights, church spires and Arthur's Seat.

'Wonderful, isn't it?' she said.

'Amazing!' I laughed and turned round with my arms at full stretch, soaking up every inch of the skyline and then looking further up at the blanket of sky where stars pinpricked the darkness. 'How did you know about this?'

'I have three older brothers and two of them came here to study medicine.' We sat down next to each other on a layer of bricks at the base of a tall chimney. 'And the third one studied medicine at Glasgow.'

'A family of doctors?'

'Just as my parents dreamed.' She leant back on one elbow and used her other hand to wrestle a packet of cigarettes and a lighter from the pocket of her dress. 'They're from Pakistan.'

'You recently moved here?'

'No, no!' She laughed. It was deep and throaty and much more grown-up sounding than I expected. 'My parents came here almost thirty years ago. I was born here. Do I sound like I'm from Pakistan?'

'No.' I blushed. 'You sound like you're from here. I'm just getting used to the accent.'

'You're not Scottish, though, are you?' She regarded me with interest. 'Southern or Northern Ireland?'

'Southern.'

We sat on the roof and talked for the rest of the evening. I told her my first name was Scarlett, but I preferred to be known by my middle name, Olivia.

'Why?' Leila asked.

'Scarlett doesn't suit me,' I said, guessing that one day I'd tell her the full story, but for now I wanted to keep the details to myself.

We discovered we had one major thing in common – we both had three older brothers and no sisters – but otherwise we couldn't have been more different. I was blonde, quiet and serious. I kept my head down, worked hard, and was too shy and lacking in confidence to make waves. Leila was fiery and intense and would speak up in class and challenge anyone to anything. I was bowled over by her and my admiration has grown into a lasting friendship.

'Mark still isn't out yet,' she says, fiddling with the stem of her wine glass, the silver bangles on her wrist catching the sunlight.

'I expect PC Bullworks is being incredibly thorough.'

'Do you think either of the boys actually understand the seriousness of it?'

'I'm not sure. It isn't cool to be afraid when you're a teenage boy and I think Robbie, in particular, is in denial.'

'He's probably still in shock,' Archie says. 'Give him a few days. I'm sure he'll feel differently.'

'And there's the thing.' I throw out my arms. 'Who would want to do this to him?'

'Liv.' She grabs my hand. 'It has to have been a mistake. Maybe one of the other boys in their group was messing about. Who could possibly want to hurt Robbie? It's absurd.'

'The police think it was deliberate.'

'And are the police always right?'

'They have more experience of this than you or I do.'

'Yes, but they don't know Robbie. We do. It might turn out to be someone who does this sort of thing.' She reaches across the table and gives me a hug. 'Let's wait and see what the police investigation comes up with.'

It sounds like a good plan but I'm not convinced. 'Has

Mark said anything to either of you about Robbie being picked on?'

'No. But make no mistake, I'll be quizzing him,' Leila says. 'If there's anything worth knowing, I'll find out. I promise.' She gives me a sympathetic smile. 'On a lighter note, how was it with Fraser?'

'Fraser?'

'Your date. *Fraser.* You went down to Leith, to that fish restaurant. The one that has all the good write-ups.'

'Oh God yes!' I lean back on the seat and feel honeysuckle tickle my cheek. 'It was okay. But after Mark's phone call I had to leave in a hurry. Left him standing there, poor man. I'll ring up and apologise.'

'So you got on with him?'

'He seemed nice enough.'

She slumps with disappointment. 'But no chemistry?'

'None. And quite honestly, I'm not sure he's over his wife.'

'What am I going to do with you?' she moans. 'It's a whole year since you and Phil separated. You spend evening after evening moping at home—'

'I don't mope!'

'—when you could be having the time of your life.'

'Much as I'm grateful to you for setting me up, Leila, I can manage my own love life.'

'Or lack of.' She folds her arms and sighs. 'How about a younger man? He wouldn't want to bore you with conversation. You can shop and spend time with your friends while he watches the football. He'd love your cooking. You wouldn't need to nag him about his health. In fact, because it will never be long term, you wouldn't need to nag him about anything.'

I shake my head at her. 'Are you actually my friend? Or has she been taken by aliens?'

'A younger man is worth considering.' She gives me a salesman's you're-missing-out face. 'Less baggage.'

'Always presuming that a younger man would consider me an option,' I say, playing along. 'I can't bring someone back here. I have Robbie and Lauren to think of.'

'You don't have to bring him home.'

'I'll go to his place, shall I? A flat-share in Tollcross, his mates coming into his bedroom to filch cigarette papers?'

'It would help to loosen you up! Stop you being so tense around Phil.'

'My sex life is not my top priority, Leila.'

'It doesn't have to be at the top but it does need to be on the list.'

'There's just no winning with you.' I look across at Archie who's wandered off to the garden shed and is rearranging the ivy on the trellis next to it. 'There's just no winning with her, is there, Archie?'

'When she gets an idea in her head, she's like a dog with a bone. My advice is to surrender now.' He flashes his wife a knowing smile. 'Resistance is futile.'

She smiles back at him and I feel a twinge of jealousy. Instead of time and teenagers wearing their marriage out, the passing years have strengthened their bond and they're united in their love for each other and for their children.

'Okay. Fraser wasn't right,' Leila acknowledges, fixing her eyes on mine. 'So we'll cast the net a tad wider.'

'I'm not Internet dating,' I say firmly. 'I'm happy on my own.' That's not exactly true and she sees it in my face. 'Okay, I'm not happy on my own but I don't want a new man enough to go on blind dates. They make me nervous and then bored.'

'Actually . . .' She looks up at me through lashes that are sleek and full without any need for mascara. 'What about the policeman in there?'

'Which one?'

'Not the weedy ginger one! The one who looks like Sean

Connery, minus the moustache. Don't you think? In his Bond years.'

'You are impossible!' I'm laughing again. 'You would have me flirt with a *detective*? Will this be before or after he finds the person who spiked Robbie's drink?'

'He *was* looking at you, Liv.'

'He was looking at *everyone*. That's what policemen do – suss people out. Anyway, he's probably married.'

'No ring.'

'Lots of married men don't wear wedding rings.' I remember his face when I was having the spat with Phil. I get the feeling he's divorced or separated but I don't say that to Leila. I don't want to give her any encouragement.

The back door opens and immediately Leila's expression changes from hectoring friend to stern mother as Mark comes out of the house.

'How did it go?' she asks him.

'Fine.' His hands are in his pockets and he gives a typically teenage shrug.

'You were completely truthful?'

'Yeah.'

'Are they going to want to question you again?' Archie asks.

'He said probably not, but if he does he'll get in touch.'

'Let's get you home, then,' Leila says. She stands up and pushes the chair in under the table. 'Have you said thank you to Liv?'

'Thanks for having me, Liv.' He looks up from his shoes. 'Sorry about . . . everything.'

'That's okay, love.'

'In the car,' Leila orders, directing him ahead of her. 'We need to collect your sisters from Granny and Granddad's.' She glances back at me. 'I'll ring you this evening.'

I follow them round to the front and see them into the car

and as I'm waving them goodbye, Erika, Phil and Lauren are coming along the pavement, Benson several yards behind them. Phil must have gone to meet them when he realised Robbie wasn't going to let him sit in on the questioning. Lauren is walking slightly apart from them both, finishing off an ice cream. Erika and Phil are holding hands, not in a casual manner but in a very deliberate way, fingers linked tightly as if they are skin-grafted together. Erika is a couple of inches short of six feet, with dark brown hair and muddy brown eyes. She's always formally dressed in expensive, pressed trousers and white or black tops. She is German but her accent is slight, her English near perfect. Everything she does and says seems to me to lack spontaneity. Communication is not casual with Erika. She is someone who chooses her words cautiously, each word carefully selected before being doled out on a measuring spoon, and I find myself wanting to finish off her sentences for her. She was a colleague of Phil's before they became involved with each other but she wasn't someone who made a lasting impression on me and I certainly never imagined that she would attract Phil enough for him to give up on his marriage and his family life.

I move back against the hawthorn hedge and watch them for a few seconds. The sight of them, so obviously happy together, ties a knot in my stomach and I turn away quickly and run back inside.

4

The next two weeks race by. DI O'Reilly and I speak most days. He tells me that the police have questioned the pub staff and Robbie's friends who were there that night. Three boys and two girls admit that they too have fake IDs and spent the evening in the pub. There is no evidence that any of them had GHB with them and, although questioned at length, they all consistently deny any knowledge of what might have happened. And anyway, none of them has any motive for harming Robbie. Dave Renwick, the boy whom Robbie fought with at school, is one of the three boys who were there. He is as shocked as everyone else at what happened. He says there's no animosity between himself and Robbie now, and their friends and teachers back this up. The police show the staff and teenagers CCTV footage of persons leaving and entering the pub, but nobody notices anyone suspicious.

Robbie's story is covered in the *Edinburgh Courier – Dr Olivia Somers, nominated for one of the City Women awards, son in drink spiking incident* – with witnesses asked to come forward. Several people get in touch with the police to say they were in the pub at that time, but, when questioned, they have nothing to add to the inquiries. 'Despite all our efforts we have nothing to go on,' O'Reilly tells me. 'It's a complete dead end.'

The lack of evidence is grist for Phil's mill as he's still convinced Robbie and Mark are lying. He uses it as an excuse to badger me for more time with the children, but the terms of our custody agreement are clear and I don't give in, not least because the children have told me numerous times that they feel uncomfortable in Phil's new home as everything is too tidy and quiet. As Lauren put it – 'I don't feel like I belong there.'

I still believe Robbie and Mark's version of events but am coming to the conclusion that it must have been a random attack as there is no evidence, or motive, for anything deliberate. Robbie has recovered from his ordeal and his first day back at school I go with him. Although the hockey club members don't all attend the same school, four of them do and were in the pub that evening. It's not as bad as Mark feared, none of them are expelled, but the head punishes them by suspending them for a week and banning them from the end-of-term trip down to London. As parents had already paid a non-refundable sum for flights and accommodation, most of them were given further sanctions at home.

'I wasn't that keen on going anyway,' Robbie says.

It's five thirty and I've come home from work to find Robbie, having discarded his uniform, wearing boxers and a T-shirt, sitting in the living room with his bare feet up on the coffee table watching one of the *Star Wars* films for the umpteenth time. There are four cereal bowls and several cups and glasses at arm's reach either side of him. He's been grounded for a month; either Phil, Leila or I drop him at school and bring him home again. He isn't allowed out in the evenings but I do allow his friends to come here. He's reluctantly accepted all of this, convinced I'm making a fuss about nothing. I don't know how I expect the incident to have changed him – Afraid? Preoccupied? Concerned that his underage drinking exposed him to such a potentially dangerous incident? – but what I do know is that he doesn't look like a boy who takes anything seriously.

'Nothing from DI O'Reilly today?'

He looks at me blankly. 'Dunno.'

'Don't know, don't care?' I bite back.

'Well, what's the point in caring?'

'Robbie!' I say harshly. 'Are you ever going to grasp the gravity of what happened to you? You were minutes, probably seconds, away from dying.'

'Yeah, well I didn't, did I?'

'I just need you to understand that it was serious.'

'I get it, Mum. There's no need to go on about it. Shit happens.'

'Don't swear, please.' I stand in front of him with my hands on my hips. 'And not only that. Look at the fallout! Several boys suspended. Parents losing money on the trip.'

'I'll pay you back.'

'With what?' My voice becomes shrill. 'You don't have any money!'

'I'll get a job.' He tips over sideways so that he can see past me to the television. 'This is a good bit.' He makes a Yoda voice and says, '"Fear leads to anger. Anger leads to hate. Hate leads to suffering."'

I sigh loudly and count to ten, knowing there's no sense in pursuing this now. I'm too tired to find a way to get through to him. I'll end up shouting and go to bed feeling like a rotten mother. So instead, I roll up my sleeves and gather together the bowls, irritation bubbling back into my speech. 'Has it ever occurred to you to rinse a bowl out and reuse it?'

He looks at the stack of bowls in my hand, his face confused as if they multiplied on their own. 'Have I had four lots of cereal?'

'It would seem so,' I say, heading towards the kitchen.

'By the way, Uncle Declan rang,' he shouts after me. 'Something about Gran and operations and could you call him.'

Declan is my eldest brother and he runs a farm back in

Ireland, close to where my mother still lives. My mother and I do not have an easy relationship, and I've been dreading this phone call. She's been on the waiting list for a hip replacement for some months now and, by the sound of it, the date for the operation has come through. Declan works full time and his wife Aisling has just given birth to their fifth child. They won't be able to manage my mother's aftercare on their own and my other two brothers now live in America. It's my turn to step up. I change out of my work clothes then sit back on my bed with a glass of wine in one hand and my phone in the other. My brother answers and we say our hellos, then he tells me the date of the op and when Mum's expected to come home. 'I don't want to have to ask you, Scarlett,' he says, calling me by my first name. 'But with Aisling just having the baby, 'n' all . . .'

'You do so much for Mammy as it is. It's definitely my turn to help.'

'You can always stay with us if the thought of being cooped up with Mammy is too much to bear.'

'I might just take you up on that.' I can't help but sigh as I anticipate the arguments and long silences ahead. 'Let's face it, she's not going to want me around anyway. If it seems like she can manage without me overnight, I'll stay with you. But tell me. How's your new baby girl?'

'She's a picture of loveliness.' His voice softens and I know that he's smiling. 'Her brothers and sisters are all doting on her.'

He tells me about the children and, as I listen, I smile too. They're a perfect family and I'm looking forward to seeing them all again, and to meeting my new niece. We talk for a while about Robbie and the fact that the police still have no idea who did it, but as Declan points out, bearing in mind that two weeks have gone by and nothing else has happened, there's a good chance it was a random attack after all.

'And is it tomorrow you'll be getting your award?' he says.

'Maybe. If I'm chosen. I can't say I'm looking forward to it, but I've got a speech at the ready in case I do win.'

'Keeping it short?''

'You bet. I'd duck out of the whole thing if I could, but Lauren's so excited about it and it's taken her mind off the attack on Robbie.'

'You can do it, sis,' he tells me. 'Nobody deserves an award more than you do.'

We talk for another twenty minutes and then I go back downstairs to make tea. Robbie's found his trousers and has been joined by Simon, Ashe and Emily – the three friends who came to the hospital on the night of the incident. None of them goes to Robbie's school and so they aren't suffering the sanctions Robbie and his school friends are. Lauren has joined them and Emily is making friendship bracelets with her. They're good kids and I don't have the heart to ask them to leave, so I end up making jacket potatoes and salad for all of us and we enjoy a relaxed evening together. In my head, I hear Phil's complaining tone – You're too soft on the children. They need more structure, firmer handling – but I ignore it because they're his words, not mine.

Next day at work, I spend the first fifteen minutes catching up with messages. I have a couple of patients in hospital and I'm pleased to hear that they're both due to be discharged later in the week. There are seven GPs in the practice and Leila is one of them. We have rooms on the same corridor and she pops her head around the door to have a chat, but before we can say anything, she's called out to the reception and we agree to catch up over lunch. I turn on my computer and begin the morning's appointments. We have an intercom installed, but I always go through to the waiting room and call my patients through personally. The waiting room is heaving with people, all shapes and sizes, most of them either elderly or under the age of five.

'Agnes Abercrombie,' I call out.

Two elderly sisters, leaning into each other like collapsed balloons, look towards me. Although it's the beginning of June, the Edinburgh wind can be punishing and they're dressed for it. Their heads are swamped in furry hats and their tweed coats, faded with use, are buttoned up to the neck. Agnes, older by three years, is a frequent patient and one of my favourites. Her sister, who's not so strong herself, helps her make an attempt to stand up but Agnes's feet have only a tentative grip on the floor and she falls back into the seat again. I walk across to help and a man to my right coughs, a great guttural roar that sets a couple of others off. This is followed, immediately to my left, by a bout of sustained sneezing.

'Warming up their instruments,' Agnes says, looking up at me, her neck held at an awkward angle.

I hold out a hand and she takes it. Her fingers are gnarled, cold and dry as paper. She is crippled with arthritis but carries on, undaunted, her sense of humour and interest in the world around her what keeps her going. I propel her into a standing position and she holds my arm, scuttling along beside me. 'Unto the breach,' she says cheerfully, and we go to my room to begin the consult. I quickly ascertain that her pain medications have stopped giving her the relief she needs and I up them to the maximum dose.

'Don't be taking them with alcohol, now,' I tell her.

'Not me, no. Although my lovely grandson brought me some whisky back from the Black Isle, Doctor. It's peaty and sharp. Wonderful stuff! I'm making it last, measuring it out in a tot glass, and only on a Friday. It should last me until Christmas.'

'Your restraint is enviable,' I tell her as I help her back to the waiting room. 'If only all my patients were as disciplined as you.'

I see the two elderly ladies to the front door and call on my next patient, sixteen-year-old Tess Williamson. She is small and plump with unbrushed hair and tired eyes.

'So what can I do for you, Tess?' Her details are up on the screen in front of me and I notice she usually sees Leila, who prescribed her the contraceptive pill last month. 'I don't think we've met before, have we?'

'I normally see Dr Campbell.'

I know Leila's list isn't full this morning and wonder why she's chosen to see me instead. Sometimes teenagers have to be persuaded into telling me what's wrong and I give her a few seconds to speak before I begin to question her. There's a glass ornament on my desk, a freebie from a pharmaceutical rep, and she picks it up then turns it over so that purple teardrop-shaped globules slide through the hole and reform on the other side. She watches this process as if mesmerised, and then flips it over to begin again.

'How can I help you, Tess?' I say, a bit more firmly this time.

'Well.' She puts the glass down and tells me she has pain on urination. I ask her a few more questions and she answers with a textbook precision that always makes me slightly suspicious. Since information became so freely available, patients often check their symptoms online and add to the list, as the information draws their attention to symptoms they hadn't even noticed.

I reach into the drawer close by my feet, bring out a plastic bottle and write her name on it. 'Do you think you could give me a sample?'

'A sample?'

'Of urine.'

'Okay.' She takes the bottle from me. 'Is there a toilet?'

'End of the corridor. Last door on the right.'

While she's gone I read back over her notes, looking for signs of past medical or social history that might indicate difficulties. I can't see anything of interest and her family aren't known to me. She returns with the sample and I fill out a form and put it and the sample in a bag for microbiology. 'Results should be back within five days,' I tell her. 'But I can prescribe you a broad-spectrum antibiotic now if you want me to.'

She shakes her head. 'It's okay. I can wait.'

I'm growing more sure that there's something she's not telling me. Sufferers of cystitis are not inclined to refuse treatment when each time they pee feels as though they're passing cut glass.

I swivel my seat round towards her. It's meant to help her relax, to indicate I've got all the time in the world, but I watch her hands stiffen into fists on her lap. 'Is everything okay with you otherwise?'

'What?' She looks at me warily.

'I'm wondering whether there's something else you want to tell me?'

'Like what?'

'Well . . .' I look back at the screen. 'I see that last month you were prescribed the contraceptive pill.'

'Yes.' She's blushing. 'Is a problem with peeing a side effect?'

'Not from the pill, no. It is a side effect of sex, though. It used to be called honeymoon cystitis, back in the day when women were virgins until they married.' I smile at her to let her see I'm not judging her. Many girls are sexually active at sixteen and I respect that choice. As long as it is a choice and not a decision that's been foisted on them. 'And you're using contraception, aren't you?'

'Yes.'

'Is it working okay for you?'

'Yes.'

'No unpleasant side effects?'

'No.'

'You remember to take it every day?'

She nods.

'Unplanned pregnancies are best avoided.'

'I know.'

'And your boyfriend. Is everything going well with him?'

She shifts with discomfort, the blush spreading to her neck.
'I suppose.'

'Are you also using condoms?'

'No.'

'Have you heard of chlamydia?' No answer. 'It's a sexually
transmitted infection and one of the signs can be cystitis.' I
talk some more about it then hand her a leaflet from my desk
drawer. 'A smear test is all it takes to establish whether or
not you're infected.'

I'm about to say more but I stop talking because I can see
she's not listening. There are half a dozen photographs on
my walls and she's staring at the one of us as a family. It was
taken about five years ago on the top of Arthur's Seat. Fat
clouds billow like candyfloss across the blue sky behind us
and the wind is blowing our hair into wayward shapes around
our heads. Our body language is easy. Both Phil and I have
our outside arms around the children and our inside ones
around each other. I haven't taken it off the wall because it's
such a happy photograph and, despite what's happened since,
it brings back good memories.

'Aren't you divorced now?'

I jerk back in my seat. 'I'm sorry?'

'It said in the papers you were divorced.'

'Yes, I am, but I wasn't when the photograph was taken.
Now,' I give her my most doctorly smile, 'is there anything
else I can help you with?'

'How's Robbie?' She says it in a rush and then immediately bites her lip.

'You know Robbie?' I smile. 'How come?'

Her cheeks are redder than a ripe strawberry. 'From school.'

'Robbie's well,' I say evenly. 'He's completely fine now.'

She nods as if this is what she needs to hear and then she takes a shaky breath. 'Have the police worked out who did it yet?'

A cold wind blows up my spine. 'What makes you say that?'

'It's just that . . .' She frowns and shakes her head. 'I know they're trying to find the person who did it and I thought that maybe they had.'

I hold her wary eyes in mine, keep them there and lean forward until we are less than a foot away from each other. 'Tess, do you know something?' I say quietly. 'Is that why you've come to see me?'

'No, no.' Strawberry drains from her face. 'It's just that I like him and I wanted to be sure he was okay.'

'He's been back at school for a week. You must have seen him there.'

'I've been on holiday and I didn't go in today and . . .' She trails off. 'Thank you.' She's on her feet and I stand up beside her.

'If you know something, please tell me,' I say, placing a gentle hand on her upper arm. 'It's important we find out what happened that night.'

'I don't!' Her voice rises with hysteria and her head shakes from side to side as if she's watching a fast playing tennis match. 'I don't know anything! I don't! Leave me alone!' She hauls herself away from me, opens the door and all but flees through it.

'Wait, Tess!' I follow her along the corridor but am slowed down by a young mother coming out of one of the other consulting rooms, her buggy pushing into the corridor in front of me, and by the time she's turned it sideways, and I'm able to pass, Tess has gone. I run out on to the street and look both ways along the pavement, but it's a busy Friday morning and she's already merged with the crowd.

Bugger.

Back in my room I sit for a few seconds trying to absorb the significance of what's just happened. I don't think Tess has cystitis at all. I think she knows the symptoms from discussions with friends or Internet research. She made an appointment with me so that she could ask about Robbie. It's the first proper lead we've had since the incident happened and I call O'Reilly at once, waiting for almost ten minutes as the person on the other end tries to find him. Twice she asks me to leave a message – 'DI O'Reilly will get back to you,' she says – but I'm not about to be fobbed off. Finally, he comes to the phone.

'Is this an okay time to talk?' I say.

'I have a meeting in one minute.'

'It won't take long.' Without breaking medical confidentiality, I tell him about Tess's appointment with me, that she was asking after Robbie and that I felt as though she was hiding something. He tells me he'll get on to it this afternoon and will be in touch again later. 'You can't go round now?' I say. 'While she's still agitated. She might have composed herself by this afternoon.'

He tells me he's working on another case and that's just as crucial. I protest some more and he stops me short. 'You need to trust us, Dr Somers.' He sounds impatient. 'We want to find out what happened just as much as you do.'

I doubt that, but I can hardly say as much because I already feel as if I'm pushing his cooperation to breaking point. Up till now, he's allocated a good number of police hours to solving this. I know I've had more than my taxpayer's worth

of attention and I'm treading a thin line between asking
politely and hassling him for more time than he has. I liken
it to behaving the way a handful of my regular patients do;
patients who are convinced there's something wrong with
them and, no matter how many investigations we do that
turn up negative, they keep coming back.

But the thing is, I remind myself, sometimes their intuition
is right – they do have something wrong with them – but the
disease presentation is atypical and it takes us a while to work
it out.

I sit for almost a minute, agitating in my seat, worrying
about what Tess's strange behaviour might mean, but I have
no further time to dwell on it as the receptionist buzzes
through to ask me whether I'm ready for my next patient. I
answer yes and spend the rest of the morning working through
my appointment list.

At lunchtime I remember I need to register for some annual
leave to care for my mother and do it quickly before I forget.

'You'll never last two weeks,' Leila says, reading my email
to the practice manager over my shoulder. 'Why don't you
arrange for the community nurses to come in?'

'And then it'll be "my daughter couldn't even bring herself
to come over and help me",' I sigh. 'You're right, though, I'll
make sure proper care is set up before I leave. It's only fair
on Declan and Aisling.' I press send and take my plastic
lunchbox out of my bag. 'It won't be so bad. We can all stay
at the farm. The kids will be on summer holiday by then and
they love hanging out with their cousins, so at least they'll
be there to keep me cheerful.' My mobile buzzes on the desk
next to me – 'Phil' is flashing up on the screen.

'You not getting that?' Leila says, sitting down opposite
me and starting on her own lunch.

'It's only Phil. His latest idea is that Robbie, and possibly
Lauren, should have counselling. He's decided that Robbie

wouldn't have got himself into this sort of trouble if he was able to talk through his feelings on the divorce.'

Leila gives a derisive roll of her eyes.

'My thoughts exactly. Robbie is refusing to go, insisting that if his dad doesn't trust him to tell the truth then he doesn't trust his dad to have his best interests at heart.'

'So Phil still thinks Robbie is lying about taking the drugs?'

'More than ever. And apparently I'm a fool for believing my own son. But anyway,' I take a forkful of salad, 'I need to tell you about this morning. Does the name Tess Williamson ring any bells?'

'I see a fair bit of her mother Audrey. She's insulin dependent and her glucose levels are often all over the place so she's been hospitalised a couple of times recently. But I don't see much of Tess.'

'She came to you last month and you put her on the pill.'

'What's the problem? Side effects?'

'No.' I fill Leila in on what was said and she listens without interrupting until I get to the part where Tess said she went to the same school as the boys.

'I'm almost a hundred per cent sure she doesn't go to their school,' Leila says. 'She goes to a boarding school somewhere.' She takes a bite of samosa. 'She was always getting head lice and her mother was obsessed with getting rid of them.'

'Strange she would lie about the school she goes to,' I say, making a mental note to share this with O'Reilly. 'And then she said to me – have the police worked out who did it yet?'

Leila pauses mid-chew. 'It's a reasonable question, isn't it?'

'Except that most people would say "Have the police found the person who did it?" Asking whether they've *worked it out yet* implies that she knows something. Don't you think?'

'I see what you're getting at.' She wipes her hands on a paper napkin. 'You should have a word with your friendly detective.'

'I already have. He's going to follow it up this afternoon. I think I'm beginning to get on his nerves.'

'How come?'

'I was pushing quite hard for him to go and see Tess immediately and he was a bit short with me.'

'I expect he's juggling several cases at once.'

'I'm sure you're right.'

'Archie was saying you'll have had more police time because of the award you're getting.'

'Might be getting.'

'The police always give more attention to victims who have clout or have the education to get involved in the inquiry.'

'Cynical.'

'Realistic.'

'I suppose.' I sigh. 'Power and money do the talking.'

'You're telling me.' Leila launches into one of her favourite topics – reorganisation of the NHS – and we spend a couple of minutes mulling over changes we would make if we held any power before she comes back to the subject of Tess. 'Don't get your hopes up.' She touches my arm. 'It might be nothing.'

'It can't be *nothing.*'

'Teenage girls can be very odd though, Liv, can't they?' Leila says. 'Maybe she just fancies him and she came to see you because she was desperate for information.'

'Or perhaps she was the person who spiked his drink. Maybe he inadvertently hurt her feelings and she's become obsessed with him and wanted to get back at him but is feeling guilty about it now.' I fork some more salad into my mouth. 'I'll be interested to see whether the urine sample has anything in it.'

'What's that you're eating?' Leila asks, her nose wrinkling at the sight of what's on my fork. She peers down into the plastic box. 'Honestly, Liv, that looks revolting!'

'It's not. The beetroot has stained everything but it tastes okay.'

'Have some of mine.'

She holds out a samosa but I shake my head. 'I'm going dress shopping when I've finished lunch. I need to go easy on the carbs.'

'Is it for this evening?'

I nod and take another quick forkful.

'Talk about last minute! You'll hardly have any time to browse.'

'You're right. I'd better get going.' I put the lid back on my lunchbox and stand up. 'I said I'd collect the kids from school and I don't want to be late.'

'Where will you shop?'

'I'm thinking I'll start with the shops in George Street and then go on to John Lewis.' I take my jacket from the hanger on the back of the door and slide it on. 'Saving Harvey Nicks as a last resort because they'll probably have something gorgeous but it'll cost an arm and a leg.'

'Choose something that matches your eyes and shows off your assets.' She looks at her watch. 'I'd come with you but I have the asthma clinic at two.'

'I think I'll manage.'

'Don't chicken out,' she reminds me, pulling the collar of my jacket out and straightening the lapel. 'Get something spectacular.'

'From love police – ' I grab my bag and open the door – 'to style police.'

'I mean it, Liv.'

'Your voice is in my head!' I shout back as I run along the corridor.

For once the parking gods are with me. I find a space immediately and it doesn't take me long to find a dress either. The assistant in the second shop I go into takes a proactive approach and has me trying on four different styles. The one I end up buying is a halter neck in charcoal-coloured silk. 'It's a very fashionable colour this season and it goes so well with your skin tone,' she says. 'And the waterfall sash falling from just below the bust is very flattering on you.'

'I feel like I'm showing too much skin,' I say, trying to pull the material in to hide my cleavage. 'Don't you think?'

'Not at all,' she tells me, standing back and appraising me from head to foot. 'Walk tall and confident. You'll be a knockout.'

With no time to dither, I buy the dress, a matching bolero cardigan and then some spectacular shoes, and make it to school just in time to collect Lauren and Robbie. Lauren is beaming with excitement. 'I can't *wait* to put on my dress,' she tells me as she climbs into the car. 'I've wanted this day to come for ages and ages and now it's here, and Mum, did you find a dress?'

'It's in the bag on the floor there, but it's all wrapped up in tissue paper so better not take it out until we get home.' I glance across at Robbie who's in the passenger seat next to me. 'We have to pick up your suit,' I say to him. 'I'll stop on the yellow lines outside and you run in. It's all paid for.'

'Do I have to?'

'We're not having that conversation again. I know you don't want to wear it, but you'd look completely out of place in a grungy T-shirt and jeans.'

'Oh my God, Mum!' Lauren cries out. 'It's gorgeous.'

I look in my rear-view mirror and see that she's torn a small hole in the tissue paper and is fingering the silk.

'Don't get any marks on it, love, will you?'

'I won't. I promise.' She leans back in the seat and closes her eyes. 'This is going to be the best night of my life so far. I can feel it.' She places a hand over her heart. 'I can't believe they're sending a car for us.' She sighs as if she's just stumbled across the gateway to heaven. 'Amber says it will probably be a stretch limo with a DVD player and a bar. Do you think it will be?'

'I doubt it, Lauren. The council's budget won't stretch to that.'

Robbie rolls his eyes.

'Don't,' I mouth towards him. 'Don't spoil it for her.'

I'm itching to ask him about Tess Williamson but can't do it in front of Lauren. She's had trouble sleeping these past two weeks and most nights she has found her way into my bed. She's ten times more worried about Robbie's near-miss with death than he is, and no amount of reassurance has helped, mostly because we don't have an explanation for what happened. While Robbie can just shrug his shoulders and accept whatever life throws at him, Lauren needs to be able to understand the reasons behind each action, whether it's something simple like jealousy between friends or the complicated machinations of her parents' divorce. Much as I've not been looking forward to this award ceremony – my short speech is burning a hole in my handbag – I know it's been a great diversion from the other stuff and has given Lauren the boost she needs.

When we arrive home, she's through the door like a shot. 'I'm first in the shower!' She runs off up the stairs and, seizing the moment, I follow Robbie into the kitchen. He dumps his school bag at his feet and opens the fridge door.

'Robbie, do you know someone called Tess Williamson?'

He pours himself a glass of milk and drinks it down before answering. 'Don't think so.'

'She's not at school with you?'

'Not in my year.' Now he's in the cornflake packet, grabbing messy handfuls and chewing fast. 'What does she look like?'

'Short. Little bit plump. Brown hair, flat grey eyes. No remarkable features to speak of.'

'Well then I'm hardly going to notice her, am I?'

'Maybe you blanked her or were rude to her or something?'

'How can I have done that when I haven't even met her?'

'She made an appointment to see me at the surgery. But she was only pretending to be ill.'

He pauses his chewing.

'It was all very suspicious.' I can feel myself frowning. 'I think she might know something.'

'I see what's going on here!' He points a finger at me. 'You're turning into Miss Marple!' The thought amuses him so much that he laughs and sprays some half-eaten cornflakes on the floor in front of him.

'Robbie!'

'All you need is a lilac cardigan.' We both watch as Benson moves in to hoover up the crumbs. 'And some brown lace-up shoes.'

'Funny, ha, ha.' I take my mobile out of my handbag and check for messages. Still nothing from O'Reilly. 'I'd just like some closure on this thing, wouldn't you?'

'We might never get closure on it.' He shrugs and gives me one of those looks that makes being a mother worthwhile. It's a kind, almost indulgent look, and underneath it I can see that he loves me. 'Mum, seriously, you need to stop worrying. It can't be good for your health.'

'Thank you for those words of wisdom, but it's common knowledge that the moment you have your first child you can wave goodbye to ever being worry-free again.'

The journey in the car could take for ever as far as Lauren's concerned. 'It's just so awesome!' There's no DVD or mini-bar but the seats are leather and the windows tinted and it's far more upmarket than the cars either Phil or myself drive. 'Nobody can see in but we can see out.' She smooths her dress down over her lap. It's a raspberry pink chiffon with a swirl of sequins across the skirt. 'This is the nicest dress I've ever had. Amber said she's never seen a dress as pretty as this.' She grins at Robbie. 'You look really handsome. You don't even look like my brother.' He goes to swipe at her head and she ducks out of the way. 'Don't touch my hair!'

The ceremony is taking place in the Assembly Rooms, and when we arrive we have to pause for a photograph taken by the *Edinburgh Courier* photographer. 'We're celebrities!' Lauren exclaims, her enthusiasm infectious, and soon all three of us are smiling into the camera lens.

Upwards of three hundred guests are gathering in the ballroom which is about fifty metres long and has large casement windows facing on to the front street. The room is painted in two shades of blue with white woodwork and opulent gold cornicing. Three massive chandeliers hang from the ceiling and the mirrors at either end reflect them into infinity. 'It's like a palace, Mum, isn't it?' Lauren says.

'It's a veritable glitter-fest,' I say.

Martin Trimble, who runs the centre, comes across to us. 'Hello everyone. You all look lovely.' His eyes home in on mine. 'We need to work the floor, Liv. I've just seen William Nash go through into the drawing room at the end.' He's breathing fast, excited because there's so much money in the room and it's the perfect time for us to secure more funding. 'Why don't you tackle Nash and I'll find Elizabeth Upton? I know she's looking for a charity to support.'

'Will do,' I say. William Nash owns half a dozen timber yards around the city and we've heard on the grapevine that he's keen to get involved in a good cause. I catch Robbie and Lauren's attention. 'Listen, you two,' I say loudly, raising my voice above the hubbub around us. 'I'm going to have to circulate. It said on our invites that there would be food and drink in the break-out rooms at either end. Help yourself and make sure you stay together.' I look at Robbie. 'Don't leave your drink unattended.'

'Mum, nothing's going to happen to me here!'

'Better to be safe than sorry.' I kiss his cheek. 'And look after your sister.'

I watch them walk away, Lauren skipping and Robbie sauntering, and feel a swell of love for them both. William Nash is more than amenable to talk about contributing to the centre and I give him a rundown on what we do and where more funding is needed. 'I run a clinic two evenings a week,' I tell him. 'A lot of my work involves directing clients to the right services. We could use a part-time paid member of staff to organise follow-ups, as often clients just disappear back into the world and we don't hear from them again.'

He agrees that this sounds like an efficient way to spend money. We talk some more and then I move on to another donor, and another, until an hour has gone by and I'm in need of something to eat. Waiters are circulating with champagne and I've already swallowed too much of it. I look around to locate Robbie and Lauren, who have teamed up with another couple of children and are happily tucking into the buffet. I'm at the other end of the long table and I choose a couple of mini-quiches and some smoked-salmon blinis and put them on my plate. Over the past year, when I've been reluctantly socialising, I've felt an acute absence of Phil, like the fourth wheel came off the car and I can't move forwards without it, but this evening I'm not missing him. Progress! I smile to myself.

'Share the joke?'

I swivel towards the voice and do a double-take. It's DI O'Reilly.

'I'm not stalking you,' he says, handing me another glass

of champagne. 'My ex-wife's up for one of the awards. She trained as a social worker and has been director of a kids' project in Wester Hailes for the last five years.'

'Fantastic!' I aim a friendly punch to his shoulder, and it's his turn to do a double-take. 'Sorry!' I cram a vol-au-vent into my mouth. 'Too much drink and not enough food.' I swallow the mushroom filling. 'And nerves.' Then a lump of puff pastry. 'And now I'm talking with my mouth full. Anyway . . . fantastic that you're on such good speaking terms with your wife that she asked you along.'

'I expect it was one of my two daughters who forced her to ask me.'

I choose another vol-au-vent and try to eat it more gracefully this time, the alcohol in my bloodstream leading me off into my imagination where I picture what O'Reilly's wife might be like. My thoughts run the gamut from small and willowy with an enigmatic smile, to tall and substantial with a bawdy sense of humour.

'I take it the other Dr Somers isn't here?' O'Reilly says, surveying the array of finger foods.

'He would have to bring his new woman with him.' I let my eyes roll with exaggerated disapproval. 'They're joined at the hip.'

'As are my wife and her new woman.'

I lean towards him, not sure that I heard correctly, the laughter of the man next to me drowning out his words. 'Her new woman?'

'That's right.'

'Ah . . .' I make a sorry face. 'Well, I'm sure it was nothing you did – or didn't – do.'

'It's quite common now, apparently.' He tips an oyster into his mouth and swallows it down. 'Women in their forties becoming lesbians.'

'Is it? I thought sexuality was an absolute.'

'Not any more. It's the modern "We can all make ourselves up as we go along" attitude.'

'Talking about making things up,' I say, 'any luck with Tess Williamson?'

He nods. 'Bullworks spoke to her earlier this evening. In fact, he'd spoken to her already because she was in the pub that night.'

'Really?' The man beside me is still guffawing and I move a foot in towards O'Reilly so that I can hear him better. 'So what's her story?'

'She was out for the evening and was sitting at an adjacent table with some friends of hers. CCTV and witness statements confirm this. None of them knows Robbie personally, but when they were leaving the pub, they saw him lying on the pavement and the paramedics arriving to treat him. She said it upset her and that she wanted to follow it up.'

'Does that ring true to you?'

'There's no reason to suspect her or any of her friends of anything sinister. They all came forward without prompting.' He spears a tiger prawn with a cocktail stick. 'Have you asked Robbie whether he knows her?'

'He says he doesn't.' I take a sip of champagne then think better of it and put the glass down on the table. 'And it still doesn't explain why she lied about where she goes to school.'

'Everyone lies to their doctor, don't they?'

'About how much they smoke and drink, maybe, but she brought the subject of school up.' I take a glass of water from a circulating waiter's tray. 'I really think she knows something. She bolted from my consultancy room like her life depended on it.'

'Her behaviour is odd, I agree.' He shrugs, as if it's all a mystery to him. 'There's something going on with her, but it may well have nothing to do with the case.'

I glance along the table to where Robbie and Lauren are

still standing talking to the other children. 'Well, I'm glad you're here.' I raise my glass to him. 'I automatically feel safer.'

He tips his head at the compliment.

'I know I've been a bit pushy,' I say.

'On the contrary, I've begun to look forward to our daily chats.'

'I bet you say that to everyone.'

He gives me an unreadable look that makes me wish there was a thought bubble coming out of his head. Leila's right, he does have a sort of craggy attractiveness that several glasses of champagne have only amplified.

'My friend Leila thinks you look like a young Sean Connery,' I blurt out.

'I've had that before.'

'I don't suppose the comparison does you any harm.'

He steps back and looks at me from my feet to my eyes. 'Good dress, by the way,' he says, knocking back another oyster. 'You've been hiding quite a figure under that doctor's coat.'

'I don't wear a doctor's coat.' His eyes are smiling and I feel the hot coals of attraction glow in my stomach. I'm not dead below the waist after all, then. Leila would be proud of me. The thought makes me laugh and I say with narrowed eyes, 'Detective Inspector, we're not flirting, are we?'

'Dear me, no. I wouldn't trust myself with a woman like you. Too brainy for the likes of me.' He makes a regretful face. 'And I can't imagine what you'd want with a crusty old copper like me.'

The champagne has made me bold and I hold O'Reilly's eyes as I imagine quite a few things I'd like to do with him; things that would warrant a private room, warm hands and detailed attention to parts of the body that don't normally see much daylight.

'Caviar tastes weird,' Lauren says, appearing at my side, her cheeks flushed and her eyes buzzing.

'It's an acquired taste,' O'Reilly tells her, breaking away from my stare.

'People always say that, but what does it actually mean?'

'It means that if you eat it often enough you grow to appreciate the flavours.'

'Ladies and gentlemen,' the MC interrupts. 'If you would all be good enough to take your seats. The time has come for us to present our guests of honour with their awards.'

'Good luck,' O'Reilly says, and I smile my thanks as we take our designated chairs towards the front.

I'm up against three other nominees – not O'Reilly's wife; she's in a different category – and the MC gives the lowdown on each of our achievements before announcing the winner. When I hear my name called, I'm aware of hugs from the children and Martin before walking on to the stage, concentrating very hard on not tripping up. My speech is short and to the point and I stare out into the sea of faces, thanking Martin, who's given body and soul to the project, and the rest of the staff at the centre, many of whom are volunteers. The award I'm presented with is a small glass plaque on a walnut stand, and when I'm back in my seat, I give it to Lauren to hold. She traces her fingers over the raised gold script and says, 'This is really special, Mum.'

The rest of the evening passes in a blur of promises and congratulations. I don't get the chance to talk to O'Reilly again but I see him on the other side of the room with a couple of girls in their late teens who must be his daughters. Twice I catch his eye. We both smile and I let myself hope that maybe, when all this is over, he'll ask me out and we'll get to know each other properly.

Then, in no time at all, we're back in the car and home again. 'I don't suppose I'll drive in a limo again.' Lauren stands at the kerb, her expression wistful as she watches the car drive away.

'I think you will, my sweet.' I kiss the top of her head. 'I think there are many sunny days ahead for you.'

Robbie unlocks the front door and we all go inside. 'Where's Benson?' he says, missing the usual rush of dog to our feet.

'Maybe we shut him in the kitchen, did we?' I ask, trying to think back, my clarity concealed in a fog of alcohol and tiredness and – dare I admit it? – interest in Sean O'Reilly, with his knowing eyes and brusque, masculine charm.

'He was on the stairs when we left.'

'What's that smell?' Lauren wrinkles up her nose and sniffs the air.

I breathe in deeply. 'Smells like paint,' I say. 'How weird.'

'I'll follow the smell and find out,' Lauren says, and she walks forward. 'It's not coming from upstairs and it's not coming from the kitchen.'

I kick off my shoes – relief! – and join her outside the living-room door. Robbie is calling on Benson and has already walked past us both and through the kitchen into the back garden.

'The smell's coming from in here,' Lauren says, her hand reaching along the living-room wall to find the light switch.

My brain is slow to engage and it doesn't occur to me that maybe I should stop her, that this smell can't be innocent, and that in our absence someone has come into our house and left their mark. At a flick of the switch, the room fills with bright light that catches us both frozen, open-mouthed, as we're smacked in the face by a message written on the facing wall – MURDERER – spelt out in block capitals. Each letter is over a foot tall and written in bright red paint, the colour of arterial blood, dripping off the end of the letters, running down the wall like massive, bloody tears.

5

We stand stock-still and stare at the wall and then at each other and then Lauren's face crumples and she starts to sob. I pull her in towards me and she presses her face into my chest. I hold her there, incapable of thinking straight. My brain is frozen on the word MURDERER and is unable to move past it.

'Benson was shut up in the shed. He was scratching away at the door,' Robbie shouts as he comes through the kitchen. 'I don't know how that could have happened. Do you, Mum?' And then he sees my face and Lauren's tears. 'What's up?' I stare at him wordlessly and he looks past me and into the living room. 'What the fuck?' He walks into the room and right up to the wall. 'What crazy psycho did this?' He looks back at me in amazement then reaches out and touches the edge of the letter M. 'It's already dry. Somebody must have come in and done this just after we left.' He stands back and loosens his bow tie. 'We'd better call the police.'

'Yes. Of course.' My brain activates with a clunking of gears. 'Robbie?' I unwind Lauren's arms from around me. 'I want you to take your sister out of here. Grab your coats and stand outside, in the middle of the path where I can see you.'

He does as he's told, speaking to Lauren the whole time, 'It's okay, Lauren. Everyone's fine. We'll look back on this in a few weeks' time and we'll laugh.'

I doubt that this will ever be funny, but I know that he's doing his best to stop her tears and it seems to be working so I'm grateful for that. I glance up the stairs and then along the hallway into the black space beyond the kitchen where Robbie just went to find Benson. *What was I thinking of letting him go out there on his own?* As soon as we came in the front door it was obvious that something wasn't right. What if whoever did this had still been out there? A few glasses of champagne and my guard is completely down. Instead of thinking about the children, I was imagining myself with O'Reilly. I can't believe my own stupidity. I take my phone from my evening bag, my hands shaking as I scan through previous calls to find the numbers O'Reilly has called me from. Mostly he's rung me from the station but once it was from a mobile and when I find the number I highlight it with my finger and the call goes through.

'Hello!' he shouts. 'Dr Somers! What can I do for you?'

There's laughter in the background behind him and I have to give him the information twice before he hears me. 'We've been broken into. The word "MURDERER" is painted across the wall in the living room. In giant red letters,' I shout.

There are a couple more seconds of background chaos and then I hear a door shut and sudden quiet. 'Are you still in the house?'

'I'm in the porch. Robbie and Lauren are on the path.'

'All of you go out on to the pavement. Just in case.' He sounds completely sober now and I hear the sound of his feet running on the ground. 'I'll have a squad car there in minutes and I'll be with you soon after.'

'Okay.' I finish the call and climb into a pair of wellies, Benson running around my feet, letting me know he's up for a midnight walk.

'DI O'Reilly says we should stand out on the pavement and wait for the police to arrive,' I tell the children, not adding the *Just in case*. Just in case there's something, or someone, waiting for us upstairs.

I shiver at the thought and Robbie pulls me towards him and Lauren. We all huddle together like this for the short time it takes the police to arrive. The first policeman goes straight into the house, the second one tells us to wait inside the car until they've finished their search. So we do, the three of us in a line on the back seat, Lauren in the middle with Benson on her knee. She's stopped crying and her expression is wide-eyed and anxious. 'I can't believe someone broke into our house.'

'It's awful,' I agree.

'Why didn't Benson attack him?'

'Darling, he's not a guard dog; he's a family pet. I'm sure that if whoever it was came in with a biscuit or a steak, he would have happily followed him to the garden.'

'At least they didn't hurt him.' She strokes his head. 'He seems completely fine.'

'He does.'

I stare up the garden path and into our house. The front door is open and I can see along the hallway to the kitchen. As the police move through the rooms, they're turning on every light so that our home is now the only one in the street that's fully illuminated. My body tenses as I wait for a scream or hurried footsteps when the perpetrator is found hidden in a wardrobe or under the bed and makes a run for it.

'The paint was dry, Mum,' Robbie says, reading my mind. 'Whoever wrote on the wall is long gone.'

'Yes, I'm sure you're right.' I look round at him and try to smile but his expression is serious, not as wide-eyed and fearful as Lauren's, but far more sombre than usual.

'Do you think this is linked to the drink spiking?' He's half mouthing, half whispering over the top of Lauren's head and I do the same back.

'I think it has to be.'

'I don't get it.'

'Neither do I.'

'I can hear you, you know,' Lauren says, her upturned face swivelling from side to side as she looks at us. 'You shouldn't try to protect me from the truth because it's much worse being kept in the dark. If I know things, I don't worry so much.'

'Sorry, poppet.' I hug her hard. 'It's just that we forget how smart you are.'

'Nosy, more like,' Robbie says. He starts to tickle her and she's giggling like a four-year-old when O'Reilly's car pulls up outside the house. We all watch him as he climbs out the passenger side, gives us a perfunctory wave and runs up the path.

'Big boss man arrives,' Robbie says.

'He seems quite nice, actually,' Lauren says, leaning forwards so that she sees him go right into the house. 'Sometimes the police can be corrupt or they drink too much.'

'Jeez, Lauren!' Robbie pokes her in the ribs. 'That's only on TV.'

She jerks out of his way and Benson ends up on my knee, his paws dragging at my dress. 'Settle down, you two!' I say, checking that Benson's nails haven't snagged the silk. 'We'll be out of here in a minute.'

'You looked like you were getting on well with him, Mum,' Robbie remarks, lifting Benson away from me.

'With DI O'Reilly?'

'Who else?'

I try to sound casual. 'Yes, we were,' I say. 'And as I've been hassling him a lot these last couple of weeks, all credit to him that he didn't plant himself at the opposite end of the room and pretend he hadn't seen me.'

'It was a good night,' Robbie says.

'It was.' I'm already feeling wistful for a couple of hours ago when it seemed as though the drink spiking was behind

us, and I was daring to imagine the possibility of a relationship with someone other than Phil. It felt, for a few heady
minutes, as if my life might shed its grey skin, left over from
the divorce, and explode with colour and texture.

'Robbie, remember the girl I was asking you about – Tess
Williamson?'

He nods.

'She was in the pub that night.'

'Who's she?' Lauren asks, and I fill her in on the back
story. 'But if she's never even met Robbie, why would she
be doing things to him?'

'Something simple could have sparked off her interest,' I
say. 'Or perhaps she's not the one doing it but she knows the
person who is.'

'Well, if it helps, I'm absolutely sure I haven't murdered
anyone,' Robbie says. 'You do know that, don't you?'

'Of course!' Lauren and I cry out, both at the same time,
and she snuggles into his shoulder.

'But if we don't take the word "murderer" literally,' I say,
'then perhaps it's something to do with you murdering her
dreams or her friend's dreams or something.'

'How?' he laughs.

'Could she have wanted to join the hockey club?' I hear
myself clutching at straws, but I'm desperately trying to
unearth a connection. 'Or could you have met her at a party
and snubbed her without realising it?'

'I don't have any control over who joins the hockey club.
And, yeah.' He shrugs. 'I guess I could have snubbed her.
Maybe. I dunno. I'm usually friendly with everyone.'

'Yes, you are.'

'Hello again.' The car door swings open and O'Reilly is
there. 'There are no intruders in the house, so we need you
to come inside now and tell us whether anything else has
been done or anything has been taken.'

We climb out of the car and follow him inside, all of us still in our finery. Robbie and Lauren go with one of each of the officers to check their rooms and I stay with O'Reilly. We walk back into the living room and my eyes are drawn at once to the livid red writing on the wall. Even although I'm prepared, it's still shocking, and I feel panic rise up through my chest. 'I want to tear the wallpaper off,' I say. 'Can I do that now?'

'We need to take photographs first,' he says. 'Forensics are on their way. They'll also take fingerprints, although that might be a long shot as so many people have been in here and the perpetrator most likely wore gloves.'

'And as soon as they've collected the evidence?'

'You can tear off the paper and have it redecorated.'

'Thank you.'

'Spot anything missing or tampered with?' O'Reilly says.

I pull my eyes away from the writing and look around the rest of the room. Benson has taken himself into his basket and is lying with his head perched on the rim, his eyes half closed. The coffee table is strewn with magazines and school-books and other stray pieces of paper. Lauren and her friends went through a stage of crocheting cushions, multicoloured fun cushions that brighten the sofas and chairs like happy smiles. Books line the back of one whole wall from ceiling to floor: classics, thrillers, how to do this or that books, collected over a lifetime. Wedgwood-blue velvet curtains are closed over the windows at the front and the patio doors to the garden at the back and some of the hooks have slipped, showing uneven gaps at the top. Hastily hung photo frames decorate the back wall, the children's ages and stages, family birthdays and Christmas mornings.

'Everything seems to be as we left it.'

'You don't have any money stashed anywhere?'

I give a short laugh. 'I should be so lucky.'

My eyes are drawn back to the wall. I expect the impact
to lessen each time I look at it but it does not. The sight is
so gruesome, like something from a horror film, completely
at odds with the décor in the living room. I realise where my
daughter gets her need to understand everything, to make
sense of what happens around her, because I know that I
won't rest until I've worked out what this can possibly mean.

'Do you think this is linked to what happened to Robbie?'
I ask O'Reilly.

'Very likely.'

I wonder whether this could have been the work of Tess
Williamson; whether she would have had the presence of
mind to break in, be friendly towards the dog and then spray-
paint this message across the wall. She didn't appear to have
that much guile, but then how would I know? I only met her
for five minutes.

'Do you think Tess Williamson could have done this?'

'We'll check whether she has an alibi for this evening and
we'll also ask her to voluntarily give us her fingerprints, but
I have a feeling her parents aren't going to like it. When we
questioned her earlier, her father hired a lawyer and he was
present throughout.'

'Doesn't that make her seem guilty?'

'I don't think so. There are a lot of people out there who
don't entirely trust the police.'

'Well, I'm one hundred per cent sure that Robbie hasn't
murdered anyone.'

'Of course,' he acknowledges. 'But perhaps we should be
looking wider than Robbie's friends. Could this be the work
of one of Phil's patients?'

'With him being a psychiatrist, you mean?'

'Yes.'

I think about this. It makes sense. Psychiatrists spend time
with people who are often seriously deluded and inhabiting

realities that aren't necessarily shared by the rest of us. 'You think this could have been done by someone who wants to get back at Phil? Perhaps he or she feels like their sense of self was murdered by the treatment they were given?'

He shrugs. 'It's possible.'

'Except that Phil has never lived here. The kids and I moved in six months ago and whoever did this would surely know that.'

'True.' He nods. 'And did you lock all the doors before you left?'

'Yes.'

'That's strange because we can't find any sign of forced entry.'

'I distinctly remember making sure all the doors were locked,' I say. 'And there were no windows left open, apart from the small ones upstairs.'

Robbie and the male police officer come into the living room. 'Can't see anything different in my bedroom,' Robbie says. He has changed out of his suit and is wearing jeans and a hoodie. 'My guitar's still there and my computer and my iPod.'

'We're just trying to work out how the person got in,' I say. 'I know I locked all the doors and none of the downstairs windows were open, were they?'

'I don't think so,' Robbie says.

'I always leave the back door key in the lock,' I tell O'Reilly, and then I explain about Robbie finding Benson in the garden hut. 'So whoever did this must have used the back door key to open the door into the garden.'

'Good,' O'Reilly says. 'We'll make sure forensics fingerprint the key.'

'The front door key I took with me.'

'You don't keep one under the doormat or under a plant pot outside?'

'No. We all carry our own keys.' I feel Robbie shifting his feet beside me. 'What is it?' I say to him.

'Em.' He's clearly uncomfortable. He pulls at his ear then makes an apologetic face. 'I meant to tell you this but I kept on forgetting. I think I lost my house key the night my drink was spiked.'

'What do you mean, *you think*?'

'Well, I haven't seen it since then. I thought it might have fallen down inside the couch, or something but—'

'So what have you been using?'

'One of the spare ones from the kitchen drawer.'

'Robbie!' I glance across at O'Reilly. 'I'm so sorry.' I shake my head and stare back at Robbie again. 'This is all because you weren't taking the attack on you seriously enough.'

'I screwed up. I'm really sorry.'

'That's just not good enough! It really, bloody isn't!' I shout, the evening's fear and frustration welling into words. 'The police are making their best efforts here.'

He keeps his eyes low and mumbles something. I'm about to wade in some more when O'Reilly speaks first.

'Well, that clears that up,' he says, matter-of-factly. 'And it also positively links the two crimes.' He sits down on the edge of the sofa. 'We should get these locks changed. I know a twenty-four-hour locksmith. Would you like me to call him?'

'Yes, please.'

'I don't think whoever did this will be back,' he says. 'But just to be on the safe side, I think you should all stay elsewhere tonight.'

'Leila will have us,' I say automatically, and then look at my watch. It's the early hours of Saturday morning and she has her cousin's wedding today. She has to organise the four children and Archie and help her parents. The last thing she needs is the three of us tipping up on her doorstep. So although I desperately want another adult to put their arms around me, I say quickly, 'Actually no, that's not a good idea. Not when it's so late.' I briefly consider the sensible option – ringing Phil so that the children can go and stay with him – but I don't want to be separated from them and I have a feeling he'll find a reason to keep them for longer than just one night. 'We can go to a hotel,' I say, putting my arm around Lauren as she comes to join us. She's also changed out of her evening clothes and is back into jeans. 'Return to the mood of earlier this evening and spoil ourselves a bit.'

'Can we afford it?' Lauren says. She leans in to whisper so that O'Reilly won't hear her. 'You could cancel my piano lessons to pay for it.'

'I think the budget will stretch to that, love.'

'We have to take Benson with us.'

'We'll find a hotel that takes dogs. Although we'll be lucky to get anywhere with it being high season.'

'I'll look on the Internet,' Robbie says, glad to leave the room. I'm avoiding his eye because I'm still angry with him for not telling me about the key. And I'm angry with myself for not being more on his case. And I'm angry with whoever did this – came into our house and spread their message across the wall. I wish I could explain it away but I can't, and suddenly it's all too clear that the attack on Robbie was deliberate. I try to take some steadying breaths but my lungs feel waterlogged, as a simmering pool of anger drains into my chest. And underneath the anger and frustration, fear is lodged, stuck to my ribs with Super Glue.

Robbie comes back with the name of a hotel fairly close by. There's been a late cancellation and they're happy to take dogs. O'Reilly offers one of the policemen to drive us there and I take him up on the offer. I go upstairs to my room and check that my small amount of jewellery is intact, then change out of my evening dress and gather some overnight toiletries. I promise to check in with O'Reilly tomorrow morning when he will give us a new set of house keys and let me know whether the forensic team found anything of note.

The hotel is not as quiet as I expected. Some wedding guests are milling around in reception and Benson goes up to say hello to each one of them. They're all cheerfully drunk and chat to Benson and the children while I register us at the desk. I book us one room with two large beds. I'm sure Robbie would prefer to be in a room on his own, but I want us all to be together.

'We can give you an extended checkout time,' the receptionist tells me. 'Two o'clock instead of twelve?'

'That would be great,' I say, sliding my credit card across the desk. 'And we'll probably have a late breakfast in the room, if that's okay.'

'Of course.'

I shout on the children and we go upstairs. As soon as we're in the room, I bolt the door behind us and satisfy myself that there are no adjoining doors into the rooms either side of us. Robbie lounges back on one of the super-king-size beds while Lauren and Benson have a look in the bathroom and then the wardrobe and the mini-bar.

'It's quite grand in here, isn't it?' Lauren says, throwing herself backwards and landing with a soft thump next to Robbie. 'It makes me wish I still had my dress on.'

Benson takes a leap on to Robbie's chest and he holds him tight, his face thoughtful as he strokes the dog's ears. 'You okay, love?' I say.

'Yeah. I just . . . I'm sorry, Mum. About the keys and everything. I thought the drink spiking was a one-off. I really did. And I don't know why that was written on the wall.' His jaw trembles. 'I don't even think I've ever really hurt anyone, never mind murdered them.'

'I'm sure you're not responsible for this, darling. I know it can't possibly be true.' I rest my hand on the top of his arm. 'It must have been written by someone who's deluded, mentally ill even. And there's no reason why you would know anyone like that.'

'Do you think the police will find out who did it?'

'I'm sure they will,' I say. 'Perhaps the forensic team will come up with something.'

'I'm really tired.' Lauren yawns and rolls on to her side. 'I don't think I've ever been up this late.'

It's a cue for us all to get ready for bed. We take turns in the bathroom and then Robbie climbs into one of the beds, Lauren and I into the other.

'I don't understand why they wrote that on the wall,' Lauren says, taking a hesitant, baffled breath. 'I mean, you've never even pulled the wings off insects like some boys do,' she calls across to Robbie. 'Whenever there's a daddy longlegs in my room, you don't kill it, you just put it out the window. Nobody in our house has ever killed anyone, apart from Benson. Benson kills rabbits and once he killed a squirrel. Remember, Mum?' I nod. 'And we made him give it to us and its fur was all matted with blood.'

'It's just some weirdo, Lauren,' Robbie says, already sounding sleepy. 'We shouldn't be giving him the satisfaction of talking about him, never mind trying to work out his rationale.'

I can't agree with Robbie because whoever is doing this is sending us a message, and working out why will be the only way to make it stop. I think about what Lauren's just said – *nobody in our house has ever killed anyone* – and it sets my thoughts off in a completely new direction. If this person *is* sending a message to someone in the house, could that someone be me?

But you're not a murderer, I remind myself. And it's true; I'm not. I've spent my working life trying to preserve life, not extinguish it. *Primum non nocere.* First, do no harm.

But.

'It was the best night of my life, and then it became one of the worst nights of my life, and now it's ended up being a bit better again,' Lauren tells me, and I stroke her hair until she falls asleep. It doesn't take long but when she's breathing soundly I don't shift into a more comfortable position. My body stays still while my mind roams elsewhere, through caves and tunnels, shining torchlight into the darkest of spaces until it finds what it's looking for . . .

I wake up with a start, rigid with fear as I blink into the darkness; what I expect to see at odds with the shadows that fill the space – large, indistinct, unfamiliar shapes that loom out of the darkness towards me. And then I remember that I'm not in my own bedroom. I'm in a hotel room with Robbie and Lauren and we're all safe. I blink several times to determine what the shadows are made of: a chest of drawers, the enormous bureau with the television and the mini-bar, a cupboard and the bed Robbie's asleep in.

My pulse begins to slow and I lean up against the headboard. My neck has been resting at an unnatural angle and I try to stretch it out, being careful not to disturb Lauren who is fast asleep beside me. The digital clock on the bedside cabinet reads 4:16. I've had about two hours' sleep but I'm not tired. Connections are coming together in my head. On the one hand they feel far-fetched, but on the other perfectly logical. Robbie hasn't lived long enough to make any serious enemies. And the same goes for Lauren. Phil doesn't live with us any more and so that only leaves me.

The grotesque image of the red-painted MURDERER is now indelibly printed on my retina. I can see it when I open my eyes and when I close them – there's no escaping it, the message is there, a larger-than-life accusation that cannot be ignored. I remember the half-dreams, half-memories of two hours ago as I slid into a short sleep, and know that I need to dredge those thoughts up again. But not here. Not while I'm in bed with Lauren, so peaceful by my side.

I ease myself out from under the duvet, tiptoe towards the door into the hallway to check it's still bolted, then head for the bathroom, easing the door shut behind me. There is a choice of half a dozen products on a shelf at the end of the bath. I choose one of the small plastic bottles of bubble bath, a blend of relaxing essential oils, and tip it into the running water. The tub is long and deep and it takes several minutes to fill, minutes I spend standing still and staring, just staring, at the plain white tiled wall. When the tub is almost full, I turn the taps off and undress, laying my clothes neatly on the lid of the toilet seat. I feel as if I am preparing for something of great significance and, while not delaying the moment, I'm not rushing it either. I slip down into the water, welcoming the warmth that covers me all the way up to my neck. The bubbles smell of sandalwood and cinnamon, winter scents that are comforting in June because I know the memories I'm about to mine will be stark and cold and grossly uncomfortable.

No, I'm not a murderer, but I have killed someone, and this truth is pulling at my sleeve like a demanding child whose voice grows ever louder – *You. You are the only person in your house who has killed another human being. You are the murderer* – on and on, and now I feel I have no option but to examine the memories, turn them this way and that, look at them with excruciating honesty to work out whether what I did can be the reason Robbie's drink was spiked and the red-painted message was emblazoned across the wall.

The first thing that occurs to me is that for something that happened over eighteen years ago, the memories are perfectly preserved. Perhaps keeping them in a dark place is what's done this. I know that psychologists have long since discovered that accurate remembering is difficult. We tend not to remember the actual event itself but are more likely to remember the details we conjured up last time we remembered it. And so, like a game of Chinese whispers, the details can be lost or changed. We have a vested interest in our own memories, after all, and so the urge to reshape them is hardwired into our consciousness. We like them to reflect the person we are now. Today I am a brave person, an honest person, so surely back then I must have been too?

With the warm water lapping at my neck and the bubbles covering my body, I scroll back through time, dredging up every little detail, every glance, every action and every misplaced step. The memories are virgin, untouched, unsullied by time and self-delusion. There has been no repackaging of the truth and there will be none now. My eyes are wide open and I look back and see it exactly as it was.

6

August 1993. I'd made it – I was a doctor! – and I couldn't stop smiling. I'd worked hard and long for this moment: in the classroom and the labs, in the library and on the wards. And it had all paid off. My plan was to become a neurosurgeon and so I chose a neurosurgical ward for my residency. I was setting my sights high, bewitched by the working of the central nervous system, the brain with its infinitesimal capacity to surprise and shock. When the ward was less busy, I spent time in the pathology lab, dissecting brains and spinal columns, eager to learn about neural pathways, and all the diseases that could affect the central nervous tissue. Every day I woke up with a sense of adventure bound to my pulse, blood and enthusiasm charging through to my fingertips. I was Christopher Columbus discovering the Americas. Neurology was a faraway land that I was making my own and I soaked up every minute of it.

I organised my life to accommodate my passion. I lived in a modern, low-maintenance flat just a fifteen-minute walk to the hospital. I didn't hanker after nights out clubbing or beach holidays in the Far East. Socialising consisted of impromptu get-togethers in a local bar with colleagues, or nights in with Phil when we watched a good movie or sat with medical textbooks, testing each other's recall. By then we had been going out for almost three years and had recently moved in together. He was two years ahead of me and was already several months into his chosen specialty: psychiatry. It was perfect. Our interests were linked but we weren't in direct competition with each other. We would discuss cases where brain injury led to psychiatric illness and vice versa. If our life together sounds boring, I would defend it by saying it wasn't so much boring as focused. We were high on our chosen careers and we were high on each other. We cooked and cared for each other and made love every other day, often wordlessly, our bodies doing the talking for themselves.

I'd never been someone with regular periods and when I started vomiting, I thought I had a virus. It wasn't morning sickness, it was all-day sickness, and it went on for two weeks before it occurred to me that I should get myself a pregnancy test. I didn't expect the result to be positive – I normally used a cap – but there was no harm in ruling out the obvious so that I could work out what was really wrong with me. During my lunch hour I went to the Gynaecology ward, where Leila was doing her residency, and gave her my urine specimen.

'It's positive,' she said, her face halfway between a disbelieving frown and a tentative smile.

'What?' I looked over her shoulder to check she had it right. 'It must be a false positive.'

'You know false positives are rare.'

'But I can't be pregnant! Do the test again.'

'Liv,' she said evenly. 'Do you always remember to put your cap in?'

'Of course!' I said, then checked myself at once, because it was an automatic of course and the truth was that there were times when I was so preoccupied with being a doctor that I forgot everything except the case I was working on. 'Shit . . . I'm not sure . . . A few weeks ago when I was on nights . . . there was so much going on and I hardly made it to bed . . . but maybe I have a tumour on my ovary or something.' I rubbed my lower abdomen. 'That could be producing HCG.'

'It's far more likely you're pregnant than you have a tumour.' We were in the small doctors' room that overlooked the ward and Leila stared through the glass partition to where rows of women lay in beds, in various stages of illness and recovery. 'You don't want to be wishing tumours on yourself.'

'Help!' I slumped down on to a chair. 'I'm so tired I can't think straight.' My head collapsed down to halfway between my knees and the floor. It felt surprisingly comfortable there. I could fall asleep, except for the hard nudge of the stethoscope that was in my pocket, digging into my middle. That, and the slowly solidifying truth that I might be pregnant. 'A baby.' I jerked up straight. 'A baby, Leila?' The bleep in my other pocket sounded and I glanced down at the number. 'That's the ward. I'd better get back.'

'Listen.' She held on to my drooping shoulders. 'There's no need to look so hopeless! Don't panic. Don't fret. Give the news time to digest. We can always repeat the test.'

'But it'll still show the same result?'

'Most likely.'

'Bloody hell!' I walked away from her and after a few steps turned back to say, 'I have to get my head around this. Please don't say anything to Phil.'

'Of course not.' She gave me a supportive smile. 'It's not the end of the world, Liv.'

It was to me. I felt as if my world was teetering on its axis and I was about to be pitched into an alternate future where I would find myself on an unknown trajectory, one I'd neither planned for nor wanted. Phil and I hadn't talked about children but, if we had, I would have said – 'Yes, of course! One day we can start a family. Not now though, not soon . . . one day.'

I resolved to tell Phil that evening, but by the time I got

home he was heading for bed. He'd spent the weekend on call and was exhausted, so I kept my worries to myself and slid under the duvet beside him, wrapping my limbs around his. He was warm and comforting and I relaxed my tired bones into his, praying that in the morning there would be the familiar bleed and all would be well.

The morning came and went and so did seven more and still nothing except continued vomiting and increasing fatigue. Phil spent several days in Glasgow on a course and was on call again all weekend, so he'd only caught me vomiting the once and I managed to fob him off with a complaint about hospital canteen food being too fatty.

Because by then I'd made a decision. My body, my life. I was entitled to do what I felt was right for me, wasn't I? I certainly thought so. I arranged for Leila to come round to the flat to sound it out with her. It was Sunday morning and I knew we wouldn't be disturbed. Leila and Archie were already married – it was the first thing they did after graduation – and, like Phil, Archie was on call all weekend. They made no secret of the fact they wanted a large family and medicine would take second place to that. Leila intended to become a GP, where hours were more flexible, and Archie was keen to specialise in radiology, a more nine-to-five branch of medicine. When she arrived, I gave her a mug of coffee and then sat her down on my worn but comfy futon, covered in a paisley patterned throw that had been with me since I was eighteen.

'Leila, I need your help.'

'Okay.' She sat up straight and watched me expectantly, her mug held high in her hand.

'I'm going to have an abortion.'

'*What?*' The mug wobbled, coffee slopping close to the rim, so I took it from her and put it on the mantelpiece. 'Why? Was Phil really angry about it?'

'I haven't told him.'

'You haven't told him?' She stood up alongside me. 'For heaven's sake, Liv, why not?'

'Sit down, please. Just hear me out.'

She gave me a disappointed look and sat back down, muttering, 'You can't keep this from him. You're closer than any couple I know.'

She was right – we were close. Phil had asked me to marry him twice over the past year and each time I said no, not because of a lack of love or commitment, but because I wanted to be a surgeon and I needed to concentrate on getting myself in with the right firm before all the distractions of a wedding. And how much worse would it be with a baby? How much would that knock the centre out of both our plans, especially mine?

I started explaining this to Leila, knowing that she would test my resolve by reminding me of every reason not to have an abortion.

'I'm too young to be a mother,' I said.

'You'll be twenty-four when the baby's born. That's not too young.'

'I'm too unprepared.'

'That's why nature gives you nine months to get used to the idea.'

'I'm not maternal, Leila.' I banged my chest. 'I swear I don't have one maternal bone in my body. I hated my time in obs and gynae – swollen bellies and ankles, and endless discussions about the best prams and cots and fucking hell! I'll go insane if I have to join that club.'

'You don't have to join any club!' she said, keeping her tone light. 'And you'll be a terrific mum.'

'You think? With my own mother as my only role model? What if I end up like her?'

'You won't! She was only miserable because she

underachieved. Like lots of women of her generation, staying at home made her depressed and bitter. You'll be a surgeon.'

'I won't be a surgeon!' I gave a dismissive laugh. 'You think when I apply to Professor Figgis he'll accept me? With a brand-new baby in tow?'

'Sex discrimination, Liv. He can't refuse you because you're a mother.'

'Think about it, Leila. Why would he pick the new mother over another doctor who's just as keen, just as committed? It wouldn't be discrimination; it would be common sense. I'd have to have the stamina of an ox to cope with both a new baby and a steep surgical learning curve. And then there are the endless hours spent on the ward and in theatre.' I shrugged. 'My dream will be over.'

'Not over, just delayed.' She urged me to look at the bigger picture. 'Real life is often uncomfortable,' she told me. 'Sure you want all your ducks to line up perfectly, but sometimes reality gives us a nudge and throws another duck into the pond.'

'A baby is a bit more demanding than a duck.'

'Yes, but it's not as if you can't afford this baby. You can set up excellent childcare. You're healthy. You have a man who loves you. Phil might be a bit taken aback at first but we both know he'll be fine with it.' She stood up and hugged me tight, trying to wrap me up into her way of thinking. 'This will be your baby, Liv. A brand-new human being! How marvellous is that?'

I didn't share her romantic ideal. Instead I saw a burgeoning stress on my relationship with Phil, both of us vying to be allowed to put career first. Leila dug up every argument she could think of to change my mind. She cited my Catholic upbringing and I told her that while I still believed in God, I was no longer religious.

'Once a Catholic, always a Catholic,' she said.

'That's not true. I don't feel like a Catholic any more.'

She told me about some of the abortions she'd seen – messy, complicated affairs; late ones where the foetus attempted to breathe.

'I'm only eight weeks at the most,' I told her. 'We're not talking viability here. It's still an embryo.'

She tried to make me feel guilty about not telling Phil. She asked me to think about how this could affect us in the future. I told her, 'We're not married yet. This is my body, my decision.'

'You're Mrs Organised,' she said. 'Maybe somewhere in your subconscious you wanted this!'

'I definitely don't want a baby, Leila.' My voice was loud and accusing and she drew back. 'When I'm busy with work, I forget to eat and sleep, and if I forgot to put my cap in then it was bloody stupid. It wasn't because I secretly wanted to be pregnant.'

She gave up then, and taking her mug of coffee from the mantelpiece, sat back down on the futon and gulped back half the liquid. I watched as her dark eyes welled up with tears.

'Leila, you're my best friend.' I knelt down in front of her. 'I know you don't agree with my decision, but please, will you help me?'

'I don't agree with you.' Her eyes were treacle pots of gloom. 'And I don't want to see you making a mistake.'

I waited as she wrestled with her better nature. With three older brothers and already eight nieces and nephews, she had been brought up in an atmosphere where every child was a gift. I felt bad making her complicit in my decision, but I knew I couldn't do this alone and neither could I tell Phil. I couldn't risk him disagreeing with me, and without his support I couldn't go ahead with the abortion. And then where would I be?

I spent the next couple of days keeping the secret. I carried it off because I was utterly determined that this was my decision and I was not about to change my mind. I saw my GP and was booked into the hospital on the other side of town where nobody knew me, and anyway, I told myself, I'd be in and out in no time; there was no way that what I was doing could get back to Phil.

I arrived at the ward for eight in the morning – Phil presumed I was off to work as usual – and Leila was taking the afternoon off to collect me. While I waited my turn, I watched a batch of first-year student doctors walk on to the ward, fold lines creasing down the front of their pristine white coats. That had been me several years ago, lit up with enthusiasm and an eagerness to learn. I'd got myself away from my mother and out of Ireland and was ready to follow in the footsteps of great men and women before me. I believed medicine was a noble profession, one that wasn't entered into lightly, one that dealt with the sacred treaty that existed between health and sickness, life and death. Although I was no longer religious, I had a strong sense of the holy ghost's presence in each one of us.

And then it hit me. When I graduated as a doctor, I took an oath – First, do no harm. I promised that my actions would be directed towards healing rather than hurt. Was I only a doctor when I was on duty? These were ideals that I subscribed to – that, in fact, I felt defined me – and yet here I was, set to very deliberately put myself in the way of life. The more I thought about it, the more the idea permeated my resolve and stole away my clarity. I was setting out to kill a living creature, and not just any living creature – my own baby, Phil's baby.

But I'm not even ten weeks, I told myself. The heart isn't beating. It's less than two centimetres in size. It's not viable, for God's sake!

No, it isn't, another voice in my head said, but it will be.

I wrestled like this for ten minutes and then, as the resident doctor approached, I grabbed for my clothes, fully prepared to make a run for it. 'I can't go through with the abortion,' I said, afraid she'd tell me it was too late and bundle me on to the trolley anyway. 'I'm so sorry for wasting your time.'

Far from being irritated by my last-minute change of mind, the doctor smiled equably. 'Good for you,' she said.

I took a taxi back to my own hospital and hunted Leila down. She was in the canteen, looking thoughtful, spooning yoghurt slowly into her mouth. When I told her I'd changed my mind she was overjoyed and jumped up and down, clapping her hands together. 'I'll get pregnant too and then we can go through everything together! Sore boobs, weepy moments, childcare. We can share all of it. Then it won't be so scary!' She put her arm through mine. 'Our children will grow up to be friends. How good will that be?'

I wasn't happy with my decision. I still didn't want a baby but I knew that unless fate lent a hand and I miscarried, I'd just have to accept it, and adapt my dreams accordingly. I knew I'd made the right decision for the baby inside me, but I felt miserable, sure that my life was no longer my own.

As I expected, Phil was at first speechless and then delighted by the news. He thought I should try for surgery anyway, but in my heart of hearts I knew it wasn't an option and all my surgical ambitions were abandoned.

More than two months went by and I was starting to show. When I lay on my back and palpated my lower abdomen, I could feel the crest of my womb rising up out of my symphysis pubis. It felt solid, like the edge of a grapefruit. I was a doctor and I knew exactly what was happening inside me, from the anatomical to the biochemical, but still I couldn't seem to visualise an actual baby. Worse still, I had a horror of being genetically incapable of loving a small baby; that I would hold it and feel nothing except the heavy weight of responsibility around my neck. I was afraid that I would end up like my mother, someone who expected too much from her children and who never listened, too obsessed with her own misery, her own lost dreams.

I thought morning sickness was supposed to stop at around fourteen weeks, but I wasn't that lucky and seemed to be stuck on a four-hourly cycle of vomiting. And I felt fatigued, deep into the very marrow of my bones. I wasn't managing more than five hours' sleep a night and fantasised about lying in my bed and never having to get up. My brain felt muddled, my back ached and the hours I spent on my feet made my ankles swell. I would have described myself as a zombie if it weren't for the fact that I was experiencing so much discomfort. I looked back down the centuries, at women who worked in the fields until they gave birth and women today in developing countries who did the same, and I wondered whether I was just a wimp and a weakling, a whiner who wanted what she couldn't have and was too self-absorbed to appreciate the blessing she'd been given.

And then one day came my wake-up call. It was Sunday evening, and we were approaching the end of a long and gruelling week. Two patients in their thirties had died, both from cerebral aneurysms. Being witness to their declines and to their families' grief took its toll on the morale of both nursing and medical staff, and there was a heavy feeling in the air. The other patients, although unaware of the details, picked up on the grave mood and several of the post-op survivors sat in their chairs, heads bandaged, drip stands like sentinels beside them as they stared out at the relentless rain.

Around teatime, I took a phone call concerning a patient who was being transferred from another hospital. The doctor couldn't tell me much, except that the woman was named Sandy Stewart, that she had raised intracranial pressure, some of her motor responses were compromised and she had extreme headaches and vomiting. 'Oh, and I almost forgot, she's pregnant,' the doctor told me. 'Thirty-two weeks.'

I phoned my registrar who was also on call that weekend but had gone home because he was coming down with the flu. 'Book her in,' he told me, through a thick, phlegmy throat. 'She'll be seen on the round tomorrow.'

So it was me who was waiting to greet her, the most junior doctor representing the team. I stood by the lift doors as it clanked and rumbled its way up to our floor. Sandy Stewart was lying on the trolley, an ambulance man on one side, her husband on the other. She was tiny, her body almost prepubescent, apart from the small baby bump just visible through the sheet that covered her. The skin under her eyes was black from lack of sleep. Her hair was a dirty blond colour and had long outgrown any styling it might have had. It was clear that, in recent weeks, she hadn't had the time or energy to care for herself but, in spite of all this, she was smiling.

'I'm Dr Naughton.' I held out my hand and she gripped it with both of hers. 'You must be Sandy.'

The staff nurse and I settled her in a bed in one of the single rooms. 'I'm glad to be getting a diagnosis at last,' she said. 'I've been throwing up nonstop and everyone kept on telling me it was morning sickness, but I knew my baby couldn't be doing this.' She stroked her stomach. 'And the headaches have been awful.'

I felt ashamed of all my complaining. I was only pregnant. Sandy Stewart, on the other hand, was housing a tumour the size of a tennis ball inside her skull, encroaching on her brain, altering its structure and affecting its function. Prognosis wasn't good. The tumour was fast growing and the space it was occupying had reached critical point. On the Monday, after Professor Figgis read the scans, he told her she had two options: leave the tumour alone or operate. Either way she wasn't set to live very long, but reducing the size of the tumour might just give her six months or a year.

'I want to see my baby. That's all I want.' She smiled up at us. 'The miracle of life; it's so marvellous isn't it?'

Professor Figgis explained to her that the obstetrician was willing to induce her at thirty-four weeks and so a compromise was reached. Sandy would stay on the ward for two weeks, being supported with fluid balance and anti-emetics, and then her baby would be delivered. She would be able to hold the baby and spend a few days with him or her before the surgery was performed.

The next morning was Tuesday and we were chronically short-staffed. The registrar was still absent with flu and Professor Figgis was lecturing in Glasgow. That was bad enough, but the resident doctor on the neighbouring ward was also off sick, so I was down to cover his duties as well. I knew I'd have to race around the ward, and still never catch up, but when I visited Sandy's room to take blood, she was in the mood for a chat.

'I don't want to be nosy but . . . you're also pregnant, aren't you?'

'Yes. I'm five months now.' I attached a tourniquet round her upper arm. 'Not quite as far along as you.'

'And is it your first baby?'

'Yes.'

'Have you been getting the room ready?'

'Not yet, but my sister-in-law is busy knitting for me,' I told her, feeling for a vein. 'I'll have enough layettes to kit out sextuplets.'

She started telling me about the preparations she'd made. The room had been ready for months: painted apple blossom white, decorated with mobiles in primary colours and pictures to interest a new baby, plus nappies and a changing mat and all the other paraphernalia that goes along with caring for a newborn. 'We've been trying to get pregnant for almost ten years and finally it happened,' she told me, exuding a *joie de vivre* that coloured the air sunshine yellow.

'Do you know the baby's sex?' I asked her, the four bottles on my tray now filled with blood.

'No. We want it to be a surprise. But still I spend a lot of time imagining what he or she will look like.' She gave an apologetic laugh. 'I think my baby will have laughing eyes, a small nose and smiley cheeks with dimples,' She laughed again. 'Trevor says the baby might not be attractive at all. It might be wrinkly and birth-marked and cry all the time but, really, I don't mind, because I know that this baby will be the best thing that's ever happened to me.' She leant back on the pillow and gazed up at the ceiling. 'If it's a boy we'll call him Michael and if it's a girl we'll call her Kirsty.' She gave a dreamy, contented sigh. 'I mean a baby? Can you imagine?'

I smiled. 'Actually, I can't. I've been trying but I just can't.'

She talked some more, and her absence of trepidation about her health during the weeks ahead made me wonder whether she understood what the professor had told her. Her husband Trevor, on the other hand, was tense and worried, and I knew that he was under no illusions about what the future held.

Later the same day, and desperate for an afternoon nap, I stood in the treatment room and made up the intravenous drugs, taking vials of steroids or antibiotics from the fridge and injecting them into one of the fifteen 100-ml bags of saline that I'd lined up in front of me. I stuck a drug and patient name label on the front of each bag, specific to the patient for whom the drug was prescribed. While I was doing this, I was interrupted three times to deal with issues on the ward. Half of the nursing staff, including the ward sister, were off sick, and a junior staff nurse, as yet unsure of herself, was in charge.

In retrospect, it was so obviously a recipe for disaster, but I didn't see it at the time. I was simply moving from one task to the next, rushing to get everything done.

During the two o'clock drug round, Sandy was due to be given one of the bags of saline with added steroids that I had prepared earlier. It was put up by one of the nurses, exactly as written on the drug chart. Within five minutes I was called to Sandy's room because she was experiencing severe itching and urticaria. Her skin was bumping up and reddening before my eyes. But worse than that was her compromised breathing. Her lips were blue and a wheeze sounded in her chest. I could see that she wasn't getting enough oxygen into her lungs and it was growing worse by the second. She was experiencing all the classic signs of an acute allergic reaction, most likely caused by the fact that she had been given an IV dose of a substance she was allergic to. I checked the IV bag and the label and the name of the steroid. Nothing wrong there. She couldn't be allergic to this; she'd had it several times already with no ill effect. My mind spooled through other options and then realisation hit me hard. All the interruptions, my tiredness and lack of concentration – I must have labelled the bags wrongly. I was the doctor who booked Sandy Stewart in so I knew about her penicillin allergy, and two of the bags I made up had penicillin in them.

Shock cracked through me like an earthquake and the baby dropped down in my womb, the head pressing on my bladder. I'd made a serious error and I needed to reverse it – now and quickly – before Sandy grew any worse. Hands trembling, I stopped the IV and asked the nurse to call the crash team while I gave Sandy an injection of adrenaline. Within seconds she was breathing more easily but I saw something in her eyes that I hadn't seen before – an accelerating sense of the inevitable.

'Sandy!' I held her hand. 'Doctors are on their way. We're going to get you better.'

I could see she didn't believe me and I had no idea what to do next. I had never felt less like a doctor. My limited understanding of neurology had shrunk to nothing and my mind was a blank page when I tried to calculate how this allergic reaction was affecting her already damaged brain.

Sandy held my hands tight and stared into my eyes, grabbing for my full attention. 'Make sure they do everything they can for my baby,' she said, her nails digging into my skin. She was struggling to breathe again and I tried to pull away to draw up some more adrenaline but she held on tight. 'And Trevor. Tell him I love him.'

By the time the crash team arrived Sandy had lost consciousness and I was ready with a second syringe of adrenaline. The doctor in charge was from another neurosurgical ward and he tried one treatment after another, but with everything else her body was going through, the chances of saving her were reduced. An emergency Caesarean section was performed and the baby, only three pounds in weight, went straight into an incubator. When the doctor recorded Sandy's time of death, there was a hush in the room and one of the junior nurses started to sob.

I took refuge in the toilet. It was as good a place as any to examine the enormity of my incompetence. I sat on the toilet seat in a locked cubicle, unable to come to grips with what I'd just done, my thoughts revolving in a tight circle of horror and disbelief.

Eventually I had to come out and by now the ward was trying to get back to some sort of normality. Patients were having their evening meal and Professor Figgis had returned from Glasgow and was telling Trevor Stewart that his wife was dead. She had passed away in a flurry of medical intervention, none of which worked. And the baby wasn't doing too great either. Unable to breathe for itself, it was immediately whisked off to Special Care. I hadn't even had the chance to see whether it was a boy or a girl, mired as I was in trying to keep Sandy alive.

I wasn't brave enough to meet Mr Stewart, so when he was finished talking to the professor and he came on to the ward, I hid in the treatment room, my head close to the doorframe, and squinted through the crack. His skin was white, his eyes stared straight ahead, unseeing and unresponsive. The nurses had packed Sandy's belongings into several bags that he lifted wearily from her bed, already stripped of all evidence that she was ever there. I watched his back as he walked towards the lift, stooped like an old man. Suffering had aged him.

Professor Figgis called me into his study, directing me towards an upright chair before he sat down behind his desk, leaning forwards on his elbows, his hands clasped together. A late afternoon sun warmed the room with a bright light that had me shielding my eyes. I told Professor Figgis the story from start to finish, holding nothing back and fully expecting to be fired on the spot. He listened, his expression serious, as he agreed that I'd made a terrible mistake.

'I'll write a letter of resignation,' I said, the words cutting me in two.

'What good would that do?' His tone was firm. 'You're a young doctor with a promising career ahead of you. Doctors sometimes have to learn the hard way and you have been both foolish and unlucky.'

'But what about Mr Stewart?' I moved my head over to one side to try to escape the sun, my hand still shielding my eyes. 'Does he know what happened?'

'Mr Stewart knew his wife was terminally ill and nothing you or I could do was going to change that.'

'Yes, but—'

'Your mistake was in not recognising your own limitations.'

'I should have asked for help.'

'You should have,' he agreed. 'But we have been uncommonly short-staffed so it's no wonder that you didn't.'

'I understand that I can't make it right but—'

'We're not *gods*, Dr Naughton. We can't fix the unfixable.'

'I know, but surely if I was honest then at least—'

'At least what? She'll rise again like Jesus? And it will all be better?' He shook his head at me, his expression resigned. 'She had a Grade IV astrocytoma. She shouldn't have died today but she was most definitely going to die at some point over the next couple of months.'

'But I accelerated her death,' I said, still squinting against the light, my eyes filling with tears. 'I killed her.'

'You're a human being, Dr Naughton, and there isn't a doctor out there who hasn't made a mistake. I was mentored by Professor Lewis Markham. You'll have heard of him?'

I nodded.

'He told me once that a doctor was never really a doctor until he had killed a patient. A dramatic statement, maybe, but unfortunately, there's often truth in it.' He turned behind him and adjusted the blinds, shutting them almost completely until the light could only filter through in centimetre strips, drawing lines across everything in the room. 'Today you've learnt that you are fallible.'

'Sir, I—'

'Sometimes we're thrown a curved ball,' he continued. 'It's not what we're expecting, but nevertheless we have to hit it back and run. If you worked in the civil service or as a teacher or a solicitor, you're never likely to directly kill anyone. But in our profession?' – he shrugged his shoulders – 'It's a possibility. Every day we have the potential to cause harm, but mostly we don't. The very fact that you're showing such remorse tells me that you'll be a better doctor because of this mistake.' He stood up and saw me to the door. 'From now on everything you do must be done that little bit better. You can't give anything back to Mr Stewart, but you can pay it forward. Be exemplary in your care for others.'

I thanked him for his time and his advice and left. I was reassured not to be losing my job, but that did nothing to alleviate the horror that gnawed away at my middle like a cancer. When I arrived back home, Phil grabbed hold of me, walking me towards the kitchen, stroking my distended stomach. 'And how's my other girl?'

'Or boy,' I said automatically. I threw myself down on a kitchen chair, bumped my ankle on the table leg and focused on the pulse of pain that travelled up to my knee. Phil had made our evening meal and I ate it automatically. It had the appearance of chicken but it tasted of absolutely nothing. He spent the first fifteen minutes talking for both of us and then he said, 'You okay?'

'That patient,' I said, feeling the day's misery and tension rupture inside me. 'The one I was telling you about. She died.' I pushed my plate away, dropped my head in my hands and started to cry. 'She died, Phil. She bloody died.'

'Hey, Liv.' He put his arms tight around me and brought me to my feet. 'You're tired, love. Come and sit down in the living room.'

'I'm not tired. I mean, I am tired but that's not why I'm crying. I'm crying because I'm not a good doctor.'

'You're way too conscientious, that's your trouble.'

'I killed her.'

'Of course you didn't kill her!' He eased me down on to the futon and took his place beside me. 'You're the most junior of doctors! Nothing that happens on the ward is your responsibility. You have a registrar and a consultant who're there to make the decisions.' He wrapped me up in arms that normally comforted me but for now just felt stifling. 'It wasn't your fault, love.'

I pulled away. 'It was!' I shouted. 'I was too tired and—' I gulped in a disbelieving breath. 'Shit.'

'You take these things too personally. It's what makes you a good doctor, but it also makes you too involved. You have to develop more of a filter.'

'But Phil, I really mean it.' I grabbed hold of his shirt. 'Listen to me, please.'

'Look what I got today!' he said breezily, taking a catalogue from the magazine rack. 'I went into John Lewis and had a look at cots.' He thumbed to a page about halfway through. 'This is the one I like.' He rested his finger on it and glanced at me to check that I saw which one he meant. 'What do you think?'

'I think you need to listen to me!' I said loudly, the pictures of cots and happy smiling mums making me think of Sandy's baby, who – if it went home at all – would return home to a room full of everything except for a mother. 'She was having a baby too.'

'We have to buy the mattress separately,' he said, his voice drowning out mine. 'And we should try out buggies. You need to think about comfort for the baby, handle height, ease of getting it in and out of the car. That sort of thing.'

I remembered the look on Sandy's face when she told me about the buggy they'd chosen. 'She had everything ready for her baby. She had a buggy with—'

'For heaven's sake, Liv!' He was growing exasperated and a vertical frown line formed between his eyes. I'd never noticed it before. It made me think about us growing old together, watching each line and wrinkle take possession of our faces. A privilege that I'd just denied another couple who loved one another, chose one another, made a baby together.

'Her name was Sandy Stewart. The baby's in an incubator

and his or her mother is dead.' I rocked back and forwards. 'If I'd only been more careful. If only I'd stayed in the treatment room until I'd finished labelling the bags.'

'I'm going to run you a bath.' He sighed and stood up. 'You need to let this go and start thinking about *our* baby.'

While he was in the bathroom, I slipped out the door and went round to Leila's flat. I told her what had happened and watched an expression of horror bloom in her eyes, quickly extinguished as she bolstered me up with words of comfort. Like Phil, her impulse was to reassure me, but while he wouldn't listen to details, Leila sat with me on the sofa and heard me out, convinced that this was management's mistake, not mine. 'You shouldn't have been left running two wards on your own!' she said, indignant on my behalf. 'It's awful!' She wrapped a blanket around my shoulders. 'This is their responsibility, not yours.'

When Phil came to collect me, Leila spent time outside the living-room door talking to him, and whatever she said worked. He was sympathetic and caring and took me home to bed where he held me tight as I cried myself empty.

I went into work next day but the weight of my own mistake collapsed my heart and I could barely function. Professor Figgis took me to one side and told me I should take the last couple of weeks of my residency off. 'Where are you going to next?' he asked me.

'To a medical ward in the Northern General,' I told him.

'Excellent! You'll feel much better after a break,' he assured me. 'A different hospital. A fresh start. Some time to bring it all into perspective.'

I felt as though he was getting rid of me, but it was no more than I deserved. I spent my first few days off half-heartedly preparing the room for my baby, but my mind was furiously preoccupied. I could see Sandy's face and hear her words and I knew that I had to go and see Trevor. I had been there when she said her last words and I needed to pass them on to her husband.

My memory was good and I remembered their address from when I booked Sandy in. I turned up at his front door and knocked several times but there was no answer. I realised he was probably at the hospital visiting his baby, and so I sat down on the doorstep and wrote him a letter, telling him how sorry I was that Sandy had died and that she'd asked me to tell him that she loved him. I finished the note by saying that if ever he wanted to chat to me about Sandy then he should call me. I wrote my phone number in large letters at the bottom of the page, folded the paper in two and posted it through his letterbox.

A couple of days passed and I waited for his call but it never came, so I asked Leila to visit the Special Care Baby Unit to find out how the baby was doing. She said she would, and that evening she came round to the flat to tell me that the baby had died.

'Oh God.' I doubled up, my guts contracting with a tight, painful spasm. Of all the bad luck – a double tragedy – the baby born too early to thrive, forced from its mother's womb in circumstances that were stressful to say the least. 'Was it a boy or a girl?'

'A boy,' Leila said.

I thought about Sandy with her ready smile and abundance of love, and hoped that there was an afterlife where she'd been reunited with her baby boy and they could spend eternity together. Leila held my hands as I cried and Phil made us both a hot drink. 'Don't you want something stronger?' I said to Leila, when I'd stopped crying long enough to look around me. 'I would if I could.'

She put down her mug of tea then reached out and gave my bump a gentle nudge. 'Can't. I'm pregnant too.' She laughed, and the hollows in her cheeks deepened.

'Really?' I hugged her hard. 'Jesus! That's amazing!'

'And now we can go through motherhood together.' She gave me a hopeful smile. 'You're a few months ahead of me but, hey! What's a few months between friends?'

We hugged again and she stayed for an hour planning our next few afternoons. She'd taken four days of annual leave and we spent time shopping for everything and anything that Leila deemed necessary for our unborn babies: cots and buggies, talcum powder and baby wipes, pastel paint for the walls and fabric for curtains. Leila's enthusiasm sparked the first inkling of maternal feeling inside me and I began to properly think about the baby I was carrying. If a baby feels his mother's pain, then my own unborn child had suffered these past few weeks and I wanted that to stop. I knew I'd never forget what I'd done, but I made the effort to shift my focus on to my baby and Phil and the family we would become, determined not to allow Sandy's death to define me.

And it didn't.

7

Robbie and Lauren eat a late breakfast in the room, Robbie coming to join Lauren on her bed so that they're both directly in front of the television. They have two trays, piled high with food, laid out in front of them. They both ordered orange juice, a cooked breakfast: bacon, egg and sausages, black pudding and tomatoes, followed by toast and jam. Benson is lying on the bed next to Lauren, eyeing every forkful that makes its way into her mouth. As they eat, they watch a film, completely gripped by the action on the screen. I tell them I didn't sleep too well – the truth – and that I need to rest for a bit longer – a lie. Rest is the last thing I'm capable of. Now that I've mined the depths of my past, I'm afraid that what happened back in October '93 is the reason for Robbie's drink spiking and for MURDERER on the wall. I didn't murder Sandy Stewart, but my actions directly led to her death and so, in effect, I killed her. I bitterly regretted my actions, and would change the past if I could, but I've not spent my life feeling guilty about it, and if that sounds callous, then I can only defend myself by saying, for my own sake, and the sake of the child I was carrying, I worked hard at letting go.

Looking at Robbie now it's difficult to believe I would have, could have, aborted him. I don't recognise the person I was then: a self-absorbed girl who wanted what she wanted and to hell with everyone else. Ambition over family and friends – a mistake I've never repeated. If I'd accepted the limitations my pregnancy imposed on me, I would have been off sick instead of struggling against it, knowing it was making me exhausted but at the same time denying it.

And now – could this be Trevor Stewart finally taking revenge? Have the articles in the newspaper sparked off a reminder? Since I was nominated for the award last September, there have been three newspaper articles about the work I do at the centre, as well as weekly reminders to the newspaper-buying public to 'vote for your favourite charity worker'. All this in-your-face publicity could have brought latent feelings to the surface. Back then, Trevor made no complaints about the care his wife was given, but I know enough about human nature to understand that feelings can lie dormant for years, and the recognition I'm getting now could be a catalyst for him to act against me.

On the one hand it seems far-fetched, and on the other, perfectly logical. I can't believe that whoever is doing this doesn't have a bloody good reason for it, and what happened all those years ago could be reason enough. I need to find out – and find out quickly – before anything else happens.

I shuffle over to the edge of the bed and open the drawers in the bedside cabinet. There's the usual information about the hotel, a bible and the Edinburgh phone book. I flick through the pages and find the letter S, my fingers moving down the pages until I get to Stewart. There are several columns of Stewart, six of them with the first name Trevor. I remember pushing the letter through his letterbox, and can recall the street if not the actual number. When I read through the addresses, I find that one of the phone book Trevor Stewarts lives in that very same street.

My heart is thumping as I close the book. It doesn't prove anything. It might be another Trevor Stewart . . . unlikely . . . So it probably is him, but chances are he remarried and has a whole new family, his first wife and child's death a painful and distant memory that only haunts him on those rare nights in the depth of winter when darkness is absolute, and the sky weeps for those long gone.

'Mum?' Robbie shouts across to me.

'What?' I look up guiltily.

He's waving his mobile phone towards me. 'It's Dad. Should I answer?'

Phil. I should have rung him before now to tell him about last night, but I've been too preoccupied with the past. 'Give it to me, love.' I slither off the bed and grab it just before the ringing stops.

'Phil. Hi, it's me.' I go into the bathroom and close the door behind me. 'I was just about to ring you.'

'Why? What's happened?'

I give him a brief summary of what we came home to last night.

'Why didn't you call me immediately?' He sounds put out.

'It was past midnight. The children were safe. I felt—'

'What if whoever did this had come back?' he cuts in.

'We're in a hotel—'

'Does Robbie have an explanation for what was written?'

'Of course not! He's never even hurt anyone, never mi—'

'And the police? What's their take on this?'

'The forensic unit came to take prints and I'm due to meet DI O'Reilly back at the hou—'

'Where—'

'Will you stop interrupting me!' I shout. 'I'm trying to explain things to you.'

'And I'm angry with you for not telling me immediately,' he barks back.

'Obviously,' I say, matching his tone. 'But you're not helping by firing questions at me as if I'm on trial.'

He doesn't reply to that. I sit down on the edge of the bath and wait, determined not to be the one who breaks the silence. Divorce turns adults into spiteful ten-year-olds – there's the constant, overwhelming need to get one over on each other. It's a game with no winners but still I seem to end up playing it.

'I'm sorry for interrupting you,' he says at last, his tone calmer now. 'I find the whole business shocking and, frankly, difficult to handle.'

'This isn't easy for any of us.'

'I'm worried about the children and anxious that we get this right.'

Phil has a veneer of being able to talk about his feelings. It took me years to work out that it's not real. I'm not saying that he isn't worried and anxious, but there will be a layer of feelings underneath this that he's not admitting to. He knows the vocabulary of openness and he uses it to manipulate situations and get his own way. He would deny that, but I've watched him do it countless times and I suspect that now he's feigning honesty because he's sweetening me up for a request.

'I know the children aren't due to come out with me until tomorrow, but would you mind if I came for them now?' he says. 'I can take them out for tea. Have a walk up the Braid Hills afterwards. It's set to be another sunny day.'

So there it is. The request. And it highlights another by-product of divorce – children are used as prize or punishment. I've seen friends and patients do it – refusing their ex-partners access if they're not in their good books.

That's a game I won't play.

'I'll ask them,' I say. 'Hang on a minute.' I leave the phone in the bathroom and go back through to the bedroom. The film is coming to an end and the breakfast trays have been massacred. Benson is lying with his nose touching the edge of one of the trays, waiting for permission to scavenge the last crust of toast. 'Dad's suggesting he takes you both out for tea and then you can all walk up the Braid Hills, feed the ducks, give Benson a run-around.'

'Whoopee do!' Robbie says. 'Just the way I want to spend my Saturday.'

'But we've just eaten,' Lauren says, her expression glum.

'You could walk first,' I say. 'And eat afterwards.'

'Does that mean we'll have to go tomorrow as well?' she says, inspecting her fingernails.

'I'm not sure.' I sit down on the bed. 'He's very keen to see you both. He's worried about everything that's happened.'

'Will Erika be there?' She finds a hangnail and picks at it.

'I expect so.' I take her hands in mine. 'But that's not so bad, is it?'

'Dad's always different when she's there,' Lauren says, pulling her hands away and collapsing on to the pillow. 'He's all weird and he hangs around her like she can't manage to do anything on her own and he was never like that with you.'

That's because he loves her. He can't help but want to be near her.

I take a big breath. 'I can talk to him about it, if you like?'

She shakes her head. 'Then he'll think it's coming from you.'

She's right about that, and I hate that we've put her in this position where she has to be aware of the discord in her parents' relationship. 'He's still your dad, Lauren.' I tickle her toes. 'Erika might not always live in his heart but you, my dear, you will.'

She draws her feet away and gives me a tentative smile. 'Do you think so?'

'I know so. Love for children endures through all the ups and downs.'

She glances round at Robbie to see what he's thinking. He's staring at the screen as if he's not listening but I can see that his jaw is already tense.

'Shall I say yes?' I brighten my face. 'You could persuade him to take you to that restaurant you really like, the one that's close to your school.'

'Robbie?' Lauren shakes his knee. 'Should we?'

'Only if we get out of tomorrow,' he says, his expression deadpan. 'And only if he doesn't go on about counselling.' He gives me a pointed look. 'Now that he can see I wasn't lying about taking drugs.'

'That's a good point,' I say. 'I'm sure he'll drop the counselling idea now.'

I go back into the bathroom and tell Phil the kids have said yes, but with reservations. 'They want to stay at home tomorrow. And also . . .' I take a breath. 'Robbie is hoping that now you'll forget about the counselling.'

'Have you spoken to him about it?' Phil says.

'The counselling? Not really, no.'

'But you haven't been positive?'

'Well, no because . . . He doesn't want to go, Phil. And as this proves he wasn't lying about the GHB, surely you can drop it?' Silence. 'Don't get me wrong, the graffiti on the wall was horrible to come home to, but the silver lining is that it proves Robbie's innocence.'

'I still think it would be beneficial for Robbie – and Lauren – to talk to someone about the divorce.'

'Well, they don't like the idea of that.'

'They could be persuaded. Some things have to be experienced before one realises the benefits.'

'I suppose so but—'

'Olivia, being a parent is not a popularity contest.'

'And I'm not making it one!'

'You need to think more carefully about the best way to support our children.'

As usual the conversation is going nowhere, and I'm too tired to get into an argument with him, so I move it on, reminding myself to talk to the children later. I give Phil the name of the hotel we're in and he says he'll be along in half an hour. We're all packed up and downstairs inside of the time. It's another lovely day, and outside on the forecourt, sun streams through the leaves on the chestnut trees that border the pavement. Benson has a quick sniff around the tree trunks, then sits at our feet and waits with us.

'Will you be okay going back to the house on your own?' Robbie asks me.

'Yes. Thank you, love. DI O'Reilly will be there and then I might pop out for a bit.'

To Trevor Stewart's. I want to get there as soon as possible so that I can rule him out as a suspect.

Listen to yourself! the voice in my head says. *You're just going to turn up at this man's door after eighteen years and say what?*

I don't know what I'll say, another voice replies, *but I do know that I have to pursue this. I have to satisfy myself that MURDERER wasn't referring to me.*

Phil pulls up in his car and climbs out. Erika's in the front seat. She looks as she always does: perfectly composed and regal in her demeanour, like an old-fashioned princess or duchess looking down on the lowly commoners. She doesn't get out of the car, but she does lower the window to say, as if addressing one of her subjects, 'May we offer you a lift, Olivia?'

'No, thank you.' *Like hell! The leftover wife in the back with the kids.* I give a broad smile. 'It's a beautiful day. I can walk.'

I leave the bags with Phil, say goodbye to the children and to Benson and start the walk home. It's all downhill and won't take longer than fifteen minutes, plenty of time before I said I'd meet O'Reilly. It's just after one and the sun is high in the sky. Warmth seeps into my muscles and within minutes I'm heated through and it feels like balm. The writing on the wall has receded to another world, a sullied place where danger festers and people hurt one another. Me, on the other hand, I live out here, in open grassy space where blackbirds sing and grass grows tall and all is right with the world.

I'm about half an hour early when I round the corner into my street and spot O'Reilly, sitting in his car at the front of the house. His eyes are closed and I realise he's fallen asleep. His jaw is relaxed and his hands are resting on his lap, defenceless as a baby. I feel my own tiredness well up in my skull, making my brain feel dense. My head grows heavy on my neck and my eyes want to close like his, but I don't let them. I stand by his car and stare down at him, remembering my thoughts last night, when I was drunk and enjoying myself and O'Reilly seemed like the most attractive man I'd met for ages. And he's still attractive now, but after last night's events I feel as romantic as a cold kipper.

I'm about to tap on the window when I change my mind. The least I can do is let him catch up with the sleep he lost because of my troubles. I leave him be and walk up my garden path to the front door, but of course my house key doesn't work because the locks have been changed and the locksmith will have given O'Reilly the keys. I contemplate lying on the grass out front to wait for him to wake, but I'm anxious to get to Trevor Stewart's house. I sincerely hope I'm wrong about the connection and I want to put my mind at rest.

I go back to O'Reilly's car and tap lightly on the window. He jerks out of sleep immediately, looks up at me with half-closed eyes and opens the car door.

'Sorry,' I say. 'I didn't want to wake you but Phil has taken the kids and I have a lot to do before they get back.'

'No problem.' He climbs out and stretches his arms up above his head. 'Forensics have finished and I have your new house keys.' He reaches back into the car and brings out a bag from the back seat. Inside are four sets of keys. 'Front, back and patio doors,' he tells me. 'The bill will come in the post. You might be able to claim the cost on your house insurance.'

'Thank you.' I take them from him. 'I'll make sure Robbie keeps hold of his keys this time. And I've been thinking . . .' I stop. O'Reilly watches me expectantly. I was about to launch into my theory about Trevor Stewart – but then what exactly will I tell O'Reilly? A long-ago tale about a junior doctor making a mistake? It's not something I'm proud of and the thought of going into all the details makes me baulk. Better to see what I find and then tell O'Reilly only if I have to.

'Have you thought of something?' He closes his car door and initiates the central locking.

'No.' I shake my head and begin walking up the path. 'I just wondered where the investigation will go now? What will you focus on?'

'Now we feel confident that the drink spiking is linked to this, we'll see whether we can confirm one person at both scenes.'

'Tess Williamson?'

'She's the obvious choice. I went round to her house this morning. She doesn't have an alibi but she's denying any involvement in this.'

'Do you think she's telling the truth?'

'No I don't but I don't think she has the wherewithal to have committed either of the crimes herself, so she may well be protecting the person who did. She's a jumpy, nervous sort of a girl, and it may come down to whether she's more afraid of whoever has committed both these crimes than she is of the police.' I unlock the front door and O'Reilly follows me inside. 'We've spoken to your neighbours on all sides but nobody saw or heard anything.'

'Do you think we're safe living here?' I ask him.

'Now that the locks are changed, yes, I do. It's important to take sensible precautions, though.'

'I'm keeping the children close,' I say. 'Neither of them is allowed out in the evening anyway, at the moment. Myself or another trustworthy adult collects them from school. They keep the doors locked; know not to answer the front door. And they would ring nine-nine-nine immediately if they suspected anything.'

'Great,' he says. 'Sounds like you've covered all your bases.'

We go through to the living room where MURDERER assaults me again, like a hard slap on the face, stark and shocking. It has all the drama of a Hollywood film and all the menace of a real-life threat and is completely at odds with our lives. Or at least it was.

'Can I tear this down now?' I ask him.

'Absolutely. Let me help you.'

'I think it will come away fairly easily,' I say. 'It's quite thick wallpaper, the sort that has two layers.' I approach the corner low down, just above the skirting, and scrape at it with my fingernail until I have hold of the edge. When I pull back, the whole strip tears upwards in one piece, taking half of the M away with it.

'Bravo!' O'Reilly shouts, and we smile at each other. 'We'll have this off in no time.' He begins at the opposite end of the wall and it's not long before we meet in the middle. Most of the strips have come away in one easy piece but occasionally we've had to tear off smaller pieces that have been left behind. Within minutes we're able to stand back and survey our work: a blank wall in front, heaps of discarded paper lying behind us.

'I never liked that paper anyway,' I say.

'You didn't put it up then?'

'No. I haven't had the time, or the money, to redecorate – and anyway,' I laugh, 'it's a horrible dingy colour. You think I would have chosen that?'

'I'm a man. I don't know what goes with what.' He smiles

some more and I'm reminded that he's got the sort of throw-away macho charm that makes my knees threaten to buckle. Suddenly I feel awkward, on my own in the house, with a man, whom only last night I imagined having sex with. As the thoughts come tumbling back to me – his hands up my dress, his mouth on mine – to my horror, I feel myself blush.

'Everything okay?' he says.

'Fine.' I walk over to the window and look out, give the fire in my cheeks a chance to die down before I turn back to him. 'You must have places to be on a Saturday.' Embarrassment makes me brisk. 'Don't let me keep you.'

'I can help tidy up this lot?' He gestures towards the discarded wallpaper.

'No.' I almost run ahead of him to the front door and hold it open. 'You've given up enough of your weekend.' I try to relax my face into a smile but find I can't because I want to start crying. I want to lean up against his chest and I want him to tell me that everything will be fine. I don't know where this ache has come from – Dredging up the past? My recent, prolonged loneliness? Or just too many films where the man comes along and fixes everything for us poor, defenceless women?

Goodness knows, I, of all people, should be disillusioned by the pull of romantic love, but there it is and my heart is sounding louder than Big Ben.

'I'll be in touch tomorrow, then.' He looks both puzzled and disappointed. 'In the meantime you know where to reach me?'

'Of course. Thank you.' As soon as he steps outside, I close the door. Shit, shit, shit! This is not a good time for me to lose control. I need to stay focused, keep my eye on what's important, not cloud the issue with misguided thoughts of romance. First things first – pull myself together and head off to Trevor Stewart's house.

I march up and down a few times, my feet making

purposeful contact with the floor, but it does nothing to diminish the build-up of feelings inside me. During these last few weeks I've been pulled every which way and, scared as I've been, I haven't allowed myself to cry. Now, though, I'm going to have to let it all out. I sit down on the sofa, wrap my arms around myself, and cry until I'm done. I let it all pour out – my fear for what could have happened to Robbie, my loneliness, my worry that my past may have erupted into the present – and then, when I'm finished, I go through to the bathroom and splash my face with cold water. The mirror confirms what I expect; I look awful – runny, red eyes, blotches around my mouth and mottled, angry cheeks. I'm going to have to give my face time to return to its normal state before I approach Trevor Stewart, and so I spend the next hour picking up the discarded wallpaper in the living room and then I clean the kitchen, clearing away debris, wiping the worktops and putting laundry in the machine. When I look in the mirror again, I still don't look great, but with a touch of blusher and some mascara I'm good enough to go.

My doctor's case is always by the front door and I carry it to the car with me then set off to Trevor Stewart's address. I'm not sure what I'll say if he answers the door, but imagine that I might want to pretend that I'm doing a house call and searching for a patient. And if he recognises me . . . ? I'll deal with that when it happens.

Like me, he lives on the south side of the city but further out towards the boundary. My hopes that he might have remarried and be in a loving relationship are dashed as soon as I see the house. It's midway along a well-cared-for street where the gardens are tended and the windows gleam. The Stewart house is the exception. The grass is as high as my knees and there are broken clay pots and a soggy cardboard box full of empty whisky bottles dumped under the bay window at the front. Giving myself no time to hesitate, I grab my doctor's bag, go through the squeaky garden gate and up to the front door. A dog in the adjacent garden starts to bark and I hear a woman's voice shout to him to stop. The front door is opaque glass and I can just about see through into the hallway. It appears as if letters and colourful circulars are piled up on the mat inside. I ring the doorbell and wait, not really expecting an answer.

'Were you needing any help?' It's a woman's voice. She's leaning over the hedge, her arms folded in front of her. The archetypal busybody neighbour. Nothing gets past her. The sort of person who can be useful when you're a locum doctor looking for a patient.

'I'm looking for Trevor Stewart,' I say. 'You wouldn't happen to know where he was?'

'Are you an estate agent?' It's another voice, a man's this time. His head pops up alongside the woman's.

'No, I'm a doctor, actually. Not Trevor's regular doctor,' I add, in case they're registered at the same practice as he is.

'Locum, eh?' he says. 'We all need the extra money now.'

'Tell me about it,' I reply, neither confirming nor denying the locum assumption. I move closer towards the hedge. 'Doesn't look like he's been around for a while?'

'You must have got your wires crossed somewhere, Doctor. Trevor's been in the Royal Ed for –' he looks at his wife – 'how long is it now, Margaret?'

'Must be three months, minimum, because I remember there was frost on the ground when the ambulance came for him.'

'Sectioned under the Mental Health Act,' he says. 'Completely lost it, poor bugger.' He shrugs, his heavy stomach rising up and then down again. 'Not even that old either.'

'He's a danger to himself,' Margaret continues. 'He's been quite a drinker. There isn't one of us in the street who hasn't met him coming out of the off-licence or rolling back from the pub late at night, falling into the gutter.'

'He never got over Sandy, of course,' her husband says. 'Love of his life, she was.'

'Brain tumour.' Margaret answers a question I have no need to ask. 'Horrible death by all accounts.'

'I was hoping you were an estate agent,' the man says. 'Could do with selling the place.' He glances back over each of his shoulders then leans in to the hedge. 'Listen, Doc, if you see a social worker and you can put a word in the right ear, Trevor won't be coming back here and the place needs selling before it falls to rack and ruin. Looks bad, you know.'

'Will do.' I make a show of checking my watch. 'Crikey! Is that the time? I should be off.' I smile at them both. 'Thank you for your help.'

'Don't forget about the house, Doc,' the man shouts after me, and I give him a wave.

I feel their eyes watching me as I climb back into my car. They've given me a lot to think about – and none of it heartening. It sounds as if Trevor's life never picked up after Sandy's death. Their love for each other was special; I know that. There was no doubting the strength of feeling they had for each other, but I always imagined that he would remarry and go on to have some more children.

Would it have made a difference if he'd had Sandy for a few months longer? Without my blunder, she would have lived another six months, maybe even a year. But, there again, as the disease advanced, her death could have been protracted and painful and I know how upsetting this can be for both the sufferer and their relatives. She would have lost function down one side. Chances are she would have been unable to swallow. She might have gone blind. Almost certainly, she would have developed epilepsy. All of this would have been extremely traumatic for Mr Stewart when he was also trying to manage a new baby.

Perhaps, either way, he would have turned to drink. The truth is, I'll never know.

And now he's a patient in the Royal Edinburgh Hospital – Phil's domain. It's the city's psychiatric hospital and is only five minutes' walk from my house. Although Mr Stewart was initially sectioned, the order lasts for two weeks, and if not reapplied for, he could have agreed to be an in-patient, in which case he will be allowed out for periods during the day to walk around the shops, get some fresh air . . . spike Robbie's drink? Come to my house?

But both of these events occurred in the evening and surely he wouldn't be allowed out then?

There is such a thing as an overnight pass, I remind myself.

I drive home, my thoughts going round in a loop, mulling over possibility and probability, and I come to the conclusion that I should go to the Royal Edinburgh to visit Trevor Stewart. I didn't get the chance to face him all those years ago, but I am prepared to do so now.

I arrive outside my door just as Phil's car is also pulling up. We say our hellos on the pavement and I give the children the new keys. They go inside, leaving me with Phil and Erika, who has climbed out of the car this time. They stand very close together in front of me and Phil glances at Erika before saying, 'Why don't you let the children come and live with us for a while?'

I take a step back. 'Why?'

'It will be safer for them. The flat is secure; the entry system adhered to. One of us can collect them from school and make sure we're always home when they are.'

'It's safe here too. I've had the locks changed.'

'Lauren is too young to be left on her own.'

'Lauren's never in the house alone. If Robbie or I aren't here, she goes round to Amber's.'

'And you think that's adequate?'

'Look, Phil.' I feel the familiar irritation simmer in my stomach. 'We've already worked out the terms of our child custody agreement.'

'True. But I've had second thoughts about it. Erika and I would like shared custody.'

'Well, I'm sorry, but I don't have second thoughts and neither, incidentally, do the children.'

'But circumstances have changed.' He leans in closer. 'Olivia, if Robbie is being targeted then he clearly needs extra protection.'

'The police will get to the bottom of what's going on. It doesn't mean the children can't live with me.'

'Are you sure you're not just being . . .' he looks around the garden until he comes up with the right word, '. . . difficult?'

'Difficult?' I repeat, my inclination to shout back at him – *Difficult? That's rich coming from you!* But I don't. I take a breath and think before I answer. Am I being difficult? Am I putting the children at risk? Phil and Erika live in a modern flat several miles from here and bang in the centre of town, the distance a welcome buffer for me as it means I never meet them when shopping or eating locally. The children have their own bedrooms in the flat but Lauren, in particular, doesn't like being so far away from her friends. Erika is on a sabbatical year and is writing up her PhD, so more often than not, she works from home.

I turn to glance at my own house, a slightly ramshackle, Edwardian semi-detached villa that could do with some money spent on it, but the children wanted to stay in the same area as they'd lived in before the separation, so moving further out of town to benefit from cheaper house prices wasn't an option. And although we haven't had much money, we have spent the last six months making it our home. Now, with the locks changed and sanction from DI O'Reilly,

I'm confident that they're safe here, in their own home, with all their belongings around them.

'I'm not being difficult,' I say to Phil. 'I appreciate your concern, but the children are better off with me.'

'You truly believe they're safe here?'

'I'm their mother, Phil. Do you honestly think I'd let them stay here if I thought it was dangerous?'

'Olivia.' Erika speaks and we both look at her. She waits a couple of seconds. 'I'm sure in your heart of hearts . . .' she pauses and I count the beats, one . . . two . . . 'you will agree, that it is best for the children . . .' another pause, '. . . to come and stay with us.'

'No, I don't agree,' I say, quick and sharp. 'In my heart of hearts, I know that there's no better place for children than with their parents. I am the primary caregiver and this is their home.'

My words are a trigger for them both to move away from me, their bodies gracefully mirroring each other. What isn't so graceful is the fact that they are now ten feet away and whispering. Phil takes his mobile from his pocket and dials a number. I hear him say 'O'Reilly' and realise he'll be hoping to bring more ammunition into the argument, but I already know that O'Reilly doesn't think we're in danger as long as we take sensible precautions. When he's finished his call, they both come back to stand in front of me again.

'DI O'Reilly doesn't share your concerns, then?' I say. Childish, but I'm back to the point-scoring.

He ignores this and says instead, 'Just now seems as good a time as any to discuss arrangements for the summer.'

'Okay.' I nod.

'Bearing in mind what's happening, I thought it might be wise to get the children right away from Edinburgh.'

'Well, as it happens, Declan's been on the phone. My mother's going into hospital and I need to fly over there.'

'When?'

'In three weeks. The timing couldn't be better. School will just have broken up for the summer.'

'You want to take Robbie and Lauren?'

'Of course.' I shrug. 'They love it there. You know they do.'

'I was hoping *I* could take them away this year.'

'We'll only be gone two weeks. I'll have to get back to work, and there's the whole of the rest of the summer.'

'I'd like to take them away as soon as school breaks up. And . . . for the whole of the summer.'

'What?' My mouth hangs open. 'You can't get eight weeks' leave!'

'In fact, I can.' He glances at Erika, whose face is lit up with a beatific smile. 'We want to take them to Erika's family home. It's in Bavaria. Lauren could learn to ride. She's wanted to do that for a while. And Robbie can fish, take the boat out, water-ski.'

'It's a wonderful place for children,' Erika says, turning that smile on me.

'Then get your own,' I say under my breath. Erika doesn't hear me but Phil does and his face tightens.

'Excuse me?' Erika looms towards me. She has large teeth, not unlike a horse. 'I didn't catch that.'

'I said—'

'Erika, darling.' Phil cuts me off, placing himself between me and her. 'Would you mind waiting in the car?'

'Of course not, my love.'

I look away as they kiss, wondering how much longer this love-in is going to last.

'Erika and I love each other, Olivia,' Phil says, his eyes fixed on Erika's retreating back. 'It really is time for you to accept that.'

'I think I'm doing rather well, all things considered.'

He stares back at me. 'Meaning?'

'A neutral party might have watched this exchange and accused you of rubbing my nose in it.' I throw my arms out. 'All this touchy-feely, look-how-much-we-care-for-each-other stuff that you're so fond of now.'

'You're accusing me of not considering your feelings?'

'Absolutely.'

'I'm not guilty of that.'

'No, of course not! Because you're never guilty of *anything*. You didn't leave me because you fancied lying between another woman's legs – oh no! It was much more worthy and much more urgent than that. If I remember rightly, you felt our relationship "was stifling you as a man and as a psychiatrist".' I pause. 'Whatever that means.'

'If I'd wanted to rub your nose in it, I would have told you that Erika and I are getting married. In Germany. In the summer.'

For several long seconds I'm completely stunned. My head says, *That figures*, while my heart gives a wail and my eyes fill with tears. It's not as if I want him back. For the first six months I did, but lately I've been so much better. It's just the fact that he was once mine – my one true love – and he has moved on seamlessly to another woman, looking much happier than he did during the last half a dozen years with me. How can that not hurt?

'You shit!' I say. 'You were going to take the children to Germany, without telling *me*, or *them*, that they would be coming to your *wedding*?'

'Because I suspected you would be like this.'

'Like what?'

'Bitter.'

'I'm not bitter.' I walk a few paces away from him. 'I'm angry.'

'You do yourself no favours taking this tone.'

'Oh fuck off, Phil.' I stare up at the sky and shake my head. 'Just fucking fuck off! I don't care. Marry Eva Braun! Move to Germany permanently. Now there's an idea.'

'About the summer—'

'Not now.' I head towards the house and he follows me. I shut the door right in his face and wait for him to ring the bell. I hope he does – there's a lot more I can say to him – and I hope he doesn't – I've said enough. I don't want to be this carping ex-wife who places hurdles at every juncture. I want to move on, and in an odd, abstract kind of a way, I even wish them happiness. It's just that the bruising hasn't quite healed and I feel as if he's kicked me in the softest of places.

I watch through the living-room window and see him climb back into his car. The thought of him marrying is bad enough, but taking the children to Germany for the whole summer? Not to see either of their faces for eight weeks? I couldn't cope with that. I need my children. I know that part of being a mother is letting go but I can't. Not yet. Lauren is far too young and anyway, I'd miss them too much.

I take some steadying breaths, then climb the stairs and find Robbie and Lauren in Robbie's room, sitting in front of his computer monitor.

'Mum, listen!' Robbie says.

I lie down on his bed. 'I'm listening,' I say.

He reads from the screen. 'Stems of plastic flowers can be filled with calcium cyanide and a crystallised acid that reacts with water to form cyanide gas.' He sits back on the seat and raises his eyebrows. 'Beware Interflora.'

'What on earth?' I lean up on one elbow and look at them both. 'What's going on?'

'It was my idea,' Lauren says, swivelling round on the seat. 'To do some research so that we're prepared for whatever comes next.'

'Somebody doesn't like us,' Robbie says.

'They really don't,' Lauren echoes.

'So we need to try and second-guess them,' Robbie says.

'Just in case,' Lauren affirms.

'What's this got to do with cyanide?' I swing my feet back round on to the floor and stand up.

'Flowers could be delivered. That could be the next thing,' Robbie says, as if it's obvious.

'So if any flowers arrive, don't put them in water without checking the stems,' Lauren says.

I almost laugh but stop myself because I completely understand their need to try to get ahead of what's been happening. 'Don't worry, I won't.' I kiss the top of Lauren's head and look at the screen. They're surfing the net and I see from the Google bar that they typed in 'Different ways to kill someone'.

'And look at this one!' Robbie shouts, pointing to a photo of someone who has huge red weals all over him.

'Don't.' I nudge him. 'You're going to frighten your sister.'

'Lauren asked me to look!'

'I did, Mum.' She pulls at my T-shirt. 'You know, once I watched a TV programme at Amber's and it was about this woman who had a stalker and she kept getting emails and text messages and then she opened her front door and there was a dead rabbit on the step.' She shivers and has a quick suck of her thumb. 'Then Amber's mum put the TV off so I don't know what happened in the end.'

'Real life tends to be a bit different from TV dramas,' I say, pulling her towards me for a hug, knowing that real life can end up being exactly like a TV drama – or worse.

'Everything happens in threes.' She looks up at me, her eyes wide with a mix of fear and imagination. 'First there was Robbie and then the house was broken into and what will be next?'

'Nothing, Lauren,' I say, holding her close. 'Nothing will be next.'

8

Sunday and I wake at four thirty, ridiculously early and not quite daylight. I pull on a tracksuit and go downstairs. Benson starts his dance around my feet and I open the back door so that he can run about in the garden reacquainting himself with all the familiar smells. Before I close the door behind him, my attention is caught by the sky. One of the reasons I love this house is that it has a southeasterly aspect, and with no tenements to block the panorama, I can see across to the horizon where the sky is churned up like raspberry ripple ice cream.

Red sky in the morning, shepherd's warning, my dad's voice automatically pops into my head. It never fails to amaze me how much of our thoughts and feelings are hard-wired at a young age; how many of our responses are like grooves in vinyl and we sing the old tunes as easily as treading the path from living room to kitchen. I remember what O'Reilly said about reinventing ourselves, but it seems to me that, for most of us, that idea is pure fantasy – our public face maybe, but our private face is never reinvented. We carry our past with us always, like clothes we can't take off, covered up by newer, more fashionable ones, but still present when we strip back the layers.

I've never been a smoker and I'm not much of a drinker. I know that a cup of coffee will only make me feel jangly on the surface, while underneath the fear and fatigue are intermingling in the same way as the pink and reds in the sky. I have to go to the Royal Edinburgh Hospital today, to satisfy this need to rule out Trevor Stewart as the man who almost killed Robbie and came to our house on Friday. As the children are no longer spending the day with Phil and I don't want to leave them on their own, I'll need to talk to them about going to friends' houses. Leila would welcome them both. She has an endless capacity to absorb other children, especially mine, into her home.

It's far too early to ring her yet, so I go through to the living room and stare at the wall. Although MURDERER is now gone, and there are no telltale indentations remaining in the lining paper, in my mind's eye I can see exactly where it was – the M was several feet above the plug sockets and the final R was above the desk where I keep bills and letter-writing materials, spare paper and pens. It's gone now, though, I tell myself. Anyone coming to the house would have no idea what had been written. It would simply look as if we were in the process of redecorating.

I make myself a cup of tea and sit down with a book, but the bare wall fills my peripheral vision and within five minutes, I'm up again. It's still only six o'clock. I can't walk Benson and leave the children home alone, so it looks as if I'm caught with my thoughts, heavy-duty reproach and recriminations. If my past mistake has brought danger to Robbie, and perhaps also to Lauren, I'll never be able to forgive myself. I may have started out as a reluctant mother, but during Robbie's first year I grew to love being a mother more than I could ever have imagined, the feelings almost frightening in their intensity. While my career is important to me, my children are my whole world. It sounds like a cliché but it's the truth. Without them, I'm nobody.

I'll drive myself to tears thinking like this, so I distract myself in the kitchen. We have half a dozen overripe bananas in the fruit bowl, a packet of chocolate chips in the cupboard and, next to it, a sticky jar of molasses and some medium oatmeal that's approaching its sell-by date. I pull bowls and scales out of the cupboards and occupy myself with making banana bread, parkin and chocolate-chip cookies, with Benson and the radio for company. And while the baking is in the oven, I rummage through the fridge and find enough vegetable leftovers to make a pot of minestrone soup. The baking is cooling on the wire rack when the phone rings.

'What's this about Friday evening?' It's Leila, her tone worried. 'Robbie sent Mark a text saying your house was broken into.'

'Not exactly broken into.' I fill her in on everything that happened, from when we arrived home to when we went to stay at the hotel.

'Why didn't you tell me?' She sounds hurt. 'You could have come here.'

'You had the wedding yesterday. I didn't want us turning up on your doorstep when you had such a busy day lined up.'

'That's what friends are for, you silly cow.' She sighs heavily. 'Sometimes you're not very good at asking for help, Liv.'

'I'm sorry, but you know how it's been since Phil left. I've grown used to sorting everything out myself.'

'Well, I hope you know I'm always here for you. A trouble shared and all that.'

'I do. And thank you.' I pull Benson on to my lap and stroke the back of his ears. 'I've been baking this morning. Fancy a visit later on?'

'Definitely. Why don't you all come for Sunday lunch?'

'We'd love to.' Problem solved. I know Leila won't mind if I slipped off after lunch to visit Trevor. 'I'll bring banana bread and some cookies. See you around two?'

'See you then.'

I put the phone back on its cradle and hold Benson on my knee while I stare through the window. The earlier promise of inclement weather is about to be fulfilled. Moment by moment, the sky is darkening as clouds roll in from the west. I haven't told O'Reilly about Trevor Stewart but should I tell Leila? Back when it happened she was sympathetic, and perhaps I should turn to her now. I hum and haw for a bit, undecided. I wonder what's stopping me and realise that I can't voice my suspicion because it feels that to do so will make it real and I'm hoping that this is a case of my imagination running away with me. I'm hoping that O'Reilly will suddenly appear and tell me that Tess Williamson has cracked, that she had some sort of obsession with Robbie and decided to act on it.

Nothing to do with me and my past.

Just one of those things.

Leila lives in a state of organised chaos. They have a huge rambling house that stretches their salaries to breaking point but, despite the usual spats between children, they are the happiest family I've ever spent time with. When we arrive, Sunday lunch is still being prepared. Leila's three daughters and Lauren set the table while the two boys go outside with Archie to chop and stack wood for winter fires. After the rain this morning, the day is now damp but fresh, the water having washed the streets clean and turned the grass emerald green.

'It's like *Little House on the Prairie*,' I say, scrubbing carrots. 'Division of labour according to sex. I thought the sixties put a stop to all of that?'

'It's nice though, isn't it?' Leila replies, closing the oven door with her foot. 'I always hankered after the sort of Sundays where everyone pitched in with family stuff, but we had to help Mum and Dad in the shop. Every day was a work day.'

'But look how you've all turned out.' I eat a finger of raw carrot. 'Your parents must be so proud. It has to be some sort of a record: four children, four doctors.'

'They were asking after you, yesterday.' She plonks a roasted leg of lamb down on the worktop next to me. 'They haven't seen you in a while.'

'I know. I keep meaning to pop into the shop but it's so difficult getting parked at Tollcross now.' I inhale the steam rising off the meat. 'Mm. Smells delicious. But tell me, how was the wedding?'

She starts a long story about the bride and the wedding party, her three girls pitching in with their comments on the clothes and the more outrageous behaviour of some of the guests. I forget about Trevor Stewart and what might be ahead for us, and it isn't until lunch is over and we're all sitting back with full stomachs and laughter reddening our cheeks that I remember what I need to do. Everyone helps clear the table, then the girls run off to play on the trampoline outside, the boys to listen to music in Mark's room and Archie to fall asleep with the Sunday papers on his lap in the sunroom.

'Leila?' I've just finished washing the pots while Leila's been stacking the dishwasher. 'Would you mind if I popped out for a bit?'

'But I want to talk to you about what happened on Friday night.' She takes two mugs from the shelf and puts the kettle on. 'I just didn't want to do it in front of the children.'

'Could you save the coffee for when I get back? I shouldn't be more than an hour.'

'Where are you going?' Her face is open, inviting a confidence, but I can't take her up on it.

'I have to meet with DI O'Reilly. Forensic results.' I hear myself speak the lie and flinch. 'No, that isn't true.'

'What do you mean? Nothing else has happened, has it?' She grabs my arm. 'Liv, you would tell me, wouldn't you?'

'Nothing else has happened, I promise. It's probably crazy but . . .' I widen my eyes. 'I have to reassure myself that I'm not the reason behind what's been going on.'

'How could you be?'

'I'm probably just going bonkers.' I kiss her on the cheek. 'I'll tell you all about it when I get back.'

'Don't rush.' Her expression is concerned as she walks me to the door. 'Take as long as you need. Archie can always drop the kids off later.'

I thank her and drive home. The Royal Edinburgh Hospital is Phil's territory, so I've been there a lot in the past but not at all recently. I know that during Sunday visiting time the car park will be full, so I leave my car by my own front door and walk on to the grounds. I pass Phil's designated parking space and groan to myself when I see his car there. He's the last person I want to bump into. I've accepted that I'll have to endure another conversation with him about summer arrange- ments, but I'd prefer it to be later rather than sooner.

Like many of the hospitals in cities all over Britain, the Royal Edinburgh is a patchwork of old and new buildings. I expect to find Trevor in one of the acute adult wards and I check in at reception to find out which one. The receptionist gives me the name and I make my way there, walking the length of the main corridor and up some stairs. I'm close to where Phil has his office and tiptoe at speed past his closed door and around the corner. The staff nurse on duty is a woman I've known for years. She's been working here almost as long as Phil and we've met often enough for us to be on first-name terms.

'Liv!' She looks up from the chart she's reading. 'Long time no see. What brings you here?'

'Hi, Sally. I'm here to visit Trevor Stewart.'

She looks surprised. 'You're not his GP, are you?'

'No. He's a friend of a patient of mine and I said I'd look him up because she's not able to get out much.' As a child I could tell lies as easily as the next girl, but I surprise myself at just how easily this lie comes tripping off my tongue.

'That's thoughtful of you.' She comes round from behind the desk and walks ahead of me into the dayroom. The television is on, and of the seven people in the room, it looks as though six are asleep, and only one is watching the screen. 'Congratulations, by the way, on your award. We all voted for you here.'

'Thank you. It's given the centre a lot of publicity which is great for fundraising.'

'Trevor's over there in the corner.'

She points her hand towards a man slumped in a straight-backed chair, the sort of chair made from wipe-clean plastic masquerading as leather, and frequently chosen for dayrooms in care homes for the elderly.

'We're trying to organise long-term residential care for him, but you know how hard it is to get beds.'

'He looks older than I expected,' I say, because even at a distance I can see his hair is completely grey and his back is rounded as if he suffers from osteoarthritis.

'You'd never think he was only fifty,' Sally agrees. 'But he's not someone who's looked after himself. He's been a serious alcoholic since he lost his wife and that was eighteen years ago.'

I'm not surprised to hear that his degeneration into alcoholism started when Sandy died. He wouldn't be the first person to turn to drink to salve his grief. What's far worse is the fact that, despite being a comparatively young man, he wasn't able to give up on the bottle.

'What was the incident that led to him being sectioned?' I ask, wondering whether he's being kept sedated with drugs.

'He was incoherent, brandishing a knife, intent on self-harm rather than hurting others. He calmed down within a few days of being in here.'

'Is he being heavily sedated?'

'Initially he was given moderate doses of anti-psychotics, but now what you see is what you get.'

'This isn't just a bad day, then?'

She shakes her head regretfully.

'I'll have a quick word with him,' I say. 'Pass on the message from his friend.'

'Be my guest. Although you'll be lucky to get any response from him.' She turns back towards the nurses' station. 'Say cheerio before you go.'

'Will do.'

I approach Trevor quietly, careful not to wake any of the other patients. The likelihood of him having the wherewithal to inflict damage on Robbie and paint MURDERER on the wall now looks like a very long shot, but I need to stare into his eyes and satisfy myself that it wasn't him.

He's dozing into his chest, his breath is rasping and he's dribbled down the front of his cardigan. It's a Fair Isle pattern with round, chunky buttons. My father used to wear something similar but my father never ended up like this – and anyway, Trevor's only eight years older than I am. I pull up a chair and sit down in front of him. 'Mr Stewart?'

No response. There's a smell of decay permeating the air around him and I keep my breaths shallow. I gently nudge his knee with my hand and he raises his head up, his movements very slow as if everything is happening through layers of cotton. Rheumy eyes peer into mine. His eyelashes are sparse; his blue iris is rimmed with an off-white discolouration. There isn't so much as a hint of recognition in his expression, just a fleeting interest before oblivion seizes him again.

And there's no recognition for me either. I try to find even a shadow of his former self, but there's no sign that he was ever the fresh-faced man of eighteen years ago whom I last saw leaving the ward after he'd been told of his wife's death. True, at that point, he looked beaten, but I never expected him to stay that way.

'My name is Olivia Somers,' I say. 'I've come to visit you.'

His eyes are closed but his tongue moves around in his mouth as if he's trying to shape some words.

'Mr Stewart.' I nudge his knee again. 'Do you remember me? My maiden name was Naughton and I looked after your wife Sandy.'

I say his wife's name quite loudly, but even that doesn't register with Trevor. His chin slides further towards his chest until it knocks against it. Within seconds his head lolls to one side and he begins to snore.

'He sleeps a lot.' There's a woman pacing beside me. Long greasy hair and stick thin, she brings her splayed fingers up to her mouth and draws greedily on an imaginary cigarette. 'Pickled his liver and his brain.' She starts to cough, and spits the phlegm from her throat on to her sleeve. The noise wakes a man further along, who fixes startled eyes on me then makes a masturbating motion with his hand and treats me to a lecherous smile.

I look back at Trevor, lost in his own world, and realise that there's no way this man is capable of walking from here to the toilet on his own, never mind being allowed an overnight pass and engineering an attack on Robbie. The woman is right – he's burnt out, his brain and liver permanently damaged by alcohol. And I played a hand in his downfall. It's a depressing thought.

'Goodbye then, Trevor.' I briefly touch his shoulder then walk back towards the nurses' station. No sign of Sally so I keep walking. I feel relieved that the trouble hasn't stemmed from my past, but that feeling is brief, as my shoulders grow heavy, guilt crowding in on me, taunting me with memories of a dead mother and her son. I remember what Professor Figgis said – 'From now on, everything you do must be done that little bit better. You can't give anything back to Mr Stewart, but you can pay it forward. Be exemplary in your care for others.'

Have I done that? Have I harmed anyone else? I sincerely hope not, and am sure that I've always given my very best attention to every patient who's come to see me.

Back in the corridor, I'm about twenty yards from Phil's

office when the door opens. Not wanting him to catch me here, I pull myself tight into the wall and then creep back round the corner and on to the ward again. It's too soon for me to feel okay about his impending marriage and, as for taking the children away for eight weeks, it's just not happening.

I walk the length of the ward looking for Sally. She's in the linen cupboard folding sheets.

'Did you get much out of him?' she asks me.

'No, you were right. He's a poor soul.'

'He is that.'

'I don't suppose he gets many visitors?'

'His daughter comes in almost every day, but otherwise no one's been in.'

'He has a daughter?' I'm frowning. After what Trevor's neighbours said to me about him never recovering from Sandy's death, I assumed he hadn't remarried. 'I didn't know that.'

'She was taken into care when she was young.'

'What about her mother?'

'Her mother died.'

I do a double take. 'Two wives died on him?'

'Just the one, as far as I know.' Sally folds a sheet into a perfect oblong and settles it on top of a neat pile, keeping all the edges parallel. 'She had a brain tumour.'

'No, that can't be right.' I lean up against the slatted wooden shelves, the strong smell of hospital laundry filling my nose. 'That baby died.'

She thinks for a second, another sheet suspended in her hands. 'You might be right. I don't know all the details. Only what Kirsty's told me.'

Kirsty. Memories of long ago – another hospital, a vulnerable young woman, me taking blood as she told me about her chosen baby names – collide in my brain with a crashing of gears. My ears ringing, I fix a frozen smile on my face and look at Sally. 'How old is she?'

'She'll be eighteen this month. She'd asked me about taking her dad out for a meal, but you see how ill he is?'

I nod, feel the skin on my face tremble.

'She's doing okay, though, Kirsty. She was lucky to get good foster parents. They encouraged her to apply for a scholarship with the performing arts school out near Livingston. She's quite an actress, apparently. One of the student nurses saw her in a production at the Lyceum last month.' She stacks the final sheet and looks at her watch. 'Better get on with the drug round. No rest for the wicked, eh?' She smiles. 'It's been good catching up, Liv. I was sorry to hear you and Phil had split up.'

I manage to almost-shrug my tight shoulders. 'Such is life.'

I say goodbye and my legs walk themselves back into the corridor, treading lightly as if on eggshells. I'm holding my breath as the neurons in my brain light up, busying themselves with making connections.

The baby lived.

Sandy and Trevor's baby – a girl, not a boy as Leila said – lived. And yet Leila told me the baby had died. I can't imagine how she could have got that so wrong. I try to envision a conversation where she asks about one of the babies in Special Care and they tell her the baby is dead. Leila would have asked after the Stewart baby. Maybe a baby boy died that day and he had a similar surname. Maybe—

'Olivia?'

The voice is loud and I jerk upright. Phil is standing in front of me.

'Are you here to see me?' he says.

'No.'

'Are you sure?'

'Yes.'

'And yet I come out of my office and find you here, frowning down at your feet.' There's an impatience in his tone and in his demeanour that makes me both shrink with embarrassment and expand with anger. He glances beyond me through the window and takes a bored, why-are-you-always-so-difficult breath. 'I'm sorry that my intention to remarry has upset you so much but—'

'Why do you always assume that everything's about you?' I cut in. 'I'm here visiting a *patient* and I was standing in the corridor thinking about his life when you appeared.'

He sighs, making it obvious that he doesn't believe me. He considers himself an expert on human behaviour and no amount of me defending myself will convince him otherwise.

'I'm not going to stand here explaining myself to you,' I say, walking past him.

'Where are the children?'

'Leila's.'

He follows me to the top of the stairs. 'We still need to talk about the summer holidays.'

'Not here,' I call back. 'And not now.'

My anger at Phil propels me out of the hospital and back home. When I get there, I stop for a breath and unlock the front door. The sight of the bare living-room wall pushes Phil to the back of my mind and catapults what I've just found out about Sandy and Trevor's baby to the front. I lean back against the kitchen counter, trying to make sense of the mix-up. It has to be a miscommunication. It's not unheard of for hospitals to give out the wrong details about the right patient and vice versa. It does seem unlikely, though, bearing in mind that Leila's a doctor, and the Gynaecology ward she worked in was close to the Special Care Baby Unit. She could have walked along the corridor and found out, seen the baby for herself.

But if it isn't a mix-up then Leila lied to me. And why would she do that?

Only one way to find out. I call Benson and take him in the car with me back to Leila's. It's a beautiful afternoon and the children are in the garden. Leila's three girls have changed into their swimming costumes and have set up a hosepipe which has a sprinkler attached and is sending arcs of water over their shrieking, running bodies. Out of range of the water, some of the hockey crowd have arrived and are lying on the grass beside Mark. They raise lazy hands to wave to me and I walk briskly towards them, concerned that I can't see my own children.

'Are Robbie and Lauren still here?' I say.

'They're round the back by the trampoline,' Emily says, sitting up with crossed legs and reaching to stroke Benson's head. 'With their dad.'

'Okay.' Phil must have hotfooted it over here after he spoke to me at the hospital, keen to talk to the children before I do. Unnecessarily, as I am not about to throw cold water on his holiday ideas – or tell the children he's getting married. I know Phil doesn't trust me, but in fact I'm more likely to encourage the children to spend time with him than not. Our marriage hasn't worked out but I don't want them to lose their dad.

'Robbie was telling us about the graffiti,' Emily says, standing up beside me. 'It's a really weird thing to happen.'

'You're telling me.' I look down at her worried face. 'The police are investigating it, so hopefully we'll get some answers soon.'

Her foot is jerked away from her as Benson drags at her laces, and she laughs, bending down to haul him off. 'You're such a silly mutt!'

'Don't let him bully you, Emily,' I say, walking into the house. 'Call me if he becomes too much of a pest.'

I find Leila staring through the patio windows at Phil, who is directly ahead of her, sitting on the edge of the trampoline, his feet dangling in mid-air.

'You're back!' She turns to hug me. 'I'm sorry about this.' She points towards Phil. 'He just turned up.'

'It's fine,' I swallow down the urge to launch straight into questioning her about the Stewart baby. Instead I keep my mind and my eyes on the conversation outside. Lauren is standing beside the trampoline, her face solemn, as it often is these days when Phil is talking to her. Robbie is lying back on the centre of the trampoline, staring everywhere except at his father: the street, the sky, towards the house and then back to the street again.

'What can he be saying to them?' Leila remarks.

'He'll be sowing the seed for summer holiday arrangements,' I say. 'And he might even be sharing his latest news.'

'What news?'

'He's marrying Erika.'

'*What?*' Leila folds her arms across her chest and her face grows disbelieving and then angry. '*When?*'

'This summer.'

'Of all the shitty timing! You've only just got divorced!' She throws her arms out, her silver bracelets colliding together with an arrhythmic shriek. 'And now with all this going on! What's wrong with the man?'

'I'm not really that bothered about it.'

Her expression is a question mark.

'I'm really not! I need some time to readjust but . . .' I take hold of her agitated hands. 'Thank you for caring. I appreciate it. I really do.' Then I tilt my head towards the garden and say, 'I just want the children to be okay with it.'

She follows my lead and stares through the window again. 'Well, if he's telling them now, he certainly picks his places.'

This makes us both laugh because Phil does look ridiculous, perched on the edge of the trampoline, swaying backwards and forwards as Robbie shifts position and Phil tries to keep his balance.

'Honestly, though,' Leila says. 'I just . . .' She trails off, shaking her head, and then says vehemently, 'I would never have believed he could be such a shit.'

'Well.' I shrug. 'People change, don't they? And not always

for the better.' I rest my finger against the glass. 'I think he's done now.'

Phil's walking away, waving to the children as he goes. Lauren raises a reluctant hand – more of a dismissal than a wave – and Robbie doesn't even bother with that. I almost feel sorry for Phil.

Almost.

I wait until he's gone, then go to join them. Lauren looks up guiltily.

'Everything okay?' I say.

'Dad was just here,' she says.

'Really?' I affect a casual interest. 'What did he want?'

'He was talking in his couch voice,' Robbie says, holding his hand up against the sun. 'I can never concentrate on what he's saying when he does that.'

'He wants us to go to Germany with him on holiday,' Lauren says. She comes across and stands beside me, nudging her body against mine. 'I'm not sure, though.' She has a long blade of grass in her hand and is tearing it into strips lengthways. 'What do you think, Mum?'

'I think . . .' I pause. 'I think it's up to you. But I also think that spending time with Dad would be good for you both.'

'We'd be going to Erika's house. She has ponies. Or her mum and dad do. They live there and she knows how to ride.' Lauren decimates the grass then throws it to one side and squints up at me. 'And I'd rather you were there, Mum, but at least if Robbie goes I won't be on my own. I mean, I don't really want to go.' Conflict is written all over her face, so that her expression changes every couple of seconds, but I can hear that Phil has done a good job of selling the whole idea to her.

'It's a long summer holiday,' I say. 'And the first two weeks we'll be in Ireland. I'm going to have to look after Gran when she comes out of hospital. She'll be grumpy and maybe a bit confused and I'll be busy trying to please her, so you and

Robbie will be on Uncle Declan's farm helping with the chores and hanging out with your cousins. A couple of weeks afterwards with Dad could be fun.'

'Do you think so?'

'I do.' I pull her in for a hug and look up at Robbie, who's still lying back on the trampoline. 'What do you say, Mister?'

'I suppose.' He gives a prolonged sigh then rolls over and jumps back down on to the ground beside us.

'And did Dad say anything else?' I ask, as we begin walking.

'About what?' Robbie immediately looks suspicious. 'He says we can forget about the counselling. That's true, isn't it?'

'I'm sure it is. He wouldn't lie to you, love.' His forehead is a scowl of irritation. 'I just wondered whether he'd been more specific about what will be happening when you're there.' *Like being guests at his wedding, for example.*

'He just went on about all the things we could do.'

'Right.'

As we round the corner of the house, Emily is organising the younger girls into cartwheel competitions and Lauren runs across the grass to join her while Robbie takes up position between the goalposts of a miniature football net. The boys start firing balls his way and there's good-natured teasing every time they score. Perfect – with the children occupied, this is my chance to speak to Leila.

'They're all having great fun out there,' I say, finding her exactly where I left her. 'We might manage ten minutes' peace before the next interruption.'

'I've made you a coffee.' She points to a mug on the table and I sit down in front of it. 'Did Phil tell them he's getting married?'

'Not yet. So better not say anything until he does.'

'I won't say a word.' She brings a chair up beside me. 'So tell me. Where did you go just now?'

'The Royal Ed.'

'Really? Why?'

'Do you remember Trevor Stewart?'

'Should I?' She frowns, her eyes moving from left to right as she places the name. 'You mean the Trevor Stewart from way back?'

'Yes.' I take a sip of my coffee. 'I thought there might be a connection with Robbie's drink spiking. The writing on the wall got me thinking about the past, back to my residency when . . .' I bite my lip, '. . . I effectively killed Sandy Stewart. It wasn't murder but it's as close as anyone in my house has ever got. So I decided to look him up and found he was still at the same address.'

Leila's jaw has dropped a couple of centimetres, her mouth open as she listens.

'His neighbours told me he'd been sectioned and I've just been to visit him.'

'Liv.' Leila reaches across and touches my upper arm. 'What's happening now can't possibly have anything to do with Sandy's death.'

'I know it sounds like a tenuous connection, but I had to reassure myself that Trevor wasn't doing this to punish me.'

'After eighteen years?'

'Yes, but look at all the publicity I've been getting lately! It would be galling if some doctor had hastened your wife's death and there she was being lauded as a star performer, wouldn't it?'

'Maybe, but . . .'

'No matter how many years had gone by, it would hurt. But anyway,' I sigh, 'Trevor's a ruined man. He's not capable of lifting a teacup to his mouth. There's no way he spiked Robbie's drink or came into my house.' I blow out a relieved breath. 'But while I was there I found out something else.'

'What?'

'His baby didn't die.'

I'm watching Leila's face closely but in truth I could be at
the other side of the room and still see the expression that
settles on her features – guilt.

'Leila?'

She's staring down at the floor; her jaw is tight shut.

'Leila?' I shake her shoulder. 'Did you already know this?'

'Shit.' She looks at me then, her right eye leaking a single
tear. 'I'm sorry, Liv.'

It's my turn to be slack-jawed. 'You *lied* to me?'

'I shouldn't have done; I didn't want to!' She throws her
arms out. 'I really didn't.'

'So why did you? Why on earth would you lie about something like that?'

'Phil told me you were obsessing about the whole thing:
Sandy's death, and the baby, and how Trevor would never cope
on his own.'

'I wasn't *obsessed*. I was having a normal reaction! Anyone
would feel bad if they'd done what I had.'

'He thought it was affecting your health. And when he told
me Trevor Stewart had called the house—'

My spine chills. 'Trevor called the house?'

'Yes. He asked to speak to you.'

'Because I left a letter in his door with my phone number
on it!' I shout. 'Leila, the man needed help!'

'But honestly, Liv, were you the right person to give him
help? He had the hospital counselling service and various
charities to support him.'

'Jesus!' I sit back, stunned. 'He must have thought I was
ignoring him.'

'Phil told him you weren't well and that he shouldn't call
back.'

'Interfering . . . bastard!' I bang my palms on the table. 'How
dare he?'

'Liv, calm down.' She tries to take hold of my hands but I

shake her away. 'I don't always see eye to eye with Phil, but in this case he really was thinking of you.'

'Was he now?' Both my palms are burning and I blow on them. 'So it's fine to treat another adult like a child, is it?'

'Think back to the person you were then. You weren't as confident and well rounded as you are now. You'd almost had an abortion!'

'Why are you bringing that up?' I say, watching her wince at my frosty tone.

'Only to indicate that . . . well . . . you weren't yourself!'

'I *was* myself, Leila.' I poke my finger into my own chest. 'That *was* me.'

'Phil was worried that you were getting involved in something you shouldn't. He thought you'd tell Trevor that you were responsible for Sandy's death and you'd lose your career too. You know how I feel about Phil, but in this case he truly believed he was protecting you.'

'And you? Is that what you thought?'

'I thought . . . You weren't looking after yourself or the baby you were carrying. You must remember how you were. You were sad and anxious and—'

I've heard enough. 'There's a fine line between care and control, Leila, and that's something Phil doesn't get.' I stand up. 'And you know what? I don't think you always get it either. Thank you for lunch. I'm going home.'

'Liv, please don't leave when you're angry. Please.'

I turn back at the door. 'The baby was a little girl. She's called Kirsty. And I'm going to find her.'

'Liv . . .'

'I don't care how crazy you think I'm being. Don't try to stop me and don't, *don't* tell Phil.'

I walk out to join the children, my eyes smarting with hot, indignant tears.

9

Monday morning surgery is always busy as, one way or another, the weekend throws up all sorts of trouble. My first patient had his shirt off when he was gardening and a neighbour told him he should have his moles checked. The second one has had diarrhoea, on and off, for six weeks and his wife has been nagging him to come and see me. And my final patient, the fifteenth this morning, has been having intermittent chest pain, so I give him an ECG and, seeing signs of cardiac irregularities, I call an ambulance.

My surgery finishes over an hour late, and it's gone half past two before I'm all done for the morning – patients seen, prescriptions printed out, emails replied to, a couple of referral letters dictated and a phone call to the hospice to check up on one of my young adults who suffers from cancer.

Leila came to my room at lunchtime, as she always does, and started to apologise for lying about the baby. I found I couldn't look her in the eye without wanting to shout at her, so I told her I still had work to do and turned my back on her until she got the message and left. Five minutes later, she snuck a chocolate-covered flapjack – my favourite – and a card around the door. The card has a picture of an apologetic bear holding a bunch of flowers and inside she's written – 'It was SO stupid of me and for years I worried about you finding out. Please forgive me. Leila.' A sad face is drawn next to her name.

Part of me wants to immediately forgive her, because she's

my best friend and she's making the effort and I know that she cares about me and the children. But a larger part of me is too hurt to let it go. She colluded with Phil in lying to me. She's as close to a sister as I'll ever get, and it hurts me to think she could go against me this way. Of course, we'll get past it, but not yet. I need time to put it in perspective.

When I left her house yesterday afternoon, I was angry and hurt, but I didn't have the chance to take myself off on my own to dwell on it. Robbie invited Emily and Ashe back home with him, and we were in the house five minutes when Lauren suggested we shop for some wallpaper. We left the older ones listening to music and trudged round a couple of shops. Lauren chose a bright, modern pattern, and by the time we got home, everyone was hungry. Emily and Lauren took charge of making supper and I forgot all about Sandy's daughter, and Leila and Phil's betrayal, and enjoyed an evening of lively chat and board games. It felt suspiciously as if they were making a concerted effort to cheer me up, but I entered into the spirit of it anyway. When Emily and Ashe had gone off home and Lauren was in bed, Robbie helped me strip the wallpaper off the remaining walls in the living room to prepare the whole room for decoration, and just before midnight I fell into bed exhausted, all thoughts of Kirsty lost in a fug of tiredness.

Now, with my morning surgery over, I have a chance to work out what to do next. Making amends is impossible, but now that I know the baby lived, I want to reassure myself that she's okay. From what Sally said, she's achieved a lot in her eighteen years and looks set to have a good career.

I wonder whether there's anything about her on the Internet. I type 'Kirsty Stewart actor' into a search engine and it comes back with a couple of relevant links. One is about her part in the play at the Lyceum – several reviewers are quoted praising her performance – and the other link mentions that she was educated at Sanderson Academy out near Livingston. I click on the link to their website and read their mission statement: 'We provide an environment where students are encouraged to develop their skills to the highest level, be that through dance, drama or music.'

My mobile is on my desk, on mute, but the screen lights up to tell me I have a call. It's O'Reilly. 'Hello?'

'Not interrupting, am I?' he says.

'No, I'm on a break.'

'I had another conversation with Tess this morning. She doesn't open up easily. Her parents told me she's been having all sorts of problems at school so is staying at home this week. As I thought, her father wanted a lawyer present but still, she agreed to allow us to take her fingerprints. There's a . . .'

I stop listening to O'Reilly because a memory spark has ignited. School. School and Tess. I try to remember back to what Leila said when I first asked her about Tess. It was something about head lice and how her mother could never get rid of them and because she went to a boarding school it made it all the harder. On the screen underneath the mission statement there are details about the length of the school day and then: 'Sanderson Academy is fully boarding by age fourteen, in order for the girls to take advantage of the programme of evening classes in all areas of dance, music and the dramatic arts.'

Boarding school isn't the norm in Scotland. In fact, I remember reading once that less than 1 per cent of children are educated this way here. Interesting then that Tess and Kirsty both go to boarding school. Is this significant? Could it be the same school?

'. . . is as far as we've got,' O'Reilly says, coming to the end of what he has to tell me.

'Well, thank you for calling. Let's speak soon,' I say, finishing the call without waiting for him to reply because my attention is back with the school website. There are several buttons down the side to click on, covering all aspects of school life from student welfare to current news. I begin with the first button and, not bothering to read much of the text, scroll through each page looking at photographs of the pupils, some playing musical instruments, others performing on stage or sitting drinking hot chocolate in the dorms. I have to know whether this is the boarding school that Tess attends because, if it is, it will link the two girls. I have no idea what Kirsty looks like, so I'm trying to find Tess and, after about ten minutes, I come across a photo entitled 'fourth years preparing for their end-of-term musical, *Annie Get Your Gun*'. My heart comes up into my throat and I gulp it down, hold my breath to keep it there. Tess is in the photo. She's standing sideways on but has turned her face to smile at the camera. She's holding a sponge in her hand and is applying foundation to the face of the girl seated in front of her.

Although I have no definite idea of what this could mean, I know I'm on to something. The first thought that occurs to me is that Kirsty Stewart and Tess Williamson could be the same person. Sally said that Kirsty was in a series of foster homes and it's possible that she was legally adopted. That's easy enough to find out because, if she was adopted by the Williamsons and had a name change, it's likely to be recorded on her medical file. I navigate back into the surgery database and find Tess's notes, scrolling through her medical history as far back as vaccinations and then her birth. She was a breech delivery and was delivered by Caesarean section, her mother's name is Audrey Williamson and she has two older sisters. No record of any adoption. That rules out my same-person theory and I go back on to Sanderson's website. There are just over three hundred children in the school, aged between seven and eighteen, and one hundred of the older children board. Kirsty is almost eighteen and Tess is sixteen, and as senior pupils it's very likely that they know one another. They could even be friends. Best friends.

I click on the contact button at the head of the home page and up comes a phone number. Swept along on a tide of apprehension and curiosity, I key the digits into my mobile and the phone at the other end rings for several beats before it's answered by a cheerful young woman.

'Sanderson Academy for the Performing Arts, how may I help you?'

'Hello, I'm interested in sending my daughter to your school and wondered whether I could make an appointment to come and see round?'

'Of course. Let me find the headmistress's diary.' I hear a door opening and closing, a rustling of papers and then the thud of a heavy book as it falls to the floor. 'You've just missed out on our Open Day, but the headmistress also sees prospective parents and pupils in the afternoons. Now let me see . . . She has a space tomorrow, at three thirty?'

I do a quick calculation. My surgery will be finished by one o'clock at the latest. I have an antenatal clinic in the afternoon but our community midwife often manages that alone and only refers to me if there's a problem. 'Yes,' I say. 'That time suits me.'

She takes my name and contact details and then says, 'Will your daughter be coming?'

'No, just me, if that's okay.'

'Of course. Can you tell me her particular area of interest?'

I quickly refer back to the website. 'She's a keen musician. She plays violin and piano but is also hoping to develop her acting skills.' The truth is that Lauren has already given up the violin and reluctantly practises piano as a trade-off for sleep-overs or computer time. And as for acting? She has only ever had minor roles in class plays and has never aspired to more.

'I'll make a note of that. It lets the headmistress tailor her talk to your needs.'

'Many thanks and I'll see you tomorrow.' I hang up the phone and am completely still for a second or two before covering my face with my hands. *What am I doing?* Is this really the right way to go about this? Setting off on my own investigation and leaving a trail of lies behind me? Should I not just hand the information over to O'Reilly, let him see whether there's any significance in it?

Not until I have something concrete, I tell myself.

But you do have something concrete, the voice in my head replies. *You have a connection between Tess Williamson and Kirsty Stewart. And Kirsty Stewart is Sandy Stewart's child.*

I take time to consider this but decide I can't tell O'Reilly about the connection yet. It feels too personal. I made the mistake; I need to find out whether it's come back to bite me. I've never before completely understood why people conceal information from the police, but now I do. It's about control and it's about self-preservation. And I'm counting on the fact that as long as I'm in the driving seat, there's a chance I can fix this before anything else happens.

Next day, my surgery goes like clockwork. I ask one of the other doctors – not Leila, it's too soon for me to be normal with her – to cover the antenatal clinic. The drive to Livingston shouldn't take more than forty minutes but traffic is often slow on the Edinburgh bypass and I head off in plenty of time. As I drive to the school, I think of all the questions a parent in my position would ask – teaching, exam results, facilities, what's their bullying policy? health policy? – so that by the time I turn off the main road, I have a list of questions at the ready. Sanderson Academy is about half a mile up a tree-lined drive, chestnut trees growing either side and farmed fields beyond. The school itself is a hotchpotch of buildings, large and small, springing up at random, it seems, and in all different sizes and styles. A sign directs me to the front of the oldest one, a square Victorian building, once grand but now slightly shabby, entirely symmetrical, apart from the modern extension to one side, flat roofed and ugly, like a carbuncle on the side of an elegant foot.

I park in a visitor space and open the entrance door into a small round glass porch, gardenias and begonias flowering in the heat of the sun. The door leading into the school is clear glass and I can see into the hallway where there's a large curved staircase and four doors leading off like diagonal points on a compass. The front door is protected by an entry system and I notice a CCTV camera just above it, in stark contrast to the rest of the décor, which is more mid-twentieth than twenty-first century.

I ring the doorbell and wait, my heart bumping nervously against my ribcage as I'm suddenly anxious about one of the members of staff recognising me. We're not that far from Edinburgh and the City Women awards have been well publicised in the *Courier*. Perhaps I should have given a false name, but then I really would have been lying, whereas at the moment, I'm simply feigning an interest in sending Lauren to school here. All I'm doing is wasting their time, I remind myself. I'm not breaking the law.

One of the doors opens and a young girl comes through it. She is tall and blonde and looks a similar age to Lauren. She unlocks the front door and smiles at me.

'Hello,' I say. 'I have an appointment with your headmistress, Miss Baker.'

'Come in.' She holds the door open. 'You should check in with her secretary, Mrs Tweedie. She's just in here.'

I follow her across the hallway. She's walking with an exaggerated bounce, her ponytails flying up and down to the rhythm. There's the melodic sound of a piano playing in a

not-so-distant room but that's immediately drowned out when
we go into Mrs Tweedie's office. The first thing I see, and
hear, are two spaniels in a large cage in the corner; they stand
up and bark, their wagging tails eager.

'Boys!' Mrs Tweedie shouts and they stop at once. She holds
out her hand to me. 'You must be Mrs Somers. Welcome to
Sanderson. Miss Baker will be with you directly.' She glances
beyond me to where the girl who opened the front door for me
is standing in the shadows. 'You can go now, Portia,' she calls.

'Thank you for showing me in, Portia,' I say, and she gives
me a practised smile then bounces off up the stairs.

'They love to gossip, these young girls,' Mrs Tweedie says.
'And as most of the school knows, Miss Baker is talking to
an agent, *from London.*' Her tone is hushed. 'We're hoping a
couple of our older students will be considered for a part in
one of the soaps. Can't say which one.' She pretends to zip
up her lips. 'All I can say is that a Scottish family will be
moving on to the *street* and two of our children are up for
auditions.' She sits back down with a happy sigh. 'Life is
never dull here, Mrs Somers.'

'I'm sure.' I lean down to stroke the dogs through the wire,
while Mrs Tweedie tells me about the history of the school and
the sorts of work some of the ex-pupils go on to achieve – in
television, theatre and music. It sounds impressive, and if Lauren
actually was interested in a career in performing arts, I'm sure
I'd be partway there to deciding Sanderson was a good option.

The door opens a couple of times as girls come in with
written messages and requests, and then, the third time, it's
the headmistress. She introduces herself and we go through
to the drawing room. She looks to be in her mid-forties and
has reddish auburn hair, cut in a neat bob, and a long swan
neck. She has the posture and poise of a former ballerina
and walks with an effortless, enviable grace.

'Do take a seat, Mrs Somers.' Her arm wafts towards a

sofa, covered in a stiff fabric patterned with roses. 'And tell me all about your daughter.'

I take a seat and speak about Lauren for a couple of minutes, not exactly making it up, but certainly exaggerating her love of music and performing. When I'm flagging, I start on my list of questions and this keeps us going until Mrs Tweedie brings in a tray of tea and biscuits. The sight of the biscuits sets my stomach rumbling. I remember that I haven't eaten lunch and take two. Miss Baker sits with a black tea, her ankles crossed and her back straight, and we talk about her career, first with the Royal Ballet and then as a teacher in Glasgow. What I really want to do is steer the conversation around to senior pupils – Kirsty Stewart in particular – but short of just coming out with it, I can't seem to make it happen, and I find myself dutifully copying down the names of a couple of dance teachers in Edinburgh.

'Your daughter may be more interested in musical theatre. Ballet is by no means a prerequisite for entry into the school. I know some girls find the self-discipline of ballet practice far too taxing, especially when they turn thirteen and boys become interesting.' A bell sounds in a far-off corridor. 'Ah.' Miss Baker stands up. 'That's the bell for next lesson and I teach a class. I've arranged for a couple of the older girls to show you around. I think it's a much better way for you to get a feel for the place.' Her right cheek dimples with a smile. 'And of course they're far more indiscreet than I am. So you'll no doubt discover all our secrets.'

'Perfect,' I say, smiling too, sure that this is my way to finding out about Kirsty but, at the same time, anxious that I don't bump into Tess, as there's a slim chance she's back at school today. She may react badly to seeing me here and I don't want to be forced to add to my lies or be ushered off the premises for being here under false pretences.

The girls who've been asked to show me around are called

Becca and Arielle. They're both fifteen and are coming to
the end of their third year. They have pretty, vivacious faces
and they talk nonstop. They show me the music block and
the theatre ('best acoustics of any school in Scotland'); the
swimming pool and games pitches ('we're actually much
better at sports than you might think'), and the dining room.
'They do make sure we eat, if that's what you're wondering,'
Arielle says, flicking back perfectly styled hair. 'My mum
always worried about that because everyone goes on about
anorexia in boarding schools, but it's not too bad here.'

I don't ask her to elucidate on what 'not too bad' means
because it's now or never and I don't want this to be a wasted
journey. 'I'm really interested in senior pupils and what they
become involved in. Do you have any information about that?'

'Come into our common room,' Becca says. 'We have loads
of photos up on the walls and we can tell you who's who.'

This sounds promising and I follow them to their common
room, which is large and slightly dilapidated. There are half a
dozen well-used couches and several mismatched rugs dotted
across the space. A table in the corner has a kettle and a toaster
on it and a fridge beside it. 'Not exactly the Ritz,' Arielle says.

'But comfortable,' I say. 'And all those photographs!' One
whole wall is taken up with photographs and newspaper
articles, and the girls lead me towards it.

'Now, I wonder whether you have a photograph of Kirsty
Stewart?' I say. 'I saw her in a performance at the Lyceum
recently and she was wonderful.'

The girls steal a glance at each other. Unfortunately, it's a
look I can't read, significant but I don't know why. 'Here's
one of her,' Becca says.

I lean in to the wall and stare at the photo. It's a girl on a
stage, wearing Elizabethan clothing, a hoop dress and wig.
From the distance the photograph's been taken, it's impossible to make out her features.

'And this is her,' Arielle says, pointing to a photo further along the wall.

A modern play this time, and she's in jeans and a checked shirt. Her face is turned away from the camera but there's something familiar about the line of her jaw and the way she's standing. It's the first time I have an inkling that I might have seen her before and it makes me feel afraid. Could I have seen her outside on the street? Perhaps she's been watching us, following me to work or the children to school.

'She can act pretty much anything,' Arielle says, her tone scathing rather than admiring.

'From Shakespeare's Ophelia to Miller's Catherine,' Becca says.

'You don't sound as if you like her, though?' I say, fishing.

Another look passes between them. 'She can be a bit of a bully,' Becca says.

'There's this girl in the year above us called Tess,' Arielle says. 'And . . .' She stops and shakes her head. 'I mean, don't get me wrong, there's not a lot of bullying here, but Tess is the perfect victim.'

'Arielle,' Becca warns.

'Well, it's true, she is! I don't know what she's even doing at this school. She doesn't try with her acting or her music.'

'That's because she wants to be a make-up artist,' Becca says, walking along in front of the wall of fame. 'This is Kelly McLeod,' she says, pointing to another photograph. 'You might have heard of her?'

'Doesn't ring any bells,' I say, still thinking about Tess. I'm not surprised to hear she's been bullied by Kirsty; she does have a downtrodden air about her. But, more to the point, this means the two girls are very definitely connected.

'Kelly's left school now, lucky her,' Arielle says. 'She moved to LA and was in three HBO pilots last year.'

'Quite a few girls leave before they're eighteen,' Becca says.

'This is Frances Scooter,' Arielle continues. 'The school wanted her to change her name so she changed it to Aimee Fox and then she got a part in a radio play,' Arielle says. 'Incidentally, what's your daughter's name?'

'Lauren Somers.'

'That's perfect,' Arielle says. 'Names are really important. I mean, would Meryl Streep be taken seriously if her name was Kylie Sidcup? Or Brittney Rusk?'

I laugh. 'No, I suppose not.'

'Normal names with a twist are good, like Emilia instead of plain Emily, Elyssa instead of just Ellie,' Becca says.

'Carrie Loftus.' Arielle points to another photo. 'Good Christian name but again the surname wasn't right – makes her sound large, doesn't it?'

'Who knew there was all this going on behind the scenes?' I say, determined to steer them back where I want them. 'Kirsty didn't have to change her name, then?'

'Her surname's not great but Kirsty sounds friendly, doesn't it?' Arielle says.

I nod.

'Which is ironic really,' Becca continues. 'Because she isn't friendly at all.'

'Truthfully, most of us are glad she left because she got all the best parts.'

The gloves are off.

'So she's left school already?' I say.

'She left at Christmas.'

'The teachers all thought she was amazing.'

'It's just a shame she's such a bitch.'

'She doesn't sound very nice,' I say. 'I'm not surprised you're glad she's left.' And then casually, 'So what's she doing now? Is she living in Edinburgh?'

'In Slateford, I think.'

'She lives in that block of flats opposite Tesco Express,'

Becca says. 'I know that because my mum met her in there last week.'

'You didn't tell me that,' Arielle says, and they start to discuss what Kirsty was wearing and has she really got an agent now and is it true she's going off to London soon? Becca's mum seems to have been short on detail so I don't learn any more, but I feel like I'm definitely making progress. And now I know where she lives, should I tell O'Reilly? Or should I just go and see her myself? Because by now I'm inclined to think that Kirsty is involved. Sure, coincidences happen, however unlikely they might seem, but the balance of probabilities is that Tess and Kirsty are significant to what's been happening to my family.

The girls tell me they have prep to do and take me back to Mrs Tweedie, who's still behind her desk sifting through piles of A4 papers. 'So, how have you enjoyed your visit?' she asks me, dumping one of the piles on the floor beside her.

'It's been marvellous,' I say. 'I'm very impressed with the school.'

'I'm so glad you've enjoyed it.' She gives me a pleased smile and takes a pen from the misshapen pottery jug on her desk. 'Give me your details and we'll send you on some information.'

'I could just take it with me now, if you like?' I say, not really wanting to end up on their mailing list.

'Well, yes. I can give you a prospectus and application form now, but we'd also like to invite you and Lauren to one of our performances.'

I can't argue with that, especially as I'm feeling guilty for having wasted their time, so I take the pen and a piece of paper and start to write down my details.

'And can I ask you something?' Mrs Tweedie continues. 'Are you the Dr Somers who's just won a City Women award?'

'Yes.' I smile up from my writing.

'My mother lives in town and she told me she'd voted for you.'

'That's very kind of her. The publicity has meant an influx of money which will really help the charity.' I pass the paper and pen back to Mrs Tweedie and notice a pile of yearbooks on a filing cabinet close to her desk; it occurs to me that I might be able to find a better photograph of Kirsty in one of them. 'Would it be okay if I looked through those?' I say.

'Of course, be my guest.' She leans over to reach them. 'They go back twenty years. Which one would you like?'

'My daughter asked me to look up Kirsty Stewart. We saw her in the Lyceum last month and we were very impressed with her performance.'

'Very talented girl, Kirsty. Can inhabit roles like a second skin,' Mrs Tweedie says, her voice lowering with admiration. 'She's one of the most gifted students who's ever stepped through these doors. She was a quiet wee thing when she arrived, but she soon found her niche.' She reaches across to the books. 'Her mother died when she was born and her father isn't a well man and somehow that makes for a wonderful actress. Sometimes children who've suffered difficulties have seams to mine that other children just don't have. I know happy childhoods are what we want for our children, but they're not always useful for an aspiring actor.' She keeps hold of one book and puts the others back. 'Here we are. This is hot off the press as Kirsty's year group is just graduating. Class of 2012.'

She hands it to me and I open it at the first page.

'She has a London agent now. We expect her to go on to great things.'

The index tells me that on page twenty-four, each student talks about their time at Sanderson Academy.

'Impeccable ear for accents,' Mrs Tweedie says. 'Why don't

you sit down there, Dr Somers?' She points to a chair positioned next to the dogs' cage. 'If you don't mind, I'll fire off a couple of emails before I forget.'

I sit down on the seat, and the two spaniels come forward for a stroke. Resting my left hand on the cage, I find page twenty-four with my right. Each of the school leavers has been pictured as if for a passport photograph, and the first two pages cover surnames A to D, the next E to K and so on, until I get to the S's. Kirsty Stewart – I see her photo at once. She's facing the camera, her eyes fixed on the lens. She is wearing an enigmatic, Mona Lisa smile and her hair is tied back into a neat ponytail.

A butterfly storm starts up in my stomach and I catch my breath from the rush of movement. I want to shout out in disbelief, holler – it can't be true! But I clamp my jaw shut, close my eyes and take a deep breath. My eyelids flutter but I keep them as closed as I am able, hectic light flickering in front of me. I count to ten and then slowly open my eyes and glance back at the book.

Nothing's changed. The girl in the picture is Emily Jones. Emily Jones is Robbie's friend. She comes to our house. She eats with us. She's good with Lauren.

Emily Jones was the Good Samaritan who resuscitated Robbie.

The supposed Good Samaritan, because it's clear from this photo that Emily Jones and Kirsty Stewart are the same person.

10

I don't hang around for any more chat with Mrs Tweedie, but wish her a quick goodbye and walk out to my car. I feel as if my eyes have been glued wide open, stuck there, staring at the truth. Pretty, vivacious Emily, whom all the boys want to date and all the mothers like because she's 'such a lovely girl', is Sandy and Trevor's baby. The truth is staggering and it sets off a tidal wave of panic that washes through me, one wave after another, and each time I feel as if I'm about to pass out from the accompanying dizziness and disbelief.

Gradually, I find a way through it, very deliberately tuning into another part of me, the part that's interested in the science behind my body's reaction. My logical mind is never afraid, never out of control. It simply observes, taking notes like a court reporter, no judgement attached, just an accurate recording of facts; my heart is now pumping blood at a rate of five gallons a minute; my breathing is deep in case I need to scream or run; endorphins are coursing through my bloodstream so that if I have to fight, I won't feel any pain; my senses are alive to everything around me – hearing more acute, pupils dilated, hairs standing on end.

A bell has sounded again and this time the girls are heading towards the dining room for tea. I stay still in my seat, far enough away from them not to be drawing attention to myself. I make out Arielle and Becca towards the back of the queue and Portia at the front. I can't see any sign of Tess and wonder whether she's still off school. It's clear from her visit to me in the surgery, and from what O'Reilly said about talking to her, that she's been badly affected by how much she knows. Or doesn't know. Because it's possible that, apart from seeing Kirsty/Emily in the pub that night, she has nothing to do with this. Yes, she lied about where she went to school, but perhaps that was because she was embarrassed and wanted to feel as if she had more of a reason to ask about Robbie.

The bigger problem is Emily. Emily joined the hockey club back in September and has been coming to my house since then. She tends to hang out with the boys but has also always been great with Lauren. They've been out walking Benson together and once she took Lauren to the cinema. I have never had any reason to suspect she's anyone other than who she says she is. But the photograph in the yearbook was most definitely her. So what's going on?

The staff nurse in the Royal Edinburgh said that Kirsty had been fostered – could her foster parents be called Jones? Or was she trying a different name for size? From what Arielle and Becca have just told me, names are important and there's much discussion about finding the one that best suits your needs as an actress and gives a favourable impression of you. Except that Emily Jones doesn't exactly fit that bill. It's a generic-sounding name with nothing special or interesting about it.

My mobile is in its holder next to the dashboard and I notice I have four missed calls from O'Reilly. I feel a swell of something like hope. He's the real policeman here. I'd be relieved to discover that I'm suffering from a bad case of paranoia. I want to find out who hurt Robbie and came into our house and I'm going about it like an amateur detective. Since Phil left me, I've spent an unhealthy amount of time watching late-night TV: *CSI* and the like, programmes where detectives follow obscure clues that lead them to uncover mysteries that stretch credulity. And here I am doing the same.

I take a breath to steady my nerves. This is me, Olivia Somers. I'm an ordinary doctor living a nothing-much-ever-happens life.

Except that in a short space of time, several uncommon events have occurred: the award, the attack on Robbie and the paint on the wall.

'Enough already!' I say out loud. I need to call O'Reilly back, check that Robbie and Lauren are where they should be and get to the centre. No more playing amateur detective.

Before making the calls, I start the car and drive out of the school grounds and into a natural stopping place just shy of the motorway. I've programmed O'Reilly's mobile number into my phone and call him at once, mentally crossing my fingers that the missed calls herald good news.

'Any news?' I say, as soon as he answers.

'No,' he says. 'Forensic results are still coming through but we haven't been able to eliminate the family's fingerprints because you didn't turn up.'

'What do you mean?'

'Fingerprinting. You were supposed to be coming with Lauren and Robbie after school.'

'I was?' I have no recollection of discussing this with him. 'I'm sorry. It's been a really busy day. I haven't had time to think about it.'

'I called the surgery to see whether you were there and I was put through to a Dr Bedford.'

My heart drops. Adrian Bedford is the doctor I asked to cover the antenatal clinic for me. I told him I needed to go and see the police about Robbie's drink spiking and about the break-in.

'He seemed to think you'd left work early to come to see me.'

'Yes.'

'Frankly, I was worried when you didn't answer your mobile.'

'It's been on silent.'

'Is that wise under the circumstances?'

'I don't suppose so. No. I'm sorry.' I scrabble around in my brain for an excuse that trumps everything else that's going on. But why make excuses? I need to be upfront with him, see what he makes of the facts. Yes, it means dredging up my past, but I can't go it alone with this. If Kirsty/Emily is a threat to my family, then I need to take steps to ensure she doesn't get near them again. And if she isn't a threat, then I can drop this once and for all. 'I had another appointment and I didn't want to mention it at work. I came out to Sanderson Academy, where Tess goes to school, and found out that another girl who goes to school here is . . .' I wince. 'Well . . . back when I was a junior doctor, I accidentally hastened someone's death. Her name was Sandy Stewart. She was pregnant and she had a brain tumour and I began to think that perhaps her death had something to do with what was going on, like you said about it maybe being an ex-patient of Phil's and—'

'Have you made a connection?'

'Yes . . . maybe . . . I think so.'

'What exactly?'

'One of Robbie's friends from the hockey club, the girl who resuscitated him, also goes to school here.'

'Emily Jones?'

'That's right. But the thing is, she's known here as Kirsty Stewart, the daughter of the woman whose death I caused.'

'You're sure about that?'

'I saw a photograph of her.'

'They don't just look similar?'

'No. It's definitely her.'

'Okay. I'll find out her address and bring her in for questioning this evening. See what she has to say for herself.'

'Do you have to? I mean . . .' I think about Emily – I like her and I know her and if she really is Sandy's daughter then perhaps I owe her the opportunity to speak to me first. 'Would you mind if I spoke to her first?'

'Why would you want to do that?'

'Because it feels personal. Her mother was lovely and I was the last person she spoke to. If Emily/Kirsty is doing this because of me then—'

'Dr Somers.' He gives a weary sigh. 'If this girl almost killed your son and caused damage inside your home, then she needs to be stopped before she does anything else.'

'Yes, I understand that.' I pause, thinking about teenagers and the mess they can get themselves into. I wasn't a paragon of virtue myself at a similar age, and if I hadn't been shown kindness and understanding, I would have lost my way completely.

'I hear a "but" coming along,' O'Reilly says.

And then I think about Robbie – how I felt at the hospital, knowing he was close to death. And two weeks later, coming back home to find the wall defaced with blood-red paint.

'You're absolutely right,' I say to O'Reilly. 'No buts. I have to put the children's safety first. Apparently she lives in a block of flats opposite Tesco Express in Slateford.'

'I'll get the exact address from the school.'

'Thank you. Will you let me know how it goes?'

'Of course.'

'Re the fingerprints. The children and I can come along tomorrow.'

'How about this evening?'

'Robbie and Lauren are with friends and I'm on my way to the centre. Tuesdays and Thursdays are my volunteer evenings.'

'Fair enough. So what's a good time tomorrow?'

'Can we make it just after six? Is that too late? It's just that the children go for tea with Phil on Wednesdays.'

'That'll be fine.'

'Thank you. I'm sorry for letting you down today. I don't know how I managed to forget.'

'Because your mind's been elsewhere.' He pauses for a second, a significant second that lets me know he has a question. 'Was Sandy Stewart's death what was preoccupying you on the path outside your house on Saturday?'

'Yes,' I say reluctantly.

'You couldn't have told me then?'

'I thought it was far-fetched. I really didn't expect it to be true. And, at that point, I thought the baby had died.' I shake my head. 'I was still praying that I was imagining it all.'

'Well, next time, however far-fetched things might seem, remember it's always worth sharing information immediately.'

'Yes. I will. I'm sorry.' My face is red. I feel as if I've been properly told off and when he ends the call I sit for a minute and let my cheeks cool. He's right, of course, I should have been upfront with him, but this does feel very personal to me and that makes honesty more difficult.

Next I call Lauren's mobile. On Tuesdays and Thursdays, when I'm at the centre, she goes to Amber's after school. She tells me they're both sitting at Amber's dining table doing their homework. She chats for a while about school and I wait until she's said all she wants to say before I remind her that I'm coming to collect her later and to make sure she's packed up and ready to go.

Robbie is with the Campbells and is in Mark's room watching television. I ask him about his homework and he tells me he doesn't have any, or at least, 'not any that's due in this week'.

'You could have it ready early. It would give you a chance to read it over and correct any mistakes.'

'That's not my style.'

'More's the pity,' I say. Then, as casually as I'm able, I ask, 'You seeing Emily tonight?'

'No. I usually only see her at the weekends. Why?'

'Just wondered.' I consider telling him where I am and what I've just discovered, but decide to leave it until O'Reilly gets back to me. Depending on what he finds out, I'll sit down with both children and tell them about the Emily/Kirsty connection.

I start the engine and drive back into town, trying to clear my head as I go. There's no point in fretting – what's happened has happened and can't be changed. O'Reilly's in charge now and all I can do is wait. It helps to imagine what I would say to someone in my position who came to see me in the surgery. I would say something along the lines of: 'What's happened is dreadful. You're bound to feel anxious and you're bound to want answers. The best way to ensure your children's safety is to cooperate with the police.' And then I would finish with, 'You need to remember to look after yourself, to relax, not to become too anxious.' I would offer sleeping pills, just for the short term, and I would tell the person to remember that talking is important, to stay in touch with friends and family. Not to bear the burden alone.

I need to take my own advice. I miss talking everything through with Leila. She's been there for me my whole adult life, longer than Phil even. So what if all those years ago she lied to me? Is it really such a big deal?

With the benefit of forty-eight hours' cooling-off period, I'm thinking it isn't that big a deal. I need my best friend back and I, of all people, know how persuasive Phil can be. I'm sure all those years ago she had little option but to go along with him. I'll have a word with her when I collect Robbie, ask her to promise never to lie to me again and then put it behind us.

I drive down into the cobbled streets of the Grassmarket, squeeze my car through the narrow alleyway and into a parking space behind the building. When I walk through the front door a big cheer goes up. 'Here she is! Our very own heroine!' Martin shouts, an electric smile lighting up his face. I'm sure he's been on a permanent high since Friday evening. 'Take a look at this.'

He holds up a newspaper in front of me. Lauren, Robbie and I are on the front page of the *Edinburgh Courier*. It's the photograph that was taken outside the Assembly Rooms. There we are, dressed in our finery, all three of us smiling and laughing. I remember Robbie and I were enthused by Lauren, who was brimming with excitement because she was having 'the best night of her life'. I look at my children's faces and feel a pull of protection that's as rigid and unbending as galvanised steel. I've always known how much I loved them, but since Phil left me, those feelings are now much closer to the surface. While my life might have unravelled over the last year, I want theirs to be rosy and safe, their future stretching out before them like the Irish blessing says: the road rising up to meet them, the wind at their backs, safe in the palm of God's hand.

'You have a busy waiting room this evening,' Martin tells me. 'But I'm guessing some of them will be here just to let your fame rub off on them.'

'I think most of our clients have other things on their mind, Martin,' I say, wishing this whole mini-celebrity business would just come to an end.

'Oh you!' He waves me away. 'Ever modest.'

I walk along the corridor towards my consulting room, taking a quick sideways glance into the waiting area. He's right – it's packed. I have a concentrated two hours of work ahead of me. My Tuesday evening drop-in clinic attracts addicts with a post-weekend determination to give up on drugs and live a cleaner life. We operate a programme of help and support to wean them off their habit and see them into employment and adequate housing. It's a long road and we don't make it with everyone, but we do have our share of successes. Winston is one of them. He's our caretaker, and in exchange for accepting a minimum wage, he gets to live in a room at the rear of the building. He's a man who's found his niche in life and I'm extremely fond of him.

'Your room's all ready for you, Dr Somers.' He takes my jacket from me and hangs it on a peg at the door. Unlike my surgery up town, this room is sparsely furnished. There's an examination couch, a desk, a couple of chairs and a pin board with leaflets shouting out safe sex and optimum health messages. Everything medical is kept in one lockable filing cabinet but none of it is worth stealing. No drugs, needles, syringes or money are kept on the premises to keep ourselves as low a break-in risk as possible. There's a mug of coffee on the desk and a sandwich next to it. 'I expect you missed your tea again,' Winston says.

I smile. 'You know me too well.'

'I'll give you five minutes then send the first one through. That okay with you?'

I give him a thumbs-up, my mouth now full of sandwich, and he goes off into the corridor to keep an eye out for trouble. He has more wisdom in his pinkie finger than the rest of us have in our whole skeleton, and I've never seen an occasion where he couldn't talk an angry or frustrated client out of a fight and into a chair.

The evening passes quickly. It's a regular mix of the hopeful and the damned and I know that an important part of my job is to show the 'damned' that their trajectory can change – not overnight; but it can be diverted, piece by piece, towards a more hopeful future.

At the end of the clinic, Martin is on the phone and,

without stopping talking, waves me towards him and points to a figure he's written on his notepad – £20,000.

'Fantastic!' I mouth at him, glad that, combined with the money we raised on Friday night, the centre's overheads and development plans are secure for the next couple of years. Winston sees me out to my car and, as I'm climbing in, our eyes catch.

'You okay, Dr Somers?'

I'm about to give an automatic upbeat reply when I stop. As a doctor, I feel as if I've seen it all: all the misery that fate or poor decisions can inflict on us and all the sordid detritus that human beings throw each other's way. And for the most part, I've managed to steer a personal path around it. But since Robbie's drink was spiked, I've felt as if I was being dragged into a more dangerous world where I have little control over the outcome.

'We might be close to finding out who spiked Robbie's drink,' I tell him, and then find myself adding, 'I think I might know who did it but I'm not sure how much is real and how much I'm imagining.' I lean my chin on the top of the open car door. 'I'm afraid that I'm right because it will mean I'm partly responsible. But I'm also afraid that I'm wrong because I desperately want it to stop.'

Winston nods as if this makes perfect sense to him. His hands are in the pockets of his baggy trousers and he's swaying backwards and forwards, but he never takes his eyes off mine. 'You feel like you're being pulled in two directions?'

'Yes.'

'If I was you, Dr Somers, I would listen to my gut.' His tone is soft but his words kick like hot chilli. 'I've watched you with people. You have good instincts.' He brings a hand up and presses his fist to his middle. 'Trust.'

'Thank you, Winston.' I don't smile – I'm feeling too serious for that – but I show my appreciation for his advice by reaching across and touching his shoulder. 'Thank you.'

As I drive off to collect the children, I keep my thoughts and feelings at bay by playing some loud music. I collect Robbie first, hoping to speak to Leila, but she's out at her fitness class. Lauren is standing at Amber's window and comes running out as soon as she sees the car pull up. She has the *Edinburgh Courier* photo in her hand and is waving it around excitedly. 'Amber's mum gave it to me for my scrapbook,' Lauren says.

'What scrapbook?' Robbie asks her.

'The one I'm starting. You never know, we could be in the paper again. Mum could get more awards.'

We arrive home to an excited Benson, the bare living-room wall a reminder – as if I needed one – that O'Reilly is questioning Emily. I go straight to the kitchen and empty the dishwasher and then the tumble drier, folding the clothes into neat 'people' piles on the worktop.

'What's this for, Mum?' Lauren is rummaging in my handbag and has found the brochure for Sanderson.

'I picked it up for one of my patients,' I say, without hesitation, my rediscovered propensity for lying no longer surprising me.

'She wants to be an actress?'

'Her daughter does.'

'I don't like acting at all.' She puts the brochure back into my bag. 'I don't know what I want to be.'

'You've plenty of time to make up your mind.'

'I know what I don't want to be.'

'Well, that's a start.'

'I don't want to be a doctor or a nurse or *anything* in a hospital.'

'I don't blame you.' I pass Lauren her pile of clothes. 'Hospital work is rewarding but it takes its toll physically and emotionally.'

'Is it okay if Amber comes to spend the night on Saturday?'

'Just Amber or the whole posse?'

'Just Amber.' She balances the clothes on her outstretched hand. 'We have things to talk about.'

'Oh?'

'Nothing much.' She affects innocence.

'Lauren, you know what happens when you girls start pairing off. Invariably, it ends up with someone feeling left out.'

'We'll be good!'

She runs off up the stairs and I follow her to the bottom and call up, 'I didn't say yes!'

On the way back into the kitchen, I notice Robbie hanging about in the living-room doorway staring at the wall. 'You okay, love?'

He shakes his head. 'I'm wondering what might happen next.' He turns his face to mine. All at once he looks a young seventeen. Gone is the bravado and the *so-what* attitude and in its place is a nervousness that I've never seen before. 'I really don't know what I did to deserve this.'

'Sweetheart.' I give him a hug and he holds on to me, dropping his face into my neck. 'I'm *absolutely* sure this has nothing to do with anything you've ever done or said and I'm also sure it's just a matter of time before the police work it all out.'

He pulls away from me and balances on the back of the sofa. 'What's DI O'Reilly saying these days?'

'Forensics are working on the fingerprints they took from the house. We have to go to the station tomorrow so that they can take our prints.'

'So basically they have nothing?'

'Well . . . DI O'Reilly's pursuing a lead but it's too early to say anything more definite.'

Robbie launches himself over the back of the sofa and

arrives within hand's reach of the remote control. 'I hope they find out who did it soon. I don't want anything else to happen.'

I go to comfort him some more but change my mind, knowing that my words will sound empty: reassuring maybe, but lacking in actual fact. And I'm determined to stave off addressing my own thoughts until I've heard from O'Reilly. When it's time to turn in, and he still hasn't rung, I can only surmise that questioning Emily is taking longer than he thought. I climb into bed and switch off my bedside light, lying with wide-open eyes focused upwards. The gap in the curtains allows a sliver of streetlight to stretch across the ceiling, illuminating a narrow pathway, a gymnast's beam, darkness waiting either side to swallow up anyone who falls off.

Another day dawns, and the good weather has given in to the bad. The pavements are running with water and wet umbrellas clutter up the practice foyer. O'Reilly calls me ten minutes before I usher through my first patient and I answer at once, clutching my mobile to my ear. 'How did it go?'

'Well, you were right about Emily Jones being Kirsty Stewart. She didn't even try to deny it. She told me she's calling herself Emily Jones now because her middle name is Emily and she's never liked the name Kirsty and because she feels very attached to her foster parents whose surname is Jones. Apparently, she has an application under way to change her name by deed poll.'

'And did she admit to any crimes against my family?'

'No. She seemed genuinely shocked when I suggested as much.'

'Seemed?'

'I wasn't entirely convinced by her. She comes across as a smart girl, and bearing in mind the sort of school she goes to, I couldn't help but wonder whether she was using some of her acting skills on me. One minute composed and cooperative, the next horrified and then weepy.'

'Did you mention her mother's death?'

'No. I simply asked her whether she had any reason to hold a grudge against you. She looked surprised and said she didn't.'

'I suppose it's possible that she doesn't know the exact details of her mother's death. What happened wasn't common knowledge, although one of the nurses or doctors on duty that day could have told Trevor, her dad.'

'What was he told?'

'I don't know exactly. I expect they told him something along the lines of his wife reacting badly to one of the drugs. I was fully prepared to resign as a doctor and to tell Trevor the truth about what had happened, but I was persuaded out of one and deceived out of the other.'

'How come?'

'My boss said my resignation would serve no purpose and, although I made an attempt to speak to Trevor Stewart, unbeknownst to me at the time, Phil prevented it.'

'Husbands, eh? Who would have them?'

I smile, appreciating O'Reilly's attempt to lighten the mood. 'So what happens now?' I say.

'She willingly gave me her fingerprints but, of course, as she's already spent legitimate time in your house, they won't be much use to us. We'll talk to the teachers at Sanderson and we'll check our databases to see whether her name has cropped up in relation to any other crimes. If it was her, she must have bought the GHB from someone. If we could tie her to the drug, then that would be a start.'

'The girls who showed me round the school said that Kirsty bullied Tess.'

'Okay. I'll follow that up too. And, in the meantime, you need to be wary of her. You shouldn't let her in your house and I think you should tell Robbie and Lauren that she's a genuine suspect.'

'Okay,' I say, baulking at the thought of holding such a conversation with the children. They both really like Emily. How will they feel when they find out she might be the person who spiked Robbie's drink? And I'll have to tell them about my link to her past. That won't be easy either. 'How sure are you that it's her?'

'She has motive, access and opportunity. I think it's very likely that she's behind it.'

He reminds me that I'm coming to the station later and I tell him I haven't forgotten. When he rings off, I go along to Leila's room, seeking comfort as much as anything else, but her door is locked and I remember that it's her day off. I'm well acquainted with the other staff in the practice but they're mostly colleagues rather than friends and it feels wrong to lumber them with my problems. There's nothing else for it but to distract myself with work and I set about my patient list with a forced jollity. Halfway through the morning, Phil calls me, and this time I pick up because he collects the children from school on Wednesdays.

'Are the children expecting me as usual today?' he says.

'Yes. And I was wondering whether you'd bring them straight to the police station? We're having our fingerprints taken. For elimination purposes.'

'No problem. Will O'Reilly be there?'

'Yes.'

'Good. It will give me a chance to find out about the investigation.'

Or you could just ask me. 'Are you going to tell the children about your marriage plans?'

'Yes. Erika's staying at home today. I'm taking them out on my own to tell them.'

I wonder whether he's showing consideration for the children or for Erika. Erika probably – the children may react badly and say something rude to her – but I decide to give him the benefit of the doubt. 'That's a good idea. They like being on their own with you. Having your undivided attention.'

'Why do you say that?'

'Because they told me. Or at least Lauren did.'

'She hasn't said anything to me.'

'She's eleven, Phil. She's conflicted. She wants her parents to be together but they're not.' I pause. 'As she sees it, her father left the whole family, and she's afraid of being completely honest with you in case you stop seeing her.'

He sighs. 'This is why I wanted them both to have counselling.'

'I don't think either of them need counselling. I just think they need to spend more time with you on their own.'

'Shared custody would make that easier.'

'I don't think either of the children are ready for that.'

'They're not ready? Or you're not ready?'

'I'm not discussing this with you,' I say, and we end the call with our usual tight goodbyes. I continue working on referral letters and other paperwork until just gone four o'clock when my mobile bleeps with a text message. My heart rate doubles when I see that it's from Emily:

It would be really good if we could talk. Will you meet me? Please?

I stare at the screen for almost a full minute, thinking about whether to text back a reply or simply ignore her. If Emily did spike Robbie's drink, then I'm not about to listen to excuses and I'm certainly not going to forgive her. It was a spiteful and dangerous act of vengeance and Robbie could have died.

But what about innocent until proven guilty? Isn't that a principle I've always believed in?

That's the reasonable me talking and it's true that, unlikely

as it seems, she might not be involved. She's been coming
to my house for the past nine months and there hasn't been
a hint of anything unpleasant. She's a good influence on
Robbie and she's always been kind and friendly towards
Lauren. She's a teenage girl who's had a tough upbringing
and I know what that's like. I'm not saying that I think I can
help her, but I don't want to make things any worse for her
and if she wants to talk to me then what harm can it do?

It might affect the investigation, the reasonable voice reminds
me. O'Reilly wasn't keen on me talking to her before he did
but, since then, he's had her in for questioning and released
her without charge. Still, I don't want to step on his toes, so
I give him a call but his mobile goes straight to answering
service. I try the station and a female constable tells me he's
in court all afternoon and could she pass on a message?

'No, I'm seeing him later anyway,' I say.

I remember what Winston said about trusting my gut
feeling and immediately an answer comes back to me – I
owe it to Sandy. I was with her when she died and even if
I hadn't precipitated her death, as a mark of respect I should
honour her memory by looking out for her child. Not
indefinitely, not forever, but now when Emily's asking to talk,
it would be heartless of me to refuse.

I text back.

Yes, I'll meet you.

She replies immediately.

Can you come to my flat? Now?

I'll be about twenty minutes.

She texts me the address and I leave the surgery and motor
across town to Slateford. It's raining hard and my wipers
move at double-quick time to clear the water off the

windscreen. I think of the children sitting in the restaurant with Phil and my mind flits between worrying at their reaction to his news and worrying about the visit I'm about to make. I'm curious about what Emily wants to say, but anxious that I don't jeopardise the case against her, should there turn out to be one.

I park in a nearby multistorey and walk along the wet pavement towards Tesco Express. I'm still in my work clothes – a serviceable grey skirt suit, tights and shoes that fall somewhere between fashionable and comfortable. My umbrella keeps water off my top half but within a minute driving rain has soaked my skirt and dirty water from passing cars has splashed up my tights. Summer in Scotland. Everyone keeps their head down and battles on through it.

The tenement building Emily lives in has one main door as the entryway into eight flats. Four of the flats have names next to the buzzers – none of them Jones or Stewart – and the remaining four are nameless. I should have asked Emily what flat she lives in and I call her phone to ask her. The automated voice tells me that the phone is switched off. Okay. I surmise that the ones without names are most likely to be rented out. The entry-phone system isn't working and I'm able to push open the door and walk inside. The stair smells damp and mouldy – 'foosty', the Scots would say.

There's an elderly lady halfway up the first flight of stairs and she calls down to me. 'Are you lookin' fer someone, hen?'

'Yes, I am actually.' I join her on the step. 'Kirsty Stewart, or perhaps Emily Jones. She's a young woman, almost eighteen. I expect she'll be in a shared flat.'

'The two flats at the top have student types living in them,' she says. Her headscarf has slipped off her head to reveal thinning hair, now damp with rain. 'They're a noisy bunch. Doors slamming at all 'oors. Makes me wish I wis deef!'

I smile and hold out my hand. 'Let me carry your shopping.'

'Would you, dear?'

'Of course.'

I lift the bags and follow her at a slow pace to the first floor where she uses three keys to unlock her front door. 'You never know nowadays,' she says.

I leave her inside and climb to the top, choose the first of the two doors and push the bell. I can't hear any far-off ringing so I guess it must be broken. I try to make a noise with the flap of the letterbox but the sound is ineffectual so I settle for just banging my fist on the door. The man who opens it is naked from the waist up. He body is lean, almost completely hairless and he's holding a bottle of beer in his right hand. 'Yeah?'

'Hi. I'm looking for Kirsty Stewart.'

'You a friend of hers?'

'Not exactly. But she's expecting me.'

'You better come in then.' He leaves the door open and walks off, calling over his shoulder, 'She's not home but you can wait if you want to.' His accent is as Irish as mine was when I first moved to Edinburgh and I surmise he must have been brought up close to where I was.

I leave my wet umbrella outside the front door and follow him into the living room where a vacant-eyed girl is lounging half on and half off the sofa. The air is pungent with the smell of a recently smoked joint, mingling with body odour and old food smells. There are dirty mugs, take-out containers with congealed food stuck in the bottom and a pizza box lying open on the floor, only a crust remaining on the greasy cardboard. Two flies have settled on the crust and several more hover just above it. Another man, his dreadlocks tied back with coloured string, is sitting on a beanbag in the corner, idly strumming a guitar, his fingers lingering on the strings, and while the sound is melodic, the whole place reeks of inertia. I want to throw open the window and take deep, cleansing breaths.

Instead, I stand next to the sofa, but the girl doesn't take the hint and make space for me to sit down. The man who opened the door has taken the only other seat, an armchair with burst springs and no cushion, so that he's practically at ground level, his legs stretching out before him almost flat to the carpet.

'You watch this?' he asks me, referring to the game show that's on TV.

'Not normally.'

'It's crap. But addictive crap if you know what I mean.'

I shiver from the water cooling on my body but more so from nerves. Emily, or Kirsty, I'm no longer sure what name I should call her, knows I'm coming, so why isn't she here? 'Is it okay if I look in her room?' I say. 'In case she came home without you realising?'

'Yeah.' He doesn't take his eyes off the screen. 'It's the one with the sunflower on the door.'

'Thank you.' I walk along the hallway, a gulp in my throat. The thin carpet, cheap to begin with, is stained beyond repair. My shoes leave wet footprints and I glance back at them before stopping in front of the sunflower and knocking quietly on the door. No answer so I turn the handle and push. It opens smoothly and her room is revealed in a slow sweep. Lace curtains hang at the window, a patchwork bedspread covers the bed, and scarves – a riot of colour: orange, petrol blue and a vivid pea green – decorate the wall above the bed. And if all this homemaking wasn't enough of a contrast to the rest of the flat, every surface and every piece of material is spotlessly clean.

I leave my shoes in the hallway and walk into her room, closing the door behind me. There are two leather Victorian tub chairs, in good condition, in front of the window. In between them is a table with an embroidered mat on it. A small glass vase with three pale pink roses is placed on the mat and beside that is a framed photo of her parents. I bend down to bring my eyes closer and the gulp in my throat doubles in size. Sandy and Trevor look exactly as I remember them. The years have not dimmed my recollection of a smiling couple, their bodies close, their eyes alight with happiness.

Shit.

I sit down on the edge of the bed, keeping my feet away from the sheepskin rug that's fluffed up and perfectly positioned beside it. Once more I'm face to face with my incompetence, an incompetence so great that it led to the early death of this beautiful, happy woman. Sitting here, with the photo in front of me, the notion that the drink spiking and the message on the wall is Kirsty's attempt at payback no longer feels far-fetched. If she is aware of the details of her mother's death, then I'm not surprised she sought me out.

Still, when I look around me at the bedroom, it doesn't strike me as the room of someone who's vengeful. In the tradition of *CSI*, such a criminal mind would surely be sign-posted. As part of her obsession, she'd have a wall dedicated to me. She'd have pinned up photographs of me crossing the street or eating in a restaurant; she'd have copies of the recent newspaper clippings and she'd have written down other details about my life.

Wouldn't she?

I remember the room I had as a teenager. When my three brothers were at home, they shared a bedroom at the front of the house and I had a tiny bedroom of my own at the back. It faced the North Atlantic and was often freezing cold. Wind blew in through the narrow gaps around the window frames and, during winter months, the moisture on the insides of the windows turned to ice. But it was mine, and although

I had far fewer possessions than Kirsty, it wasn't dissimilar to this. Just like her, I had a dressing table with collections of lipstick and pots of eye shadow, hairbrushes and jewellery. I had schoolbooks in a pile in the corner, as she does, and posters of my favourite music artists on the wall – Kirsty has the side wall dedicated to a band that Robbie also listens to. This room is tidier than most teenage girls' rooms but – apart from the tub chairs and the table in between – it is a teenager's room.

And there is another significant similarity between myself and Kirsty – the name change. By the time I reached eighteen I had stopped calling myself Scarlett and went by my middle name instead. I needed to be a new me, and Scarlett was burdened with expectations I could never live up to. It wasn't an easy transition and there came a point when I was in over my head. If it hadn't been for my brother Declan, I would be leading a very different life.

I I

My mother called me Scarlett as an act of defiance. Everyone in our village was called Bridget or Mary or Anne – good girls' names full of Catholic history, denial and guilt woven into the alphabet. While my mother spent her afternoons cleaning the church and arranging the flowers, her mind was in Hollywood – *Seven Brides for Seven Brothers, Show Boat* and *Gone with the Wind.* By the time I was ten I knew my mother didn't want a daughter who flushed red and penitent when the nuns walked past, their black veils billowing out behind them. My mother demanded that I stand up to authority in a way that she never could. She wanted rebellion. She wanted a daughter who didn't listen to threats of hell and damnation – only a few misplaced footsteps away and usually involving the opposite sex; she wanted a daughter who walked tall through school, sure of her own self, her own destiny.

'Scarlett O'Hara didn't bend to any man's will. She rolled up her sleeves and took charge. She made things happen for herself.'

I'd seen the film a dozen times and it seemed to me that for all her feisty rebellion, Scarlett wanted nothing more than a man – first, the insipid, wet rag Ashley Wilkes who was blond and fey and flimsy as a dandelion clock. And then, latterly, she realised that the dark and dangerous Rhett Butler was, after all, just the man to tame her, but by then he had already gone.

'Bugger that nonsense,' my father said. He was an

easy-going man who came home each evening smelling of fresh air and cigarette smoke, let me rest on the arm of his chair and gave me the last of his tea, crystals of sugar like silt in the bottom of the mug. 'We live in a modern world, Scarlett. You listen at school; you get yourself a career. Education is the way to freedom. You'll have a home of your own. You can have a husband and children if you want. It will be your choice. That's what education and a career will buy you – choice.'

I had three brothers – Diarmaid and Finn who were two and four years older than me, and Declan who was a full ten years older and was the responsible one. He made sure that the loan for the tractor was paid on time, that my father didn't drink too much whiskey and that we always had a shilling each for the collection plate on a Sunday. And unlike my father, who experienced my mother's mood swings as a disinterested observer rather than a player in her life, Declan managed our mother with an enviable finesse. He intuited her moods with an accuracy that my other two brothers and I never learnt how to match. My mother sang every note on the emotional range – from untrammelled joy to a limb-trembling anger – and Declan was like a human tuning fork. Pitch perfect, he persuaded my mother out of her temper, saving me from her tongue and from her fists that lashed out in my direction. When my mother was down, as she often was, weeping by the sink or railing against fate, Declan would pick wild flowers for the kitchen table or do odd jobs for the solicitor whose land bordered ours, and come home with a leg of lamb or a pound of cheese. He was the only one of us who ever put a smile on her face.

Diarmaid and Finn were as wild as the weather allowed them to be. They were boys with precious few morals and almost no conscience, feral creatures of the earth. My mother ignored them both. She put food in front of them and washed their clothes but otherwise, as long as they stayed out of her way, she was oblivious to them. If a farmer turned up at the door complaining that they'd been worrying his sheep or taking his rowing boat out fishing without asking him first, it was Declan or my dad who doled out the punishment.

So, most of the time, the full force of my mother's attention was focused on me. The nuns told me I was clever enough to go on to university, but, unlike my father, my mother had little respect for education and when she heard what the nuns had said to me, her displeasure filtered through to her hands which slapped and dragged me around the kitchen. 'The answers aren't in books!' she bawled. 'The answers are in there.' She prodded close to my heart. 'You need gumption, not a degree! Courage not learning, otherwise you'll go the same way as all the other women around here.'

She'd been university material herself and where had that taken her? Nowhere. Pregnant at seventeen, she'd left school and moved into the cramped and leaky farm house that remained her home for over thirty years. She wanted me to break the mould, to 'be different', to 'be an entrepreneur', like Finuala Finnigan, a former classmate of hers who lived mostly in London, and spent August in a huge house on the edge of our village. My mother idolised her because she had made a success of herself; she travelled, she wore expensive clothes, and every third or fourth summer the man she brought back to Ireland was an updated model. She was famous 'in the places that matter' and she had most of the village scampering around after her – cleaning, shopping, catering, driving her and her London friends to and from the airport. My mother, who cleaned for her, seemed to see it as a privilege. 'I'm not doing it for the money, Scarlett. I'm doing it for the friendship.'

It was an unequal friendship – my mother the poverty-stricken relation living at the edge of Finuala's rich and glitzy showcase of a life. The summer I turned fourteen, my mother came back from Finuala's estate bursting with enthusiasm. She'd asked Finuala if she would be kind enough to be my mentor. 'Why?' I said.

'Why? *Why?*' she shrieked. 'Isn't it obvious? She'll open doors for you.'

I didn't want to do it, of course, but refusing my mother would have invited a storm of temper so I spent three long weeks 'shadowing' Finuala. I learnt exactly how she liked her morning coffee, her afternoon smoked salmon sandwiches and her fruit tea. Most of her morning was spent on the phone cajoling or downright bullying members of her London staff. She'd opened a company that sold authentic Far Eastern artefacts and it had grown from a turnover of less than a million to over one hundred million in ten years. Every afternoon brought a steady stream of people in and out of the house – masseurs, beauticians, professional chefs, business people, lawyers and accountants. I was allowed to sit in on her 'entrepreneurial' meetings, but mostly whatever was being discussed went over my head. She had a grasping quality about her that made me cringe and she was forever giving me knowing looks and arch little stares. I hadn't a clue what she was on about.

I did my best to 'learn my way to success' but I knew I wasn't fooling her. On the final day of her not-exactly-a-holiday because 'holidays are for wimps', my mother was taken into the drawing room, which overlooked the water, a spectacular view of slate-grey sea and white-topped waves, stark cliffs with a sheer drop to the shore, a view that always stopped me in my tracks but Finuala told me she didn't see it any more – 'it's just land and water. The beauty is in the owning of it.' I listened at the door while she reported my failure to my mother. 'Scarlett won't make anything of herself, Maureen. She has too little drive. No imagination. No business acumen.'

My mother left Finuala's house with her head down and her furious steps tearing holes in the ground. I knew I was in for it when I got home, and sure enough, I'd no sooner come through the front door than my mother was a whirling dervish at my side. 'What was the point in me naming you after someone with courage when you—'

'Scarlett O'Hara isn't real!' I cried out, and she slapped me so hard that I fell over sideways and banged my head on the floor. It detonated an explosion inside my skull – fireworks, lights, crackles and pops, whooshing . . . and then burning pain and a ringing ear, intense throbbing that would last for days. I didn't get up from the floor straight away. I kept my eyes shut and lay there until teatime. I thought about what had just happened and decided that was the last time she would ever hit me.

So help me God.

I stopped talking to her and she to me. Whenever she did throw a comment or a question my way I either ignored her or I lied. Declan was the buffer, but he wasn't home much because he had a mortgage on his own little place and he was courting – a beautiful, serene girl who I'd always imagined was going to become a nun because stillness emanated from her like morning mist from the earth. Her name was Aisling and I was there the first time she and Declan laid eyes on each other. He'd come to collect me from school and Aisling was also waiting in the car park. She was four years older than me and about to leave school to study nursing in Dublin. When their eyes met, I swore that I could see a channel open up between them. Like the falling in love of a fairytale, or one of my mother's films, they walked towards each other and said a few shy words before arranging to meet up later.

I was happy for him but afraid for myself because Diarmaid and Finn were living in Galway City and it meant long evenings on my own with my mother. My father was often busy in the evening – either still at work in the fields or, when darkness fell, he could be found in the pub. He could never sit still for long unless there was a pint in his hand and he wasn't allowed to drink at home – only my mother was allowed to do that. And whenever she was drunk, I was treated to the thrust of her advice: 'Don't be marrying any of the men from around here. Drunkards, every last one of them. You'll be stuck with four children. I was seventeen when I had Declan – *seventeen*.'

When I was sixteen, I got myself a boyfriend. I met him at Mass, of all places. He was only there because his mother had broken her leg and was needing an arm to lean on. He was two years older than me and, although we'd never met before, I knew who he was because Diarmaid and Finn often spoke of him.

'Mam was feeling optimistic when she named me after Gabriel the Archangel,' he told me. 'Means strength of God.' Mass was over and he was waiting for his mother to finish talking to Father O'Riordan. 'It's all horseshit though, isn't it?'

'Don't talk to me about mothers and names,' I said. 'I haven't lived up to mine and now my mother hates me.'

'What's your name then?'

'Scarlett.'

'As in scarlet woman?'

I laughed. 'As in Scarlett O'Hara. *Gone with the Wind*.'

He turned his head to one side and blew cigarette smoke across the tops of the gravestones. 'Hard to live up to a someone from the films.'

'I tried to tell my mother that. Couldn't hear out of my left ear for a week.'

I went out with him because of his dark eyes and roguish air. He wasn't rough with me like Diarmaid and Finn were.

He wasn't forever elbowing me out of the way or pretending he hadn't just tripped me up. And he wasn't always walking away before I'd finished my sentence. He treated me like Declan did – he was kind and he listened. He made me laugh. He stuck two fingers up at convention and I admired him for that. He was brave and defiant and when I was with him I felt the same.

Of course it was going to end badly, but tell that to a sixteen-year-old girl who has fallen in love. The last time we were together, we spent the early evening outside, just the two of us, and for months afterwards I relived every word and action, savouring the memories like a sweet-toothed child savours each square of her weekly bar of chocolate.

We were sheltering from the wind, protected by the thick trunk of a lone ancient oak tree, a welcome windbreak on the otherwise treeless landscape. Gabe had come back from his brother's in Dublin with some marijuana and had just rolled a joint. He lit it, cupped both hands around it and inhaled deeply. I was telling him about how much I wanted to leave Ireland and that I'd do anything to get away. When he didn't comment I snuggled closer and said, 'Are you listening to me?'

'I'm listening.'

'Do you believe me?'

'Of course. Who doesn't want to leave Ireland?'

I smiled and slumped against the tree, my back supported as I looked up through the bare branches to the sky. It was a perishing cold night and my breath froze in front of me but the sky was cloudless and the stars were sharp and clearly defined. I stared up at them, counting, making patterns, imagining other galaxies, other earths, other girls like me. I wished I knew the names of some of those stars, as if by naming them, they would somehow be more real, more tangible. Why did they never teach us anything useful at school?

'Honours leaving Cert,' Gabe said.

'What?'

'Mr Byrne was teaching us. I'll bring my binoculars next time. You can see Saturn and Mars really clearly at this time of year.'

My mouth dropped open. 'Are you reading my mind, or what?'

'Or what,' he said. 'Now give me a kiss.'

I brought my face slowly towards his, then, at the last moment, swerved off to one side and took the joint out of his fingers.

'I knew you were going to do that.'

'Transparent, am I?' I drew a draught deep into my lungs.

'As glass.'

It felt very daring to be puffing on the joint. I knew if I was caught I'd be damned to hell and back, and never be allowed out again but with Gabe I felt invincible. My eyes narrowed as I drew the smoke into my lungs then I passed the joint back to Gabe and gave in to the feeling. I let the drug swirl inside me like a Mr Whippy ice cream, turning and coiling through my blood until I feel unscrewed, relaxed into a better version of myself, where time stretched and I lived in a safer part of now.

'When I was small,' I said languidly, 'I imagined that the night sky was a blanket . . . and the stars were holes in the blanket . . . and behind the blanket was the light.'

Gabe stretched his arms upwards and then let them drop back to his side. 'We have a budgie and at eight o'clock every evening Mammy puts a cover over the cage. There may even be some holes in it.'

'Exactly! Just like God's blanket. He covers us up at night so we can all get some sleep!'

We chuckled for a while and then we fell silent again. My mind was like still water broken occasionally by thoughts that

bubbled to the surface then escaped into the air where, unac-
knowledged, they evaporated. I felt so at ease with myself
that I wanted to live in the moment for ever. Not to stop
time so much as to suspend it, like in a photograph.

When we finished the joint, Gabe started to kiss me. His
tongue was warm and wet and teased its way around the
inside of my mouth. His hands were broad, the fingers long
and agile and he slid them inside my coat and under my
jumper. I let them roam. He moved them up and around my
waist, then down to the small of my back. It felt good and I
relaxed into him. He was about six inches taller than me and
we fitted together perfectly, my curves melting into his angles.
His hands found the inside of my bra and he snuggled closer.
He coaxed my nipples awake with his fingers and I felt
something pull deep in my stomach.

'Better stop.' I nudged him away. We'd had sex already,
just the once, the details lost in a drunken haze and I was
hoping the second time would be a bit more romantic.

'Come on, Scarlett.' He was kissing my neck, making my
blood heat up. 'You know how crazy you make me.'

'I can feel it growing against my stomach,' I giggled, and
held him back from me. Then suddenly I was serious again.
'I don't want to get pregnant.' Imagining the shame it would
bring to my family made me shiver and Gabe drew me close
again.

'I'll pull out just before I come.' He lowered the zipper of
his jeans. 'I promise.'

His hands pulled at my jeans and I slapped him around
the head with my gloves, ineffectually, because in my heart
I'd already given in. There was a brief gust of freezing cold
air before his warmth covered me and he lifted me up, my
back against the tree. His voice whispered persuasively in my
ear but it was unnecessary because I was already a slave to
my nerve endings and couldn't think past this moment,

couldn't really think at all; I was simply living the experience.

Afterwards, we zipped and buttoned up our clothes and collapsed down to the ground. I sat across his knee, wrapped up, warm and close. And when we heard his friends coming I slid my hands under his jacket and turned my face up for one last kiss before our peace was shattered. I didn't like his friends. They were coarser than he was. They were like Diarmaid and Finn, always pushing and shoving and trying to outdo each other.

We left the protection of the tree and started walking across the field. They say that Ireland is the greenest place on earth and that's because it's usually raining, and that night the rain was in our faces and the wind blew us sideways so that we moved like crabs, scuttling right and then left. Gabe had hold of my hand but he was talking to his three friends and I had to run to keep up. The moon was almost full but still there wasn't enough light for me to see by and the grass, ruptured by furrows and clumps of weeds, caused me to stumble. Each time Gabe pulled me upright again.

The pond at the bottom of the field was half frozen and his friends wanted to slide on it, had some mad idea about racing each other. They were pumped up with foolish bravado that had them egging each other on to bigger and faster feats. I watched Gabe's face as he made up his mind whether to stay with me and risk being called a sissy or join in with the competitive jousting. Before we got as far as the pond there was a barn on our right-hand side. 'Why don't you wait in there, Scarlett?' Gabe asked me, pulling a bottle of whiskey from his pocket. He took a mouthful and then handed the bottle to me. 'I'll need to go with those three, otherwise God only knows what will happen to them.'

Like an obedient child, I trotted off to the barn. I knew I was trespassing but was too far from home to know who

owned the farm, and so somehow that made it all right. I
slid open the latch and went inside. Meagre light seeped in
through holes that spotted the wooden roof and sides. The
barn was about thirty feet in length and full of hay, piled five
bales high and ten bales deep. There was a gap at ground
level and I squeezed myself in between two of the bales. While
I waited, I drank a third of a bottle of whiskey and my
thoughts grew less joined up with each mouthful. What would
Declan say if he knew that I pretended I was asleep in bed
but, most nights, at ten o'clock I climbed out through the
window? God help me if I was pregnant. My mother would
skin me alive. I'd end up like her. Bitter and twisted. I didn't
want to disappoint Declan but I loved Gabe. He made me
feel like I belonged. Sex made me feel like I belonged. Sex.

My eyes were closing when I heard shouting and the sound
of thundering feet. I stood up and went to the door, expecting
to see just Gabe and his friends, but they'd been joined by
almost a dozen others and they were all running up the hill
towards me. Not far behind them were two men with guns.
One man fired his gun into the air and shouted, 'Get off my
land, you thieving bastards!'

As the young men drew level with me, I heard my name
being called and then a hand grabbed mine and hauled me
along with the crowd. It wasn't until we reached the road
that I realised it wasn't Gabe who'd grabbed me but my
brother Diarmaid. 'What are you doing here?' I asked him,
knowing full well that Diarmaid and his crew could turn up
anywhere. Both Diarmaid and Finn were part of a
marauding, adrenaline-fuelled pack of young men who
couldn't stay home and were banned from most of the pubs
in the neighbourhood.

'I could be asking you the same.'

I turned away from him. 'I have to go back and get Gabe.'

He yanked me back by the hair. 'What's he to you?'

'My boyfriend, if you must know.' He yanked my hair again. 'Ow! Stop it.'

I tried to get his hands off me but he held me fast. 'Sure you haven't been having sex with him, Scarlett?'

I didn't answer but the look on my face must have given me away and he punched the air beside me. 'You dirty little slut!' He shook me hard. 'Don't you move. Don't you feckin' move.'

He whistled on Finn who ran off to fetch his car and they drove me to Declan's house. It was a small two-bedroom cottage on the rise of a hill and Diarmaid pushed his way into the house without knocking, dragging me behind him. Aisling was sitting by the fire – her sister Deirdre had given birth to a baby boy and Aisling was knitting a tiny blue cardie – and when we burst into the room she jumped up from her chair. 'Scarlett! What's going on?'

I was crying so hard that I couldn't answer her. In the car, Diarmaid had called me all the names under the sun, the tone of his voice not dissimilar to my mother's.

'We need to see Declan,' Finn said.

'Well, Declan isn't here,' Aisling said, reaching for my hand and bringing me over to her side of the fire.

'You need to tell him about *her*,' Diarmaid said, pointing a vicious finger at me. 'She's been whoring it around the village.'

'How dare you!' Aisling said quietly. 'I'd like you to think about your language in front of your sister.' She shooed them both towards the door. 'Be off with you! And don't be coming back until you've found your manners.' For a small woman she had an authority that brooked no argument and they were in the car and away before I could say so much as a Hail Mary.

'Oh holy hour!' Aisling said, holding me by the shoulders. 'What a carry-on for a Friday evening! Declan will be home soon and in the meantime you can have a nice hot bath and get warm by the fire.'

Again, I did as I was told, and while I was drying myself Declan arrived home. I could hear his voice in the living room, the low murmuring tone of his and the higher tones of Aisling, soothing and placatory. I gathered that he'd met Finn and Diarmaid further along the lane and heard all about where I'd been and who I'd been with. When I came out of the bathroom, I was wearing Aisling's nightie and dressing gown and a pair of Declan's thick socks. Declan held me tight against him for an age and it set me off crying again.

'You could have been hurt, Scarlett. You mustn't hang out with boys like Gabe Duggan. He's like Diarmaid and Finn, only worse.'

'He's not like them! He's good to me.'

'He's a menace! Promise me you'll never get in touch with him again.'

'I can't!'

'Promise me, Scarlett!'

I promised him because I'd never seen him look so sad and I couldn't bear to be the cause of it. I never found out what he said to our parents, but I moved out of my home and in with Declan. Aisling was training up in Dublin and only came to stay once or twice a month. So it was just me and Declan and their dog Captain, a retired sheep dog, half blind with cataracts but blessed with an ever-wagging tail. Being with Declan made me the happiest I'd ever been. We lived on bowls of soup with bread to dip in and big pots of stew, and I tried very hard not to be jealous when Aisling came to stay. She was kindness itself, though, and I thanked her for sharing her Declan-time with me.

'It's you who's sharing him with me, Scarlett,' she said. 'Declan told me all about when you were born, how you were always smiling and how excited you'd get when he took you on the tractor with him.' She was a tactile person and she hugged me then. 'You know your brother loves you, now don't you?'

Declan took me to talk to Sister Mary-Agnes to see whether she'd give me extra lessons after school. She was Aisling's aunt and already my science teacher. She agreed at once. 'You have an aptitude, Scarlett Olivia Naughton,' she told me, steering me into a chair. 'And what God has given you should never be wasted.'

'I don't think I believe in God any more.'

'Scarlett Olivia Naughton!' Her hand clutched the crucifix that hung down on her chest. 'How can you say such a thing? Do I need to have a meeting with your mother and father?'

'No, Sister. I'm sorry, Sister.'

'And so you should be. The good Lord believes in you, so that'll be an end to such talk.' She swooped around me, moving books from shelf to table so that I ended up with a bigger pile in front of me than I could carry. 'Have you seen the way a workman shapes a copper pot?'

'I don't know why I should have, Sister.'

'Well let me tell you, Scarlett. He holds a hammer in his right hand and bashes the outside, while his left hand shapes, gently and persuasively, from the inside. That's the way God will work on you.'

As the days passed, Sister Mary-Agnes dropped my first name – 'Scarlett is a colour, not a name' – and began calling me by my middle name, Olivia, chosen by my father because I was born on 10 June, which was St Olivia's feast day. The patron saint of music, she lived in the ninth century and was as unlike me as any girl could be, but it was a better name than Scarlett, and as it was a name I'd been writing down between Scarlett and Naughton for the last ten years, it still felt like me. Just a different me.

I never saw Gabe again. I found out that he'd been caught

by the farmer and I worried that he was only caught because he slowed down to look for me. He was charged with criminal damage because two of the farmer's rowing boats had been spun out on to the ice, the surface cracking under their weight so that the boats were lost in the water. I suspected this had happened before Gabe even got there but he accepted the blame for it anyway. I worried that he would be sent to prison and I worried that he'd think that I'd abandoned him, but I didn't dare break my promise to Declan. I did, however, keep my ears pricked for any gossip, and after a few months I heard that Gabe was given a suspended sentence and went to stay with his uncle down in Cork where he could finish school away from distractions.

If I'd been a lover of the dramatic, as my mother was, then I would have felt sorry for my poor self and stood on the cliff edge with a shawl wrapped around me, but I knew I was just an ordinary girl who'd lost her way. I wasn't especially intelligent but I had an almost photographic memory, and Sister Mary-Agnes made sure I had a slew of facts to memorise. Soon, though, her presence wasn't necessary, and I studied because I enjoyed it. When I got the letter to say I'd been accepted to study medicine at university, the first person I told was Declan. He sat staring at the letter and grinning, as if the dream had come true for him, not just me. When I told my daddy I'd got in to medical school, he stood on the pub table and announced to all his cronies that his daughter was going places and then he bought them all a round of drinks. I asked Daddy not to tell my mother because I knew she'd be less than impressed. We were so rarely in each other's company now, anyway, but I didn't want her seeking me out to tell me what a failure I was making of my life.

Before I left for university, Declan and Aisling were married in the local chapel. She wore a white broderie-anglaise, full-length dress and a crown of pink roses on her hair. If someone had asked me to describe what happiness was, I would have said it was Declan and Aisling, holding hands on the church step.

I left on the bus that evening and by the time I'd got to Edinburgh I was looking forward to making my future.

12

The front door opens and slams shut. I listen as footsteps come along the corridor. There's a slight pause outside the door – I imagine she's spotted my shoes – and in that space of time, I take a deep, preparatory breath. The door opens and Emily comes in. Her eyes meet mine and she doesn't miss a beat. She closes the door behind her and smiles. 'Olivia,' she says. She has the strap of a canvas bag across her body and she pulls it over her head, putting the bag down neatly beside a row of shoes. 'Thank you for coming.'

I don't speak immediately. Now that we're face to face, I feel calm. She is so much the Emily Jones I know: a sweet-natured, patently non-threatening slip of a girl, just five feet tall. But then, when I look at her more closely, I see that she is also Kirsty Stewart. She has traits in common with her parents: her mother's almond-shaped eyes and wide mouth; her father's hair and eye colour.

'This is awkward,' she says. 'I don't suppose there's any point in pretending I have an identical twin?'

'No, I don't think there is.' I smile. 'Should I call you Emily or Kirsty?'

'Kirsty,' she answers at once. 'I'm not sure I'm quite cutting it as Emily. Parts of Kirsty just keep on bubbling through, if you know what I mean.'

'Yes, I do.' I give a short laugh. 'I do know what you mean. Most people know me as Olivia, but during my childhood I was called Scarlett and my Irish family still call me that.'

'Really?' She pulls across one of the tub chairs and places it about three feet away. 'Why the change?'

'It was a hard name to live up to.'

'Right.' She nods as if she knows exactly what I mean and then she sits down, smoothing the material of her light summer dress over her knees. The dress is a pale cream with a faint pattern of flowers across it and, like my skirt, it's wet at the bottom. Her legs and feet are bare, her toenails bright with a rainbow of different coloured polish. 'I would offer you a cup of tea but I'm sure you've seen the state of the place? Hygiene isn't their strong point.' She screws her toes down into the sheepskin rug. 'Sorry I wasn't here when you arrived. I missed the bus.'

'That's okay.' I clear my throat. 'I tried to call you but your phone was switched off.'

'Was it?'

'Is it your foster parents who live in Murrayfield, then?'

'What do you mean?'

'At the hospital, when I was booking a taxi, you said you lived in Murrayfield.'

'Did I?' She shrugs. 'I don't know anyone who lives in Murrayfield. My foster parents lived in Lasswade but they recently moved up to Inverness. I don't see them any more.'

'Really?' I start back. 'I thought that was why you'd changed your name to Jones?'

'No. I . . .' She stops and purses her lips. 'You've been talking to the police.'

'DI O'Reilly told me that he'd had a chat with you.'

'Interrogation more like.'

'I'm sorry if he was tough on you, Emily—'

'*Kirsty,*' she says. 'I said you should call me Kirsty.'

'I'm sorry.' I hold up my hand. 'It's just that I've known you for nine months as Emily. It's hard to make the leap.'

'But you do remember, don't you?' She stretches her hand

to the table and takes hold of the photo frame. 'You do remember this couple?' She holds the photograph at chest height and I look at Trevor and Sandy's smiling faces, then up into their daughter's more serious one.

'Yes, I remember them,' I say quietly.

She turns the photo towards her and for a moment her expression softens before she puts the frame back on the table.

'I went to see your dad on Monday.'

'I know. One of the nurses told me. That's why I asked you to come here.'

I wait for her to elaborate but she doesn't. She's staring at her feet, pointing and flexing her toes several times before saying, 'What made you realise that my dad was part of the puzzle?'

'Well . . .' I look up at the ceiling, not seeing what's there, but instead seeing the red-painted MURDERER, shouting its message with a deafening roar. 'You know about what happened to Robbie and you also know that someone came to my house and covered the wall with paint. The police told me to think about who might have done it and when I looked back into my past I realised that . . .' I stop, unsure how frank to be.

'Go on,' she urges, leaning forward now, her face pale and serious, her hands clutched together on her lap.

'Did your father speak to you about how your mother died?'

'My father never talked about my mother. But he kept diaries. He wrote them all his married life and then for five years after Mum died. It was hard for him to cope and I wasn't always an easy baby.' She looks thoughtful. 'He was a professional writer, you know? Did you know that?' I shake my head. 'He wrote articles for the *Edinburgh Courier*. Ironic really, when the woman who killed his wife then goes on to be celebrated in the very same paper.'

She doesn't say it with any emotion. It's a throwaway comment, a casual acknowledgement of life's funny little coincidences. But for me, her words feel like an ice grenade that scores a direct hit and freezes my brain.

'I was taken into care when I was ten. A nosy teacher at school said that she could tell I was forging permission slips. Annoying really, because we were doing all right, me and Dad. Most of the time he was drunk, but he never hit me or anything, and I could cook, do the washing, stuff like that.' She's very deliberately not looking at me. She's examining her fingernails and then she reaches into a drawer and brings out a nail file. 'But when social services got their hands on me I was slotted into the system. I was with three families that didn't work out and then I got the Joneses and they were nice. They didn't foster children for the money; they did it because they believed in giving something back. They encouraged me to apply for the scholarship to Sanderson.'

'I'm sorry, Kirsty.' I find my voice. 'I'm sorry that your childhood has been so tough at times.'

'You've been to Sanderson.' She stops filing and stares at me. 'Haven't you?'

I nod. 'I gather you're a talented actress.'

'I bet Mrs Tweedie gave you the whole spiel about me arriving all shy and retiring and leaving with the world at my feet?'

'Something like that.'

'Couldn't you see through them?' she says, astonished. 'They are churning out *actors* after all. Performance is everything.' She throws the nail file on to the bedspread and stands up. 'Let me show you.'

I watch as she lurches across the room, slurring words under her breath. Her coat is hanging on the back of the door and she reaches for it, but her hand is slightly too far to the left and she re-reaches, grabs it and fights to put it on. The battle with the coat sleeves causes her to break into a cackle of laughter and then, in the space of a lengthy, exhaled breath she slides down the emotional spectrum into maudlin self-pity. I catch some of her rant, 'dinnae care', 'life's a bastard', 'fuck the lot o' them' as she tosses the coat aside and drags her limbs around the room, her head jerking from side to side.

Part of me can't help but be impressed. Her act is not a parody of a drunk – it is a drunk. She is utterly convincing. And then, like the flick of a switch, she turns off the performance and comes back to her seat. 'That was one of the pieces that got me my scholarship.' She inhales slowly. 'And then there's this.'

The room grows still. We're both barely breathing. I watch as her lower lip begins to tremble and her face reddens. 'Okay, so I know I go too far sometimes,' she says. 'It's just . . . it's just . . .' There's so much pain in her eyes that I flinch. 'I know I alienate people, and I want to be a better person, but I'm just not sure how.' She takes a halting breath. 'With my dad and everything, my life's been a mess.' Her fists are tight and she draws her dress into them until the remaining material bunches up over her thighs. 'All the time drunk. Never talking or spending time with me. Just drunk.' Tears flow in two steady streams down her cheeks. 'I'm a horrible person.' She shakes her head at me. 'I hurt people and I hurt myself.' Her tiny frame shakes with emotion. 'Can you help me?' It's a whisper, and it echoes the look of shy hopefulness that brings a dull light back into her eyes. 'Do you think you can . . .' She bites her lip, her expression conflicted, and brings her face closer to mine. 'Do you think you can help me get revenge?'

Her eyes flare with heat, compelling me not to look away, and I don't, I can't. A couple of seconds to make her point and she withdraws, stands up – I can breathe again – walks over to the cupboard in the corner and rummages around before sitting back down. 'I have to keep my food in my room because if I leave it in the kitchen they steal it.' She tears the wrapper off a muesli bar and takes a bite. 'They get the munchies at night.' She breaks off a piece, being careful with the crumbs and holds it out to me. 'You want some?'

I shake my head.

'So.' She swallows her mouthful. 'Back to my mum.'

'Yes.' I nod, keen to get this over with. 'Did your dad's diaries mention why your mum was in hospital?'

'She had a brain tumour.'

'That's right. A grade IV astrocytoma, a highly malignant tumour that infiltrates the brain and can be a considerable size before it becomes symptomatic.'

She finishes the muesli bar and crosses her arms and legs. 'The diaries make it sound like everyone gave up on Mum the moment she got the diagnosis. Especially Dad.'

'That's not fair on him, Kirsty. They were so much in love and they were finally having a baby they'd longed for and she had cancer. It was unbearable for him.'

'But what about *her*? How unbearable must it have been for her?'

'I'm sure in her blackest moments she was very afraid. But what I remember most about her is that she was incredibly brave and very happy because she was having the baby she'd always wanted.'

'A baby she never got to hold.'

'That's true. But your mum did know that she was not going to live much longer than a few months.'

'How can you say that?' She throws out her arms. 'You're not God!'

'I saw her neurological scans. She didn't have a healthy brain and, statistically, to live for any length of time with an aggressive tumour of that size is not possible.'

'So you do think you're God?'

'No, I—'

'And if she *was* going to die, then what difference would kill her a few months early make? Is that what you thought?'

'Absolutely not—'

'No need for you to feel guilty. Poor woman was already on her way out.'

'Kirsty!' I try to take hold of her hands but she stands up and moves to the other side of the room.

'That poor woman was my mother!' she shouts. 'And in a few months they might have found a cure!'

'They didn't find a cure. They still haven't. There are treatments but—'

'But they could have found a cure! They might have operated on her and got some clue from the way her brain was working. The right forensic team with the right surgeon at exactly the right moment. They could have developed a treatment from studying my mother's case. From *my* mother.' She rushes towards me and I stand up before she lands on my knee. 'Tell me that's impossible,' she says quietly. '*Tell me.*'

'It's not im-poss-ible,' I say slowly. 'But it's so improbable as to be extremely unlikely.'

'But it isn't *impossible*.' She pushes me in the hollow of my shoulder and I stumble back towards the window, my arms automatically stretching forwards to keep her away from me, but there's no need because she's turned her face into the wall and has her arms wrapped around herself, not making a sound. Sunshine is filtering through the lace curtains, spilling honey-coloured light on to the carpet, and I move the curtain to one side, looking out on to the front street where people are far below me, hurrying about their business. It's still raining, but the sun has dodged the clouds and I know that somewhere out there, people will be admiring a rainbow.

'A monkey's wedding,' Kirsty says, coming to stand beside me, her expression calm again. 'That's what my dad always said. When it rains and shines together, it's a monkey's wedding. Daft, isn't it?'

I look at my watch. It's already after five o'clock. In exactly an hour I need to meet the children at the police station, even although it now seems pointless to go through the rigmarole of taking prints when Kirsty's all but admitted to doing it.

'Do you have somewhere to be?' she asks me.

'I do.'

'I'm sorry I lashed out just now.' She looks genuinely contrite but then how would I know? She's already made a point of showing me her acting skills. She returns to her seat, patting the space on the bed in front of her. 'Please sit down again.'

I consider my options – there are only two: I leave or I stay. I came here to give her a chance to talk and to find out whether my past mistake was responsible for what's been happening and clearly it is. So I can leave the rest to O'Reilly, or I can stay and pursue the details myself.

It doesn't take me long to decide that I'll stay. I want to hear what she has to say about the night Robbie's drink was spiked. And I want to know whether she's planning anything else, because if she is, then I need to stop her.

'What do you want from me, Kirsty?' My skirt's beginning to dry but it still feels cold and uncomfortable, and I sit down on the remaining chair to benefit from the patch of sunlight. She reacts by pulling her chair towards me so that we're only a foot away from each other.

'Good. I'm glad you're staying.' She smiles. 'I want us to work out a way to fix this problem that we have with each other.'

'I don't have a problem with you.'

'Even when I admit to what I've done?'

'Tell me.'

'I wasn't the only one.' She looks up at me through dipped lashes. 'There was someone else involved too.'

'Tess Williamson?'

'Tess Williamson,' she affirms, shaking her head, as if simply saying Tess's name speaks volumes in itself. 'She was on the phone just now having a meltdown about the whole thing and – well,' she widens her eyes, 'you've met her. She has all the courage of the lion from *The Wizard of Oz*.' Her expression is contemptuous, and I can easily imagine her manipulating Tess until she does as she says. 'Okay, so I suppose I haven't always been that kind to her but Tess wants friends.' She shrugs. 'Some people have to buy their way into friendships. Others don't. That's the way it works.'

'What do you mean by "the whole thing"?'

She looks at me blankly.

'You said Tess was having a meltdown about "the whole thing".'

'We came to your house,' she says lightly. 'We wrote "murderer" on your living-room wall.'

My feeling of shock is brief – isn't this what I've been expecting? It's almost a relief to know that I've got to the source. But behind that relief is anger and I can't risk unleashing it. *If she wrote on the wall, did she also almost kill Robbie?* I shake my head to clear the thought.

'Why did you write "murderer" on the wall?' I say.

'It was Tess's idea. When you were first put up for the City Women award I was really upset and Tess told me I should get revenge.'

'This was last September?'

'Yes. I'd known about you for a while because I'd found my dad's diaries earlier in the year when he had another stint in hospital and I was clearing out the loft.' She tilts her head. 'Just imagine it. I'd recently found out that a Dr Naughton had killed my mother and I was wondering what to do with that news when I read all about you in the papers. How you were Irish and your maiden name was Naughton and that you'd trained in Edinburgh and worked in neurosurgery. And now you were a GP into do-gooding on a grand scale. Like you were curing cancer or something. When in fact you're nothing special, are you?'

'No, I'm not. I'm a flawed human being, capable of making wrong decisions. And living to regret them.'

'Tess thought I should take revenge there and then but I was curious about you. I wanted to get to know you and when I saw you had a teenage son I thought that was the best way.'

'So you joined the hockey club?'

'Luckily, the club standard isn't very high. Meetings are on Fridays and I was already a weekly boarder at Sanderson.' She shrugs. 'It worked like a dream.'

'You were operating under a false name and you came into my house under false pretences.' I hold her eyes. 'That's a bit extreme, don't you think?'

'My life has always been extreme.' She thinks for a moment, her expression serious. 'You have a nice family, you know?'

'Yes, I know.'

'I've lived in a few families and mostly they're teetering on the edge of misery. But you three are generous and friendly and you laugh a lot. For a while I really thought I was over it. I was being Emily and people like Emily and it feels good being liked.' She laughs. 'That's an ironic laugh because Kirsty isn't anyone's favourite. I'm sure when you spoke to the girls at Sanderson they told you that.'

'They did.'

'You're newly divorced, aren't you?'

'Yes.'

'Did you want to fight back at your husband – hurt him, kill him even?'

'I've never thought about killing him, but I have been angry, depressed at times and spiteful.'

'Did you do anything?'

'Kirsty.' I sigh. 'Can we just stick to the point?'

'This is the point.' The fire in her eyes keeps me tied to her. 'Did you do anything?'

'I thought about all those things women do – emptying joint bank accounts, cutting up his suits, sewing prawns into curtain seams so that the smell of rotting fish would drive him nuts – but I didn't do any of that.'

'Nothing at all?'

'Well . . . I gave some of his stuff to our local charity shop and he had to buy it back.'

She smiles. 'Go on.'

'And I hung about outside his flat a couple of times, waylaid him, made a fool of myself until he called the police on me.'

'Bastard,' she says, her voice hushed with empathy. 'Sounds like you're better off without him. And you've not turned to drink?' She affects an accent. 'You being Irish 'n all.'

I shake my head. 'No.' In fact I have been drunk a few times when the kids were with Phil and I only had Benson for an audience.

'And did you have the perfect upbringing? Cut flowers in a vase on the kitchen table, the smell of baking when you opened the front door?' She's shifted mood again and now she's an interviewer, all teeth and exaggerated interest. 'A mother who dried her hands on her apron then threw her arms wide to hug you?'

'No. I had a mother who was depressed. She got very little joy out of her life, her children included.'

'But even a bad mother's better than no mother at all, wouldn't you say?'

'Maybe. Maybe not,' I say flatly. 'As a doctor, I've seen both ends of the spectrum and all the stops in between.'

'Well, I would have liked the option of a mother.' She leans forward in the seat. 'You took that away from me.'

'Kirsty.' I steady my voice. 'Did you spike Robbie's drink?'

'Yes.'

Her admission triggers a noise from my throat. It's a sound I've never heard before – a visceral concoction, a witch's brew of anger and hatred and willingness to tear the flesh off bones. It scares me rigid and my face flushes with the effort it takes to keep myself in check.

'You're shocked,' she says, her mouth widening into a pleased smile.

I close my eyes, glue my lips together and let myself breathe. *Do not let her get to you,* I tell myself. *She's a mixed-up teenager who's got in way over her head. She needs to understand how badly she's behaving and then we can put this behind us.*

I clear my throat and just about manage to look her in the eye when I say, 'Tell me about that night.'

'Well.' She muses for a bit. 'It was Tess's idea. She bought the GHB and . . .' She shrugs. 'Spiking his drink was easy.'

'So why did you save him?' I say.

'I never wanted to *kill* him. And when I saw him lying there, I knew I'd given him too much.' She pauses, her eyes bright with revelation. 'His house keys had fallen out of his pocket and I realised I needed to take revenge on you directly, not hurt Robbie.'

'Kirsty, you almost killed him.'

'You *actually* killed my mother. I think I have the moral high ground here, don't you?'

'Listen!' I lean towards her. 'I know you're angry and you have every right to be. I completely understand that. But look at what you've done. Your actions against Robbie were *deliberate*. What happened with your mother was an accident.'

'But you didn't come forward to tell the truth?'

'I did own up to my mistake. I told my boss exactly what had happened.'

'And?'

'He persuaded me that resigning wouldn't serve any purpose and that I should pick myself up and make sure I became a better doctor because of it.'

'And that made it okay?'

'No, it wasn't okay. I was very upset by it and I did consider giving up medicine.'

'But you didn't?'

'No.'

'And then you moved on?'

'Yes. But it was difficult. Believe me, I did not take your mother's death lightly. I'm extremely sorry that it happened.'

'You're sorry that you killed her?'

'Yes.'

'Then say it.'

'Kirsty.' I take both her hands in mine and pin our eyes together. 'I'm so sorry I killed your mother.'

Her body rears up and she takes a breath, broken by a suppressed sob that she confines to her throat. I try to hug her but she pulls away and drops on to her knees on the rug. 'My father never moved on.' She drags out a box from underneath the bed and when she takes off the lid there are four piles of A5 notebooks. She looks through them until she finds the one she wants and sits back on the chair, holding the book on her lap. When she opens it, a sheet of paper falls out. 'Do you remember this?' She thrusts the paper in front of my face. It's a faded piece of Basildon Bond writing paper.

'It's the letter I sent to your father.' I recognise my own writing – *Dear Trevor, I am sorry to have missed you when you came on to the ward and even sorrier that Sandy has passed away . . .*

'He already knew that Mum's death had been caused by a doctor making a mistake with the drugs – he'd overheard a couple of nurses talking about it.' She clears her throat and gives me a pointed look. 'Let me read you what he wrote in his diary.'

'This letter came today from Dr Naughton. I think she must be the one who made the mistake with the medicine. I'm sorry if Dr Naughton was the person who made the mistake because Sandy liked her and I'm not going to make a fuss. Nothing will bring Sandy back.'

She turns the page and reads on.

'Dr Naughton gave me her phone number and twice I've called her home, but the doctor she lives with said she wasn't well enough to talk to me. He told me not to call again because Dr Naughton isn't well. I hope she's not having problems with her pregnancy.'

Kirsty stops reading, closes the book and crosses her ankles. 'If that was all that had been written, I would never have been sure that you'd done it, but do you want to know what happened next?'

She can't hide the look of triumph on her face and I know that what's coming is likely to upset me but still I have to say, 'Yes.'

'See for yourself.' She holds out the book. 'It's about halfway through.'

I find the right page and start to read.

This morning when I was visiting Kirsty in the baby unit (she grows stronger by the hour and is almost breathing for herself – how happy Sandy would be to see her!), Dr Naughton's fiancé came to talk to me. He's a brusque sort of a man, a psychiatrist, I think. He doesn't have much of a bedside manner, more time for doctors than patients, was the impression he gave me. He told me that I was never to ring their home again. I said I never would have, if it hadn't been for the fact that Dr Naughton asked me to. 'You're upsetting her,' he told me. 'Dr Naughton is a good doctor and she doesn't deserve to have this incident colour her future.' I had no answer to that. Sandy's death reduced to 'an incident'. I turned away from him and he walked back into the corridor. He didn't even ask after the baby. Somehow that made me sadder than anything.'

I close the book and stay very still, tension locking my diaphragm.

'Just as well you divorced him really, isn't it?' Kirsty says. 'Or else you'd be filing for divorce as soon as you get home.'

I'm struggling to breathe in and, on numb legs, I lurch towards the casement window, tugging it up from the bottom until it's open about a foot. I steady myself on the sill as cool air floods on to my face and into my lungs.

Phil. *How could he have done that? What gave him the right to recklessly interfere in my life?* I feel the urge to shake him and shake him until all his arrogance and self-importance has emptied out and he's forced to see his behaviour for what it was. Despite the fact that I no longer love him, I feel gutted for the woman I used to be, blindly trusting a man who could happily go behind her back and manipulate the situation as he saw fit.

'Did you know my father called your house?' Kirsty asks me.

'No, I didn't. I only found out a couple of days ago. Phil kept it from me.'

'Why did you marry him in the first place?'

'Because I loved him.'

'And love is blind?'

I shrug a reply and sit back down, my body heavy with the weight of murky, churned-up feelings and nowhere to empty them out, clean myself up and move on.

'For years I looked at other girls' mothers and imagined what it would be like to have one of my own,' Kirsty says. 'I imagined what it would be like to have someone who tucked me in at night and read me stories, who sewed on nametapes and took me shopping.' There's a reedy, fragile tone to her voice that makes her sound as if she's on the edge of tears. 'When I'm acting I can lose myself in another person's life. I'm like clingfilm. I can wrap myself around characters, around people. I can take their shape. I don't find that difficult because I don't really have a self. I spent too much time wishing I was one of those other girls, the ones who had mothers.'

'This room doesn't belong to someone without a self.' I gesture at the walls, the bedspread and the vase of flowers on the table. 'There's so much love and care gone into this room.'

'I'm playing the part of someone who has a room like this.'

'Why? When you could be like the people you live with.'

'I like to pretend I'm a different sort of girl. An Emily.' She narrows her eyes. 'Your daughter thinks that you're not a proper family any more because her father left her. But she has no idea how bad it can get.'

'I know Lauren has found it difficult since Phil left, but she will come to terms with it.'

Kirsty picks up her parents' photo and stares at it before looking back at me. 'Do you believe in fairytales?'

'Wicked stepmothers and handsome princes?' I sigh. 'Real life is never that black and white.'

'Still, you might remember that in fairytales, bad deeds don't go unpunished.'

'Fairytales are stories, Kirsty. Nothing more.' I know what

she's driving at and I don't want to hear any more. I look at my watch again and stand up. 'I'm sorry, but I really do need to go now.' I'm going to be almost an hour late for O'Reilly.

'You want your children to stay safe.' Her eyes are challenging. 'Don't you?'

'Of course. That's what every mother wants.' I glance across at Sandy's photo. 'Do you think your mother would want you to avenge her death in such a violent and dangerous way? Setting yourself on a path of prosecution and prison?'

'I have no idea. I never knew my mother.'

'Well, I did. I knew her. And she was full of beauty and light and love for everyone. But mostly for you, Kirsty.' I pause, hoping that somewhere inside her wounded heart, my words will take root. 'She wanted you more than she'd ever wanted anything or anybody in her whole life.'

I continue to talk about Sandy, but within moments Kirsty has stuck her fingers in her ears and started humming, all the time watching my lips, and when they're no longer moving, she takes her fingers out and says airily, 'You done with the eulogy?'

'Kirsty—'

'My mother's dead – *dead* – while you're a public figure with your City Women award. How can that be fair?'

'Life isn't fair. Life is complex and confusing. It's unpredictable. There are no certainties and no forevers.'

'That's easy for you to say!' She points a finger into my face. 'You have it all!'

'I don't!' I almost laugh. 'Life has never been easy for me. I've worked hard for everything I have and still my marriage failed and still I've made mistakes that haunt me.' Her frown softens. 'I'm sorry that your life has been hard and I'm sorry that I played a part in that, but you have taken your revenge. You spiked Robbie's drink and caused me to have the worst few hours of my life. You befriended

my family under false pretences. You've lied to the police
and used Tess as a shield.'

'A lot of it was her idea.'

'I don't believe that.' I take hold of her shoulders. 'Kirsty,
I know what it's like to be a teenager and to get in over your
head but really – you have to stop now.'

'Or what? You'll tell the police? Have me arrested?' She's
trying for bravado but her lips are trembling. 'They don't
have any hard evidence and I'll deny everything you tell
them.'

'I'm not threatening you, Kirsty. I want you to see that this
course of action is not healthy for you. Hard as it is, you
need to let it go.'

'I don't think I can.' It's a whispered admission of weak-
ness. 'It feels too important.'

'You don't have to get through it alone. I could find you
someone experienced to talk to. Someone who will help
you put all of this into perspective.' I reach for the door
handle and pull. 'Why don't we meet up tomorrow and talk?'
I step into the hallway and into my shoes. 'I promise you'll
get through this.'

'You'll call me tomorrow?'

'Yes.' I place a hand on her shoulder. 'Don't worry. It's all
going to work out.'

13

I run from Kirsty's flat back to my car and experience a further soaking, and now the car's steamed up and the heater's going full blast. I drive far too fast because I'm well over an hour late for my meeting at the police station. Phil will already be there with the children, pacing up and down, no doubt, and O'Reilly will be wondering what's stopped me turning up this time.

I keep my shaky hands on the wheel as I negotiate my way through the late evening traffic, accelerating through amber lights that change to red just as I cross the intersection. A van driver sounds his horn and I fix my eyes up ahead. Despite the warm air that's circulating through the car's interior, my teeth are chattering. I feel drained from the emotional intensity of my meeting with Kirsty. Although I'm angry about what she did to Robbie, I can't help but feel sorry for her. At times she was childlike, bitter about life's inequalities and unwilling to accept the enormity of her own lies and acts of vengeance. But at other times, I could see through her mistrust and hurt feelings to the real girl underneath. I think she'll respond well to counselling. The talking cure doesn't work for everyone, but for Kirsty, who's able to articulate her feelings, I think it will help her see her situation more clearly. Not only does she have her mother's death to properly come to terms with, but her father is not going to recover. He may not live much longer, and that is bound to be another tipping point for her.

When I get to the police station, I can't find a parking space. I have to park further along the road and then run back a hundred yards or more. Another drenching and I'm aware that by the time I enter the building I'm beyond bedraggled. My hair is both dripping on my shoulders and frizzing up over my skull like candyfloss. My skirt has been soaked twice and is now misshapen and flapping against my tights, which are splashed with dirty water.

'Where on earth have you been?' Phil shouts as I enter the foyer.

'I'm sorry. I got stuck with a patient.'

'You couldn't have answered your phone?'

'No,' I say sharply, my eye catching that of the desk clerk, who's clearly seen it all before. 'Otherwise I would have done, wouldn't I?'

'You're dripping wet.' He's frowning, shaking his head at my perceived incompetence. When we were married, this side of him manifested itself as solicitous and caring, but now it's critical and nagging.

'Where are the children?' I say.

'They're in the staff room watching TV. I've spent the last twenty minutes calling you.'

'I'm sorry . . .'

'Erika is waiting for me.'

I can't help but roll my eyes. He doesn't notice because he's staring at the floor, twisting his ring on his finger – a present from Erika, it's a signet ring embossed with a seal of some sort – his expression worried. 'The children didn't take the news well.'

'What news?' I say, a split second before it comes to me – his impending marriage.

'What do you mean, what news?' he snaps.

'All right!' I snap back. 'I remember now. I'm sorry.' My third apology in less than two minutes. I take a moment to slow down and try to see this from his point of view. He wants to be a good father and the children are upset that he's remarrying. He needs me to help smooth the way. And I will. For the children's sake, not for his. 'So what did they say?'

It turns out Lauren burst into tears as soon as he told them, and Robbie sat with his arms crossed and refused to comment. 'Neither of them spoke through dinner. Lauren ate nothing. Robbie wolfed his down and then ate Lauren's as well.'

'Good old Robbie!' I say, trying to introduce a lighter note. 'Nothing comes between him and his appetite.'

Phil manages a weak smile. 'I'm not sure where to go from here.'

'I'll have a word with them,' I say. 'They just need some time to get used to the idea.'

'Thank you.' He looks momentarily humbled. 'I appreciate that.'

'How very grown up we're being!' I say breezily and then, just like that, I remember what was written in Trevor's diary. My face flushes and my eyes fill up with angry tears as Phil's eighteen-year-old deception barges to the forefront of my mind.

'I know this is difficult for you, Liv.' Phil brings a tissue out of his pocket. 'But my getting married—'

'It's not that.' I take the tissue from him. I'm not crying but I use it to wipe the rainwater off my face. He's watching me, his expression softer than I've seen in a long time but I'm not about to be diverted. 'I want to talk to you about what's been happening,' I say.

'Don't worry.' He lays a comforting hand on my upper arm. 'O'Reilly is confident they've made a breakthrough. Forensic results have come through and there's a positive match on prints with a girl called Tess Williamson. She came to your surgery, I believe?'

'She didn't do it.' I shake my head. 'She was bullied into taking part.'

'Olivia, you can't possibly know that.'

'I do know that, actually. I do *bloody* know that and I'll tell you why I know that. Because this,' I hiss, my temper rising through me like steam, '*this*—'

'Keep your voice down.' He takes my elbow and leads me over to the side where we're well out of the desk clerk's earshot. 'Why are you shaking?'

'Because I'm angry, Phil. And shocked and hurt and . . .' I bite my lip but it doesn't stop me from spewing out, 'Fucking, *fucking* furious with you.' His face shuts down and he steps away from me. I hear O'Reilly's voice further along the corridor and I reach for Phil's lapels and say, '*This* is about Sandy Stewart's death and the baby that you and Leila told me was dead.'

'What on earth are you talking about?' His expression is a sneer. 'What can this possibly have to do with Sandy Stewart?'

'Dr Somers, you made it.' O'Reilly is coming towards me. He's smiling. I can't smile back.

'You look like you had to battle through the rain to get here,' O'Reilly says. 'Toilets are that way if you want to freshen up.'

I take the cue and walk off in the direction of O'Reilly's pointing hand. The toilet is just round the corner and as I push open the door, I'm greeted by a guffaw of laughter. There are two women in front of the mirror, applying make-up as if this is a nightclub not a police station. Their hilarity is exactly what I need to dispel my anger. I choose a sink next to the two of them and rummage in my bag for a hairbrush. I do intend to take Phil to task about his inter-ference eighteen years ago, but I want to do it without losing my temper. I don't want him to have the excuse of focusing on, not so much what I'm saying, but the way I'm saying it. He loves to take the high ground on 'respectful communication'.

My eyes sting as I envisage Phil going home to Erika and telling her that I'm losing it, and all the more reason for him to have shared custody of the children. I can hear Erika playing devil's advocate, being sympathetic to me because that's how she sells herself – angelic, thoughtful, always willing to help the downtrodden. The fact that she stole another woman's husband is conveniently forgotten – yes, I know Phil wouldn't have gone if he wasn't willing, and the way I feel about him now, she's more than welcome to him – but still, she did that. She came between a husband and his wife and now they're planning their wedding.

'You get caught in the rain without a brolly?' one of the women asks me.

'And some,' I say, staring at the horror that is my hair. Frizzy and flyaway at the best of times, it looks as if I've deliberately combed it into a bird's nest tangle for Halloween fancy dress. I spend a couple of minutes brushing it out and the two women tell me why they're at the police station. They are mother and daughter, and the daughter's soon-to-be ex-husband has been harassing them. They took matters into their own hands and slashed his car tyres.

'Not very mature,' the mother says. 'But ever so satisfying. You married?'

'Not any more,' I say. 'My husband's out there doing his best to make me want to stab him. He makes me *so* mad.'

'Ignore him,' the daughter says. 'Even better, build yourself some armour. This is what I do, I look in the mirror and I say "Dave Smith is an arse".' She turns to me and gives me a quizzical look. 'And who wants to be married to an arse?'

I smile. 'Not me.'

'There you go then. You try it.'

'Okay.' I'm willing to try anything. I square my shoulders in front of the mirror, take a breath and say quietly, 'Phil Somers is an arse.'

'You have to mean it,' the mother says, nudging me. 'Have another go.'

So I say it three more times and find that they're right – it's surprisingly helpful. It hardens me up. Makes me see that he has no control over me any more. It's not all about what he thinks and – truthfully – he does behave like an arse. It's worth reminding myself of that.

By the time I leave the bathroom, I'm smiling. O'Reilly is still in the foyer waiting for me. 'You look better.'

'I was having some therapy in the toilets,' I say.

'Oh?'

'A couple of women are championing the way forward for women without men.'

'All men are useless and all women are fools for putting up with them, is that it?'

'Not exactly. But it is about not feeling cowed by their opinion. Phil is in the habit of making me feel small,' I say, as if O'Reilly hasn't witnessed it for himself. 'I have to be careful not to take it on board because he always uses it against me.'

'Good for you,' he says, not in an offhand way, but with a sincerity that lets me know he means it.

I walk along the corridor with him and into a bare, grey-walled room with a metal table and three metal chairs, all of which are screwed into the floor.

'Is this one of the interrogation rooms?' I say, my eyes drawn towards the camera in the corner.

'These days we call them interview rooms. But, don't worry, the camera isn't switched on.' He waves his arm. 'Take a seat.' I sit down at the table and he sits opposite me. 'I hear you called me this afternoon?' he says.

'You were in court.'

'Was there a problem?'

'No. Not really.'

'We have some good news.' He smiles. 'Forensic results came back on the fingerprints. Tess Williamson's were found in two places in your house: on the living-room wall and on the door handle.'

'Phil told me.'

'We'll pick her up this evening and charge her with breaking and entering. We can't tie her to the drink spiking yet but—'

'I don't think you should charge Tess,' I say loudly.

'And why's that?'

'Emily . . . Kirsty texted me earlier and asked me to meet her.'

'And did you?'

'Yes.'

His eyes narrow. He has a pen in his hand and he taps it several times on the table.

'That was why I called you,' I say. 'To ask you whether you thought it was wise for me to meet up with her. But I couldn't reach you, and I remembered that all you'd said was that I should be wary of her and not let her in my house.'

The look on his face tells me that this doesn't quite get me off the hook. He clears his throat. 'So what did she say?'

'A lot.' I summarise about half of what was said, telling him about her bitterness towards me for ending her mother's life but also the softer side of her and the vulnerability she showed when talking about her parents. 'I think she could do with some counselling. There's a very good chance she'll be able to get past this—'

'Did she say she was planning on taking more action against you and your family?'

'No.'

'Did she admit to coming to your house?'

'She told me that she and Tess did it together.'

'Did she admit that she spiked Robbie's drink?'

'Yes.'

He bangs the palms of his hands on the table – not that loud and not that hard, but the room is otherwise quiet and I jump. 'I'm sorry.' He stands up. 'Excuse me a moment. Until I have the whole story, I need to stop Bullworks from bringing Tess in.'

He leaves the door open and goes off along the corridor, clearly irritated. I imagine myself in his position: he's busy – too many cases and not enough time; members of the public blundering their way around his investigations; it has to be annoying. It's like patients who ask for an NHS referral. I spend time sourcing treatment, writing emails, checking budgets and then I find out, almost by the way, that they've changed their mind or are getting it done privately and all my effort has been for nothing.

When O'Reilly comes back into the room he has an A4 pad with him. 'Okay. Let's just write down exactly what was said.'

'I hope I haven't caused you more work.'

'Dr Somers, I think it's important you don't lose sight of what Kirsty did to Robbie.' His face is serious. 'This could have been a murder investigation.'

'I know.' I swallow quickly. 'I haven't forgotten that, but I think Kirsty got out of her depth with the drink spiking. She said she didn't intend to give Robbie enough to make him lose consciousness. It was malicious, but she didn't mean any real harm. She was trying to upset me. She perceives me as being someone who has everything, and that's made her bitter.'

'Forgive me if I don't share your bleeding heart,' O'Reilly says tartly. 'But this is a girl who has a sustained ability to lie, to assume another persona and to bully an accomplice into aiding and abetting her. She doesn't need counselling; she needs some time in a prison cell.'

'I said I would talk with her tomorrow and . . .' I trail off and look around the room. 'Is that not a good idea?'

'You should stay away from her. I understand that you feel a sense of responsibility because of what happened with her mother, and I understand that you are in the business of helping people, but with all due respect to your medical training and your people skills, you should keep out of this investigation.'

'Okay.' I bite my lip. 'I'm sorry. I just thought I might be able to point her in the right direction. She's only seventeen. She's never had a mother.' My eyes fill up again and I let my forehead drop on to the table. 'She presses my buttons.'

'Well don't go anywhere near her and then she won't be able to,' O'Reilly says. 'And remember to tell your children she's a danger.'

'I will.' I jerk myself upright again. 'Can I go now?'

'Let's just quickly write down as much as you can remember and then I'll bring Kirsty in again. And we can bring Tess in. And eventually, we'll get the truth out of both of them.'

I spend the next twenty minutes dredging up everything I can remember, from the number of foster homes Kirsty stayed in to the contents of the diary. When I get to the part where Phil went behind my back, O'Reilly whistles through his teeth. 'You're going to let him get away with that?'

'No. I almost tackled him about it tonight, but it's better if I pick my moment. I might even do it in front of Erika. Or would that be mean?'

O'Reilly weighs this up with a tilt of his head one way and then the other. 'In situations like that, it's usually the messenger who gets shot.'

'She should know what he's capable of. They're getting

hitched in the summer. Today, he told the children about his impending marriage, and I don't think they took it very well.'

'That's why they don't look too happy, then?'

'Yes. And I should really go and get them and – ' I wave my arms around – 'drive them home.'

'Of course. There's no need to take your fingerprints now we know who the culprit is.' He winks at me and I smile then follow him to the staff room. I like him, and in another time, another place, and I might have had an opportunity with him, but there's nothing I can do about it now. Timing is everything and, at the moment, any involvement with him would be a complication too far.

'Hello, you two.'

Lauren and Robbie are in the staff room watching a football match on the television. They both jump up when they hear my voice and Lauren automatically puts her arms around me. Before her face buries into my chest I see that she has indeed been crying – an extended bout by the looks of things.

We say goodbye to O'Reilly and I take them both home. A quick stop in their bedrooms to tear off their uniforms and they flop down on the living-room sofa with Benson between them. I remove my suit and leave it on a hanger to dry, then climb into jeans and a blouse and make the children some food.

When I go into the living room, Lauren's just handed Robbie the remote control. 'Anything but football,' she says, as he starts flicking through channels.

'Food for you both!' I set a tray down on the coffee table in front of them. I've made them cheese and ham toasties with rocket salad and sliced tomatoes.

'Great, Mum.' Robbie reaches over and takes a plate.

'Chocolate mousse for afters,' I say, pouring them some juice. 'Dad said you didn't eat anything at dinner, Lauren.'

'No wonder after what he came out with.' She takes her

plate and breaks off the end of the toastie. 'Do you know what he's planning to do, Mum?'

'I do,' I say, sitting down opposite them. 'Do you want to talk about it?'

'I suppose.' She squirts some ketchup on her plate and dips the toast into it. 'He went on about how he wants to share his special day with us, like we want him to marry Erika, like we'll think it's special too.' Her expression is incredulous. 'He just doesn't get it. He doesn't get *anything*. I mean, he wants me to be a *bridesmaid*. I don't even want to *go*, so why would I want to be a bridesmaid?'

'You'll get another dress,' I say, in my most persuasive tone.

'Mum, this is *serious*.'

'I know. I'm sorry. I stand corrected.'

Robbie already has tomato sauce on his chin and he wipes it off with the back of his sleeve. 'Don't help him, Mum. Don't take his side.'

'I'm not doing it for his sake. I'm doing it for yours. I want you to have a dad you can turn to.'

'We brought out the best in him; Erika doesn't,' Lauren says. 'I don't understand why he doesn't see that.'

'I know what you mean,' I say. 'And before I forget, I think you're both great kids and I'm very proud of you.' I kiss them on the tops of their heads. 'Of course, you have the advantage, Lauren, because you don't make a mess with food like your brother does.' I hold a plate under Robbie's chin to catch a sliver of tomato that falls from his mouth.

'That's why we have Benson,' he says.

'No one will ever marry you if you eat like a pig,' Lauren tells him.

'Yeah, and I really want to get married.'

She sticks her tongue out at him.

'Another small matter,' I say, rubbing my hands on my

jeans. I'm nervous about broaching the Kirsty/Emily connection, but know it has to be done. I daren't spurn O'Reilly's
advice. He's right about me and my bleeding heart. I tend
to see the good in people and that's not always wise. 'I need to
talk to you about the case.'

'It's fine,' Lauren says. 'Detective Inspector O'Reilly told
us that they have someone with fingerprints.'

'Everyone has fingerprints, Lauren,' Robbie says, laughing.

'You know what I mean.' She nudges him hard in the ribs.
'They've got matching ones. It's that girl you talked about,
Mum. Tess Williams.'

'Williamson,' I say.

'Yeah, her.'

Robbie, the king of distraction, is back to flicking through
the channels, and he finds an old episode of *Doctor Who*.
'Look, Lauren!' he says. 'This was the one where that kid
went around saying "Are you my mummy?"'

He says, *'Are you my mummy?'* in a spooky voice and
Lauren immediately starts giggling.

'It was a really scary episode!' She collapses on to his
shoulder. 'I'll never sleep tonight.'

'Watch it through your fingers,' he tells her.

'Pause it just now, Robbie,' I tell him. 'I really need to speak
to you both.'

'What about?' Lauren says.

'About trusting people.'

'What do you mean?'

'She means taking sweets from strangers,' Robbie clarifies,
pausing the action on the screen just as the Doctor comes
out of the TARDIS.

Lauren makes an incredulous face. 'I'm *eleven*, Mum. And
I'm not a complete idiot.'

'I know and I don't mean to insult either of you, but what
we're going through is unusual and dangerous. And danger

often comes from the most ordinary people. People who you might not expect to hurt you — for example, teenage girls.'

'Like Tess?'

'Well, no . . .' I stop. 'I'm thinking of Emily Jones.'

'Emily?' Robbie says. 'Why her?'

'Emily has not been completely honest with any of us. Her real name is Kirsty Stewart and she has very deliberately engineered a way to get to know us all.'

'What?' Robbie starts laughing. 'Mum, this isn't more of you playing Miss Marple, is it?'

'No. What I'm telling you is absolutely true.'

'Emily wouldn't make stuff up!' Lauren cries out, and with her attention diverted Robbie swipes a piece of her toastie. 'She's really nice!'

'You're right. There is a side of her that's really nice, but there's also a side of her that . . . isn't. She admitted to me today that she was the one who painted on the wall and that she was also the person who spiked your drink, Robbie.'

Both children are staring at me with their mouths open. 'I'm sorry I had to tell you this but, for your own safety, you mustn't have anything else to do with her. I don't expect she'll come to the hockey club on Friday, Robbie, but if she does—'

'Hang on, hang on!' Robbie brings his hands together in a T-shape. 'Time out, Mum. This doesn't make any sense. Why would Emily do all that?'

'Well . . .' I'm loath to tell them about the exact circumstances of Sandy's death. 'Emily feels she has good reason not to like me.'

'But she does like you, Mum!' Lauren says. 'She told me! "Your mum's really cool," she said.'

'Lauren.' I take both her hands. 'Please believe me when I say that some people are very good at lying. What school has Emily told you she goes to?'

'The high school in Barnton.'

'She doesn't. She recently left school – Sanderson Academy. It's a school for the performing arts.'

'But, why?' Her eyes grow as large as an antelope's. 'Why would she lie to us?'

'Because she has a grievance against me.'

'What grievance?' Robbie says.

'It's complicated.'

'You can explain it to us,' Lauren says, trying to smile. 'You're good at explaining things.'

'It's not . . .' I look at both their faces: solemn, still and listening hard to everything I say. 'I don't want to tell you exactly what happened because it . . .' *shows me up in a bad light* . . . 'because it's not . . .' I take a big breath. 'I'm ashamed.'

'Mum, you're scaring me!' Lauren says, grabbing at my knees and shaking them. 'Just tell us!'

'Okay . . . well.' I run my tongue around the inside of my mouth, find it dry and take a sip of Lauren's juice. 'Back when I was a junior doctor, I looked after Emily's pregnant mum. Emily, who as I've explained is actually called Kirsty, hadn't been born yet and her mum was very ill. She had a brain tumour.'

'No wait, Mum!' Lauren butts in. 'Emily and Kirsty can't be the same person, because Emily's mum's not sick. She's a teacher at a primary school.'

'No, sweetheart. That isn't true. Emily *is* Kirsty, and her mum died eighteen years ago. Her father never remarried. Kirsty has been in foster care since she was about ten.'

Lauren deflates back in her seat, thinking hard, trying to come up with some fact or observation that will prove me wrong.

'And you were the doctor when Kirsty was born?' Robbie says.

'Yes. I didn't deliver the baby, but I was working on the

neurosurgical ward that Sandy, Kirsty's mother, had been admitted to.'

'So . . .' Robbie looks up into the corner of the room as he thinks. 'What made Emily or Kirsty or whoever she is come after us?'

'I made a mistake,' I say quietly. 'And Kirsty read about it in her father's diaries.'

'A mistake with her mother's care?' Robbie says.

'Yes.'

Robbie stares up at the ceiling again, thinking it through. He gets there before Lauren does and I watch his face blanch with horror. 'Jesus, Mum. You didn't hurt her . . . did you? I mean, you didn't . . . kill her or anything, did you?'

'I did. I caused her premature death.' There are tears on my cheeks and I wipe them away with the back of my hand. 'It was an accident and her mother—'

'What?' Lauren stands up and her plate falls to the floor and breaks into four pieces, the cracking sound loud enough to make Benson squeal and run for his bed. 'You killed Emily's *mother?*'

'Kirsty's mother. And it was—'

'Oh my God!' Lauren's face is crumpling. I recognise her expression from my own face in the mirror on recent occasions. Everything feels so bleak that she can't even cry. 'You're the murderer?'

'Lauren, please give me a chance to explain.'

'I'm not listening to you!' she shrieks and pushes past me, running up the stairs, her footsteps heavy, her breathing erratic, and when she gets to her room she slams the door so violently that the whole house shakes.

'Lauren!' I stand at the bottom of the stairs and call up to her. 'Please come back so that we can talk about it.' No answer. 'Lauren, please!' Still no answer, and I know from past experience that I'm wasting my time. I'll have to give her a chance to absorb the information and make sense of it as best she can before she'll be willing to talk to me again.

And then there's Robbie's reaction. He's not as shocked as his sister, but still, his limbs are trembling and he's looking at me warily, as if I've suddenly grown another head. 'That's heavy shit, Mum. That's really heavy shit.'

'I know, love.'

'How did it happen? Why did we never know about this? What's . . .' His head shakes from side to side. 'I mean . . . did you get into trouble for it?'

'No, I didn't get into trouble. I tried to resign, but my consultant said I needed to just get on and be a better doctor because of it.' Benson, upset by the commotion, jumps up on my knee and I stroke him under his chin. 'I'm sure I would have told you when you were older. I certainly would have told you if you'd trained to be a doctor. Patients dying because of medical error is not as unusual as you might think.'

'So how did it happen?'

'I gave her a drug she was allergic to.'

'And was she going to be cured or . . . ?'

'She wasn't going to be cured. She was going to die from the brain tumour. But the fact remains that I did cause her to die sooner than she should have.'

'Jesus.' His arms are still now, but his legs are shaking up and down and his eyes are wide and blinking every couple of seconds. 'Does Dad know?'

'Dad and Leila and Archie all know. It was a huge deal for me and it took me a while to get over it, but I was pregnant with you and I had to put it behind me.' I start crying again. Telling the children has been harder than I thought. I feel a mixture of intense shame and regret and I can only hope I haven't damaged my relationship with them, especially Lauren, who's too young to appreciate the complications that adult life can bring.

'Mum.' Robbie comes across and puts his arms around me. 'It's okay. You're not a bad person. Everyone makes mistakes. You were just really unlucky.' He rocks me in his arms and I let him, touched by his kindness and understanding.

When I've stopped crying, we both go upstairs to see whether we can tempt Lauren out of her room. She's wedged a chair against the door and is refusing to talk to me, so I leave Robbie to see whether he can get through to her and go back downstairs to work my way through a pile of ironing, Radio Four on as company. Before I start on it, I call Leila at home, hoping that she might be able to pop round for an hour. Archie answers and tells me that Leila is out with her brothers' wives and he isn't expecting her home until late. I'll have to wait a bit longer for my heart-to-heart – lunchtime tomorrow, not ideal when we're both at work, but, weather permitting, we can always go out and sit on a park bench. I need to talk to her about what's going on before I burst open with the worry of it all. Leila will have a reasoned, balanced perspective on the whole thing. She's known for giving sound advice and I need her now more than I ever have.

Robbie comes downstairs just before ten to tell me that Lauren finally opened the door for him and is now in her bed. 'She's pretty upset,' he says.

'Do you think I should try and have a word with her?'

'I'd wait for a bit, if I was you.' He gives me a hug. 'You know what she's like, Mum. She makes a massive fuss and then she comes round.'

'This is quite a big bombshell for her to recover from, though, isn't it?'

'Yeah.' He rests against the worktop and blows out a lungful of air. 'It's weird. I've known Emily for nine months and I had no idea she was scoping our family. Bit of a dark horse.' He sighs. 'Well, I'd better go to bed. See what tomorrow brings.' He kisses me on the cheek. 'See you in the morning, Mum.'

'Sleep well, Robbie.' I hug him tight for a second. 'And thank you.'

I stay downstairs for a while longer to finish the ironing and tidy the kitchen. When I go up to bed the house is completely still apart from the usual creaking and settling of floorboards. I open Robbie's door and tiptoe into his room. I could in fact be banging a drum or playing a trumpet because he's a sound sleeper and would slumber through a rocket launching in the back garden. He's splayed out all over the bed like a starfish, his duvet kicked off and his clothes lying in a heap beside him. I look down at him for a minute or more and then I sneak into Lauren's room and find her fast asleep and breathing softly, curled up in a ball at the very edge of her bed because most of the space is taken up with her soft toys: a menagerie of animals from a furry brown mole to a tiger larger than a toddler. When her friends come to stay she hides them at the back of the cupboard, and as soon as they're gone she pulls them out again and arranges them on top of her duvet. Like most children, in some ways she's mature for her age, in others she's not. She's ahead of herself academically and is a good runner because she's small and fast, but physically and emotionally, she's a late developer.

I kiss her gently on the forehead, letting my hand rest on her hair for a few precious seconds before she turns over in her sleep, resettling herself next to a gorilla and a short-necked giraffe. As I'm creeping out again, I notice a pile of torn-up paper on her desk and I open the door a tad more so that the light from the hallway shines directly on to the pieces of paper. It's the newspaper clippings and scrapbook. She's torn the photograph of the three of us, taken just before the award ceremony, into tiny blow-away pieces. A larger photograph of me, published in the paper some months ago, has a red pen through my face, obliterating my eyes and tearing through my mouth.

14

The next day I get up at six thirty, as I always do, and spend the first half an hour showering, dressing and preparing for the day ahead. I'm still worried about Lauren's reaction last night and I'm hoping that she'll have calmed down – things never seem quite so bad in the clear morning light. She's not a great eater but she does love waffles for breakfast, so I haul the waffle maker out from the back of the cupboard and make a start on the batter, then go up to Robbie's attic room and knock several times on his door, shouting loudly, 'Time to get up, love!' No reply. 'I'm making waffles!'

'Okay.' I hear the wooden boards creak as his feet hit the floor.

'They'll be ready in five minutes.' I take a deep breath, go down the stairs and stop in front of Lauren's door. *Act normal.* 'Seven o'clock, Lauren! Time to get up!' No answer. 'Is it okay if I come in?' Still no answer, so I turn the door handle and peek my head around the door, seeing first her empty bed and then Lauren herself, sitting at her desk, in full school uniform, her hair brushed and her bag next to her feet. 'You're up already! Well done!' I come into her room and stand next to her. 'I'm making waffles for breakfast.' She doesn't look at me. She's keeping her eyes focused on the pile of torn-up newspaper. 'Lauren, I'm sorry about last night.' I hunker down beside her and look up into her pinched and solemn face. 'I know you must be very disappointed in me.' I reach my hand out towards her but she shrinks away from my touch. 'Lauren?'

'I want to stay with Dad.'

'I know you're hurt. I understand that.'

'I want to stay with Dad!' she shouts, the force of her words sending me backwards into a sitting position on the floor. Her face is a challenging glare and I realise that being apologetic isn't going to work. It looks as if she's been stewing in her own anger and disappointment all night.

I bring myself back up on to my feet and say, 'Breakfast will be ready in a few minutes.' Then I leave her bedroom door open and go back to the kitchen, beating the batter with a whisk until some of my nervous anxiety dissipates.

Robbie appears moments later and collapses on to a stool at the breakfast bar. 'Lauren still in a mood?'

'I'm afraid so.'

'She'll get over it.' He tips cornflakes and milk into a bowl. 'It's just a bit of a shock, that's all.'

'The trouble is, though, at her age you see your parents as good people and first her dad has disappointed her and now I have. Big time.' I drop batter on to the hot waffle iron. 'So big, in fact, that she's saying she wants to go and live with your dad.'

'No way.' He shovels a spoonful of cereal into his mouth. 'She hates being there. Erika's too strict and they only ever play classical music. It's like being at a funeral.'

'Still, I think Lauren sees it as the lesser of the evils.'

'Have we got that squirty cream that comes out of the can?'

'We do.' I fetch it out of the fridge and show it to him.

'That'll bring her down. I'll go and get her.'

I stand at the bottom of the stairs and listen as he tries to persuade her to come for breakfast. I can hear what he's saying but not Lauren's replies. 'Come on, Lauren. Don't be so moody.' A couple of seconds, and then, 'So Mum made a mistake! It's not the end of the world. She's still our mum.' Almost a full minute before Robbie says, 'Everybody has to lie sometimes! Mum's no different.' And then, finally, 'You know how much you like waffles. And we've got that cream as well. Are you coming, or not?'

I'm back in the kitchen by the time they both appear. I arrange a cluster of food on the breakfast bar: half a dozen waffles, cream, sugar and a big pile of strawberries. Lauren gets on to her stool and stares down at the surface but doesn't put anything on her plate. I hold a glass of orange juice out towards her. She doesn't take it, so Robbie does, putting it directly in front of her hand. Then he puts a waffle on her plate and one on his own. 'Cream?' He shakes the can beside her and she moves her head away. 'Suit yourself.' He squirts some cream on to his waffle, layers strawberries on top and bites into it.

I sit down opposite them with a coffee and it triggers Lauren into speech.

'Everything that's been happening in our family is because of you,' Lauren says, her eyes glittering with an intensity that makes me wince. 'We were all really worried and it turns out this is all your fault.' I don't remember her ever looking at me with so much hatred, but at least she *is* looking at me now. It feels like an advance on being ignored.

'I know. And, believe me—'

'You lie. You say that Emily's a liar but you lie too.' She grabs my bag and pulls the Sanderson Academy brochure out of it. 'You said this was for a patient of yours, but it wasn't, was it?'

'No, it wasn't. I was following clues and I ended up there.'

'That's not what you said to me.'

'Parents don't always tell their children everything because it isn't always appropriate.'

'So you lie instead?'

'Not usually, I—'

'Everyone thinks you're *great*,' she says. 'My friends think you're the best mother ever. You're always nice to everyone. You do charity work. You won that award.' She pushes her plate away and stands up. 'I thought you were great too, but you're not.' She picks up her school bag. 'No wonder Dad left you.'

'Lauren!' Robbie says, looking from her to me and back again. 'Steady on!'

Lauren's not listening. She's opening the front door and is out on the path just as Leila pulls up and sounds her horn. Robbie grabs the rest of the waffles and I carry his school bag out to the car. Leila's doing the school run this morning and already has her four children in the back of her seven-seater. She sees me coming and gives me a hopeful look. We haven't spoken since I found out she'd lied about Sandy's baby, but that's of little consequence now, and I come up to her open window and say quietly, 'Can we talk today? I could really do with a friend.'

'Of course!' She jumps out of the car to hug me. 'Archie told me you'd called. I'm glad you've forgiven me. I will never, ever lie to you again. Cross my heart and hope to die.' She moves her finger in a cross-shaped motion over her chest, and looks at me with earnest eyes. 'Are you okay?' She holds my shoulders. 'You look like you've been crying.'

'I have. And I think I'm about to start again.'

'Oh, God, Liv. What's going on?'

'I don't want to be late, Mum.' Jasmine's leaning out of the window. 'I have to practise my recorder before music lesson.'

'If you practised it in the evening like you're supposed to,' Leila calls back, 'it wouldn't always be such a rush.'

'You should go, Leila,' I say, smiling. 'I'll catch you at work.'

I kiss her cheek. 'Set aside your whole lunch hour. It's going to take a while.'

I wave goodbye to them all – everyone waving back apart from Lauren who's making a point of looking in the opposite direction – then I go inside to gather myself together for the day. Just as I'm locking the front door, the post arrives and I have a quick glance through it. The one that gets my attention is a thick, textured, vanilla-coloured envelope, made from the sort of paper that only lawyers can afford to use and when I open it, sure enough, it's from my solicitor telling me that Phil's solicitor has been in touch. A photocopy of the 'request' from Phil's solicitor that we review child custody arrangements is also enclosed. There's no obligation for me to do as much – it's barely five months since we drew up the agreement – but in light of Phil's marriage and his future wife's commitment to 'provide a nurturing environment for Lauren and Robert', my cooperation would be appreciated. I stare at the letter for a few long seconds then put it into my doctor's case and set off for work. I'll call my solicitor after nine. It's typical of Phil to neglect to warn me that a letter was on the way and I try not to let it unsettle me, but inevitably it does because I'm already perched on the curve of a towering set of worries and one more might just unbalance me completely.

When I arrive at the surgery, I close my door behind me and check through my emails – good, normal, doctorly stuff for me to get my teeth into. It works for about ten minutes and then I start to worry about the promises I made yesterday – two conflicting promises: one to Kirsty and the other to O'Reilly. I promised Kirsty that I'd call her today and that we would discuss ways to help her put her mother's death into perspective. And I promised O'Reilly that I wouldn't have anything else to do with Kirsty. I don't want to let Kirsty down but, equally, I have to take O'Reilly's advice. If only

Phil and I weren't at such loggerheads, I could ask him for help with Kirsty. Professionally, he is well respected, and I'm sure he'd be able to refer her to one of his colleagues.

Thinking of Phil reminds me about the letter and I bring it out of my bag to reread it. It's long-winded and jargon-heavy, but I use a neon highlighter to illuminate the sentences that concern me and then make the call to my solicitor. It takes a couple of minutes before I'm put through and when we start speaking, I'm mindful of an imaginary meter ticking away, like in a taxi, except this one goes up in tens of pounds, not tens of pence. 'Would you mind just giving me the bottom line?' I say, cutting through his legalese. 'Sorry, but my surgery starts in a minute.'

'Absolutely. Scots law is concerned with the child's best interest. Unless there's evidence that you're no longer providing a stable environment for the children then the current agreement will stand. As Robbie is almost eighteen, this really only concerns Lauren.' He gives me a couple more details and finishes with, 'I'll word a suitable reply to Phil's solicitor and send you a copy in the post.'

'Thank you.' I put the phone down and it rings again immediately, a button flashing to tell me it's reception.

'Could you squeeze in an extra couple of patients, Liv? Leila's not coming in this morning.'

'How come? I saw her less than an hour ago. She was taking my kids to school.'

'It's only just happened. Her daughter fell over in the playground and has broken her arm. Leila won't be in until later, if at all.'

'Which daughter?'

'Jasmine, I think. She's the only one at primary school now, isn't she?'

'Yes, she is.' My heart sinks for Jasmine and Leila but mostly, I must admit, for myself and our missed lunch date.

'Okay. No problem. Just give me ten minutes to organise myself.'

I send a quick text to Leila, sending my love and sympathy, and she comes back almost immediately.

I'm so sorry. Really wanted to catch up with you. Hopefully we won't be waiting in a long queue. Hospitals L

My morning passes in a rush – a conveyor belt of patients and their relatives, and I try to give each one the attention they deserve. It keeps me too busy to think about my own life, and when lunchtime comes and goes and Leila still isn't back, I offer to take half of her home visits too. I collect the list from the receptionist and head off without even looking at the names. The first two are fairly straightforward and I read their notes in the car then go in for the visits. The third and final one is Audrey Williamson – Tess's mother. According to her notes she called up this morning asking for an urgent visit from Dr Campbell. I call the surgery to ask the receptionist what the problem is and the receptionist tells me that Mrs Williamson refused to say, but insisted that it was very important she see a doctor today. 'And in light of the fact that she has diabetes and isn't long out of hospital,' the receptionist tells me, 'I didn't feel it was my place to push too hard.'

'Fair enough.' I pull up outside their front door, wondering whether the police have spoken to Tess again yet, and wondering also what O'Reilly will think about me going into her house. *But you're going as a doctor, to see her mother,* I remind myself. *And Tess should really be at school.*

I ring the doorbell and Mrs Williamson answers. 'Dr Somers!' She tries to smile through her anxiety. 'I wasn't expecting you; I was expecting Dr Campbell.'

'I know and I'm sorry about that. Unfortunately, Dr Campbell has had to take the day off and I'm covering her cases.'

'I see.'

'If you'd prefer to only see Dr Campbell then I completely understand.'

'Not at all.' She opens the door wider. 'In fact, I think it's better that it's you. Please come in.' She hustles me through the front door and into the living room, where two ginger cats, sitting at either end of the windowsill, appraise me disdainfully then go back to licking their paws.

'How are you keeping, Mrs Williamson?'

'Not too bad, thank you.' Her smile is easier now but nevertheless, she doesn't look well. Her skin lacks lustre, her hair is chopped into an unflattering bob and she has a visible tremor in both her hands. 'I worry far more about Tess than I do about myself.'

'Is she back at school today?'

'She's upstairs. The police were here this morning and her father's on business in Germany so I sat with her while they questioned her but . . .' She stops and shakes her head, stares up at the ceiling and then back at me. 'I know your family has been having some troubles, and somehow Tess has been brought to the police's attention, but I really don't think she has anything to do with it.'

'I don't think Tess is behind it either,' I assure her. 'But let's talk about what's troubling you.'

'Tess. Tess is troubling me.'

'But you asked for Dr Campbell to come out and see you, didn't you?'

'Yes, but only because I didn't want to say what the real problem was.' She takes a step towards me. 'Between you and me, Dr Somers, her dad will not be happy about this. You see, Tess is not like her two older sisters.' She waves towards the wall, where two girls wearing graduation robes smile into the room. 'I know we have high standards in our family and have always expected a lot of the girls, but Tess doesn't have their drive or their confidence. This is another week when I haven't been able to get her to go to school. And now all this trouble with Kirsty Stewart.' Her voice cracks. 'Frankly, it's difficult to remember I'm a Christian when I think about that girl. She's a nasty piece of work. She's bullied Tess since day one, and have the school listened? No. Because she's a wonderful actress and she'll no doubt go on to great things and the fact that she's an *impossible* bully and a downright *bitch* will all be forgotten.' Her cheeks flush. 'Pardon my language but you can't believe what . . .' She shakes her head. 'I'm at my wits' end.'

'I can see that,' I say, unsure as to how Kirsty can still be causing Tess such serious problems when she no longer goes to Sanderson. 'Now, why don't we try to plan a way forward?'

'George, my husband, says we shouldn't give in to bullying and I agree with him. But you have to understand that we're a conventional family and choosing Sanderson Academy for Tess was not a decision we took lightly. Wherever Tess goes, she struggles to fit in, and we thought this school would help but . . . well.' She purses her lips. 'Tess has a lot of growing up to do.'

'Why don't we wait for Dr Campbell to come back tomorrow? I know that Tess usually sees her.'

'But Tess saw you last time, didn't she?'

'She did but . . .' This is difficult. 'To be frank, Mrs Williamson, I don't want to step on anyone's toes and bearing in mind the fact that Tess—'

'What's going on?' We both turn and see Tess standing at the entrance to the living room, her mouth hanging open in surprise. She is still in her pyjamas and is wearing thick socks and a long cardigan. Her shoulders are slumped and greasy hair hangs down over her face.

'Hello, Tess,' I say. 'How are you feeling?'

'Fine.' She sits down on the couch, holding herself towards the edge.

'I'll just make us a cup of tea while you two chat,' Mrs Williamson says, running off to the kitchen. 'I bought some homemade shortbread at St Bede's coffee morning.'

'Thank you but I'm not able to stay for tea,' I shout out, hoping to make a speedy exit. Much as I believe Tess to be Kirsty's victim, I'm not inclined to get involved. The waters are muddy enough as it is. 'I need to get back to the surgery.'

'It's not my fault,' Tess says, grabbing my arm. 'I don't want to do what Kirsty says.' She shudders and uses her other hand to pull her cardigan in around herself. 'She forces me to go along with her.'

'Tess.' I try to move past her but she's holding on tight and, to make matters worse, one of the ginger cats has jumped off the windowsill and is wrapping itself around my legs. 'Have you told the police the truth about your involvement with Kirsty?'

'Yes.' Although she goes to a school for the performing arts she is patently lying, the wash of uncertainty that passes across her face a dead giveaway.

'Look, Tess, I don't blame you for any of this,' I say, detaching her fingers from my sleeve. 'I know Kirsty is bullying you, but in order for you to break free of her, you need to be honest with the police. And as she doesn't go to school with you any more, I can't imagine it will be that difficult.'

Her eyes are downcast. 'You don't understand.'

'What do I not understand?'

'You didn't tell my mum I was on the pill, did you?' she says, raising her eyes just enough to see into mine.

'Of course not. That information is confidential.'

'My parents are really strict.'

'They don't know you have a boyfriend?'

'They don't know anything about me.' She blushes. 'If they did they'd go mad. They'd throw me out.'

'Well . . . it's difficult being sixteen. Parents don't always see us the way we see ourselves. But you're of an age where your sex life is your business, and if you want to talk to me about it then you should make an appointment and come to the surgery.'

More downcast eyes, and I'm beginning to wonder whether she has a genuine reason to be afraid of her parents. It's a sad fact that child abuse is always a consideration when a young person is unhappy and unable to express the exact reason why. 'You know, we have a counsellor attached to the practice who could help you with any worries you might have. Worries to do with your parents or your boyfriend—'

'Kirsty won't stop,' she says, and for the first time there's conviction in her eyes. 'Not until she gets what she wants.'

'The person Kirsty wants to hurt is me,' I say. 'I'm sure she'll leave you alone now.'

'You're wrong.' It's barely a whisper and I lean forward to hear more. 'You don't know what she's like.'

'Why does Kirsty have such a hold over you?' I say.

'She knows about me.'

'Knows what about you?'

Her eyes dart across to the window and then over to the door. 'She saw me doing something and she said she'd put it on Facebook.'

'What sort of thing?'

'I can't say, but she has pictures.' Her face flushes. 'My parents, they just wouldn't . . . I mean, I couldn't . . .' She gives up, defeated.

'Tess, I can see that life is tough for you at the moment,' I say slowly. 'So it's no wonder your confidence has taken a knocking, but—'

'It'll be over soon,' she says, standing up beside me. 'I know it will be.'

'How do you know that?'

'I just do.' She shrugs. 'She has more in store for you, you know.' Her expression is pitying. 'You should be careful.'

When I get back to work, I'm feeling brittle enough to break. I can't get Tess's final comment out of my head. I know she's only sixteen and I know teenage girls are prone to melodrama, but in this case I don't think her reaction was an exaggeration. I try calling O'Reilly but he isn't available and once more I wish I had Leila to talk to. Her phone is switched off so I call Archie. It isn't good news. He tells me that Jasmine's fracture was complicated and she's been given a general anaesthetic to insert a metal pin. She has to stay in hospital overnight and Leila will stay with her. 'So Leila won't be in to work tomorrow, I'm afraid,' he says. 'I'd take time off but we're backed up here.'

'Give them both my love, won't you?' I say to Archie. 'I won't bother Leila today. I'll wait and talk to her when she's home.'

It's my evening for volunteering at the centre but I'm wishing now that I'd cancelled. Lauren is never far from my mind and I hope she hasn't had too miserable a day at school. I think about the impact my confession will have had on her. Nothing's ever as simple with Lauren as it is with Robbie. Even when he was small, Robbie was able to shrug his shoulders and make the best of things. But Lauren has sensitive feelings and a strong sense of right and wrong. She wants everything to be fair and just, and so learning that her mother is only human – she makes mistakes; fatal ones that have ongoing consequences – will be a challenge for her.

I need to try to speak to her again, see whether I can help her to understand. I call Martin at the centre to cancel my evening surgery. 'I have a lot going on at home at the moment and really need to be with my kids.' Buoyed up by our recent success, nothing can dampen his mood and he tells me that it's not a problem. We have a small list of volunteer doctors who'll cover for me and he'll start making calls at once.

Lauren should be at Amber's house by now and I call her mother Elizabeth to tell her that I'm coming to collect her early. 'Lauren's not here, Liv,' Elizabeth tells me. 'She says there was a change of plan and that she was going to her dad's today.'

'But it's Thursday. She always comes to you on a Thursday.'

'That's what I said, but she told me she'll be spending more time with her dad now.'

I shut my eyes.

'Sorry, Liv. Should I have said no?'

'It's not your fault. It's mine. I should have warned you she was in a foul mood this morning and she's doing this to punish me.'

'I rang Phil to check, of course, and he said he'd come down to the hospital entrance to meet her. I dropped her off there. She was with him when I left.'

Great. Can my life grow any more difficult? I grab my keys and bag and head out to my car. I'm sure Phil was delighted to get the call. More power to his campaign to have shared custody of the children. I don't want to make a scene – goodness knows I'm in Lauren's bad books enough as it is – but I want her to see that I'm making an effort to speak with her. I just need to make sure that I don't end up having a full-blown argument with Phil.

I'll be calm, I tell myself. *I will.*

There's a space in the hospital car park – first stroke of luck – and I'm feeling like fate might just give me a little bit more of the same, when I bump into Erika in the corridor. 'Hello,' I say. 'I'm looking for Lauren and Phil. Are they in his office?'

'Olivia.' She smiles. I wait. 'Yes, Philip is in his office but—'

'Thank you.' I run past her and up the stairs, feeling rude

for not listening to the end of the sentence but I can't bear
the slow rhythm of her speech. When I get to Phil's office, I
don't bother knocking; I just go straight in. Phil's the only
person in the room and is sitting behind his desk talking on
the phone. 'Where's Lauren?' I ask him.

He puts his hand over the mouthpiece. 'She's in the canteen
with her friend.'

'What friend? Elizabeth didn't mention that she had one
of her classmates with her.' Phil ignores me and resumes
talking to whoever's on the end of the line. 'What friend?' I
say, much louder this time, and he frowns across at me.

'I'll call you back later, Ed. Thank you for your advice.'
He puts the phone back on the cradle and stands up. 'Olivia,
I don't appreciate you barging into my office like this.'

'And I don't appreciate you allowing Lauren to come here
when she's supposed to be at Amber's.'

'She's my daughter and she was upset. What did you expect
me to say? No?'

'Well you don't appear to be looking after her!'

'She met a friend downstairs and they've gone to have a
Coke.'

'What friend? And how could she have met a friend
here?'

'The girl was visiting a relative.'

'And Lauren knows her? Are you sure?'

'Yes. She was playing with Lauren on Sunday, at Leila's.'

A queasy panic fills the spaces inside my skull. 'What's the
girl's name?'

'Emily, I think she said.'

'Sweet Jesus.' I hold my hand over my mouth to contain
the maelstrom of sound that's building in my chest.

'Erika's just gone down to fetch Lauren,' Phil says. 'She's
going to do her homework with her. Ah! – here she is.'

The door to Phil's office is still open and Erika glides in.

'Lauren isn't downstairs, Philip.' Pause. 'I looked in the toilets too but—'

I have my phone out of my bag and am calling Lauren's mobile before Erika finishes her sentence. It goes straight to answering service. 'Lauren, it's me,' I say. 'Please call me at once. Or call Dad or Robbie. We're extremely worried. Please call.'

'What's going on?' Phil says.

'That girl is Kirsty Stewart!' I shout. 'Trevor Stewart's baby from all those years ago. The baby that you and Leila told me was dead.'

'What are you talking about? She said her name was Emily.'

'She was lying!'

'How would Lauren know her?'

'Hello?' I'm on the phone again. 'I need to speak to DI O'Reilly. It's extremely urgent.' I keep the phone to my ear but look at Phil. 'Lauren knows her as Emily Jones, a friend of Robbie's.'

'Dr Somers?' The sound of O'Reilly's voice releases some of my tension. I fill him in on what's happened and he says he'll come to the hospital immediately. 'Get hold of Robbie,' he tells me. 'He should come to the hospital too. Better to keep you all in one place.'

'Okay.' I end the call and give Erika my mobile. 'Could you call Robbie for me, please?' I say. 'The police want him to come here immediately. Ask him to get a taxi. Perhaps you could meet him at the door and pay for it.'

'Of course.'

She leaves the room and I close the door behind her. There's a hollow ache inside my throat and I reach for the glass of water on Phil's desk and drink it down. 'Please call Lauren's mobile,' I say to Phil. 'She might answer when she sees it's you.'

He does it without question, his jaw tight and his face pale, but she doesn't answer him either, so he leaves a message. Panic is building inside me, a pressure cooker of fear and trepidation. Tess warned me that Kirsty had more in store for me, but she couldn't have known that Lauren would be coming here instead of going to Amber's. It has to have been a chance meeting which means that Kirsty won't have planned anything and that must be good, mustn't it?

Phil is pacing the floor, up and down, up and down, and then he stops beside his desk and bangs a book down hard on the surface. 'Why didn't I know about this connection with the two girls?'

'Why didn't you know? *Why didn't you know?*' I step right into his personal space. 'Because you don't live with us any more. And because you buggered off from the police station instead of sticking around to listen to what I had to say!'

'You weren't making any sense in the police station!' He throws his arms out. 'Now, will you please tell me what's going on?'

'Okay.' I fold my arms across my chest and tell him about the Kirsty/Emily connection, the fact that she befriended Robbie and the fact that she admitted to spiking his drink and painting on the wall.

'Why didn't you warn the children that this girl was dangerous?'

'I did! I told them last night. But I also had to tell them about Sandy Stewart and how she died. Robbie was okay with it but Lauren was angry and shocked. She could barely look at me this morning.'

'So help me God, Olivia,' he says, his expression steely. 'If Lauren is hurt because you've kept me in the dark—'

'Yes! Let's talk about keeping people in the dark!' I walk a few short steps around in a circle and come back to face him again. 'I found out that you went to see Trevor Stewart and told him he shouldn't call our house any more.'

He doesn't even falter. 'That was to protect you.'

'Protect me from what?'

'From yourself!' he shouts, uncharacteristically venting his anger. 'God knows you needed protecting!'

'Really?' I say. 'You honestly think that interfering in my life was about protecting me?'

'Hard as you find it to believe, throughout our marriage I did my best to protect you.'

'Well, in your *protecting* of me, you told Trevor I was the person who made the drug error that ended up killing his wife and that's the *only* reason Kirsty knows to take revenge on me and the children.' Fear washes across his face. 'So look to yourself, Phil. Look to your bloody self.'

The door opens. Erika again. 'Robbie is on his way,' she says. 'I had to come back upstairs because I forgot . . . my purse.'

'Erika?' I say loudly.

'Yes?' Her expression is startled.

'You should be very careful of marrying Phil. Soon he'll be deciding what you eat and drink, who your friends are, and when and where you're allowed to spend time with them.' I'm addressing Erika but I'm eyeball to eyeball with Phil. 'And if you do something he really doesn't like, then he'll start lying to you. He'll tell you it's for your own protection but it won't feel like that. It'll feel like a betrayal.' I should stop now because the air is beginning to crackle around us. 'You'll never be enough for him and you'll always have to try harder than he does because love isn't about giving for Phil, it's about control.'

Phil raises his hand then, and before I have time to react, he slaps me, quick and hard across my face. His signet ring is embossed, and the raised edge tears the skin across my cheekbone.

'Philip!' Erika shouts, and I stumble to one side, almost falling over with the unexpected force of his anger. Erika helps me right myself and Phil shrinks back towards the window. I haven't been hurt like this since my mother last hit me, and I'm shocked by the intensity of the pain and the humiliation. My skin is on fire, the sensation similar to a burn, and when I cup my aching cheek, I feel blood on my palm.

'You have a cut,' Erika says, frowning at my face with a concern that feels comforting and motherly. 'Philip, go down and meet Robbie,' Erika says, her tone surprisingly stern. 'He will be arriving in a moment.'

Phil walks towards the door and, as he passes me, he throws me a vicious stare. Erika takes my hand and leads me towards one of the two soft seats at the side of the room, then she busies herself in the small alcove where there's a fridge and a sink. When she comes across to sit next to me, she's carrying an ice pack, a glass of water and some painkillers. 'Anti-inflammatories,' she tells me.

I try to smile my thanks but can't locate the necessary muscles because my face pulses with an all-over pain that leaves no room for directed movement. She holds the ice pack against my swollen cheek and I flinch away from the intense cold, but she persuades me back towards it, making soft clucking noises with her tongue. Her kindness is so unexpected that I feel humbled. As I swallow the pills, my tongue gets in the way and my hands shake and some of the water spills down the side of the glass on to my top. And that's it. I've reached my threshold. I start crying loud, gulping tears, bigger than the biggest raindrops. I sound like a crazy person – a confused, tormented patient who has suffered more than she can bear. Erika holds my hands and supplies me with tissues and doesn't let up on her support until I empty my eyes. 'Thank you, Erika,' I say.

'You're most welcome.' She holds my hand. 'Is there anything else I can do to help you?'

'Do you still have my mobile?'

'Yes.'

'I want to call Lauren again.' My left eye is watering, my vision blurred, so Erika presses the buttons for me. Once again, Lauren's number goes straight to answering service. And then I remember that I have Kirsty's number too, so Erika connects me to her – 'this mobile is switched off.'

'Shit. It's hopeless.' My eyes fill up again just as the door opens and Phil, Robbie, O'Reilly and PC Bullworks come in to the room. 'What happened to your face?' O'Reilly says at once, and Robbie echoes him.

'I was dizzy. I fell and bashed my cheek on the table.'

Robbie puts his arm round me and O'Reilly turns narrowed eyes on Phil, who's in the corner whispering with Erika. O'Reilly and Bullworks seem to have mobilised half of the Edinburgh police force, and uniformed officers come in and out of the room, their radios crackling high up on the front of their stab vests. Every few minutes O'Reilly gives me an update – the hospital grounds have been searched and the girls are nowhere to be found; they're not at my house or Phil's flat; police officers have gone to Kirsty's flat but there's no sign of them there; no joy at the hockey club either – on and on, until my head is bursting with information that only increases my anxiety to a high-pitched scream. Robbie is holding my hands, agitating his legs up and down. 'Don't worry, Mum,' he keeps saying. 'She'll be fine.'

I nod as though I believe him. 'I'm going to the toilet,' I say, slipping out quietly before I draw more attention and have to listen to more bad news. There's a staff toilet at the end of the corridor and I walk there on shaky legs. A large, well-lit mirror reflects my face back at me. The left side is puffed up, my cheek pushing outward and upward to meet my bloodshot and watering eye. The cut along the crest of my cheekbone has stopped bleeding, the edges already coming together and, bad as it looks, I'm sure it's only soft tissue injury and will completely heal within a couple of days.

I'm still holding the ice pack and I take it with me into the cubicle, locking the door behind me before sitting down on the lid of the toilet. The numbness from the ice pack spreads from my cheek right through my head until I don't think or feel anything. I'm not me. I'm not here. Lauren is not in danger. I sit so still that I lose all sense of future and past and exist in an emotion-free state where my surroundings have flat-lined.

When my mobile rings, I jerk upright and my heart kicks in a rapid rhythm to remind me that I'm still alive. I'm both relieved and afraid to see that the name flashing on the screen is Emily. I answer at once. 'Kirsty? Is Lauren with you?'

'Yes.' There's a smile in her voice. 'Do you want her back?'

15

'Is Lauren okay?' I ask Kirsty, my mobile wedged to my ear.

'Lauren's fine. We're out walking. She's playing frisbee with Benson.'

I hadn't thought to ask the police whether Benson was at home. 'Can I talk to her?'

'She doesn't want to talk to you. She's a nicer kid than you deserve.'

I shut my eyes. 'Kirsty, please—'

'She asked me about my mother and I told her what you'd done.'

'Kirsty—'

'I know you went to visit Tess.'

'I wasn't visiting Tess. Her mother requested a home visit for herself.'

'You were supposed to call me today.'

'I couldn't call you.'

'Why not?'

'It's complicated.'

'I had this foster mother once, and she always used to say that. But what she really meant was that she didn't have time for me.'

There's no answer to that. I've told her I'm sorry and I know it isn't enough. I feel as though there's nothing else I can do or say, so I just let her talk.

'I was straight with you and I thought you were being straight with me. But all you've done is pass the buck to the police.

My flatmates told me the police have been looking for me all day today so I couldn't even go up to the ward to visit my dad in case the nurses had been told to report on me.' She gives a shaky laugh. 'But I have something else up my sleeve and I was about to set it off when Lauren texted me. She said she needed to speak to me and I thought – well, why not? She said she wasn't living with you any more and that I could meet her at the entrance to her dad's hospital. My dad's a burnt-out wreck taking up space on one of the wards while hers is a kingpin, but hey! As you pointed out, life isn't fair, is it?'

'What do you want, Kirsty?'

'I want you to call off the police and I want you to meet me tomorrow.'

'Okay. I'll try.'

'You need to do more than *try*,' she shouts.

'I realise that. What I mean is, I'll definitely meet you. But as far as calling off the police is concerned, I can try but I can't make—'

'Any promises?' She laughs. 'Well, we both know what your promises are worth.'

'Please, will you let Lauren go home?'

'Where are we meeting tomorrow?'

'You choose.'

'How about the café at Holy Corner? Ten o'clock. And don't tell the police.'

I tell her I won't and then say again, 'Please will you let Lauren go home?'

'I've not been stopping her.'

She tells me that they're in the park close to my house and that she'll leave Lauren there. I come out of the toilet and run back along the corridor to tell everyone the news. O'Reilly has a police officer stationed at my house and he calls him at once. Within minutes he reports that he's in the park, has found Lauren and that she's safe and sound.

'See, Mum!' Robbie says. 'I knew it would all be okay!'

I can't smile because my face is too swollen, but relief floods through me like water through a burst dam and I tip to one side, my legs caught in the flow. 'Let's get you home,' O'Reilly says, catching hold of my elbow to stop me from slamming up against the wall.

Grateful for his steadying hand, I let him lead me outside, and as I don't feel up to driving, I go in his car with him. We're just leaving the hospital grounds when he says, 'Did you really bash your cheek on the table?'

'Yes,' I say, unwilling to elaborate on my argument with Phil.

He gives me a quick, sideways glance before saying, 'What else did Kirsty say to you?'

'That she knows the police are looking for her.'

'We've been trying to find her all day but she hasn't been going to any of her usual places.'

'And she also said that I should persuade the police to leave her alone because she hasn't done anything wrong.'

He pulls up outside my front door and turns to look at me. 'And do you believe she hasn't done anything wrong?'

'No. I think she's definitely gone too far.'

'Good.' He climbs out of the car and opens the door for me. 'No more bleeding heart?'

'No more bleeding heart,' I say. 'Wait a second.' I hold his shirtsleeve to keep him on the pavement where no one can overhear us. 'I said I'd meet her at ten o'clock tomorrow, in the café at Holy Corner. She told me she has something else up her sleeve.'

'Okay.' He smiles. 'Well done. We'll pick her up and charge her with, at the very least, reckless endangerment and breaking and entering.'

We go indoors and Lauren's eyes widen with shock when she sees my cut and swollen face. She's about to run towards me when her expression shuts down and she hovers beside

Phil instead. 'You should never have left the hospital without telling me,' Phil is saying to her. 'We were all very worried.'

'I needed to speak to Emily,' Lauren answers, throwing herself at the sofa and pulling Benson up beside her.

'You know her name's not really Emily, don't you, Lauren?' O'Reilly says, sitting down opposite her. 'You understand that she's been lying to you.'

'She's not the only person who's been lying,' Lauren says, spearing a glance my way.

'Why don't you tell me how you met up with each other?' O'Reilly says, and Lauren sighs as if it's all a bore, then informs him that she was the one who got in touch first because she wanted to find out if what I'd told her was true.

'So Kirsty didn't force you to go with her?'

'No, I wanted to go,' Lauren tells him. 'We bought ice creams and then we took Benson to the park.'

'And what did you talk about?'

'Just about life, and how my mum killed her mum, and how her dad doesn't recognise her any more.' She thinks for a second then sends another piercing glare in my direction. 'You think waffles make everything better but they don't.'

'And did Kirsty ask you to do anything?' O'Reilly says to her.

'What do you mean?'

'Well . . . did she ask you to give her something from your house . . . or maybe she told you something that you have to keep secret from your parents?'

'No.'

'Are you sure?'

'I don't tell lies. Not like some people.'

'That's good,' O'Reilly says. 'But you do know that you can't trust Kirsty?'

'She's only behaving like this because of what happened to her mother.'

'But she's been threatening members of your family, Lauren,' he says. 'You need to stay away from her.'

'Okay.' She looks down at her feet. 'I want to go back with Dad.' Her eyes swing around to Robbie. 'Are you coming too?'

'No.' He shakes his head at her, clearly annoyed. 'This is where we live. You need to stop being such a child.'

'I *am* a child. And I'm going to pack.' She flounces out of the room, shoulders back, feet stamping, but it's more posture than real defiance because her eyes are full of tears. Robbie follows her and I'm left with O'Reilly, Phil and Erika. My face is pulsing with pain and I want nothing more than to lie down and lose myself to sleep.

'I'll be off, then,' O'Reilly says, and I see him to the door. 'I'll come here for eight o'clock tomorrow and we'll talk about how the meeting with Kirsty will pan out.'

'Okay.'

'And in the meantime we'll continue looking for Kirsty but I expect she'll be hard to find, so lock all your doors and remember to ring me if you're at all suspicious.'

'I will. Thank you.'

When he's on the front step he turns back towards me and reaches for the side of my face, gently laying the back of his hand against my sore cheek. 'He hit you, didn't he?' he says quietly.

I nod.

'Has he ever done it before?'

'No.'

'Were there any witnesses?'

'Only Erika.'

'You should let me file a report, charge him with assault.'

I make an aborted attempt at a laugh, stopping immediately because it hurts too much. 'There's enough animosity between us as it is.'

'You think it's okay for people to hit each other?'

'Of course not.' I remember the years of abuse meted out by my mother. 'My mother was handy with her fists. It's probably why I'm so soft with my own children. I can barely even bring myself to shout at them, never mind hit them.'

He moves a step closer. 'You going to be all right?'

'Yes.' His eyes are kind and it makes me want to cry again, so I fold my arms across my chest and look down at the step. 'I think so.'

'I'll be back first thing in the morning.' He rubs his hand down my upper arm and walks off along the path. 'Remember, I'm always on the end of the phone.'

I wait until he's driven off and then I go back into the hallway. Lauren has filled two huge blue Ikea bags: one with clothes, the other with soft toys and schoolbooks. She walks straight past me, dragging one and balancing the other on her shoulder. She has Phil's keys and she opens his car, then levers the bags up on to the edge of the boot and tips them in.

'Did you get my solicitor's letter this morning?' Phil says.

'Yes, and it changes nothing,' I say. 'I know Lauren is angry with me at the moment but she'll come round.'

'You need to stop being stubborn about this.'

'I'm not being stubborn. I have no intention of becoming a part-time parent. We drew up an agreement. We presented our affidavits to the court and they were accepted. That's the end of it.'

'Not as far as I'm concerned. My circumstances are changing and so must our arrangement.'

'Well, you should have thought of that sooner.'

'I will be pursuing it, Olivia. Erika and I are committed to greater involvement with the children.'

'You go for it, Phil. No judge will give you the time of day.' I tilt my head so that he has a perfect view of my bruised cheek. 'Now, if you don't mind, I'd like to get some ice for my face.'

I go into the kitchen and close the door behind me. Robbie is already in here, spooning dog food into Benson's dish. 'I've poured you a glass of wine, Mum,' he says, pointing to a full glass of red on the breakfast bar. 'And I've put two pizzas in the oven.'

'Are you perfect, or what?' I say, taking a bag of peas from the freezer and moulding them against my cheek. 'Boy, do I feel glad that today's almost over.' I drink back a few mouthfuls of wine and lean against the work surface to wait until the coast is clear. I don't want to set eyes on Phil for some time, if I can help it. I've had enough of him for one lifetime. And after the way Erika helped me this afternoon, I feel she's too good for him. She has to be shocked by the way he slapped me. O'Reilly's right – I should have him charged, or at the very least visit a doctor and have the incident recorded in case I need to use it against him in the future. Except that he's the children's father and the circumstances were extreme. I'd much rather we could keep a respectful distance and move forward with a semblance of harmony than be forever fighting in court.

When I hear Phil's car pulling away, I go through to the living room and sit down on a soft seat, putting the television on to distract me from the blank wall. Robbie stays in the kitchen to 'organise our meal'. I know he's trying to make up for Lauren's rejection of me and it warms my heart to see that he cares so much.

I keep the television volume low and think about what O'Reilly said about me and my bleeding heart. Up till now I've done my best to give credence to Kirsty's grievance against me, but what happened today was a step too far. I'm wondering what else she's planning and try to remember her exact words from the phone call – 'I have something else up my sleeve and I was about to set it off when Lauren texted me.'

I wonder whether the police will arrest Kirsty on her way into the café. Or perhaps O'Reilly is going to make me wear a wire. Does that really happen, or is it the stuff of television? I have a voice-recording facility on my mobile phone. It would have been useful if I'd recorded the first conversation I had with her, but at that stage I still saw her as the more harmless Emily. However, after today's phone call, she's lost my sympathy. It's as if she has no sense of boundaries. Sure, she might have mitigating circumstances, and as a doctor I can see that she's more in need of skilled counselling than she is of prison, but I'm not her doctor, I'm the mother of two children and I'm the object of her revenge. Life can't go on like this. Enough is enough.

I wake around six, early, because the skin on my face feels tight and each beat of my pulse sends an ache through my eye socket, down into my cheekbone and around my jaw line. I come down into the kitchen and swallow two painkillers then look out through the window. The birds are singing a vigorous morning chorus in between darting from tree to feeder and back again. The sky is a rich blue and I open the back door to go outside with Benson and breathe in the fresh morning air. It's still quite nippy but the sun is already lifting its face above the horizon, promising us a beautiful day, the sort that shows Edinburgh off in all her glory, especially if you have the energy to climb to a high point and admire the view.

'What happened to your face?'

For a split second I freeze, and then I turn around slowly in the direction of the voice. It's Kirsty. She's wearing jeans, a dark blue hoodie and flat shoes, and she's carrying her canvas bag.

'I spent the night in your garden hut.' She shivers and rubs her hands together. 'It was bloody cold! But beggars can't be choosers and all that.' She picks Benson up and hugs him into her chest. 'It helps that Benson likes me.' She tickles his tummy and he licks her face in appreciation. 'It crossed my mind that you wouldn't be able to resist telling that nice DI about your meeting with me with today. Am I right or am I right?'

It's still two hours before O'Reilly arrives. My neighbours on either side have families of similar ages to mine. If I was to scream loudly, and their windows were open to the rear, they would surely hear me. Or I could run into the house. I'm closer to the back door than Kirsty is. I could slam the door behind me and call the police. But in both cases she'll get away and that'll mean she'll simply pop up somewhere else when really we need her in custody. I don't trust myself to wrestle her to the ground. She's small, but I have no experience of physically subduing someone and I expect she's the sort of girl who would scratch, bite and kick out at me – probably targeting my already sore face.

All these thoughts go through my head in a constant stream of data, and Kirsty second-guesses me. 'Before you think about screaming or alerting a neighbour, I think you should know that I've done something which will impact very badly on you. But in this case what's done *can* be undone, so it's worth your while cooperating with me.' She puts Benson back down on to the ground. 'Are you going to invite me in?'

My options limited, I walk back towards the house and she follows me inside.

'I need to use the toilet and you're going to have to come with me,' she says. 'Because I don't trust you not to call the police.'

She heads straight for the downstairs loo and I go with

her. I'm wearing my dressing gown and I put my hands in my pockets, hoping to find my mobile phone, but there's nothing in there except clumps of old tissues and a couple of dog biscuits. My mobile must still be lying on my bedside cabinet. I didn't bring it down with me first thing, like I normally do, because I was so keen to take the painkillers. Shit. So much for my bright idea that I could record the conversation. Perhaps I can delay her long enough so that O'Reilly gets here before she leaves or perhaps Robbie will wake up and come downstairs. We'd certainly both be able to detain her. I consider shouting up to him, but he isn't easy to wake and I don't want to make matters worse. If she really has done something that will damage me then the sooner I know about it the better.

She leaves the bathroom door open as she pees. 'You'll have seen a lot of this sort of thing being a doctor,' she says, wiping herself with toilet paper. 'I expect nothing embarrasses you.' She pulls her trousers up and pushes the flush. 'I'll wash my hands. It's not the cleanest of huts.' She washes and dries her hands and has a quick check of her face in the mirror. She's far paler than when I last saw her and there are dark circles under her eyes.

'So.' She turns to look at me. 'Could I have a cup of tea?'

I make tea and toast. I do it because it uses up time and I'm banking on Robbie or O'Reilly appearing. She sits opposite me at the breakfast bar and eats four slices of toast with peanut butter and raspberry jam and she drinks two mugs of tea. She does all the talking – I have yet to speak because I don't want to encourage her. I don't trust her. I don't like her. I don't want her in my house. But for now, I'm playing along. She tells me about parts she's had in the theatre, what it feels like to wear another person's clothes, kiss someone she doesn't fancy, cry tears for injuries that have happened to the character, not to her. 'It's all about immersion and imagination,' she tells me, chewing noisily. 'Inhabiting the character from the inside out.'

When she's finished eating and talking, she exhales a deep breath and says, 'That was good.' Then she hops off the stool, grabs her bag and I follow her through to the living room where she flops down on a seat. 'Shame about the wall, but then the wallpaper wasn't great, was it?' Her eyes are restless, flitting from lamp to television to wall and back to me. 'Lauren told me she chose a new pattern.' Her eyes keep moving: window, television, fireplace, me. 'You're not saying much,' she says.

I shrug.

'I should just stop with the silly nonsense and be a good girl, is that it?' she says tartly, her upbeat mood cracking at last.

'I'm sorry, Kirsty,' I say. 'But it seems like everything's a performance for you and I just can't join in.'

'Is that what you see when you look at me? A patchwork person, who lives a made-up life?'

'Not only that. I also see an articulate, highly intelligent young woman who is using her energies in all the wrong ways. I think you should be spending time with your father because I'm sure the doctor on the ward has told you that he might not be long for this world and death is absolute. There will be no second chances for the time you missed.'

She stares up at the ceiling and sighs.

'I understand you're angry about your mother's death, but you're ignoring the facts of her cancer.'

'I stole some of your prescriptions,' she says loudly.

'Pardon?'

'When I came to your house that night, I stole three of your prescription sheets.'

'Why?'

She delves into her canvas bag and pulls out a green

prescription sheet, which she passes across to me. Nowadays, most of our prescriptions are printed out in surgery, but we still carry a pad for home visits and this script looks as if it's been written by me. It's not difficult to work out how she got hold of my pad. I always leave my doctor's case by the front door and when she came here last Friday evening, knowing full well we were at the award ceremony and that she had plenty of time to snoop around, she must have been delighted to come across my doctor's case. The script has Tess Williamson's name and address handwritten at the top and the prescription is for a dozen, 10-ml vials of morphine for injection. Most definitely not something I would have prescribed for Tess.

'I did my research,' she says. 'I went into a pharmacy and asked them how to correctly write a prescription. I said it was for a part I was playing and they were surprisingly helpful. And then I spent a few days practising your signature. And bingo, here's the finished article. What do you think, Dr Somers? Does it pass muster?'

'So you've been very clever,' I say, laying the prescription down on the table. 'What's the point of it?'

'It's my back-up plan. Look, I don't want to ruin you – I just want people to see you for who you are and, short of taking a time machine back to 1993, we're stuck with the fact that my mother died and you caused it.'

'I don't see what the prescriptions have to do with your mother's death.'

'Well . . . as I said, they're my back-up. I've been thinking a lot about how this can be made right and I've hit upon an idea.'

'And?'

'Over the past nine months there've been three full-page articles about you in the *Edinburgh Courier*, all singing your praises. I want you to go and see the journalist who wrote them – she's called Carys Blakemore, isn't she? – and have her put the record straight.'

'You want me to tell Carys about your mother's death?'

'Yes. All of it. How and why she died, what happened to my father and to me. Let people see that you're not perfect.'

I think about what this would mean for my career. My work as a GP would continue. I expect some of my patients would be shocked; others would feel it was too long ago for it to be relevant. The centre is a different matter, though. We're pulling in more funding because my profile looks deserving, and without a squeaky clean past, some of the donors are bound to opt out.

'I can't do that,' I say to Kirsty. 'The negative publicity would jeopardise the centre's work.'

'At the moment, there are two other prescriptions, just like this one, waiting to be handed in to a chemist. They both have Tess's name on them.'

'So?' I shrug. 'I'll tell the police that you stole them and forged my signature.'

'That's what I want you to do. Then Tess will say you made her cooperate with you because you wanted the drugs for yourself.'

I give a short laugh. 'The police aren't going to believe Tess over me!'

'Not solely. But those guys I live with? They owe me a couple of favours. One good thing about having a dead mother is that I have money from the insurance policy she left me. I pay their rent; they help me out, get me drugs, set stuff up for me. They would lie for me too. I know they would. I'll ask them to start a whispering campaign. A word here, another word there and suddenly our celebrity doctor isn't all she seems.'

'No one is going to believe that I take drugs.'

'Why not? People do that, you know. They turn to drugs

when they're unhappy. You're recently divorced. You're hard up. You spend a lot of evenings on your own. You wouldn't be the first doctor to become addicted to illegal substances.' Her eyes bore into mine. 'I've seen you in action. There's nothing more important to you than your family and your job, and both would suffer. I could throw enough doubt on your character for your carefully constructed world to collapse. Lauren already thinks you're a liar. How much worse would this make it?'

Benson, who's been lying in his bed close to my feet, senses the tension in the room and jumps up beside me, a low growl in his throat. 'My thoughts exactly, Benson,' I say and lean in to Kirsty until we're only inches apart. 'Get out of my house,' I say quietly.

She smiles. 'It could take you years to gain Lauren's trust again. She's already lost some of her faith in you.' Benson growls a little louder and Kirsty stands up. 'You have until the end of today to get in touch with the journalist. The article needs to be in the paper next week and then you'll have paid me and my mother back. Think about it, Dr Somers. Sure you can fight your corner but remember – mud sticks.'

The front door slams as she leaves.

'Sweet Jesus.' I rest my elbows on the table and rub my forehead with my fingers. Kirsty's been in and out of my house enough over the past nine months to know that my children and my job are all I have. But what she can't possibly know is that her threat is made doubly dangerous because of Phil's bid for shared custody. I can't have any links to illegal drug use because, if I do, Phil will use it against me, citing my past behaviour as evidence.

I think about what my solicitor told me on the phone earlier. The crux of it was that the court would only take another look at custody arrangements if I'm no longer providing a stable environment for the children. I wish I could trust Phil not to go for the jugular but I can't. I know that if he gets wind of any wrongdoing on my part, he'll use the information and I'll risk losing custody of Lauren.

Sure, handwriting experts could detect that my signature was forged. And with sustained questioning, Tess would be bound to crack and confess that I had nothing to do with the prescriptions. I'm sure Kirsty could get her friends to lie for her, but if they were up against a doctor of good moral character then would their testimony be believed?

No. Except that opposing counsel could argue that 'on the surface, Olivia Somers appears to be solid gold, but when one delves a little deeper, one finds dubious personal incidents, including a period of Class B drug abuse in her mid-twenties, that throw doubt upon her character.'

16

Robbie's birth was a difficult one. A fortnight before my due date, I was admitted to hospital with pre-eclampsia. My blood pressure was through the roof and there was protein in my urine. I stayed on the ward for the whole two weeks before they decided that it was time to induce me. When labour started I agreed to an epidural because it was recommended as a way to bring down my blood pressure. 'But now I might not feel the urge to push,' I said to Leila. We'd been going to antenatal classes together and were both hoping for natural births. 'I don't want to end up with a forceps delivery.'

'It's more important to get your BP down, though, isn't it?' Leila said, and from a medical standpoint I agreed with her.

The labour progressed slowly and then the baby started to show signs of foetal distress. I ended up with Keilland's rotational forceps, the baby's head turned around while he was still inside me and then hauled down the birth canal, dragged into the world with metal instruments gripping on to his precious, little head. By this time I'd drifted into unconsciousness because I'd lost so much blood, and when I came round, Leila was holding one of my hands and Phil the other. I could see that Leila had been crying.

'Is the baby okay?' I said.

'He's a beautiful boy,' Phil told me, and he wheeled the Perspex cot closer so that I could take a look. 'Seven pounds, six ounces; little bit of jaundice but otherwise absolutely fine.'

'Can I hold him?'

'Of course!' Phil laughed, and Leila helped me sit up in bed. I felt dizzy and had to wait for several seconds to let my head clear, and then Phil rested my son on my lap, keeping his hand around the back of the baby's head as a support. The baby was wearing a hospital gown, which resembled a mini cotton dress with ties at the back, and he had on a tiny nappy, his scrawny legs growing out of the bottom of it. 'He's long,' I said.

'Aye, he's going to be tall,' Leila said.

Wrapped around one of his perfect miniature feet was his nametag, which I couldn't read because my eyes were misty and wouldn't focus on the letters. My arms felt heavy but I managed to bring them under his body so that I could snuggle him up towards my breast. Phil took his hand away from around the baby's head and I saw the purple bruising and misshapen cranium that's typical of a forceps delivery. I couldn't bear it. I started to cry, horrified that my sweet little boy had come into the world this way. I began gabbling to Phil and Leila about forceps complications: the risk of intracranial bleeding or cranial fracture.

'He's fine, Liv,' Phil soothed. 'He's just a bit bruised, that's all.'

'Has he opened his eyes? Is he responding to stimuli?'

'He's tired, poor little man. He's had a busy day.'

Leila and Phil crooned over him while I worried. Could I not have pushed a bit harder? Would it have been better if I'd had a Caesarean section? What if he had lasting damage?

'Your haemoglobin's only eight point two,' Phil told me. 'They'll give you a couple of units of blood and you'll feel much better after that.'

When the second bag of blood was going in to my vein, my temperature climbed two degrees in thirty minutes. 'Your body's not happy,' the nurse told me. 'We'll have to abandon the transfusion. A couple of weeks on iron tablets and you'll be right as rain.'

I left hospital after six days feeling as if I'd been cast adrift in foreign seas. Phil couldn't take any more time off and Leila and Archie had moved across town. She didn't have a car back then and was now so heavily pregnant that getting on and off buses was a chore. I didn't have a car either and lived up two flights of stairs. I'd had problems with my sacral joints when I was pregnant and, even though I'd now had the baby, it still wasn't getting any better. Most days I had shooting sciatic pains down my right leg and when it was really troubling me I walked with a limp, barely able to lift my leg off the ground. Going to the local shops was a mission in itself, as I juggled bags and baby and my sore leg. The thought of taking the baby on a bus to visit Leila was more than I could cope with.

Robbie's first few weeks, I felt as if I was running to catch up. Other mothers spoke about the rapturous joy on seeing their baby for the first time and I felt as though I might be rumbled because, although I knew I loved him, I looked at the tiny red-faced child and felt scared. Responsibility was written in neon-bright letters across his forehead and I was terrified I'd get it wrong. I kept his crib close to my side of the bed and I'd wake at night with pins and needles in my hand because it would be hanging into his crib, touching his firm little body, making sure he was still breathing.

Phil had an explanation for my fears. I had been poorly mothered myself and my father was too much of a man's man. So it would take a bit of learning, but heavens above! – I was a doctor, a member of the caring profession – I'd be fine.

The midwife was kind and motherly and she came to visit every day for a week. I envied her ease with my baby. I watched her and learnt from her but still I was all fingers and thumbs and Robbie was forever sliding in the water when I bathed him. I had no idea how I ended up being so utterly inept. I'd been confident with babies when I was training but now it was as if I'd never even seen one, never mind held one.

'You are taking your iron tablets now, aren't you?' the midwife asked me. 'Your haemoglobin will still be low and that affects your energy levels, and energy levels affect confidence.' She gave me a hug. 'You're doing fine, Olivia. Don't be too hard on yourself.'

Phil was a natural father and, when he was home, he handled his baby as though he'd been doing it all his life. He held Robbie's body with one confident hand, the tiny sleepy head snuggled into the crook of his neck as he wandered round the house: answering the phone, cooking dinner, reading psychiatric journals. I tried to copy Phil but Robbie's head was forever flopping to one side and my hand wasn't large enough to cover his whole back and hold him safe.

I was determined to breastfeed but very quickly my nipples were red raw with his fierce sucking. The midwife told me I needed to be firmer with him. 'Don't let him latch on for too long. He needs to feed and then come off.'

Easier said than done. He'd suck hard, then toy with my nipple, suck again. Then he'd fall asleep. I'd change him, wake him up, put him on the other breast, but he'd get crotchety and refuse to take a full feed. And usually after feeding, he wriggled and struggled and then he'd start to wail, the loud animal cries of a creature who'd been abandoned. 'I think my milk must be off,' I told the health visitor.

She laughed. 'He's just a bit colicky, that's all.' She was the epitome of common sense. 'Are you watching what you're eating and drinking?'

I was watching what I was eating and drinking. I was doing everything everyone told me. I was trying to relax. I was making sure we both got fresh air and socialised with other mothers. I introduced routine and rhythm into his life and I made sure he got loads of cuddles and fun time. But none of that helped. He wasn't gaining weight so it was suggested I supplement with a bottle. 'He's a hungry boy. It's not your fault,' the health visitor said. 'Don't take it personally.'

When Phil came home to find half a dozen bottles and a sterilising unit in the kitchen, he stood with open mouth. 'What's this for?'

'He's not gaining weight. I've to supplement feeds.'

'He looks all right to me,' Phil said. 'I think you should persevere for a bit longer.'

'Well, that's easy for you to say!' I shouted. 'Because you're not the one with cracked nipples and a desperate need to sleep!'

'He's a *baby*, Liv!' He gave me one of his disappointed looks. 'Honestly, how hard can it be?'

Phil walked out of the kitchen and I spent a minute crying and feeling pathetic and then another minute deciding that I'd give Robbie formula and to hell with Phil's opinion. I started Robbie on a mid-morning bottle and one before bedtime and within days he made his preference clear. He reared away from my breast and howled because all he wanted was the rubber teat. As soon as he caught it in his mouth, he sucked with great gusto then fell into a deep, peaceful sleep.

I was determined not to feel a failure, but Phil gave me the silent treatment for a while, and when I tried to talk to him about it he told me, 'I didn't see you as a quitter.'

'Well, perhaps if you were home more . . .'

'Somebody has to earn the money.'

'I feel isolated, Phil!'

'Well join some clubs, or something! Visit Leila!' He left the room again, shouting out, 'Jesus, Liv! You're an intelligent woman, work it out!'

I was already in a couple of mother and baby groups and I was slowly making friends, but mostly the chat seemed unnecessarily competitive – my baby can do this, my baby can do that. All I wanted was to feel normal and most of the time I left feeling inadequate.

Leila and I made an effort to see each other once a week but she was on course to become a GP and had returned to work when Mark was just two months old. And with such a large extended family all living in Edinburgh, she was spoilt for childcare and for company. I hadn't even completed my final residency yet and planned to return to work when Robbie was six months old. I wasn't sure whether I was looking forward to it or not, because much as I still wanted to be a doctor, I hadn't exactly left on a high. I had been well and truly hammered for my own fallibility. A woman was dead and no amount of studying or practising or striving to be an exemplary doctor was ever going to change that. And now that my own baby was born I couldn't help but think about the other life lost along with Sandy's – her newborn son's. At times when I held Robbie, I felt the ghost of another mother and another baby just beyond my reach. I had to work hard not to let it get me down but some days the enormity of my mistake clung to me, infecting the air like city smog until it was all I could do not to hide under the covers and cry.

Still, I tried to take my silver linings where I could find them, and there were two advantages to not breastfeeding: Robbie slept better and so, therefore, did I; and I was able to take painkillers for my aching leg – not that they helped much. I'd attended a course of physio, but there was still no improvement; in fact, if anything, my leg was worse than ever. One afternoon I'd taken Robbie to the park and met a couple of other mothers there, done some shopping, and by the time I got home, I was almost crying with the pain, the prescribed anti-inflammatories barely knocking the edge off it.

I stood in the stairwell wrestling Robbie out of his buggy, but he was over four hours without a feed and in the middle of a sustained bout of hungry wailing. Since he'd started on the bottle, he'd grown heavier, and I managed to hoist him on to my shoulder but, for the life of me, couldn't manage the bags as well. My heart started to race and within seconds I was sweating and gulping down an almost overwhelming feeling of incompetence. And it was at times like this that Sandy's spectre taunted me – she was born to be a mother. But me? I was just playing at it.

The main door opened and our neighbour came in. His name was Ben but everyone called him Porky. 'Because of my belly,' he'd told me the first time we met. 'Give me a pie and I'm happy.'

'Need a hand there, Liv?'

I nodded, not trusting myself to speak. He took Robbie off my shoulder, lifted the bags and went ahead of me up the stairs. I managed to get myself up to my front door but by then I was struggling to hold back tears. 'Sorry, it's my leg.' I told him about my problems with sciatica. 'Every movement seems to aggravate it.'

'I had that a few years ago when I was still playing rugby.' He took my key from me and unlocked the door. 'It's a killer. Had to give up the game, but even then it took a long time to shift it.' He followed me inside. 'Let me help you get the wee man sorted.'

He gave Robbie a bottle and then I changed him and settled him into his crib for a nap while Porky put the shopping away. 'Got some sticky doughnuts back at my place if you want to come over.'

'Love to.' I put my slippers on and Porky lifted Robbie's crib and we went across the landing. We'd been in Porky's flat before, Robbie and I. He'd taken us in when we were having the boiler replaced and again a couple of weeks later when my TV was on the blink. He lived with a couple of other post-grad students – they were all doing PhDs – and the atmosphere in the flat was always lively without being too chaotic.

'You know, you're very good with women,' I told him, trying to settle my leg into a comfortable position, but wincing from the pain. 'A lot of men are bored by tears or else they run away.'

'I've got something that can help you with that leg.'

'Oh?'

'Wee bit of wacky baccy.'

'I shouldn't.'

'Doesn't agree with you?'

'Actually it does agree with me,' I said, thinking about my evenings with Gabe. 'Haven't had it for years, though.'

'It's mild, the stuff I smoke. Grow my own.' He looked at me with a little boy's excitement. 'Do you want to see?'

I followed him to the hall cupboard, four foot square and close to the kitchen. It was where I stored my ironing board, tumble drier and shelves of sheets, towels and odds and sods. Porky had the cupboard walls lined with tinfoil and half a dozen cannabis plants growing to fill the space, five hundred-watt bulbs shining down on them.

'Want to try some?'

'Better not. But thanks for the offer.'

Two weeks later the same thing happened again but this time it was worse – my leg was almost paralysed and pain shot from my toes to the base of my spine. I accepted Porky's cup of tea and sympathy and when he offered me a hash cookie I didn't say no. 'It's a pure resin,' Porky told me. 'Comes from Afghanistan.'

Within minutes, a feeling of relaxation flooded into every cell of my body. I settled back on the sofa, and we watched a French movie, Robbie asleep in his crib next to me. For the first time in months my leg didn't hurt and I felt all the tension leave my body.

I began to spend more time next door – just an hour or so every other evening. Phil was usually out until at least eight o'clock and Robbie enjoyed the company. He was often grumpy in the evening but the post-grad students always had him giggling and gurgling within minutes. I felt so relaxed when I was with them, and it made me realise that, when I was a student, I missed out this whole phase because I was always so busy studying.

Coping skills, I told myself, when I developed a habit of saying yes to a hash cookie. *That's what it's giving you.*

I became a much better housewife – I didn't forget to buy milk or bread and Phil's shirts were always ironed. To be fair to him, he knew how to roast a chicken and scramble eggs and he could do his own ironing – he didn't subscribe to the concept of women's and men's work – but still, he loved that I was looking after him. 'You're certainly cheering up,' he told me. 'I feel like I've got the old Liv back.'

Robbie was five months old when Phil and I were due to get married. I'd had to fight hard to keep the wedding small and would have been happy with just Leila and Archie and a few other close friends but Phil wanted more than that. 'What about Declan?' he said. 'Don't you want to share your happy day with him?'

'Sure I do. Declan and Aisling and their kids would be fine. Dad would be fine. Finn and Diarmaid can come too if they want, although I can't see them making the effort, but I don't want my mother to come.'

'Liv . . .'

'Really, Phil, I don't want her to come.' We were in bed and we'd just made love. With my new-found ability to relax, we were making love almost every night and it was bringing us closer. 'I still feel fragile, and she'll see that, and she'll kick me when I'm down. I know what she's like. And the fact that I'm getting married in a register office would be the perfect reason for her to have a go at me.'

'It would be good for you to let go of old patterns.'

'I don't feel strong enough, and anyway, it's all very well for me to be letting go of old patterns but she won't.'

The day dawned and I wore a cream silk dress and delicate sandals. I'd lost all my baby weight and I felt young and carefree. Porky had made me a batch of hash cookies that I pushed to the back of the cupboard because I was sure I could get through the day without needing to have one. Carrying Robbie was what usually set the sciatica off, and that triggered a vicious cycle – the pain made me tense and when I grew tense, it increased the pain. But today Phil would carry him and I would be able to relax. I'd got my way and it was to be a small ceremony with a dozen friends. I'd spoken to Declan and we'd agreed that time and money were tight for them – they'd recently taken a mortgage out on their own farm that Declan was busy building into a solid business. It made more sense for Phil and me to go and visit them at Christmas time and then the cousins could get to know each other and the adults would have time in the evenings to catch up with one another.

We arrived at the register office for a quarter to eleven. Leila, Archie and baby Mark were there to meet us. Leila was my maid of honour and she was dressed in a green and gold dress that one of her sisters-in-law had made for her and it set her colouring off to perfection. The ceremony was simple but satisfying and I felt happy to have my baby and my man and enough friends to make a party sing. We walked down the road to the pub where we'd hired a reception room. Archie and Phil were carrying the babies, Leila and I were in the centre of the pavement holding on to our husbands' free hands and talking to each other.

And then I saw my mother. She was standing on the pub step, ramrod straight, the look on her face a picture of undisguised disgust. 'What's she doing here?' I said to Phil.

'Honestly, Liv, I thought this was the perfect time for you to make amends.'

'I don't have any amends to make,' I said. I pulled Leila to a stop beside me and the men walked on ahead. 'Did you know that Phil was planning this?'

'As God is my witness, I didn't,' she told me. 'I wouldn't have let him do this to you.' She looked as stunned as I was. 'What do you want me to do? Shall I ask her to go?'

'It's okay,' I said. 'I'll do it. You go on inside.'

I waited until everyone had gone through the front door and then I approached my mother. 'What are you doing here?'

'Well, that's a fine welcome.' She looked me up and down. 'You've put on weight, Scarlett. It doesn't suit you.'

'Did you see my baby?'

'Trust you to do things the wrong way round. Who takes a baby to their own wedding?'

'Is Daddy with you?'

'Why would he come?' She puffed up. 'How can a marriage outside of the church ever be a proper marriage?'

I didn't believe my dad would make that sort of judgement and while, in my heart, I knew that my mother was only here to have a go at me, I still hoped for a chink, an unbending, a fraction of a smile. 'Are you proud of me, Mammy?'

'Why would I be proud of you?'

'Most mothers would be proud if their daughter had a lovely husband and a baby and was happy. Not to mention being a doctor.'

'Well, I'm not most mothers,' she said, rounding on me, her pupils pinpricks of concentrated anger. 'You stupid, stupid girl! You could have been someone.'

'I am *someone* and this is my wedding day.'

'Finuala was right when she told me you'd never make anything of yourself.'

'Jesus Christ!' I shouted. 'Who cares about bloody Finuala?'

'*Do not* take the Lord's name in vain, Scarlett Olivia Naughton!' my mother shouted back, crossing herself fiercely, her rosary beads coiled round her hand. 'Don't cheapen Him in the same way as you've cheapened yourself.'

'My name stopped being Naughton over an hour ago and I haven't called myself Scarlett in years,' I said, the base of my spine beginning to tighten and burn. 'Just go away. Now. *I want you to leave.*'

'Why should I leave when I've come all this way at your husband's invitation?'

'Then I'll go.'

I knew that I was letting her win, walking away from my own reception, but I couldn't stay there. I couldn't stand her toxic mix of bitterness and religion. I hailed a taxi and went home and when I got there I rang Porky's doorbell.

'Back so soon?'

'I need a bolthole,' I said, limping inside. 'Just for an hour. Then I'll go back to the reception. My leg's on fire and I want to murder my mother.'

They were smoking dope and I shared a spliff or two and then I threw caution to the wind and snorted some coke. I meant to go back, I really did, but Porky had some friends round and they were funny and interesting. Three hours went by and I began to miss Robbie. My arms felt empty and my heart was sending out sharp, poignant signals like a distress beacon.

'I need my baby,' I told Porky. 'I'd better get back.'

As I passed my own door I could hear voices inside. I didn't have keys with me so I rang the bell, and when the door opened there was Phil, a frantic, surprised look on his face. 'Where the hell have you been?'

'Where's Robbie?' I walked through the hallway and into the living room.

'Are you okay?' Leila kissed me on either cheek. 'We were so worried.'

'I'm fine!' I walked past her. 'Here he is!' Robbie was next to the window in his bouncy chair, kicking his legs and sucking on his fist. I lifted him up and kissed his forehead and his cheeks, a dozen little kisses that made him giggle. 'How's my boy been?'

'What's going on with your pupils?' Phil said, standing in front of me, hands on hips. 'They're dilated.'

'I'm in love,' I said, smiling at him. 'You look so handsome in your best suit.' I leant forward to kiss him too but he pulled his head away from mine.

'I was looking for biscuits,' Archie said, coming through from the kitchen waving a Tupperware. 'And found these. Is it okay to have one?'

'Oops! They're mine. Hash cookies.' I balanced Robbie on one arm and grabbed the box from Archie with my free hand. 'Sorry! They're for my sciatica.' Silence flooded the room, bringing with it the constricting weight of shock and disapproval. 'What?' I said. The three of them were staring at me as if I'd just admitted to a smack habit. 'It's only marijuana! It's not such a big deal.'

Phil lifted Robbie from me and handed him to Leila. 'Would you mind taking Robbie out for an hour or so? Olivia and I need to talk.'

'No!' I tried to step between them but Phil held me away from Leila. 'For goodness' sake! Why are you overreacting?'

'You're taking drugs,' Phil said, his disappointed look bruising me. 'You've been looking after our baby when you're *stoned.*'

'The hash is for my *leg*,' I said, keeping my tone subdued. 'It does *not* affect my ability to look after Robbie.'

Leila was backing out of the room.

'Leila?' I was hurt by the expression on her face – shock and judgement and a hint of embarrassment. 'Help me out here!'

But she didn't. Archie closed the living-room door behind

them both and I was left alone with Phil, my husband. We'd been married less than six hours and already we were fighting.

'I take it you've been spending time with the degenerates next door?'

'Degenerates? How can you say that? You don't even know them!'

'They're leeches, Olivia. Perennial students, bleeding taxpayers' money because they're too feckless to get jobs.'

'When did you become so bloody superior?'

'And when did you become so bloody irresponsible?' he threw back.

'Irresponsible? You're a fine one to talk!' I poked my finger into his chest. 'I asked you not to invite my mother. I told you why. I *bloody* told you. But still you went on and did it anyway because you never listen!'

We carried on like that for half an hour or more until I was crying from frustration and disappointment with myself and with Phil, and the spoiling of my wedding, and he was telling me that he loved me and he was sorry and now he understood how painful my leg really was and how justified my negative feelings were towards my mother. We sealed our apologies by making love on the couch, a tender coming together that made up for all the harsh words. And we agreed that we would always remember to talk to each other, to share what we were thinking and feeling and respect each other's differences; that we loved each other enough to make our marriage work.

I meant everything I said and it was years later before I wondered whether he did too.

17

It's just after seven when Kirsty leaves and I tell Robbie it's time to get up. He reminds me that he doesn't have a lesson first thing – he isn't expected in school until eleven – so I leave him to sleep some more and have a shower.

While I'm under the water, I turn what Kirsty's just told me every which way in my head, distil the argument down to its essence and know that I can't risk my name being linked to drug abuse. My career will survive a newspaper article telling the truth about what happened all those years ago – I can recover from that – but Phil taking Lauren? I can't risk it. I had become hooked on my daily cannabis cookie and this fact is recorded in my medical records. And because of the dependence, I was slow to wean myself off it. The pain relief and relaxation it brought me helped me through a couple of difficult months, but when Phil found out, I had to find other ways to cope and that meant doctors' visits and pain clinics and months of Phil watching me for signs of a relapse. I'm sure a good solicitor could argue that there's no smoke without fire – the business with the prescriptions, the fact that I worked with recovering addicts: both are ideal ways to access drugs – and past history could be seen to indicate that I have a predisposition to drug taking when I'm unhappy. Just like Kirsty said, I wouldn't be the first divorcee to turn to drugs for comfort. And for the sake of an impressionable child of eleven, Phil might be given full custody. The fact that I've done nothing more than grow overly fond of an extra gin and tonic would be hard to prove.

I dry myself quickly and plan my morning – four phone calls, two meetings and then maybe I can take a breath. As soon as I'm dressed – jeans and a T-shirt and flat sandals – I call O'Reilly and ask him if I can meet him at the police station instead of here. 'Why?' he asks.

'Can I tell you when I see you?'

'Okay.'

Next I call the surgery and leave a message to say that I'm sorry but I won't be in to work. 'I had an accident yesterday,' I say. 'I injured my face. Nothing serious, but it needs a couple of days to calm down.'

My third call is to Kirsty. 'I'll do it,' I say without preamble. 'But how can I trust that you won't just go along with your whole back-up plan anyway?'

'When I see the newspaper article, I'll give you the prescriptions and that will be that.'

'But the article won't be in the newspaper before next week. I don't want to wait that long.'

'Too bad.'

'Wait! Don't ring off.' I pull thoughts together in my head. 'I have an idea. I'm going to call Carys Blakemore, the journalist, and ask her if she's free for lunch. You could come too.'

'As the dead woman's baby?'

'If you want.'

'I don't want.'

'Then I can say you're a soon-to-be medical student who's shadowing me. You'll hear me tell her about what happened and you can give me the scripts.'

'Well . . .'

'I'm not bullshitting you, Kirsty. I want to put an end to this. Today. Once and for all.'

'You're not going to have the police there to arrest me, are you?'

'No. But they will keep looking for you. That's completely out of my hands.'

'I know that. And I have an idea how to fix it. Nothing that concerns you.'

'Okay. So will you come to lunch?'

'Looks like it.'

'I'll text you with the details.'

Feeling like I'm getting somewhere, I call Carys and tell her I want to give her a story – the other side of Olivia Somers, as it were. 'Intriguing,' she says.

'Let me take you to lunch,' I say. 'We can talk about it then.'

We agree to meet up town and I text Kirsty the details, then drive to the police station and find a parking space just in front of the building. I'm feeling nervous about meeting O'Reilly because it isn't easy to lie to him – firstly because I like him and secondly because he's practised at lassoing lies and dragging them to ground.

'DI O'Reilly will be with you directly,' the desk clerk tells me, and I smile my thanks then walk in circles round the foyer, stopping a couple of times in front of the poster board to look at advice about crime prevention, my eyes reading the words, my brain incapable of processing them.

'Dr Somers.'

O'Reilly is by my side and I try to swallow my anxiety before saying, 'We need to have a chat.'

He waves his arm in the direction of the interview rooms. 'After you.'

There's a kerfuffle going on further along the corridor with a suit-clad middle-aged man swearing and flailing punches in all directions while two policemen talk him down. O'Reilly opens the door of the room we were in last time and I walk in ahead of him. 'You need a lot of patience for this job,' I say.

'As you do with being a doctor, I expect,' he says. 'They're similar roles in some ways, aren't they? There's a certain amount of detective work involved in your job, I'm sure.' He points me towards a chair and sits down on the one opposite. 'So what's going on?'

I rub my hands on my jeans. 'Kirsty isn't going to show up today.'

'Why's that?'

My mouth is completely dry and I run my tongue around it, but there's nothing happening. Saliva production has stopped in favour of adrenaline that's coursing through my blood, flooding my capillaries like a river in spate. 'Is it possible to have a glass of water, please?'

'Of course.' He jumps up. 'In fact, I'm sure we can stretch to tea or coffee.'

'Water's fine.'

He opens the door and shouts out, 'Tea and a glass of water, Jenny!' He waits for her reply which is out of my earshot. 'Cheers, love.' On his way back to the seat he says, 'I hear you went to see Tess Williamson yesterday.'

'It was for her mother. She'd requested a home visit.'

'And did you speak to Tess?'

'Briefly. I'm sorry, I meant to tell you, but with Lauren going missing it slipped my mind.'

His face is impassive. 'How do you know Kirsty's not meeting you at ten?'

'She slept in my garden hut overnight.' I've decided that the best way forward is to be economical with the truth, telling O'Reilly almost everything except the lunch details. I begin by recounting my dilemma when I found her in the garden – should I shout for help or should I tackle her? 'I didn't feel confident with either and didn't have the chance to use my mobile, so I felt the best thing was to let her talk. And we did. And then we came to an agreement.'

He sighs. 'Tell me you've not gone soft on her again?'

'Not exactly, but I have agreed to a compromise.'

'And that would be?'

'I'm going to speak to the journalist at the *Edinburgh Courier*. She can write the truth about me. Redress the balance a bit. Let readers see that I'm not so perfect.'

'"Let readers see that I'm not so perfect."' He repeats my words very deliberately and then scratches his chin. 'And this will make Kirsty happy, will it?'

The door pushes open and Jenny bustles in. 'Tea and some water.'

'Thank you, Jenny,' O'Reilly says.

I lurch for the glass of water and take small sips, each one temporarily easing the parched ache inside my mouth.

'What interests me,' O'Reilly says, 'is why you won't help us convict the person who almost killed your son?'

'In her mind, she has a genuine grievance.'

'And in your mind?'

'In my mind . . . well . . . I think she does have a point.'

'So she's just going to get away with it? Almost killing your son, causing damage inside your home. Those events are justified, are they?'

'Not exactly, but they are understandable.'

'Intimidation is fine in your book, is it?'

'Of course not. But there is a certain justice in the public seeing me as I am.'

'Warts and all?'

'Yes.'

'From hero to zero in one fell swoop?' He gives me a challenging look. 'You'll go from Dr Somers, shining example to the rest of us, to Dr Somers with a skeleton bursting out of her closet.' He drums his fingers on the desk. It's a jagged sound and it makes my teeth vibrate. 'I expect the centre will lose some of its charity funding when your name is splashed across the front pages of the *Edinburgh Courier.*'

'I just have to hope that doesn't happen.' This worries me and I can't help but show it. 'I don't want the centre to suffer for my mistakes, but I do have to stand up and take responsibility for what I've done. I don't think there's a time limit on that.'

'Olivia?'

'Yes?' His eyes are calculating but kind and I feel a hairline crack in my resolve.

'Why not just tell me the truth?'

'I'm not lying.'

Our eyes fix and hold but I don't give in; I grip my hands together under the table, hard enough for it to hurt.

'Well . . .' His sigh is regretful. 'In that case, I'll have to write a report and there'll be a decision made as to whether or not you'll be charged for wasting police time.'

I baulk at this, drop my head and blink furiously. 'I . . .' It hadn't occurred to me that this might happen. 'In your opinion, am I likely to be charged?'

'Put it this way. We are pursuing a girl who spiked your son's drink and had him admitted to hospital in a coma. You, quite rightly, reported this as a crime. We speak almost every day for two weeks. You're keen to ensure the police service are doing all they can to find the culprit and then she comes, uninvited, into your home and causes criminal damage. This sends you off on your own investigation which you share with me only when pushed.' He takes a mouthful of tea. 'It's a matter of the law that we pursue Kirsty Stewart and I also would have thought that for you and your family it's important she's brought to justice. But strangely enough, one minute you're on side and the next you're not. Yesterday, you tell me you'll help us bring her in. Today you tell me you're sorting it out yourself.' He gives a hearty, not altogether amused, laugh. 'In my opinion, you've definitely been wasting police time. Will you be prosecuted?' He shakes his head. 'That's not my decision.'

I can't look at his face so I stare instead at what's on the table: a mug, a glass and his arms. His shirtsleeves are rolled up to his elbows; his forearms are tanned and warm looking. There's a white mark on his left wrist where his watch should be. 'Have you been out in the sun?'

'I have an allotment.'

'I didn't see you as a gardener.' It makes me wish I could have got to know him better. There's something comforting about a man who spends time on the land. Perhaps I feel this way because my father was, and Declan is, a farmer. I don't know. But what I do know is that O'Reilly is a better man than my half-baked truths are allowing him to be and it makes me feel ashamed. I briefly consider telling him about my lunch appointment and the fact that Kirsty will be there but I know he'll want to arrest Kirsty and bring her in. And then what? Allegations of drug taking, none of which O'Reilly will believe at first, but if Phil gets wind of it, and has a word in O'Reilly's ear, will he be swayed? He knows I haven't always been straight with him. He knows I kept my suspicions about the Sandy Stewart connection to myself and, he's right, I only give him information when I have to.

'Well! I have things to do.' He's clearly had enough. 'You know your way out.' He stands up and walks away from me, not bothering to look back.

'Thank you,' I say.

'For what?' he shouts, and keeps on walking.

I head outside into the sunshine and into my car, my heart heavy with shame and disappointment. There's no way for me to make it right with everyone, especially not O'Reilly, and I just have to live with it, put what needs to be first, first and get this day over with.

When I arrive home, I chase Robbie out of bed and have breakfast with him. He's not much of a morning person and most of his replies are monosyllabic, but his company is precious to me and I enjoy just being with him. As soon as he heads off to school, I get ready for my lunch date. It's not for over an hour yet but I want to try to disguise the injury to my face. The swelling is receding, the cut is healing and the bruising is a plum/raspberry stain that I manage to conceal with some heavy-duty foundation. Then I apply some eye make-up and lipstick, change into a summer dress and use curling tongs to style my hair. I arrive at the restaurant exactly on time and find that Carys is already there. She's in her mid-forties, with short, black, well-groomed hair and an easy smile. She always dresses in single-coloured shift dresses and a matching cardigan. Today, her dress is a flamingo pink and the cardigan a fuchsia colour with delicate lace edging. She's good company and has interviewed me twice before. Both times we ended up kicking back our heels and discussing everything from our upbringings to our job satisfaction. She has a son with autism and we spend the first few minutes talking about how he's doing before she says, 'The table's set for three?'

'Yes.' I look around the busy restaurant to see whether I can locate Kirsty. 'I have a young girl spending time with me – a week in the life of a doctor, kind of thing.' My eye catches a flash of movement by the front door. 'Ah, here she is!' I stand up to wave and Kirsty comes towards us, her head down. 'Emily, this is Carys Blakemore, a journalist with the *Edinburgh Courier*. Carys, this is Emily Jones, a would-be medical student.'

'Pleased to meet you, Emily.' Carys shakes her hand and Kirsty gives her a shy smile then takes the remaining seat.

She hasn't changed her clothes since I saw her this morning and her navy blue hoodie is out of place with all the summer colours around us.

'Let's order first, shall we?' I say. 'And then we can get down to business.'

The restaurant is Italian and the food has mass appeal. I order bruschetta as a starter and a main of tuna steak and green beans. Carys orders similar dishes to mine while Kirsty, who's staring at the menu with undisguised hunger, orders a pasta starter and the largest pizza they have with three extra toppings.

'Oh to be young again!' Carys says, smiling at Kirsty. 'Gone are the days when I could get away with eating so many carbs.'

'My mum says I have hollow legs.' Kirsty looks at me. 'Takes a lot to fill me up.'

It's something she's heard me say about Robbie and I wonder whether she's trying to goad me or just letting me know that she has her tentacles out, reaching into my life, reminding me that she can hurt me.

'I can't wait to hear what you have to tell me,' Carys says, placing her digital recorder on the table. 'Is it okay for me to record it?'

'Of course.'

She switches it on and I begin by saying, 'I want to be more upfront about who I am. The previous articles you've written about me have been about the successful side of me, and I thought it was time to reveal another side.' I take a drink of water and lean my elbows on the table. 'One of the principles of the Hippocratic oath is that doctors should first do no harm. Unfortunately, early on in my career, I did do harm. I mixed up two very different drugs and they were given to a pregnant woman.'

Carys draws in her breath, her interest piqued.

'I went into medicine to save lives and I was very unlucky

that the mistake I made ended up costing a young woman her life.'

We talk for some time as Carys's nose for a good story leads her to ask all the right questions: the particulars of the case, how it happened, what I felt, and the professional repercussions of my actions. Our starters are eaten and cleared and we're almost finished our main course when she says. 'So this woman was terminally ill?'

'She was. But I denied her a few extra months. She would have seen her baby born and perhaps her husband would have coped better. Who knows?' I place my knife and fork together on the plate. 'It's all what-ifs-and-maybes but—'

'And she might have been cured,' Kirsty interrupts. She's said very little throughout the meal, keeping her attention on her food, only looking at me when I say something personal about her mother.

'Well, that's extremely unlikely.'

'How can you be sure? It's like chaos theory. Every action, however small, produces another action that throws off the trajectory. And this wasn't a small action.' She bites into the last of her pizza. 'You might have thrown the whole course of medical science off balance.'

'That's a bit dramatic!' Carys says, clearly surprised that Kirsty has seen to challenge me like this.

'Perhaps you have a point, Emily,' I say. 'But the truth is we'll never know. And part of being human is accepting that there are things that you can't conceivably know about or change.'

She throws me a malevolent look, gets up and marches off towards the loo.

'She's a strange one!' Carys says, laughing into her napkin. 'One of the reasons I avoid these youth opportunity schemes is that you never know quite what you're going to get. I hope you're going to make her pay for her own meal?'

'She's all right really.' I smile. 'I'll just go and make sure she's okay. Something I said might have touched a nerve.'

I weave through the tables, the restaurant buzzing with happy diners and tempting plates of food and find Kirsty in the loo, staring at herself in the mirror. 'I've done what you asked,' I say. 'Now will you please give me the prescriptions?'

'That journalist's a *bitch*,' she cries out. 'She enjoyed hearing about how sick my mother was. My mother *died* and—' She stops, her head falling forward until the crown rests against the mirror. 'My mother was a real person.'

'Kirsty, that's what journalists are like. They love a good story, especially if it involves downfall of any sort. The public are often far more comfortable reading about failure than they are about success and this is a story about my failure. It's what you wanted, isn't it?'

'I hate her. I hate people.' She rummages around in her bag and pulls out the two prescriptions. 'I hate everyone.'

She passes the prescriptions to me and I tear them in half and then in half again and again until the pieces are tiny and I'm able to flush them down the loo. When I'm finished Kirsty is still standing in the same place but now her body is shaking, tears dripping from her cheeks into the sink in front of her.

'Kirsty.' I place a hand on her shoulder and she jumps as if stung.

'Fuck off!' she shouts. 'I hate you! I fucking hate you!' She lurches past me and I watch her charge through the restaurant and out on to the pavement where she quickly merges into the crowd.

'Emily's had to leave,' I say, rejoining Carys at the table. 'Period pains.'

'Is that what she calls it?' Carys says drily. 'I saw her running out the door just now. She looked like she was being chased by the grim reaper.'

There's no reply to that and, once more, in spite of all the trouble she's caused, I feel an ache of sympathy for Kirsty.

'You know, Liv, I'm willing to call the whole thing off,' Carys says. 'We can delete the tape and it will be like it never happened.'

'The story needs to be told,' I say. 'Publish it as it is.'

'If you're absolutely sure?'

'I am.'

We finish up with some coffee and chat about family and work, then I pay the bill and we say our goodbyes. Carys heads back to her office and I check my phone before setting off home. I read a much earlier text from Leila telling me she's heard I'm not at work and she's at her house with Jasmine and do I want to pop in?

I buy a couple of things to keep Jasmine busy then drive to Leila's, glad to know the time has come for me to get my friend back. Leila answers the door immediately because she's in the porch with Jasmine and they're both sliding their feet into flat summer shoes.

'I've brought something for the invalid,' I say, passing a magazine and some sweets to Jasmine.

'Thank you!' She reaches forward and kisses me on the cheek and then glues her eyes to the front cover of the magazine. 'I didn't have any pocket money left to buy this and I really wanted it!'

Leila kisses my other cheek and says, 'Lovely to see you, Liv. Is your face okay? You don't usually wear so much make-up.'

'You're not going out, are you?'

'We're on our way back to the hospital.' She rolls her eyes. 'When I texted you earlier all was well, but now the cast is slipping.' She turns to her daughter. 'Jasmine, show Aunty Liv.'

I feel the crush of my own disappointment – circumstances

are definitely conspiring against me – and try not to show it. Jasmine's attention is still with the magazine but she obligingly holds out her injured arm. The cast runs from halfway up her fingers to an inch below her elbow and I see at once that it's twisting around on her arm far too easily. 'The swelling must have gone down quicker than they thought,' I say to Leila.

'I've been on the phone to them and they said to come in straight away and have it recast.'

'Poor you,' I say to Jasmine. 'You have been through the wars.'

'Dad says the pin inside my wrist will set off the metal detector when we go through airports,' she tells me, briefly looking up from her reading.

'Honestly, it's all such a bore,' Leila says, pushing Jasmine ahead of her and locking the front door behind them. 'You know this is the fourth bone she's broken in as many years? They'll be sending social services after us next.'

'Well at least it happened at school this time.'

'I know. Why does she have to be the only girl who can't climb a wall without falling off?' She gives her daughter an affectionate hug. 'In the car, love. How are things with you, Liv?' She's walking away as she asks me.

'Complicated.' There's no point in launching into the whole sorry tale. All I want is for someone to put their arms round me, someone I know and love, and my thoughts circle and land on Declan. 'Leila, will you do me a favour? Could Robbie and Benson come and stay with you for the weekend? Lauren's with Phil and I'd love to see my brother. I could easily fly over to Galway for the weekend.'

'Of course! They're more than welcome. But you'll be going to Ireland for your mother's hip operation in a few weeks, won't you?'

'I want to see Declan sooner than that. I need a bit of time out. Change of perspective. What with all that's been going on . . .'

'I understand.' She aims a swift kiss at my cheek. 'Archie's doing the school run. I'll let him know to collect Robbie too.' She climbs into the car. 'I'm sorry I've been such a rubbish friend lately. I'm not forgetting that we need to catch up.' She starts the engine. 'Save all the details and we'll have a real heart-to-heart on Monday.' She begins reversing and calls through the open window. 'Okay?'

'Yes.' I wave her away. 'I look forward to it.'

Ireland's west coast is like the edge of the world. Peaty soil is covered with green grass and grazing sheep. Jagged, rocky cliffs slice into farmland, beyond which white-topped Atlantic waves batter the sandy shore. I feel the pull of the childhood familiar – the smell of grass, the heat of farm animals, the taste of fresh, damp air on the back of my throat. I think about my brother and his family, good people who love me and will throw open their doors without judgement or question.

I book an evening flight to Galway City and spend the rest of the afternoon packing and sorting the house. I text both children to let them know what I'm doing: Robbie wishes me a good time, Lauren doesn't reply. I try not to feel disappointed and set off to the airport with music playing and my windows open. When I've parked my car, I make my way to check-in and then through to the departure lounge where I buy a gin and tonic and drink it slowly, staring out on to the tarmac where the taxiing planes weave a space around each other. When my flight's called I join the queue of boarders and collapse into an aisle seat. The plane takes off, exhaustion breaks over me and I fall into forty minutes of dreamless sleep.

18

I check in to a hotel in Galway City but before I go up to my room, I ask the receptionist whether there's somewhere I can access the Internet. She points me in the direction of what she calls 'the business centre' – a small alcove, where a couple of desktop computers are switched on and waiting for action. I feel unhappy about the way I left things with O'Reilly but don't feel up to talking to him. Instead, I call the police station to find out his email address then I log on to my email and begin a message to him, typing and deleting for almost ten minutes before I hit upon the right tone. Firstly, I thank him for all he's done, and then I apologise for not always being upfront with him. I finish by telling him where I'm staying and that, come tomorrow, I'll be heading off to visit my brother, 'somewhere to lick my wounds and stay out of trouble'.

I hesitate over a postscript – 'I hope we'll bump into each other sometime in the future'; change it to 'perhaps we could catch up over a drink one evening?', change it again to 'please stop in if ever you're passing my way'. That doesn't sound right either, but I leave it at that and press send.

I wake around six, my cheekbone throbbing from where I've been lying on it, have a quick energising shower and get dressed before making myself a cup of tea and sitting by the window to watch the river run past the back of the hotel and down into the bay. Only a week ago, Robbie, Lauren and I stayed in a hotel in Edinburgh and I had my first inkling that Robbie had had his drink spiked because of me. Now, here

I am, giving in to an eighteen-year-old girl who managed to find my weak spot. I can only hope that the newspaper coverage is enough to get Kirsty off my back and away from my family for good.

Hungry for breakfast, I pack my few toiletries and pyjamas into my suitcase then phone Declan. He's surprised to hear I'm close by and offers to come straight over to collect me, but I tell him that I want to potter around the city and will hire a car and drop in to see them late afternoon. 'You know Mam's op isn't for another couple of weeks, don't you?' he says.

'Yes. I haven't forgotten about that. This is an extra visit. I need to talk to you.'

'Nothing else has happened to Robbie, has it?'

'No. I'll tell you all about it later.'

Declan knows about my reliance on cannabis and, before that, my part in Sandy Stewart's death, but I've yet to tell him about the graffiti on the wall and the unravelling of my life thereafter. It's going to take an hour or so of explaining and I hope he thinks I've done the right thing cooperating with Kirsty.

I leave my suitcase with the receptionist and walk out into the street. The weather forecast is fair to middling and I grab a quick coffee and bacon buttie then spend the morning shopping for presents for my nieces and nephews. It's rare for me to have time on my hands and at first I feel self-conscious. I was brought up an hour's drive away from Galway City and have been gone so long now that I'm unlikely to see anyone I know, but the place is still familiar to me and I expect, at any moment, to bump into Gabe or Sister Mary-Agnes. I don't, of course, and gradually I begin to relax and value the breathing space. I carry on shopping until I have a present for each of Declan's children, then hire myself a car and drive back to the hotel to collect my suitcase.

In front of reception there is a large foyer and my eyes are drawn to two groups of tourists talking loudly as they plan their holiday. And then my gaze passes over a lone man, seated and facing the front door, engrossed in a newspaper.

I stop breathing, momentarily stunned.

It's O'Reilly.

'Oh, my God. Has something happened?' I stumble towards him. 'Please tell me nothing's happened.'

'No. No. Nothing like that.' He stands up and reaches across to lay a hand on my arm. 'I'm sorry to give you a fright.'

I step back and look him up and down. He's wearing off-duty, heavy cotton trousers and an open-necked short-sleeved shirt. 'So why are you here then?'

'I got your email last night and . . .' He shrugs. 'I worked the last couple of weekends and I'm due some time off. It's a while since I'd been to Ireland so I thought I'd join you.'

'All the way from Edinburgh?'

'I was hoping you could show me around. My folks were from Cork. I've never been to Galway.' He throws his newspaper on to the seat behind him. 'And I was rude to you the other day. I'd like to take you out to lunch to make up for it, if you'll let me?'

He leaves a few seconds for my reply, but I'm too busy working out what this could mean – him reading my email, dropping everything and catching the early flight out here.

'But I can . . .' He shifts his feet. 'Perhaps this wasn't such a good idea.'

With each word uttered he's growing more unsure of himself and I know it's because I'm frowning when, if I'm honest, I'm ridiculously pleased to see him and all I want to do is smile. So I do. I ignore the pain in my cheek and smile, and like magic his uncertainty evaporates. He smiles back and I feel a blush creep up from my neck to my cheeks. 'I'm due at my brother's later but . . . Yes! It's a while since I've had breakfast.'

'Good.' He nods, staring at me with an expression of calculation and kindness and it makes my heart beat faster. He's come all this way to see me and it can't be as a policeman so it must be because he likes me, mustn't it?

The thought makes me smile even wider and then the receptionist calls me over to collect my suitcase. I take it from her and O'Reilly comes outside with me to lock my case and carrier bag of presents into the boot of the hire car. 'I know a place close by where we can eat,' I say, and we fall into step beside each other as we cross one of the stone bridges that straddle the river.

'Were you brought up in the city?' O'Reilly says.

'No. We lived on a farm further up the coast.' I point towards an area beyond his head. 'Over to the west you have Connemara, with its granite and turf bogs, famous for sturdy ponies, and still a place where people speak Irish. And then, to the east of the river you have porous limestone. It's not so boggy and it's less mountainous . . .' I stop. He's staring at me with an amused expression. 'Am I sounding too much like a travel guide?'

'No! It's great. I can see you love it here.'

'It's perfect for holidays but I'm not sure I'd want to live here again. It's an artistic, bohemian sort of a place. Nationally, four per cent of the population go to the theatre and in Galway it's fifteen per cent. This is a city for creative people who play instruments by the fire and are good with their hands. I never really fitted in here.' As if to prove my point we round the corner and pass the market stalls, weighed down with arts and crafts, and a couple of buskers playing a musical accompaniment, the melodic sound of traditional Irish music perforating the air.

I wait until we've walked further on before I speak again. 'Sure I love the wide open space, and the weather doesn't bother me, but really all I ever wanted was to get out of here.' I push open the door into a modern café/bar. 'This is one of the famous eating places. A bit overpriced but worth it for the view.'

O'Reilly stops to stare through the enormous window that overlooks the bay just at the point where the Corrib empties into the Atlantic Ocean, churning salt and river water into an impatient cocktail. Brightly painted boats are anchored in the bay, dotting the sea with blocks of colour. 'It's fabulous,' he says. 'Makes me wish I was a fisherman.' He follows me to a table and the waitress comes for our order. O'Reilly chooses a crock of mussels and I choose a salmon salad and we spend the first ten minutes talking about the history of Galway and the direction it's moving in now, as recession bites harder and the construction that dominated areas of the city has ground to a halt.

'And does your brother farm?' O'Reilly says, settling his elbows on the table.

'Very successfully.' I tell him about my father's farm and how – no matter how hard he worked – he could barely make ends meet. 'My brother Declan, on the other hand, has turned the same acreage into a thriving business. He made the transition to organic farming before it was even fashionable and he has a top spot in the market. They've created something really wonderful there, the two of them.'

'You sound proud of him.'

'I am.' I stare beyond O'Reilly and out of the window to where a photographer has set up his tripod and is taking photos of the harbour. 'Phil often teased me for idolising Declan, and I do idolise him, because he was so important to me when I was growing up and he still is the person I most look up to.'

'Are you going to tell him about everything that's been going on?'

'Yes.'

'All of it?'

'He already knows about Sandy Stewart's death.'

'And the rest?' His eyes are challenging.

I allow a second to pass before saying, 'What rest?'

'The arrangement you've made with Kirsty.'

My happy heart wilts with the realisation that O'Reilly might be here as a policeman after all. 'You haven't come all this way to get me to talk about Kirsty, have you?'

'No. And if you don't want to talk about her, you don't have to.' I look out of the window to indicate that the subject is closed, but he continues undaunted. 'So she found out your secret, is that it?'

I stare back at him but I don't speak.

'She must have some leverage over you, otherwise you wouldn't have taken her with you when you lunched with the journalist.'

Our food is ready and we both lean back so that the waitress can put the plates down in front of us. O'Reilly's eyes stay on my face, daring me to respond to him. I lift my knife and fork to begin eating, then change my mind because my stomach has shrunk to nothing. O'Reilly doesn't have any such problem. He takes a mouthful and says, 'Edinburgh's a small city. When I dropped off my youngest daughter last night, my ex-wife was having one of her soirees and I heard your name mentioned. Carys Blakemore was there, telling her companion that you'd given her a story.' He sees my expression. 'I'm a detective. I ask questions. I make no apologies for that.' He leans in closer. 'Was the would-be medical student Kirsty?'

'You know, I thought you came here because . . .' I stop, shake my head at my own foolishness. 'When we met in the police station, I said all I needed to say and you informed me that I could well be prosecuted for wasting police time. I accept that. And I have nothing else to add.'

'Not even off the record?'

'Are you ever off the record?'

'I can forget that I'm a policeman.' He drops his fork to hold both his hands in the air. 'I promise.'

Up close, his dark eyes have a seductive quality that threatens to break me open like a piñata and I draw back from the table.

'My first name's Sean.'

'I know.' Behind my ribcage, my heart gives a shiver of delight while my head warns me against him – *He wants to arrest Kirsty. He's not interested in you. Be careful! You'll only end up getting hurt.*

'Sean, you know . . .' My head and heart are neck and neck in the race to make me speak their words and I try to find a middle ground. 'You have this whole empathetic male thing going on,' I say quietly. 'Don't make me like you too much. Not if you don't mean it.'

'I do mean it,' he says. 'I wouldn't come all this way just to ask you about Kirsty. I came all this way because I like you and I thought that if we were away from Edinburgh you might find it easier to talk to me.'

My heart blooms with colour, and my head is forced to admit defeat – *God help me*; I hope I can trust him not to hurt me. 'Ok*ay*,' I say slowly. 'I'll tell you. As a man, not a policeman, mind?'

'I'm listening.'

'Well . . . When I made the mistake with Sandy Stewart it shattered my faith in myself. I'd never had much self-esteem, and being a doctor made me feel worthwhile.' I pause, not wanting to sound as if I feel sorry for myself. 'I think that's why I was attracted to Phil. In many ways he's the opposite of me. He's capable and confident and he believes a person can control what he thinks or feels or . . . fears.' I move a forkful of salmon from one side of my plate to the other. 'After Robbie was born I was struggling to cope. I tried to speak to Phil but either I didn't explain myself well enough or he didn't understand what I was going through. I felt ashamed and I felt lost. I loved my baby but I wasn't in a good frame of mind and to make matters worse I suffered from painful sciatica. I coped by becoming addicted to cannabis. Phil found out and took a strong line.'

'He wasn't sympathetic?'

I laugh. 'Phil doesn't do sympathy. Don't get me wrong – he's not all bad; he's a better father than he was a husband. He expected me to move on from Sandy's death and take to motherhood easily, but I didn't.' I shrug. 'Anyway, he's trying to get shared custody of the kids. Robbie's almost eighteen and in a few months custody won't be an issue with him. But Lauren is still only eleven and Phil wants her to spend more time with him and Erika.'

'And what does Lauren think?'

'A week or so ago I would have said she'd be dead against it. But now she's angry with me and she's likely to go along with it and then I'll lose her.' My eyes fill up and I blink rapidly. 'Phil's very determined and he always gets what he wants.' I explain about the solicitor's letter and the terms of our agreement. 'When Kirsty broke into my house, she stole some prescriptions from my case. I don't know much about police work but I do know something about human nature and Kirsty isn't your average girl. She's intelligent and manipulative – exactly the type of girl that you'd never want your own daughter or son to go near because she's destructive. She susses out people's weaknesses and homes in on them. She's done it with Tess Williamson and now she's done it with me.'

'So what's she going to do with the prescriptions?'

'She took time to learn how to write the drug name – morphine – and the dose accurately – harder than you might think – and then she forged my signature. The prescriptions were in Tess's name and she was going to collect them then use the information against me.'

'How?'

'Tess would say that I had asked her to get the morphine. She's in Kirsty's pocket. She does what Kirsty tells her and I think she'll continue to do so until Kirsty no longer has any use for her.'

'And that's why you've agreed to the story in the paper?'

'Yes, because I couldn't let Phil get wind of any illegal drug use. I know he would use it against me.'

'No procurator fiscal could make a case out of what you've just told me.'

'Not a criminal case, maybe. But a custody hearing? Most people believe there's no smoke without fire. I have a past history. I work with rehabilitating drug addicts who have contacts in the illegal drug market. Not only that, but Kirsty has flatmates who she assured me would be happy to take pot shots at my character. I don't want to be a part-time parent. Losing Lauren is the worst thing that could happen to me and so I can't take the risk.'

'I still don't think you should give in to her,' Sean says.

'Well . . . You know what? A long time ago, I set this in motion. It was an honest-to-god mistake, but it cost a life and, like it or not, we are affected by everything we do. I thought I hadn't let Sandy's death define me but it just might have.' With my confession out of the way, I feel my appetite returning and I shovel a couple of forkfuls of salmon into my mouth. 'Why do I work at the centre when I could be at home with my kids? If I want to work extra hours, I could do locum work, because God knows I could do with the money, but I don't because I'm always striving to be a better person.'

'You don't deserve to have your mistake made public. You mustn't think that you do.'

'And yet my success has been made public?'

'You didn't ask for the award.'

'No. And believe me, I never expected Sandy's death to

come back to haunt me. I haven't gone around feeling guilty about it. The system supported me in putting it behind me and I did.'

'But?'

'But . . .' I sigh. 'I need to take responsibility for my mistake.' Sean has finished his mussels and I take one last mouthful of salad then stand up. 'Do you want to meet my brother?'

We set off in the tiny hire car, our shoulders knocking together. Sean is on the same flight as I am on Monday morning so, 'We can stay a couple of nights with Declan and Aisling,' I tell him.

'Shouldn't you call them? Tell them you have a friend with you?'

'They won't mind. They have plenty of space.'

On the journey, we talk about our upbringings, and I find out that he is the middle of three boys and his brothers are both living with their families in Glasgow. His mother and father died within a couple of years of one another, 'back in the nineties when Tony Blair was promising us a whole new world,' he says, bracing himself against the door as I negotiate a mile of corkscrew bends. 'And your parents? Are they alive?'

'My father died ten years ago. My mother's still alive but I don't talk to her if I can help it. Although, she's having a hip operation soon and I'm coming back to look after her.' I sigh. 'It won't be easy. We don't get along.'

'Aren't there any community nurses around here?'

'There are, but she'll be uncooperative, and then Aisling will end up having to go round and make the peace. When you meet my sister-in-law you'll see that making the peace is something she's good at, but it isn't fair to lumber her with it. She's only just had a baby. Their fifth.'

As we get closer to the farm, I start to get excited, and can't sit still for pointing out landmarks. 'That's the convent school I went to, and over there is the best chip shop in all of Ireland, and I lost my virginity against that tree. He was called Gabriel, after the angel.'

'How romantic!' Sean laughs. 'Wasn't it uncomfortable?'

'No, it was very nice actually.'

The road winds through the village and when we're about thirty yards from the church I see Father O'Riordan standing on the pavement, his hands behind his back, looking up and down the street. It's too late to reverse and impossible to make myself invisible, so when he steps out in front of the car and waves us to a halt, I apply the brakes and lower my window.

'Is that you, Scarlett Naughton?'

'Yes, Father. Good to see you, Father.'

'You've come a long way, Scarlett.'

'Yes, Father.'

'Will we be seeing you at Mass then?'

'I expect so, Father. But not this visit.'

'How's your mother?'

'Fine, Father.'

'She's a difficult woman, to be sure.' He bends his head to see into the car and reach his hand across me. 'And who will you be, then?'

'Sean O'Reilly. Pleased to meet you.'

'Now that's a good Irish name.'

I half listen to Sean make conversation with Father O'Riordan while I look along the street and see faces that I recognise and shop fronts that seem to have exactly the same window displays as when I left.

'. . . all that malarkey's for over there,' Father O'Riordan says, and then he bangs the roof. 'On your way now and stay longer next time.'

A few yards on, Sean is laughing when he says, 'Why does he call you Scarlett?'

'Scarlett Olivia Naughton was the name I was christened with, but I dropped the Scarlett when I came to Edinburgh.'

'I'm seeing you in a whole new light.' He laughs again. 'I don't suppose I'd be allowed to call you Scarlett?'

'I don't suppose you would,' I say drily, and he laughs again, mischief in his eyes.

I turn off on to a narrow track, uneven ground bumping under the wheels as we drive towards the farm, situated almost a mile from the road, but easy to spot because the sun is shining on the roofs of the outbuildings, making them sparkle. When we pull up in front of the house, my nephews and nieces run out to meet me and then Aisling comes out too, her new baby in her arms, and we all hug each other. I introduce Sean and Aisling to each other but all the while I'm impatient to see my brother, and my eldest nephew runs off to fetch his dad while I stand talking, my eyes darting off to one side, knowing that Declan is only seconds away. When he comes around the corner of the barn, he shouts my name and I run to him as if I'm still the child I was. He lifts me up and hugs me for twenty seconds or more and I start to cry from the love of him.

'Those two,' I hear Aisling tell Sean. 'They have such a bond. I'm hoping my children will be as close as they are.'

The evening passes in a whirl of catching up. Declan takes Sean round the farm and they talk vegetables and yields, cattle and prices. The first opportunity Aisling gets she takes me to one side. 'Aren't you the dark horse?' she whispers. 'He looks like Sean Connery, don't you think? That lovely accent. Those eyes.' She nudges me. 'Tell me you don't see it?'

'I do see it.'

'Will you be sharing a bed?'

'Ssh! No.'

'Are you sure?'

'Yes. We haven't even . . .'

'Sweet Jesus, Scarlett, you're blushing!'

When the children are down for the night, the four of us

spend the evening talking, and it makes me happy to see how much Declan and Aisling enjoy Sean's company, and he theirs.

Early the following morning, I borrow Aisling's wellingtons and walk the farm with Declan. He shows me everything he's done since I was last there and I hang on his arm, my hand in the pocket of his jacket, just like I always used to. It's my opportunity to tell him about everything that's been happening and he listens without judgement until he hears all the details and then he says, 'I'm sure it was a difficult decision, but you've done the right thing, Scarlett.'

It's all I needed to hear and, next day, when we leave for the airport, my heart feels light. My nieces and nephews hug Sean as though they've known him a lot longer than a weekend and he promises them he'll be back soon and next time he'll stay longer.

Sean and I sit in companionable silence in the departures lounge, as if we're a long-married couple returning from a weekend break. Sean buys a copy of *Gardener's World* and gets lost in an article about composting. He doesn't fidget or pace the way Phil always does but is a relaxed, comforting presence next to me. It's all I can do not to lean my head on his shoulder and I dare to hope that I might be getting a second chance at love.

When we arrive back in Edinburgh, Sean goes to the toilet while I wait at the belt for the luggage to come through. I switch my mobile back on and see that I've a missed call from Robbie. I check my watch – almost six o'clock; they should both be with Phil by now. Lauren was there anyway and Robbie arranged to go there for the evening. I don't want to interrupt dinner so I send Robbie a quick text message saying I'll call him after seven. It's no sooner sent when my phone starts ringing, his name flashing on the screen. Sean's back from the toilet and points two fingers at his eyes and then at the luggage belt, which has just started moving. I mouth 'thank you' and step away from the crowd and over to the wall where I'll be able to hear Robbie better.

'Hello, Dr Somers.'

I freeze. It isn't Robbie's voice; it's Kirsty's.

'Are you there?'

'Why do you have Robbie's phone?' I say.

'If we're going to answer questions then you need to answer mine first.'

I briefly close my eyes. *Please God, don't let her be pulling another stunt.* 'Go on.'

'Why couldn't you have just played it straight?'

'I don't know what you mean.'

'Was it after I left? Is that when you and that Blakemore bitch decided to stitch me up?'

I watch O'Reilly take my suitcase off the conveyer belt. He seems far, far away, as if I'm looking through the wrong end of binoculars. 'There was no stitch up, Kirsty,' I say. 'You were there with me. You heard what I said.'

'You're a liar.'

'Why do you have Robbie's phone?'

'Because he's here with me.'

'Where?'

There's the sound of heavy traffic in the background, so I'm not surprised when she answers, 'On the Forth Road Bridge.'

I take a big breath in. 'Kirsty, I've done exactly as you asked. You promised me that would be the end of it.'

She says nothing for several interminable seconds; my heart is suspended in my ribcage, waiting for the hammer blow.

'Too late,' she says. 'A life for a life. That's fair, don't you think?'

The line goes dead and I'm left staring at Sean.

19

'What's happened?' Sean takes hold of my shoulders. 'Tell me!'

'Kirsty answered Robbie's phone.'

'So where's Robbie?'

'With Kirsty on the Forth Road Bridge.'

'Call her back.'

I gulp down my rising panic and do it, listening, wishing, praying, for the sound of Robbie's voice but . . . nothing. 'She's switched it off,' I say.

'Okay, Olivia. Think.' He holds my shaky hands still. 'What did Kirsty say?'

'Something . . .' The space in my head is cluttered up with confusing messages and fragments of fear and I dart around until I find a remembered phrase. 'A life for a life,' I blurt out.

'But why would she say that when you've done what she asked?'

'She said something about me stitching her up.'

He drops my hands and lifts both of our cases. 'We need to see a copy of the *Edinburgh Courier*.'

We run a few yards to the airport shop where people are wasting time browsing the shelves. The newspapers are in a pile close to the floor and Sean picks one up. On page five there is a large photo of me, smiling, and the headline says: *When good doctors just keep getting better.* We both read the first paragraph, which begins: 'Olivia Somers, our recent City Women award winner, has a confession to make – she's only human. Just like the rest of us, she's made her fair share of mistakes. But, unlike the rest of us, not only is Olivia Somers able to admit to her mistakes, she's also able to learn from them.'

'Shit,' Sean says softly. 'The interview's slanted completely in your favour.'

Barbed wire grips my ribcage and I daren't breathe in for fear that I'll tear myself wide open. I know what this will mean to Kirsty. When I last saw her, running from the restaurant, she was close to breaking point and this article will have dealt the final blow.

'Come on.' Sean moves off at a run and I keep up with him, weaving around the throngs of people that crowd the arrivals area. When we're outside, he holds my suitcase up against the traffic and we sprint over the road. His car is close by and we're in it and moving off before I have a chance to think. The screech of his police siren sends my heartbeat even higher and I bite down hard on my lip.

'Put your seatbelt on,' Sean shouts across at me, swerving out of the car park on to the access road. 'And call Mark Campbell's phone to see whether he knows anything.'

I put my belt on and concentrate on using my mobile. I have Mark's phone number programmed into my phone but it seems to take me forever to find it as my fingers press the wrong places on the screen and I end up opening functions I don't want. All the while Sean is driving faster than can possibly be safe, but up ahead of us cars slow down and pull in to one side to allow us to pass. I finally manage to connect with Mark's phone but, just like Robbie's, his phone is switched off.

'Mark's phone is off,' I tell Sean.

'He might be with them,' Sean says. 'But don't worry, we can be there in ten minutes. She won't be expecting that.'

It's a good point and my spirits feel the ghost of a lift. Sean takes his police radio from the holder on the dashboard between us and talks to the South Queensferry police. 'Two, possibly three or even four young people,' Sean says, using his other hand to steer us around the roundabout and on to the motorway. 'They might be driving on to the bridge or they might be walking on to it. We're not far away and I don't want them to know we're on to them, so I'll shut off the siren when I get close. I'm driving a black, BMW 5 series.' He speaks his number plate using the phonetic alphabet. 'I'll stop just before the bridge. Meet me there.'

In the distance, one of the bridge's two metal towers rises gracefully into the air, cables slung across the top and falling in an arc towards the centre of the bridge. There are two lanes of traffic moving in either direction; on the outside of the roadway is a cycle track and pedestrian walkway – all the better for admiring the scenery – and people regularly walk from one side to the other, taking in the view along the Firth of Forth that cuts into the east side of Scotland separating North and South Queensferry.

Early evening traffic means the queue is long. Sean has silenced the siren but is overtaking the cars and lorries anyway, his light flashing a warning as he encroaches into the path of oncoming vehicles.

Every second is meaningful. Every second holds my son's life in the palm of its hands. I imagine the hands of a clock wrapping themselves around Robbie, holding him safe. *Please, please keep him safe.* I know how easy it is to die. I've seen people die, suddenly, in an instant, their lives snuffed out in the time it takes to make a cup of tea.

An oncoming car sounds its horn and I jump in my seat. Sean doesn't even flinch. He forces every last millimetre of air out of the space to either side of us and I tense against the imminent collision of wing mirrors. A split second of heightened alert and the vehicles pass each other, the different mirror positions preventing an explosion of glass and plastic.

My mind is chasing itself, circling on possibilities: Kirsty trying to push Robbie over the handrail or threatening him with a knife or attempting to drug him again. Or maybe her intention is simply to scare me and this is a complete over-reaction on our part. We could get there and find that Kirsty ran off immediately after she spoke to me.

Except that Robbie and Mark's phones are switched off.

And Kirsty's last words were *a life for a life*.

And she's already proven that she's adept at forward planning.

The article in the *Edinburgh Courier* was supposed to mark the end of Kirsty's revenge and instead it has brought us to crisis point. I curse myself for not asking Carys to show me the copy before it went to print, but it never occurred to me that it would go to press so quickly, and nor did I expect her to turn the story around. *I should never have gone to Ireland. I should have stayed in Edinburgh and kept my children locked up beside me.*

'You didn't know this was going to happen,' Sean shouts over to me. For a moment I think I must have been speaking aloud, but then I realise that he's already guessed I blame myself. 'We're almost there. We'll get her before she does anything. Don't worry.'

I daren't ask Sean what he thinks Kirsty intends to do. His take on this may be even worse than mine, and I'm already battling to hang on to my emotions when all I want to do is howl up at the sky.

Facts are normally a comfort to me, but I know more about this bridge than I care to. About five years ago Phil had a patient who suffered from hypermania and she was continually reeling off facts and figures. Phil came home and told me about whatever subject was obsessing her. One particular day she'd given him the bridge's vital statistics – opened in 1964, 2.5 kilometres long, etc. – but what I remember most are the suicides. Every year about twenty people jump off the bridge and in all the years since it was built only three of those people have survived. Entering the water from over a hundred metres up is like hitting concrete, so even if they're picked up by one of the boats that pass along this waterway, they're likely to die from their injuries.

Sean stops the car just before the bridge begins and we both climb out. All forms of motor vehicles accelerate past us up the sloping lanes and on to the bridge. Exhaust fumes and engine noise assault us both and I hold my hand up where my forehead meets my eyes to see whether I can see past the sun and on to the bridge, turning back around when a car comes to a stop beside us and two uniformed police officers climb out.

'There are four people walking on this side, away from us,' one of the officers shouts, his eyes sparking with emergency. 'They're about two hundred metres in.' He hands Sean his binoculars. 'You'll be able to see whether or not you can identify them.'

Sean has a quick look then passes the binoculars to me. 'I think it's Kirsty with Robbie, Mark and Tess.'

I hold the binoculars up to my eyes. It takes me a few seconds to focus and, when I do, I only have a moment to look before my hands tremble and I drop the binoculars down to my side. 'Yes, it's them,' I say, trying to process what I've just seen. Both boys were walking a few paces ahead of the girls and Mark had his face turned towards Kirsty. I couldn't see the expression on Robbie's face but Mark was definitely afraid. And Tess was walking very close to Kirsty, as if she was physically tied to her.

'We need to stop all traffic going on to the bridge.' Sean's voice is raised as he instructs the uniformed officers. 'And you need to call in one of the armed response vehicles.' He turns away from me so that I can't hear what he says next and then the policemen jump back in their car and speed off.

'Okay, Olivia, listen to me.' Sean pulls me in close to the car, managing to identify a small pocket of quiet where the traffic noise is muffled and we don't have to shout. 'I'm going to follow the last car on to the bridge and then I'm going to talk to Kirsty.'

'I'm coming with you.'

'I think I have a better chance of talking her out of whatever she's planning than you do.' He glances away from us to where large neon signs are warning vehicles to slow down and come to a halt. 'I need to go. Stand to one side.'

'No!' I resist the pull of his arm. 'It makes sense for me to come. I'm the person she wants! Everyone who's on the bridge is only there because I'm not.'

'It's not appropriate for you to come with me. You're emotionally involved—'

'Which is exactly why I should be there.' I climb into the passenger seat. 'I'm coming with you. You can't stop me. This is my problem, my son.' I brace myself against the side of the door, ready to resist in case he tries to physically throw me out, but he doesn't. I watch him take a nanosecond to decide between wasting time trying to talk me round and getting on to the bridge before the situation worsens, and then he runs round to the driver's side and starts the engine.

'Olivia?'

'Yes?' I swivel to look at him and register the strain on his face.

'I don't want you putting yourself in danger.'

I don't reply because I think we both know that it's already too late for that.

'I think Kirsty might have a gun.'

'A gun?' I hadn't factored that into the equation and my heart, an aching sore behind my ribcage, squeezes another shot of alarm into my bloodstream. 'How could she get hold of a gun?'

'It's difficult but not impossible to get hold of one.' We fall in behind the last car and follow it on to the bridge. 'It looked like she was holding a handgun into Tess's side. I can't be sure but it would explain Tess's stilted walking and also why the boys are cooperating with her.'

We're on the bridge now, less than twenty yards away from them. Kirsty's wearing a black leather jacket and biker boots – a tough and uncompromising look. And I see that Sean's right. She's carrying a handgun.

But what frightens me more is the position that Tess has taken up. As Sean brings the car to a stop beside Robbie and Mark, I'm horrified to see that Tess has climbed up on to the handrail. She's sitting on the rail, facing inwards, her flipflops kicked off and her hands in her lap. All that's preventing her from falling backwards are her toes, which curl into the vertical rails, the muscles in her feet keeping her still and safe. There's over a hundred-metre drop behind her and yet she's staring straight ahead with an almost blank expression, as if she's watching a boring programme on television.

I'm out of the car before Sean has the chance to stop me. I step between the two boys and Kirsty and see her eyes widen before she says, 'Dr Somers! Well, what do you know?'

'Mum!' Robbie shouts. I don't turn around but my peripheral vision catches every movement. Sean has hold of the boys and is pulling them away from me.

'This is about you and me, Kirsty,' I say, looking only at her. 'I'm here now. So let everyone else go.'

'Mum! I'm not leaving you!'

The uniformed policemen have followed us on to the bridge and I hear Sean commanding the boys to go with them so that they can be taken to safety. Robbie calls out to me again but I ignore him. Now that Robbie and Mark are out of danger, a liquid relief fills all the empty spaces inside me. All I need to do is get Tess to safety and then it'll just be Kirsty and me, and we can go all the way back to the beginning of the story, to the woman I admitted to hospital and the newborn baby I thought was dead.

Keeping my eyes on Kirsty, I speak to Tess. 'Whatever hold she has on you, Tess, it stops right here and right now. It's me she wants.' I risk a quick glance in Tess's direction. The wind has lifted her hair off her shoulders and it's streaming back behind her. 'Please come down.' I don't move towards her but I do hold out my hand and Kirsty raises the gun. Since he passed the boys back to the uniformed officers, Sean has been behind me, and now he tries to step in front of me, but my arm automatically bangs across his chest. 'Don't!' My eyes are focused on Kirsty again. 'Please let me handle this.'

I sense his reluctance but still he moves back behind me, whispering, 'Keep her talking.'

She's still pointing the gun at the centre of my chest. I've never even seen a handgun before and I've no idea what make or calibre it is. When I was growing up, my father used a rifle. He shot foxes and rats, and when we were old enough, he taught my three brothers and me how to shoot. Aiming accurately is harder than people think. You have to know the gun and you have to have a steady hand and a certain aptitude for it.

Still, Kirsty is only six or seven feet away from me and is unlikely to miss from this distance. Plus, I already know that preparation is important to her. She could have anticipated this moment, practised for it until she knew she had it right.

A slow smile is spreading across her face. She's sure of her ground. Whatever she's threatened Tess with, it's going to take more than a request from me for her to get down. It's as if she's under Kirsty's spell and only Kirsty can release her.

'Why don't you let Tess go, Kirsty?' I say. 'This has got nothing to do with her.'

'She's my insurance policy.' She lowers the gun. 'While I have her, I know you'll stay put.'

'I'm not going anywhere.' I throw my arms out in surrender. 'I'm as keen to end this as you are. So what do you suggest we do?'

'Well . . . my original plan was to have your son sitting on the handrail, ready to fall, but hey?' She laughs. 'You're here now. Either you go over the edge or – ' she throws her head sideways towards Tess – 'she does.' Her stare is challenging. 'So what's it to be?'

'I saw the story in the *Edinburgh Courier.*' I put my hands together in the prayer position. 'I didn't know she was going to take that slant. I swear to you, I didn't.'

'My mother's death has become another reason for you to be classed as a superstar.'

'Let me get in touch with them. I can call them. I'll demand to be given a right to reply.'

'It's too late. Look at all this . . .' She gestures around us. 'Traffic stopped, police involved. Whatever way it goes, I'm heading to prison.'

Sean steps forward again. 'Not necessarily.'

'Get back!' She points the gun at him. 'I *will* shoot you.'

He moves a couple of baby steps backwards, his hands in the air. 'Let's keep it calm,' he says.

'It's make-your-mind-up time, Dr Somers.' She tilts a defiant chin towards me, and points the gun at my chest again. 'You or Tess?'

Her body is standing firm; her legs are slightly apart, her feet planted firmly on the tarmac. I don't want to push her into firing the gun. I don't want to die and I don't want Tess to die either, and somewhere in the space between Kirsty's threat and my own fear, I find a moment of peace. I glance up at the bluebell-coloured sky and take a deep breath, then allow my eyes to slide down the horizon and meet Tess's. She's no longer bored and distant. She's focusing on me with an intensity that matches Kirsty's. She's trying to tell me something. Her eyes flick to the gun, then to me, and she mouths the message again, her lips exaggerating each syllable.

I get it. I know what Tess is saying and it propels me forward at once. My feet are moving but I'm not aware of the pavement beneath them.

Kirsty and Sean call out at the same time –

'No!' shouts Sean.

'I'll kill you!' screams Kirsty.

The gun fires but I don't stop; I'm heading towards Tess who's smiling at me. There's no despair in her eyes, only a slight hesitation, a shallow in-breath and then . . .

Seconds are concrete units of time, always identical, regardless of how much we need to shorten or lengthen them. I want this to be a Hollywood moment, where I s-p-r-i-n-t and r-e-a-c-h, just catching Tess's ankles in my grip, holding her there until O'Reilly's by my side and helps me pull her back on to the bridge.

But real life is seldom so accommodating and, although I run the short distance between us, using my longest, fastest strides, nothing happens in slow motion.

In real time, her feet let go of the railings.

– I'm three metres away . . .

She tips backwards.

– two metres . . .

Her legs fly up.

I reach the rail and grab for her but my hands miss her ankles by a metre or more.

My arms should be rubber. I throw them over the barrier but my gesture is useless, Tess is accelerating away from me faster than I can blink. She has a small, hopeful spectre of a smile on her face that tells me she isn't afraid, and then her body twists in the air and she hits the sea with the whipcrack sound of a life being taken.

'Help her!' I scream. 'Do something!'

There's movement all around me. One of the uniformed officers takes hold of my shoulders and pulls me away from the railing. 'The coastguard's boat is already on the water. The girl will be picked up straight away,' he tells me.

'Her name is Tess.' Desolation surges inside me. 'Her name is Tess Williamson. She's sixteen.' My eyes move past him and find Kirsty. Sean has her face down on the ground and is cautioning her.

'You bitch.' I fall down on my knees beside her, take a handful of her hair and jerk her head back.

'Olivia!'

Sean tries to prise my fingers away but I hang on tight and lock my eyes with Kirsty's. 'It should be you down there.'

Sean is standing over me, one foot on Kirsty's back, both his arms underneath mine, pulling me upwards but before he has spun me away from her I spit in her face.

'Olivia!' He gives my shoulders an urgent shake. 'Enough!' I step away and wipe the back of my hand over my mouth as a shudder of fear and anger arc through my chest.

'Mum, Mum!' Robbie is running towards me and then his arms around me and he's crying into my neck. 'When I heard the gun go off, I thought she had shot you.'

'The gun isn't real,' I say. 'It's a good imitation, most likely a theatre prop. Tess told me it was a fake just before she . . .' I shudder again and Robbie hugs me tighter.

At the entrance to the bridge, police cars are gathering in force and there's the high-pitched sound of the advance response unit arriving – but they're too bloody late. I think about Tess, down below, in the water. The horror of her fall. The horror of the sea when it made contact with her body.

Sean has Kirsty handcuffed and is leading her to a police van, a slight, girlish figure who kicks and struggles and shouts obscenities, most of them directed towards me. I allow another couple of policemen to bundle Robbie and me into a police car and drive us to the entrance of the bridge where two paramedics come forward to check us over.

'My son,' I say. 'Please look after him.'

One paramedic takes Robbie to the ambulance while the other one places a foil blanket over my shoulders and clips it under my chin. I'm grateful that he doesn't try to stop me when I walk over to the side and attempt to see down to the shore, but the angle of the land obscures the water's edge. I see boats further out but they're all moving either east or west. They must have Tess on the boat by now and be trying to save her.

My stomach heaves and I vomit by the side of the road, emptying acid and what little food there was inside me on to the grass verge. Then I stand where I am. I don't want to talk or move or speculate. I wait . . . and in that time I pray. Three people in almost fifty years have survived the fall. I remember that one of the three people who survived did so because he was wearing a rucksack, and the medics reckoned this had cushioned his entry into the water. Tess was wearing a simple summer dress but her body twisted halfway down. Is that good or bad?

Please let her be miracle number four.

But her chances of survival are less than one per cent. In fact, the likelihood that she'll live through the ordeal is about one in three hundred.

But there is a chance, I argue back. It's a slim chance, but it's still a chance.

It's almost fifteen minutes before O'Reilly comes over to me and by now, despite the foil blanket and the sun, I'm freezing cold and shivering. 'Is she alive?' I say.

He shakes his head.

That's when the world grows black. I lose control of my bladder and my legs and it's only O'Reilly catching me that prevents me from cracking my head on the road.

20

In my dreams there's an alternative reality where I catch Tess's ankles and hold on. She doesn't shatter her pelvis, nor does she fracture her two femurs and her patellae. Her facial bones aren't rearranged on impact with the water because she doesn't fall in face first. She doesn't fall into the water at all.

In my dreams she's smiling. She looks trouble-free and rested. She has the two family cats on her knee and she's idly stroking their fur while she talks enthusiastically about the school play and how much she likes to work behind the scenes.

I pray her mother has the comfort of such dreams because the reality is unbearable. Fourteen bones make up the face and they're not built to absorb shock. Tess's facial bones fracture into so many pieces that her face no longer exists. Without a structure for the flesh to wrap around, her face is loose and poorly defined – bruised, battered and unrecognisable.

Her death feels like an obscenity. I spend the first couple of days asking myself why. Why did she take her own life? Why did she do it when she knew that the gun was a fake? Nobody needed to die that day, least of all Tess, who had nothing to do with Kirsty's vendetta against me.

And then Sean tells me that evidence recovered from Tess's bedroom shows she was anticipating her suicide, and had been for three months, since one of her fellow pupils left Sanderson.

It turns out that Tess never had a boyfriend, her prescription for the pill an attempt to fit in with the other girls at school. They spent evenings talking about their boyfriends, discussing first sex and all it entailed, and Tess wanted to be like them. In fact she'd had a relationship with another girl called Tilly Revere. Kirsty found out about it and threatened to expose them both. Tilly left the school but Tess's parents, unaware of what was going on, insisted that Tess stay and complete the academic year. Tess was sure her parents would disapprove of any sexual relationship, but a same-sex one was completely outwith the bounds of what they would feel was 'decent'. Kirsty continued to dangle the sword of disclosure over Tess's head, and for a girl like Tess, already shy and lacking in self-confidence, the threats were too much to bear.

The only small lining in an otherwise black cloud is that Tess had the forethought to record the instances of bullying – dates, times, what was said, what she had to do for Kirsty and the action Kirsty took against her, which proves invaluable when the police build a case against Kirsty.

Tess's funeral is attended by almost two hundred people. Her sisters arrive at the church with their parents. They are straighter-backed, thinner, prettier versions of Tess. They wear tight black tailored skirt suits and black silk shirts. They look stylishly attractive, in control of their emotions and their interactions with other mourners. This is in complete contrast to their parents, who appear hurriedly clothed and wear the stunned expression of people who have just survived a major incident. And when their protracted case of shock has evaporated, grief will seep in, molecule by molecule, until their skin is porous and everything – absolutely everything – will be a painful reminder of their daughter's absence. Shopping, cleaning, driving in the car, watching TV, not watching TV, every meal, every cycle of the washing machine, every leaf that falls from every tree.

My heart aches for them. And underneath that ache, I feel

angry. Angry at myself and all the other adults, every last one of us, who didn't realise the seriousness of Tess's state of mind. And I'm angry at a world that allows such futility.

But mostly I'm angry at Kirsty for her sustained and wilful destruction of another girl's life.

Kirsty is being held in custody in the women's prison outside Glasgow until her trial begins. Because of the evidence left by Tess, and corroborated by several girls at school, she is charged with culpable homicide and culpable and reckless conduct. She's also charged with Robbie's attempted murder and breaking and entering my home. Her defence counsel is already suggesting that some of the evidence is inadmissible, but Sean is convinced we have a good shot at proving all four charges.

'She'll be sentenced to six or seven years at the very least,' he says.

'Which means she could be out in four.'

'Five, maybe,' he says. 'But honestly, Liv, bearing in mind the extent of her planning and the force of her behaviour, I think the judge will recommend she serves a full sentence.'

I go back to work in the surgery immediately after Tess's funeral. Everyone is sympathetic towards me apart from Leila. She is adamant she won't forgive me – not ever. I didn't make enough effort to talk to her and that put her son at risk. I understand her hurt feelings and let her rage at me, punctuating her anger with apologies until she dares me to apologise one more time.

It takes only a week before she comes into my room, closes the door behind her and says, 'Okay. I'm letting it go. I'm striking it out. It's like it never happened. But if you *ever* . . .' She stops, smooths her skirt down and takes a deep breath. 'It's gone.'

Sean and I have become players in each other's lives. It happens slowly. At first he tiptoes around me, careful not to intrude. I'm quieter and more serious than I've ever been because I find it difficult to recover from what happened on the bridge. I'm grateful that Robbie and Mark got through it unscathed – they were upset at first but bounced back within a week or so – but I feel a lasting horror and shame at Tess's death. Sean and I talk about it and I discover that he has his own demons to fight. She died in front of him too, and I know that he also wishes to relive those last few minutes and do it differently.

'I should have realised that the gun was a fake,' he says. 'Then we could have got to Tess sooner.'

'How could you know it was a fake? It was a good imitation, wasn't it?'

'It was the perfect weight and size, an exact replica of a Glock.' He shakes his head at this. 'But still . . .'

I take indefinite leave from the centre – the latest article in the *Edinburgh Courier* has done the centre no harm at all and a stream of new funding continues to flow into the centre's bank account – because I want to spend my evenings with the children. Lauren has forgiven me and is back at home again, her scrapbook restored. 'Dad's flat makes me feel tense,' she tells me. 'Erika's quite nice and everything, but it's not like being here with you and Robbie.'

Sean spends at least three of those evenings a week with us too. 'I need bodies to practise my cooking on,' he says, always arriving with a colourful selection of vegetables from his allotment. He makes beetroot salad with a raspberry vinegar dressing, sweet potato mash and a leek and cheese flan. All of it made with love and care and I've never eaten so much nor felt so deliciously spoilt.

The children grow to enjoy his visits just as much as I do, and he's considerate enough to cook his way around their likes and dislikes. Robbie pronounces him as 'cool' and Lauren think he's 'really easy to talk to and makes the best chicken salad *ever*'. Being with Sean is a revelation for me. He's more sensitive than I expected. Not sensitive about himself, but sensitive to the world and people around him. He works in a boys' club in one of the poorer housing estates on the outskirts of town. He plays football with them and has planted vegetables there too, already nurturing several of his helpers towards careers in gardening. He's straightforward without being one-dimensional or dull, although when I meet his two daughters, Ailsa and Susie, for the first time, Ailsa says to me, 'Dad can be very boring about his garden. In fact he can be very boring about a lot of things, but don't give up on him, will you?'

'I don't find him boring at all,' I say, laughing at her candour. 'I love him.'

'You do?' She gives me a huge smile and kisses my cheek. 'I knew he'd get someone nice eventually! Mum's always been too much of a hard ass.'

Phil comes to see me at the end of June and apologises for his loss of temper when we knew Lauren was missing. 'I hope you're able to forgive me,' he says. 'It was unacceptable. As was my interfering in your life back when Sandy Stewart died.'

I acknowledge this with a half-smile, wondering whether this apology is Erika's doing but he surprises me further when he says, 'I know both Robbie and Lauren are happier living with you and so I've called off my solicitor. I won't be pushing for shared custody.'

'Thank you.' I manage a full smile this time because I can see that he's really trying.

'Erika and I do want to stay involved in the children's lives, though.'

'Of course.'

'Perhaps we can share them in the holidays? And maybe another evening during the week?'

'I don't see why not.' We eye each other for a couple of long seconds and I feel the past catch up the present. Here. Now. We're separate people, but with two healthy, precious children, proof of days past, shared love and loyalty. 'Erika's good for you, Phil,' I say, giving him a quick hug. 'I really hope you're happy together.'

I linger by the window to watch him walk back to his car and let my feelings for him relax into a groove somewhere between acceptance and respect.

Who would have thought it?

The summer holidays pass by without a hitch. My mother's operation is cancelled so I don't go to Ireland after all, although Sean and I book flights for all four of us to spend the October week with Declan and co. The children fly off to Germany for a couple of weeks and send me an email with wedding photos attached. Brides invariably look radiant and Erika really does. I feel a genuine, untarnished happiness for them both.

While the children are in Germany, Sean all but moves in. What started as a chaste kiss on the doorstep accelerates into a no-holds-barred love affair. I'm hardly a veteran where love and romance is concerned, and Phil was only the second man I ever had sex with, but I know when I'm on to a good thing. Sean embodies combinations that I never even knew I wanted in a man – kindness and strength, activity and tranquillity, wisdom and a thirst to learn.

Falling in love makes me happy, but I don't feel like a young woman again, all trembling and unsure. Instead I discover distinctly adult appetites. Like digging in your back garden and coming upon an oil well – I can hardly believe it myself. Part of the reason Phil left me was because he needed 'a greater degree of intimacy', and here I am, being the most intimate I've ever been, with a man I've known for only a few short months, but feel like I've known all my life.

Tonight we go to bed early. We're careful not to flaunt our attraction in front of Lauren and Robbie, but they're both at friends' houses. Sean has had a tough week at work, staying out late three evenings in a row to close a case. So when he comes home we go straight into the shower. We make love in the cubicle, urgent, racy sex that makes every part of me zing. When we're finished I towel-dry his hair and then comb it through. 'You smell so good.' I kiss his Adam's apple. 'Let me wet-shave you. You're scratchy.'

I get a basin of warm water, some shaving foam and a razor. He sits back on the bed and I straddle him. We're both still naked. I put the towel over his chest and begin. I can't stop smiling. Being close to him feels like eating chocolate after months of dieting; the best, most exquisite chocolate, bitter on the outside and sweeter than sugar on the inside.

'Do you think I'm good at this?' I make the last few sweeps around his neckline.

'I'm enjoying it.' His eyes are closed and he's smiling.

I cut him a tiny bit and lick the blood off. 'Spoke too soon.' I use the towel to wipe off the rest of the foam then start to kiss him. He doesn't kiss me back. He lets me have his neck, his cheeks and his mouth like a gift. When I stop to look down at him, his face is relaxed. The lines on his forehead are smoothed out and I kiss the crow's-feet at the corner of his eyes then climb off and pull his head on to my breasts, shifting myself into a comfortable position against the headboard.

Within seconds he's asleep and I arrange his limbs across mine, then cover us both with a duvet. I stroke his hair and think about the nature of love. There are songs and poems about love, books and films about love. Clichés and idioms: love's young dream, the look of love, puppy love, cupboard love, all is fair in love and war, he loves me, he loves me not. In some languages there are separate words for the different kinds of love: love for a child, a parent, a friend, a husband, a lover.

Sean's love for me has chipped away at my rock of loneliness until it's no bigger than a grain of sand. All there is left to haunt me is the injustice against Tess. *She wasn't your child*, I tell myself. *Your children are alive. Be thankful.* It would be up to her family to avenge her death. And, anyway, I don't believe in revenge. It's short-term satisfaction for long-term damage.

So I'm not looking for revenge but I am looking for something – security, assurance – impossible while Kirsty's state of mind remains the same. I spoke to Sean about it. 'If Kirsty serves five years, Lauren will only be sixteen when she gets out of prison,' I said.

'She'll get help inside,' Sean told me. 'She'll have to talk about what she's done. She won't be allowed out until they're sure she's no longer a danger to the public.'

I want to believe him but I don't. Kirsty won't be a danger to the public but she will be a danger to me and my children. I spent some time doing research. I felt as if I was going behind Sean's back, so I did it when he wasn't staying over and the children were in bed. I found several cases where people were in prison for years and came out to commit the same or similar crimes. Sustained hatred and determination don't die easily.

'What are you thinking?' Sean sits up and stretches his arms above his head, then flops back down beside me. 'You're looking serious.'

'I was thinking about how much I love you,' I say.

He stares at me with those eyes of his, the ones that see into every part of me, except the darkest corner, right out back, where only ghosts lurk. He rolls on to his side and I turn off the light then spoon into his back. My last thought before I sleep is a cautionary one. I know what I don't want. I don't want to spend another evening in A & E. I don't want to hear Kirsty's voice on the other end of the phone. I don't want her anywhere near my children.

I'm still a doctor. I believe in the sanctity of life. I believe in doing no harm.

But if I have to, I will.